Death Never Forgets
(A Mike Cannon jumps racing mystery)

Eric Horridge

DEDICATION

This book is dedicated to all those suffering from or living with Cancer. To their families and friends who support them, and to those who grieve for the ones who have passed on from the disease.

To those who search for answers and cures.

Let us continue the fight ....

Prologue

The sound of bone on bone was lost, dissipated in the vastness of the stadium, and drowned out by the roar of the crowd. Twelve thousand people jumped to their feet in unison. Some screamed obscenities, while others shouted support for the man in red who ran away from the prostrate figure in white. The latter rolled around on the ground clutching his left leg a grimace etched on his face as the impact of the clumsy tackle seared through his body.

"I think it's broken," he said to his captain who had quickly crossed the pitch from the opposite side and was now kneeling beside his teammate.

"The bastard!" the captain replied, looking across the field at the perpetrator of the foul, pointing viciously at the player. "You'll get what's coming to you for this," he shouted, indicating his own player still lying immobile on the ground. Turning to his teammate, he tried to reassure him saying, "just take it easy for a second. Let's see what the Physio says hey?"

The player in white nodded, closed his eyes then lay backward, his arms behind his head, the soft turf cut like a bowling green felt comfortable. He felt no pain, just a numbness.

Parts of the crowd, the home team supporters, began booing and chanting. They had seen many players pretending to be hurt, especially the so-called high-quality imports, and they believed this to be no different. Some players earned thousands if not millions of pounds playing in the highest league in the land and to those watching, the play-acting was unnecessary.

"How does it feel?" asked the team physiotherapist who had reached the player and had begun a physical examination of the injury. A deep gash was evident in the lower shin, blood was slowly seeping through the sock. He noticed that the player was not wearing any shin pads.

The man in white raised his torso, sitting up, his arms supporting himself. He was about to speak when he noticed the man in control of the game, the referee, a few yards away, raising a yellow card in the direction of the player who had tackled him. Despite the pain now starting to crease through his leg and the baying crowd, the man in white somehow felt calm, at peace. He answered the Physio.

"I'm sure it's broken. I felt it crack."

The physio told the player to lie back again while he began talking softly into a small microphone attached to the lapel of his own tracksuit.

"We'll need a substitute and a stretcher," he said, slowly rolling down the players' sock, revealing part of the player's tibia protruding through the skin. The physio was surprised that the player wasn't screaming with pain, given the injury. He knew the man was likely in shock and wasn't fully aware of how bad the break was.

The referee walked over to the huddle of the physio and other support staff who had now surrounded the player and were working on getting him safely off the pitch.

"How is he doing?" he asked.

"Not good," the physio replied, "we're dealing with a bad break here."

"Okay," replied the referee, "how long do you need?" he continued, looking at his watch. The game was tied at one goal each and there were only a few minutes left of extra time. If things remained as they were, then a penalty shootout was likely needed to decide the winner. It wasn't something any of the officials wanted as there was always controversy afterward when penalties were used to conclude the tie.

"It will take as long as it takes," the physio replied, disgusted at the very question.

In the technical area, the manager of the away side began reorganizing his team. He was angry, extremely angry. He had lost one of his star players to a reckless challenge and now he needed a substitute for the injured player, and he needed one not afraid to take penalties. He made his decision.

The stretcher-bearers bore the weight of the injured player who was now covered with a grey blanket, his leg immobilized with a plastic splint. They brought him to the side of the field laying him down carefully. The referee blew his whistle for the game to recommence.

The captain of the away side took control of the free-kick, launching the ball forward towards the eighteen-yard box of the opposing side. A group of four players jumped for the ball but as it soared across the goal face, a stray elbow deliberately aimed, smashed into the eye of the home team player, the defender who had just been booked for the bad foul on the player in white. The man crumpled to the ground like a discarded bag of potatoes, blood streaming from his left eye. As he fell he didn't see the grass hurtle towards him, he only felt the surrounding darkness close in on him, as his head hit the ground.

CHAPTER 1

"It's a very nice set up isn't it, Mike?" Rich Telside said.

Mike Cannon looked around at the wood-panelling that covered three sides of the room. It gave him and the others standing around at the bar, a sense of warmth, a sense of comfort, especially when compared to the snow lying outside that could be seen through the wall-to-floor window making up the fourth wall of the room.

"Not bad at all, Rich," Cannon replied. "A bit of money has gone into this. I mean just look at that driveway."

Telside turned his head to look out of the glass window. Despite the snow covering most of the paddocks that stretched away to the right and seemed to blend into one, the driveway leading up to the building they were standing in, the *visitors centre*, snaked like a ribbon away into the distance. Only a single set of tyre marks disturbed the virgin covering that lay on the ground. The road was ultimately lost from view, the low white cloud and mist seemed to swallow everything in its immediate surrounds.

Telside nodded in agreement with his boss. The investment in setting up the stables, building the admin and visitors Blocks as well as developing the staff facilities had cost millions. It was a very special place owned by someone lucky enough to have achieved their rewards through the talent they had been given.

"Another drink, Mike?" interrupted the man with sandy coloured hair and a moustache to match.

"No thanks," Cannon replied, "I've still to finish this one," indicating the glass in his hand containing a rum and coke that he had not yet touched.

"No problem," Brendon Harris responded, smiling as he always seemed to do. "We'll get going in a minute or so if that's alright with you?"

"Of course," Cannon replied, "whenever you are ready."

"We're just waiting for Alex, then we'll start."

Cannon smiled his understanding. Harris turned and walked away, taking a few steps towards another group of people standing around the bar, again letting them know that the meeting would start in the next couple of minutes.

The drive up to Cheshire had been uneventful, but long. The snow that had fallen was heavier than forecast and the roads had been full. The journey on the M40 had been reasonable but when Cannon and Telside had hit the M6 the trip had seemed interminable. Between Birmingham and Stoke-on-Trent, the journey had blown out by an hour, taking the trip to well over three and a half hours overall. They had been glad to finally arrive at their destination, but the start of the meeting had been delayed due to other syndicate members also arriving late. Eventually, everyone had managed to find their way to 'Stonely Park' and had been adequately fed and watered. Now it was just a matter of concluding the arrangements and then everyone could go home or get to their accommodation for the night.

As Cannon and Telside continued chatting to themselves, they suddenly felt a buzz around the room, then the voices slowly soften until a silence seemed to descend upon the assembled groups. A sense of anticipation filled the air. To Cannon, it seemed that there was an unnecessary ripple of excitement permeating through the collective. Heads were turning towards the single door, the entrance, and the sole exit of the room. Voices could be heard getting louder as two men climbed up the stairs, unseen but not out of earshot of those standing with their drinks and awaiting the arrival of the two.

Alex Stone and the trainer of the horses housed at the facility, Dominic Wingrew, entered the room, both men smiling at the assembled group. It was clear to Cannon that the two men were experienced at such entrances. They had done the very same thing many many times. That's how you become a well-known personality, Cannon thought. A smile, an entrance, a glittering career, and a spot on national television.

Spontaneously the room began clapping. Telside who was standing beside Cannon whispered quietly to him, "A bit dramatic don't you think?"

Cannon could just hear what Telside had said. He nodded. "A bit of theatre Rich. Never really hurt anybody."

Telside didn't respond. He briefly put his hands together joining in the acknowledgement with the others of the two men's arrival.

Stone and Wingrew remained standing just a few feet inside the room, waiting for the applause to die down. Eventually, the clapping stopped, and Stone took the opportunity to thank everyone for their kindness.

"I hope everyone has got a drink?" he asked pointing towards the bar, still occupied by the two female bartenders who were both dressed in white blouses and black slacks and who had been serving the group for the past forty-five minutes.

"I think everyone has been well catered for Alex," Brendon Harris said, "We really appreciate your hospitality and would like to thank you for hosting our little get-together."

"It's my pleasure," Stone replied. "As you can see, we cater for these types of events fairly regularly. Whether it be the buying of a horse, the selling or moving on of one, or indeed the establishment of a syndicate like this one, we try to create good relationships, and this is how we do it." He turned to Wingrew who nodded, smiling as he did so, indicating to all his affirmation of what Stone had said.

Cannon watched Wingrew's face, noting the man's body language as Stone spoke. Cannon wasn't sure if Wingrew was in full agreement with his boss, but he was practiced enough not to give away too many of his own feelings.

Cannon noted that Wingrew's face had remained static as Stone had spoken. Was he really happy losing such a good horse to Cannon?

"That's great, Alex," Harris said, once Stone had finished his practiced *patter*. Continuing he said, "I am sure I speak on behalf of everybody in the syndicate when I say that we are privileged to be able to visit this amazing facility of yours and yet, despite the loss of the horse, you are still willing to host us as we arrange for the formal move of *Titan's Hand* to Mike Cannon's stable. We are truly appreciative of your magnanimous gesture."

The group clapped again showing its appreciation. Cannon squirmed internally. Harris was really *laying it on thick*. What Cannon was offering, was taking responsibility for the care of a prize thoroughbred and the promise of hard work. He wasn't offering first-class surroundings and *special events*, he just hoped that Brendon had advised the syndicate members accordingly. Stone held out a hand, professing modesty, flapping it towards the group and indicating that they should stop clapping him.

"I'm sure Mike will do wonders with the horse," Stone said, smiling again in Cannon's direction. "We'll be sorry to see him go, but sometimes a change can work wonders with a horse with so much talent. We know he has the capability, and we know Mike does too," he went on, "remember I am still the largest individual percentage holder in the horse, so while he is moving stables, he is still close to my heart."

"Well, with that, should I suggest we start the meeting?" Harris asked.

"I think so," Stone replied, "let's do it."

Stone pointed towards a room just behind and to the left of the bar, accessible via a single door. He walked towards it, pushing it open and inviting everyone to join him.

Inside the room was a board table made of highly polished oak. It was surrounded by a dozen high-back chairs. It was just large enough for each of the syndicate members to take a seat leaving a spare for Telside. Dominic Wingrew stood at the door for a short while as the group settled down, then excused himself from the meeting. The room had windows facing the long drive that Cannon and Telside had discussed before but also had similar windows facing the stable Blocks situated behind the building. Cannon looked behind him, glancing through the window just as Harris brought the meeting to order, Cannon noticed Wingrew entering into one of the stable Blocks, his footprints leading up to the door clearly outlined in the snow. Cannon noted that each of the Blocks had a large letter painted on the side of the specific building. He noted that Wingrew went into Block C.

"Okay, bringing the meeting of the Titan-H syndicate to order," Harris said, "I would like to thank each of you for coming, I note it's been a long way for some of you and I appreciate you making the effort to get here despite the poor weather conditions."

The group laughed quietly, acknowledging the sentiment.

"Once again," Harris continued, "I, on behalf of everyone here, want to thank Mr. Stone for his generosity in hosting this very meeting and looking after us so well."

Stone smiled. It was a practiced gesture.

Suddenly, without warning, a voice was raised, a woman's voice. "Oh, for goodness sake Brendon! Could you please get on with it? We haven't got all day and already it is starting to get dark. I've got to get to Newcastle tonight, so I'll need to be on my way in the next hour or so. I have a taxi booked already to take me to the station at Northwich. "

Harris looked at his watch as did others in the room. Currently, it was two thirty-five. The sun would be down shortly, and it would be dark by four-thirty.

"In addition, I still want to see the horse before I go," the woman continued, "so can you please get a move on?" she repeated.

Harris sighed. "Okay Sarah, just give me a chance."

Some of the group smirked into their hands, Sarah Walters owner of a chain of nail bars was an extremely impatient woman and she made no bones about it. As part of the original syndicate that had bought the horse when he first came up for sale, she was well known for being forthright. Cannon had been introduced to her when he and Telside had arrived. She was small in stature, just over five feet tall. Aged in her mid-fifties, she was as skinny as a rake. She never seemed to eat anything. Those that knew her believed that she lived on the vapours from her e-cigarette which she was constantly puffing on. Fortunately, she had accepted that she was not able to *vape* in the meeting, but she played continuously with the *device* that she held in her hand. Cannon noted a smell of pomegranates wafting in his direction as she constantly turned it over and over.

Harris continued, trying to regain his composure, lost temporarily by Walters' outburst. "Right, so for the record we, the Titan-H syndicate, made up of the following people, have agreed to move our horse, *Titan's Hand,* from the stable of Dominic Wingrew to that of Mike Cannon. The reason being is to give the horse a chance to fulfill his potential in a stable which is smaller but more focused than the current arrangements? Is that what we all agree?" he asked.

"Yes," "Yep," "Agreed," came voices from around the room.

"Okay," Harris continued, "if that's the formal acceptance then let's confirm the percentage split that each of us now holds given that Mr. Cannon has taken a share in the horse. Is that okay with everybody?"

Again there were nods of acceptance around the room, so Harris plowed on. He noted that Sarah Walters was checking her watch again.

"Mr. Stone," he said, "after the sale of some of your stake, and as you mentioned earlier, you remain the single largest stakeholder in the horse at

30 percent."

"Agreed," replied Stone.

"And Mr. Cannon, Mike, you have now acquired twenty percent of the horse. Correct?"

"Correct," repeated Cannon.

Addressing the rest of the meeting, Harris said, "The willingness to buy into *Titan's Hand* is an act of good faith on Mr. Cannon's behalf and I think we should thank him for doing so. Don't you agree?"

There was consensus in the room and murmurs and nods made towards Cannon. It was fairly low-key, but Cannon accepted the acknowledgement graciously. Inwardly he hoped that the relationship between horse, his fellow owners, and himself would be a positive one. He looked around the room as Harris carried on. Most of those assembled seemed genuine. He wasn't sure about Sarah Walters, and he knew a little about Alex Stone, but being a major stakeholder and now the trainer of the horse, he hoped for a relatively smooth ride through the horse's remaining career.

It was the first time he had the dual responsibility of trainer and part-owner of any horse. He had taken a stake through the encouragement of Michelle. She had suggested for a while that he take advantage of his talent. "Why not own as well as train?" she had said one evening as they sat in their lounge. "Sharing in the prize money can only be good," she had continued, a smile upon her face. "And I'm sure Rich will agree."

The seed had been planted, so when the opportunity arose to join the Titan-H syndicate as well as train the horse, Cannon had assessed the risk, looked at the outlay, and decided it was worth a shot. Before making a final decision he had discussed the matter with Rich. The horse that he was buying into had potential and had been successful in several races already. Cannon and Telside had looked at the various races the horse had run in and won. During the first half of the current season, the horse seemed to have lost its will to race. It was jumping badly, seemed tentative, and yet in the preceding season, it had been one of the most successful hurdlers racing. Neither Cannon, nor Telside could establish from watching the films what the reason was, but once they were able to get the horse into their stable they would be able to find out firsthand what the issues could be. At least that was their hope.

"Alright, so with Mike here taking 20%, the balance of 50%, given Mr. Stone keeps 30%, is split amongst the rest of us as follows," Harris continued.

The sale by Stone of 45% of his shareholding had allowed both Cannon and several others to join the syndicate. The other remaining 25% holding had not changed despite Stone's sale. It was split into:

10% Brendon Harris (as the syndicate manager)

10% Richard **'Dick'** Swiftmann

5% Sarah Walters.

"So for those that bought into the horse, from the 25% Mr. Stone has now sold," Harris continued, "I am happy to formally welcome you all on the journey with us," he smiled. "And those people are....Fred and Mary Punch, 5% between the two of you. Peter Brown, 5%, Cindy Higgins 5%, Melanie Freed 5%, and last but not least Tony Clairy 5%."

The room fell silent, the new owners not really sure what to do next. After a few seconds, Richard Swiftmann echoed Harris' welcoming words and suggested the new owners say a few words about themselves.

"After all, given we are partners in the horse, it would be good to know if we can be partners outside of the syndicate as well. Maybe our business or personal interests could be useful to each other at some stage?" he asked.

Harris agreed, noting that he knew a little about each of the new syndicate members as they had completed the necessary forms when they applied to join, but such detail was quite limited in scope.

"At least I know where some of you live," he said smiling, trying to appease those that may have felt their privacy had been compromised.

Cannon watched, intrigued. It was the first time that he had seen a syndicate meeting run in this way. Normally syndicates were established with some people living quite remote from others, resulting in many people rarely meeting the other members. If they did meet, this would have often been at a racecourse and even then not everyone in the syndicate would always be in attendance. He noted how some of the people around the table seemed uncomfortable about sharing their background, but before anyone could respond to Harris, Sarah Walters spoke out again forcefully.

"I'm sorry to do this to everyone," she stated standing up, "but I need to leave. I have a meeting up North, and I need to be on my way." She reached into a handbag that she had placed on the floor, placing her vaper onto the table, and extracting a dozen or so business cards which she then threw across the table towards Harris sending them fanning and spinning in all directions.

Some around the table reached out towards them, picking up the brightly coloured laminated cards.

As she picked up the vaper and readied herself to leave, placing a grey *Teddy* coat around her shoulders, she exclaimed. "As you probably know, I'm Sarah Walters. I own several nail bars across the country. I'm no longer married, and long may that be the case," she added enthusiastically, "and if you need any further information about me. Google it!" she said. "Plus, my website is on my card!" and with that, she left the room.

Some in the room giggled behind their hands. Cannon looked at Telside, who looked speechless, aghast. Cannon's face remained like stone. How he felt was not reflected in his features. His mind was running, however. What was he letting himself in for, he thought? Was this the start of something he would regret? He had been involved with many difficult owners previously. Owners of all types. In addition, he had met many people, good and bad, when he was in the police. As a Detective Inspector, he had come across many different types. Individuals, often with their own agendas. He guessed Sarah Walters was one such type. He parked his thoughts. It wasn't his place to speak just yet, but the way Walters had acted certainly, didn't auger well for the future. The syndicate, he concluded, could have some interesting times ahead and he, being the trainer of their horse, and being a larger stakeholder than most, could put him in the firing line. Time would tell.

Harris looked embarrassed. Cannon noted that Stone seemed distant from the goings-on of Walters, almost disinterested. Others around the room appeared shocked, unsure of what they had seen and heard. They found the entire incident amusing.

"Ahem, I'm sorry about that," Harris said finally. "You must excuse, *Ms.* Harris, she can be a little…..*flighty,* can we say?"

"I'd use stronger words than that," Peter Brown said, "In fact where I come from she'd get a mouthful from me and maybe more if she acted that way."

Brown, a farmer from Sheffield, stocky, just short of six feet tall, mid-forties, and someone who could look after himself sat to the left of Cannon. He hadn't said much when they were first introduced, preferring instead to take a beer from the bar and to sit on a chair watching the racing channel that was being shown on a large flat screen attached to one of the walls. Later, while the TV had been muted, Brown had shown more interest in what was showing than in meeting his fellow syndicate members.

"I'm sure that's true," Harris replied to Brown, "and yes, Sarah was indeed very rude, but she *did* say that she was in a hurry," he conceded.

"Aye, okay," Brown replied, folding his arms across his chest. It was clear he disagreed with Harris' view.

Harris took a deep breath. "Let's move on," he said, "If we still want to see the horse before Mr. Cannon…sorry, Mike, and Mr. Telside…"

"Rich!" interrupted Cannon's deputy, "call me Rich," he continued.

"Rich…" agreed Harris, acknowledging Telside's request. "So, before Mike and *Rich* take the horse down to Oxfordshire, if we still want to see him before he goes, then we'd better get a move on. It will be getting dark in a short while and I'm sure they will want to be on their way as soon as they can be?"

He left the question hanging.

"Mr. and Mrs. Punch. Fred and Mary," Harris said pointing at a youngish couple seated opposite Cannon. "Tell us briefly about yourselves," he asked. Cannon had observed that the couple had stayed very quiet so far, keeping to themselves. They seemed embarrassed to be in the room. He also noted they appeared to be holding hands underneath the table.

"Well, there's not much to say really," Fred Punch said. "I'm originally from Whitstable in Kent and Mary here is from Portsmouth." Mary Punch lifted a hand and waved, waggling her fingers in a gesture that seemed like a royal who couldn't be bothered to put in any energy. She was a waif of a woman, early thirties, similar in age to that of her husband. She had jet black hair cut in an asymmetrical bob. Her skin had a pale color, almost translucent. The contrast with her hair was stark. Cannon wasn't sure if the hair was dyed but it seemed to suit her. Her thin fingers and arms were covered by a pale blue cardigan which sat atop a white blouse buttoned up to her throat. Blue denim jeans and sensible blue trainers completed her outfit.

"We met at University, Leicester," Fred Punch continued. "I was studying Economics and Mary, Film art. We've been married now for just over two years."

"And what do you do?" asked Cindy Higgins.

"Oh, well we make a range of documentaries and lifestyle programs now," replied Fred Punch, "we have a contract with channel 4."

Cindy Higgins seemed impressed. An ex-model she had been in the limelight quite often during her career. Having cameras pointing at her was one of the things she missed. She wondered if in the future she might be able to use what the Punch's were selling? Certainly, her lifestyle could be something worth documenting. She was a very attractive woman still. At forty-seven but still pretending to be in her thirties, she smiled at Punch, her eye's conveying more than a thank you for his explanation. He blushed. Mary Punch gripped his hand tighter. He felt her annoyance.

"Yes," she jumped in, speaking for the first time. "We've filmed everything from the Emergency services in Hull to Maternity Units in Devon, through to Swinger parties in Manchester," she added with a slight smirk on her face.

"As I said," Fred Punch concluded, clearing his throat, "a whole range of subjects."

"Thank you, Fred....and Mary, for that. Who is next?" Harris asked. "Cindy? Perhaps you?"

Cindy Higgins continued to lock eyes with Fred Punch. He stared back, eventually dropping his gaze. Higgins noted that in comparison to his wife, Fred Punch was a man in his mid-thirties, medium height with light brown hair. He was well built. He had a flat stomach, strong thighs, an attractive man to most women. His chiselled features, a solid chin, and nose, deep green eyes made him seem incongruous when placed against his wife. However, Cindy Higgins soon put that thought to bed. There was no telling for taste.

"I'm thirty-eight," she lied. "Former model. Catwalk. Now I represent a medical firm."

"A rep?" Brown said somewhat cruelly.

"A *consultant!*" Higgins retorted, "to clinicians, doctors, and other medical professionals."

"A rep, selling drugs," Brown replied, laughing. "Let's call a spade a spade, darling," he added. "As I said before, there is no need for fancy stuff. Where I come from we…."

"I'm sure that will be enough, Mr. Brown," Harris jumped in. "We are all friends here, no need to go any further," he added, trying to play down an issue that he thought was potentially getting out of hand. He was beginning to think that the free drinks that had been served at the bar had perhaps not been the best of ideas.

"Let's move on, time is passing," he said, tapping his watch, and nodding towards the window where the sky was darkening, and snow had begun to fall again. "How about you Melanie. You've been extremely quiet so far."

"Hey what about m….?" Brown interrupted.

"Mister Brown, we'll get to you in a minute. If you don't mind, I'd like Mrs. Freed to introduce herself first."

"Very well," Brown conceded.

Melanie Freed took a deep breath. She was a woman in her early sixties. Her grey hair was tied back in a bun. She wore a beige woollen jumper under a mohair coat which she had kept on all the time despite being inside, a plaid skirt, stockings, and shoes with large buckles. Her outfit screamed *Grandma,* however, it turned out that she was the widow of an ex-RAF pilot. She did not have any children and she was from Lincolnshire. "I hope that helps?" she asked once she had told everyone her background.

"Yes, that's fine, Mrs. Freed," Harris advised. "We are very glad to have you on board," he said as kindly as he could. Before turning back to Brown, he asked Tony Clairy if it was okay for the farmer to formally introduce himself ahead of Clairy. There was no objection.

"Okay, Mister Brown. Go ahead. Introduce yourself," Harris said somewhat bluntly.

The tone wasn't lost on the man from Yorkshire, but he ignored it, saying, "My name is Peter Brown. I'm a farmer, sheep. I'm originally from Sheffield but now I have a farm about 25 miles to the East of the city, not too far from Retford. I'm married, two kids, but none of that is any of your business really," he said. "Oh, and by the way," he continued, looking at Cannon, "I've had a few racehorses in my time. Even trained a few point-to-pointers myself, so I know a little bit about the game," he stated condescendingly.

Cannon nodded at Brown deciding not to say anything in response. He felt Rich tense up beside him. Cannon patted him on the arm and shook his head slightly. He didn't want Rich rising to the bait, however, he heard him say something under his breath.

Harris thanked Brown for his input, happy that they had almost gotten through everyone. He wanted everyone out into the stables to look at *Titan's Hand* in the first instance and then the rest of the impressive setup that Stone had built.

"Mr. Clairy?" Harris said, "if you don't mind, the floor is yours." He raised a hand, palm upwards, and gestured towards the table, indicating Clairy could speak when he was ready to do so.

"Hi everyone," Clairy said. "My name is Tony Clairy. I'm an ex-footballer. I played most of my career in the Championship and the league below that, League one. I retired a few years ago. Since then, I've followed my hobby which is photography. My living is now selling photographs to newspapers, magazines, and the wider media, TV, social media. I specialize in pictures of and about nature."

Cannon looked around the room at the nods of appreciation and acceptance of Tony Clairy into the syndicate, though he did notice Stone look a little quizzically at the man. Clairy was tall, around 6 feet two, aged roughly forty, his stomach had started to show signs of a paunch. No longer playing football and training hard for a living, the body was beginning to slow, and muscles were beginning to turn fatty. Despite this, he was still very well-groomed, a few scars on his face reflecting perhaps his days of taking knocks on the field.

"I used to play in the midfield or defence if needed," he said, noting one or two of the group seemed curious about his sporting prowess. "Had to retire. Too many injuries," he continued, "however I am glad to be adding another string to my bow, and I look forward to the success of *Titan's Hand* in Mr. Cannon's care."

Despite the obvious knocks, Clairy was still quite good-looking. Cindy Higgins noted the man's dark eyes, his strong nose (still straight), and chin. He had a full head of brown hair, cut stylishly. He wore no ring on his wedding finger. Cindy would follow that up when she had the chance.

"Thank you, Tony," Harris said once Clairy had concluded his comments. There was a short silence before Swiftmann made a small coughing gesture into his hand. Harris immediately recognized his mistake.

"Oh, sorry everyone, I nearly forgot." He pointed towards Dick Swiftmann. "Richard has been in the original syndicate since day one and has been on the journey with Alex, myself, and Sarah, so he is almost part of the furniture, should we say? I'm sorry Richard. Over to you," he continued apologetically.

"Thank you, Brendon," Swiftmann replied.

Facing those around the table in turn, he said, "Firstly, could I ask that you all call me Dick rather than Richard? I know the name is sometimes used in a derogatory way, but it's what I've been called nearly all my life," he went on, "and I prefer it."

There were a few giggles around the room, however, Swiftmann ignored them. "We also have another *Richard* with us anyway," he pointed towards Telside, "who I'm sure we will get to know in the coming months and also next season, when we visit Mike's yard in Stonesfield, down in Oxfordshire. So, to avoid confusion, I'm Dick and that's Rich," he again nodded at Cannon's assistant. Continuing on he said, "As mentioned by Brendon, I've been with the horse since day one. He's done well in the past but for some reason, he has run some bad races in recent times. We hope by changing stables to Mike, and a thank you again should go out to Dominic for the success achieved to date, that the horse will return to winning ways," he smiled. "No pressure Mike!" he added, to the delight of the others.

Cannon just smiled. Normally the transfer of horses in and out of his stable wasn't done as formally as this was, but to move a horse away and change the syndicate members at the same time, especially from such a high-profile stable as that of Stones to that of Cannon, was quite a big thing.

"So, that's me," concluded Swiftmann, suddenly. "I guess we can now go and see the horse before everyone goes home? What do you think Brendon?"

Harris nodded, then before turning to Stone, to get the go-ahead, he pointed out of the window. The snow had begun to fall even harder making it appear even darker outside.

"Everyone, I see the weather is turning against us, so I'm not sure how many of you want to tour the stables after you have seen the horse, however, I understand from Alex and Dominic that you are free to do so. At least to around about six o'clock, when the stablehands will be closing everything up, feeding the horses etcetera. Mike, I suspect you will be well on your way by then? Is that right?"

"Yes," Cannon replied. "Ideally if we can be on our way by around 5 pm that would be great. We have quite a long way to go. Rich here will drive the horse down in our horse-box, and I'll be meeting him back at the stables."

"Thanks for the clarity," Harris replied. "Alex, is it ok for us to go and see our charge now before he moves down south?"

"Of course," Stone replied. "I'd just like to suggest that we all congregate outside his stable in Block B. It's stable number three for those unaware. We can have a quick look at him and then if you like follow Mike and Rich out into the yard again to see him load up. It might take a while, I guess?" he looked towards Cannon who nodded in agreement. Continuing, Stone said, "Once you are out of this building and on the pathways or grassy areas please can I ask you all to be careful? I think with the snow and ice underfoot, things can be a little messy so it would be better if we are all careful and stay safe rather than be sorry. We don't want any injuries from anyone falling, do we?" he concluded.

Harris echoed Stone's words then invited everyone to move towards the stables at their leisure. The group stood up from the table, a murmur of thanks, a few handshakes took place, and the group slowly dispersed after some had finished their drinks. Cannon noted that most of those assembled had been drinking beer or wine, but Clairy was drinking what appeared to be coke. Perhaps a legacy of his sporting days? However, all that sugar wouldn't be helping his waistline, Cannon thought.

CHAPTER 2

It took around twenty minutes for the group to re-assemble. Most were standing outside the stable of *Titan's Hand*, however, Cannon and Telside were inside, preparing the horse for travel. Head collar, a poll guard to protect the head, tail guard, leg bandages, shoe covers, and finally blankets to keep the horse warm were all needed for the trip. The assembled group noted how much care was taken with their horse. It was an owners' precious cargo, and they had every right to ensure things were done properly, but some were surprised at how much attention was given. Cannon insisted that all and any of the horses under his care were treated correctly. In this case, he was now part-owner as well, so he took even more care.

Speaking from inside the stable, he said to those outside. "As you can see, it takes a while to get the horse ready, and sometimes if they are skittish or agitated it can take much longer. *Especially* if the latter," he emphasized. "It can be extremely dangerous if a horse is cranky and kicks out. I've seen people have legs broken or some coming close to being killed."

Some in the group nodded their understanding. Cannon continued. "As you can see this boy is being very good. Nothing appears to bother him, which makes Rich and my job so much easier."

"If he's so laid back," jumped in Peter Brown, "Is that why he's not racing well?"

Cannon smiled to himself. A typical owners' question, he thought, and one from an owner who had strong views on most things. He recalled Brown's earlier comments about knowing about the game and training point-to-pointers.

"I'm not sure," Cannon replied honestly, neutrally, moving to the side of the horse and away from the animal's head in order to see Brown more clearly. The mornings' hay, to be replaced shortly, crunched under his feet. "I'll need to get into his head a little bit once I've got him in my yard," he said, "so, I can't answer just yet. What I can say is that the horse has got great potential as a hurdler. He's got speed and I know he can jump better than he has been doing, so we'll see. Does that help?"

"I guess so," replied Brown unconvincingly, his furrowed brow indicating what he was really thinking.

"Any more questions?" Cannon asked.

There was silence from the group. "In that case, If I could just ask you to stand back, Rich can bring the horse out and we can load him up. You are welcome to follow or as mentioned earlier by Alex and Brendon, have a wander around of the facilities. For those that haven't had the chance to see them yet, they really are amazing."

The group stood to one side as Rich led the horse out of the stable, his hooves clacking on the cement floor that ran down the middle of the stable block. Some of the other horses looked out through the bars of their doors at the departing animal. It was a much different sound from what they normally experienced. Hay would normally be laid twice per day which would deaden the sound of the individual horses' movements so the sound of metal shoes on cement at that time of day piqued the interest of a number of the stable occupants.

Rich led the way to the exit of the stable Block. Cannon noted some of the group decided not to follow and guessed that they were likely on their way home or had decided to take a walk through the rest of Block B and then see the other animals in the other Blocks.

Cannon knew that there were some blueblood horses in the other blocks. Horses were owned by sheiks, ex-football managers, actors, film stars, and other personalities. Wingrew was a successful trainer in the main and Stone's money had built a fantastic facility. State of the art. Cannon hoped that his fellow owners had tempered their expectations about his own stables?.

He had been chosen to take *Titan's Hand* because he had done so well with some other horses, and he believed the horse had good potential. Despite not having a champion horse in his care, he had once almost won the Grand National, but a crazed owner had stopped him from doing so. This had increased his profile, enhanced further by another horse that had also done extremely well in the *Tingle Creek Chase* at Sandown, only losing the race by just a few inches. Those had all been *Chasers*. Cannon still had to prove himself with *hurdlers*. He had trained a few and had been reasonably successful, however, the hurdlers he had been given to train were never really the top-quality horses, the cream of the crop. He did however have hope that *Titan's Hand* would be able to change that. If so and noting the horses' potential, Cannon believed that he could become a Stayers' Hurdler or even a Champion Hurdler. Time would tell. If he was as good as hoped and was able to qualify for the best races, then Cannon would be over the moon.

They began loading the horse into the horsebox. The snow was starting to come down harder. On the grassy areas and out into the paddocks along the drive, the snow appeared inches deep. Untouched, virgin. The driveway no longer showed signs of tyre tracks, the snow having covered those that had previously left their mark. The sky appeared to be just a few metres above them. It was a dishwater grey with no sign of any break in it. The black of night was not too far away, despite the relatively early hour. How long the snow would fall was also anyone's guess, however, it was clear that the trip back to Oxfordshire would be much longer and more treacherous than preferred. Roads were bound to be impacted, some potentially blocked.

"I don't think we'll be racing soon," Cannon said to the few people assembled around him. He noted that Fred and Mary Punch, along with Clairy and Swiftmann had either already left for home or had gone off on their tour. "With all this snow, courses are bound to be closed for a while, but let's hope for not too long," he said. "I'd like to give the horse a run as soon as he seems ready," he went on, "but I'll let him tell me when that is."

As they settled the horse inside the box, some of the others decided to leave, saying their goodbyes. Only Brendon Harris and Peter Brown remained behind as Cannon and Telside ensured they were happy that the horse was secure and comfortable. They began folding up the ramp, before finally closing the door. As they began securing the bolts and clasps on the box, checking that it was fully closed, through the deafening silence of the snowfall they suddenly heard a scream, A scream that got louder and more hysterical as each second passed. Cannon's police training kicked in. Despite the years that had passed, he recognized that the scream was one of fear, of horror, not of surprise. The sound continued. Brown and Harris stood immobile. Rich stayed next to the horse box. Cannon ran!

He ran towards the sound that now curdled his blood. His senses took him towards stable Block B. Others from the syndicate were suddenly behind him, following, curious, frightened. He saw Swiftmann out of the corner of his eye a few yards behind him, jogging, but without any sound emanating from his shoes as they hit the ground. Footsteps were deadened by the snow. Soon he felt more people behind him, he could sense their heavy breathing, their gasps for air as they ran.

Upon arrival at the entrance to Block B, Cannon ran inside slowing slightly to get his bearings and to hear where the screams were coming from. Curiously it was silent, the only sound the odd rustle of an animals' movements, rolling around upon the straw laid on the floor of a stable. The other people behind Cannon came to a halt just inside the Block's door. Harris arrived a few seconds later, puffing. Brown came in last, he bent doubled over, hands on knees as he came to a halt.

Cannon and the others listened for a few seconds before another scream rent the silence. "Block A?" Swiftmann suggested.

Cannon agreed and barged through the crowd that had now grown in size due to the addition of some of the permanent staff, the stable-hands, and others who had heard the commotion. Behind Cannon a snaking line of people, some walking almost in single file, and a few running abreast of each other headed towards Block A.

As he got closer to the entrance of the Block, he noticed the sound, the wailing, echoing off the sides of the interior walls. Slumped against the left wall, sitting on the concrete, in the semi-dark was Mary Punch. She had wrapped her arms around her legs. She was sobbing deeply, her head bent down, the sound subdued as she rocked backward and forwards.

Cannon looked beyond her. She was sitting in front of a hay store. He walked slowly towards her, pointing at the others to stay back as they reached the main entrance to the Block. As he got closer to the entrance to the hay store, he noticed a shadow on the wall near the back of the Block. A door slightly ajar, the last of the winter light just creeping through the crack and illuminating some small movement.

Cannon reached the distraught figure of Mary Punch, whose whimpering continued, softer now but unabated. He bent down and touched her on the shoulder. She flinched in fear before raising her eyes and looking into his. Her sobs became louder, Cannon seeing the horror in her face. He stood, then slowly walked into the hay room. He noticed those who had followed him originally had now slowly entered the Block, stepping quietly perhaps 20 feet behind.

Inside the hay room towards the back, he noticed a figure in the shadows. Standing vertically, arms flat against his side, head lolling to the left was Fred Punch. Through his stomach was a large fork pinning the man to one of the hay bales. The force of the blow had sent the tines right through the body, severing the spinal cord and likely causing almost instant death, certainly within seconds. Blood seeped through Punch's mouth. A large amount of blood had already been lost through the immediate injury as well. It was clear to Cannon that the man's heart had continued pumping for a few short seconds after the initial injury, resulting in a mass of the sticky liquid spreading onto Punch's clothes and the ground in front of him. Cannon found a light switch just inside the door to the room. Turning the light on he noticed that the man's face had somehow stayed in situ, the grimace, fear, and shock that he would have experienced as he was struck, attacked, pierced, was etched onto it.

"Call the police and get an ambulance here quickly!" he shouted to no one in particular, just the group of people that he could sense were now standing outside the room.

Harris peered inside, "Oh my G….," he began to say, however before he could finish the sentence, Stone came rushing into the Block from the open back door, knocking it against the wall and making it rebound on its hinges, slamming it shut again through the barging action as he charged through.

"What the hell's happened?!" he exclaimed, "I heard all the screaming. What's..?"

Stone suddenly realized that everyone around the door to the hay room was either attending to Mary Punch or were on their phones. Harris had thrown up, vomited by the sight of the dead man.

He heard Cannon call out again.

"Alex, get in here quickly," he said, "but be careful not to touch anything. I need your help."

Stone moved inside slowly advancing towards Cannon.

"It looks like the fork is coming loose from the hay-bale behind, it won't be long before it no longer holds him up. Let's just get him onto his side on the ground, the police can do the rest," Cannon said. "But don't touch the fork-handle or shaft, it may have fingerprints or other DNA on it."

"Okay," Stone replied.

They took the body by the shirt and trousers and with one man on either side, slowly eased the dead man to the ground. As they did so, Stone's hand slipped, and he lost hold of Punch's shirt. As the body fell away from him, towards Cannon, Stone reached out to grab what he could, his hand reaching the fork handle which he took hold of.

"Shit!" he shouted.

Cannon had no choice but to accept what had happened. He was curious but he had not seen any intent on Stone's part to let go of the body deliberately. He stored the incident in his memory before repeating, "Let's ease him down now. Slowly!"

The deadweight of the man caused them to struggle slightly, but they eventually achieved their objective. Standing up after their exertions, both men looked at the corpse. It was an obscene sight. On its side the piercing of the man's back was evident, and pieces of flesh and muscle almost dripped from the tines that now showed clearly through the man's clothes.

"Get her to your bar, give her a strong drink," Cannon demanded of Stone concerning Mary Punch. "Hopefully the police will be here soon, and the ambulance too."

"An ambulance won't help him," Stone said, nodding towards the ground, his face beginning to turn an uncomfortable grey.

"Agreed," Cannon replied, "but hopefully it will help her," he said, flicking his head in the general direction of Mary Punch who was being comforted by some of the others outside. She was still wailing despite the attempts by some to calm her down.

"Okay," Stone replied. He turned and quickly walked out of the room. He began ushering everyone outside, as Harris helped Mary to her feet and held her under her arms. Her legs had *gone*. She seemed unable to walk but with the help of Stone, Harris was able to manhandle her out of the Block and back into the now fading light. They took her across the snow-covered ground, leaving trails and tracks from the many feet crisscrossing the area, and sat her in the very bar that they had left no more than thirty minutes before.

Cannon stayed with the body. It was quiet for a while, and he was left alone with his thoughts. Death was never far away. He had seen it so many times. He could never forget what he had experienced over the years while he was in the police force. His dreams were often filled with faces from the past. Some haunted him more than others. Some came back to him and some never returned. Some were still alive, many were ghosts. It appeared to him that Death never forgot where to find him. It seemed to visit too often. In the most unlikely places.

He heard a noise behind him. *Rich!*

"You okay, Mike?" he asked.

"Yes, I'm fine," Cannon replied, the dark memories that he had just recalled disappearing like smoke on the wind. "Not something I expected though," he continued.

Telside wasn't fully aware of what had happened. He had continued to settle *Titan's Hand* in the horsebox as the others ran off towards the screams. He looked down at the body lying on the ground then looked back at Cannon.

"Bloody hell, Mike," he said, "what the hell is going on?"

Cannon shook his head, suggesting that he had no idea. He knew very little about the man and had no inkling as to who would have wanted Fred Punch dead. Then he looked down at himself. He noticed his shoes and jeans were all covered in bloodstains. The sticky, viscous liquid had permeated his clothes and onto his hands. He dropped to the floor, scraping his palms with hay and rubbing furiously between his fingers. Pieces of material dropped to the ground like little red matchsticks, as the friction from rubbing the coarse fibres against his skin broke the hay into smaller pieces.

"Look Rich," Cannon responded eventually. "I suggest you get going with the horse. I'll tell the police when they arrive that I told you to get on your way. I'll take responsibility for you if they complain, but as we both know, neither of us was anywhere near this place when the *murder* took place…"

"Murder?!" questioned Rich.

"Absolutely," Cannon replied. "This is about as cold-blooded as you can get."

"Fuck," Rich replied.

As he was not one for swearing, Cannon knew that Rich was shaken up. He wouldn't normally issue any expletive no matter what the issue was. Cannon knew that Telside felt uncomfortable with what he was seeing in front of him.

"Get on your way. Now!" Cannon said.

With the ringing instruction in his ear, Telside turned and left the hay room, almost running towards the horsebox outside which was now illuminated by a bright light situated above the door of the Block. It appeared to be an automatic light that was activated by movement around or in front of the door. Telside guessed that it came online once the daylight had reduced to a certain level. The area outside however was empty of people. The horsebox was as he had left it, its doors firmly closed, the horse still inside.

He made another quick check of the bolts around the base and top of the back door then jumped into the cabin, started the engine, put the inside heater on to clear the windscreen, and with a jerk due to his haste to leave, began the slow drive between the paddocks and on towards the main road. Snow continued to fall, and it made the journey slower than he expected. As he reached the main road and turned to begin the long journey home, he heard sirens in the distance coming from his left. He could just make out the blue and red flashing lights which he believed to be the emergency services drifting in and out of his view. They raced along the road, their lights disappearing, then reappearing as they sped along, up the hills and down into the many dips that the road traversed.

Leaving Cannon behind was not something he was happy to do, but he realized he had no option. He would give Michelle a call as soon as he could. He knew that Cannon would spend most of the time helping the police and would likely forget to give her any thought while the initial investigation got underway. The taking of statements, the initial interviews happening, would make it a long night. As soon as he could, Telside stopped driving and pulled the horsebox into a small layby about five miles from Stone's stables. The area was quiet, it was now very dark. A wind had come up and drops of compacted snow and ice fell from the surrounding tree branches onto the roof of the horsebox, creating a thudding sound each time. *Titan's Hand* kicked out, his hoof hitting the side of the van every time a thud was heard on the outside of the vehicle.

Telside picked up his mobile and despite fighting bad reception, made the call.

CHAPTER 3

Inspector Tim Cummings was young for his rank. Cannon was surprised that the man with whom he, and the others, would likely need to engage with concerning Punch's murder, was as youthful-looking as he was.
Cannon was glad. He didn't need to be put in his place by an arrogant, self-absorbed fool that wanted to be the centre of attention in a murder inquiry. He had been through that once before. What he had hoped for was someone with an open mind. He observed that in Cummings.
The Inspector was standing in the bar area along with the other syndicate members, plus Wingrew and several of Stones staff that had been on the property when Fred Punch was killed a few hours earlier.
Seated on a chair beside Cummings, was Sergeant Paula Alton. Outside, a crime scene tent had been set up and a number of SOCO's were searching the area. Lights had been brought in, to augment those already in place, and to give the officers a better opportunity of finding the clues they needed. It was now pitch dark and the wind that had come up over the past few hours was starting to push the still falling snow across the paths of the officers who were searching the grounds. Beams from their torches seemingly impotent as the snow and the light merged.
The men inside Block A had a slightly easier task than those working outside as the lighting was much better. Being a feed, tack, and storage facility, it needed more light, than the other buildings. With no horses stabled within, it was a working area for people, therefore, needing to meet the necessary Health and Safety requirements. The only negative was that being a feed store primarily, it did not have any CCTV cameras within it or even at the entrance. CCTV was expensive and with little of value to guard, it had been deemed an unnecessary expense. Cannon thought it an ironic situation, a false economy. What if there was a fire in the Block, wouldn't it be good to know how it may have started to prevent a reoccurrence?
The sun had set at least an hour ago and Cummings had kept everyone waiting before he requested the group, now assembled in the room, to meet with him. He had wanted to ensure that there were no slip-ups, he wanted to do things properly. Getting the SOCO's working, the body of Punch removed, and then maintaining the integrity of the immediate area where the body was found was his main priority. Everything else would fall into place as the investigation continued, he thought.
Introducing himself and his Sergeant formally, Cummings let everyone in the room know that the investigation into Punch's murder would require their complete cooperation. He expected that each of them would be able to provide a detailed statement about what they knew of the *incident*, and

once they had done so they could leave. He advised them that follow-ups were to be expected and that none of them should try to leave the immediate area of where they lived and certainly not try to leave the country.

"And another thing," he added, "I know that what has happened will likely be a shock to many of you, but for the record, murder is what we see, what we investigate every day," he nodded towards his Sergeant. "So, with that in mind, I want to promise you one thing. We *will* get to the bottom of this."

He looked around the room, surveying each face in turn. He was looking for any tell-tale signs from those in front of him, that could give him an inkling, a first clue as to who the guilty party was. No one moved. Every face was as if carved from stone. No one appeared to blink. Ten seconds of silence seemed to stretch into eternity.

"If it helps Inspector…..?" Cannon asked, breaking into the void.

"And you are?"

"Mike Cannon, Inspector. Can I have a word?"

Cummings eyed Cannon somewhat suspiciously. From experience, Cummings had found that the first person to walk into the empty space of silence was often the guilty party. The partner, wife, or husband of a murdered family member were often the police's first thoughts, the first considered as the main suspects. It was frequently found that the killer was those closest to the deceased.

"I think….Mr. Cannon….,"

"Mike,"

"Mike," echoed Cummings, "I think that it would be best if everyone can give their statements first, including yourself, and then if you'd like, I am happy to talk with you later. That can be tonight or tomorrow depending upon how much available time I have," he said.

"No problem," Cannon replied, holding up his hands in mock surrender, "I was just hoping that I could help speed up the process, that's all."

"I appreciate the offer, Mr. Ca….Mike and I will probably take you up on it, however, we have a lot to do in the next few hours as I'm sure you would appreciate."

"Of course." Cannon reconsidered his initial thoughts about Cummings. He wasn't sure now if youth screamed over-confidence or something else?

"Right," Cummings continued, "if I could ask everyone to wait here in the bar please? My Sergeant here will use the room behind you," he pointed towards the door of the room where only a few hours earlier the syndicate had met, "and she will take a statement from each of you in due course."

"How long is this going to take, Inspector?" Peter Brown asked.

"That depends, Sir."

"On?"

"On everyone's cooperation."

Brown shrugged at the vague response. "I'm sorry Inspector, but some of us have places to go. We need to get home and with all this snow about, the roads will be bloody treacherous. I need to let people know where I am."

"I agree Sir...er, Mr....?" he left the question hanging.

"Brown. Peter Brown."

"Well Mr. Brown, if you need to call anyone, please go ahead and let them know you are safe and well and that you will be somewhat delayed. However, if I could..."

"Somewhat...! What the hell does that mean?" Brown said, his voice raised in anger.

A smattering of concern began to filter across the room after what Cummings had indicated. The very thought of a delayed departure home had begun to resonate within the group. The potential for a very long night ahead was becoming more and more evident.

"Mr. Brown," Cummings replied calmly, "what it means is quite simple. Everyone cooperates, everyone gets to go home....at least initially."

The subtle meaning was not lost on Brown nor the others. It was clear that Cummings and Alton were likely to be nothing if not thorough.

Harris jumped in to try and calm things down. "Inspector, if I may?"

"Yes, what is it?"

Harris cleared his throat. "Inspector, my name is Harris, Brendon Harris. I'm the manager of the syndicate that Fred Punch, the victim of this terrible crime, was a part of."

"And your point is, Mr. Harris?"

"Well Inspector, I just wanted to say that I think it is highly unlikely that anyone here, in the syndicate, was responsible for the murder of Mr. Punch. I can assure you...."

"Assure me of what?" Cummings asked, visibly annoyed.

"That there was no reason for anyone in the syndicate to perpetrate this terrible crime," Harris replied. "We only met a few hours ago for the very first time. How could anyone..?"

"Exactly, Mr. Harris. How could anyone kill someone else?" Cummings responded. "It's an interesting question," he replied sarcastically, "but one that we need to answer, and that's exactly what we aim to do...so if you wouldn't mind, could we please get on with your statements? Oh, and should you need to make a call to families or loved ones, can I suggest that you do so now? Thank you."

Alton stood up and called out Cindy Higgins by name. Higgins identified herself and was told by the Sergeant to go through into what she called the *interview* room.

Cannon observed Higgins walk slowly into the other room and watched as the door closed behind her. He had noticed the Sergeant counting heads as Cummings had been talking. She had a folder with her into which she had inserted a list of names of those in the room. It had been the first request that Cummings had made when he had originally corralled everyone into the bar area. A list of names of all those on-site at the time of the murder was what he had asked for. Cannon noted that with the obvious exception of Sarah Walters and Fred Punch, all the members of the syndicate were surprisingly present. In addition, there was Dominic Wingrew and a total of six full-time and part-time staff members. Two were the bar staff, two others from the administration team, and two stable-hands.

He knew that Harris and Brown could not have been involved with Punch's death as they had been with him and Rich as they were loading *Titan's Hand* into the horsebox. In fact, they had followed the horse all the way from the stable that he had been kept in, all the way to the horsebox, even as others drifted off to take their tour of the facilities.

While Higgins was being interviewed, Cummings left the room after asking a police Constable who had been standing outside the door of the bar area, to ensure that no one left the room while Cummings himself was away.

Cannon suspected that the Inspector was on his way to get an update from the head of the SOCO's team. He also noticed a rise in the volume level within the room. Several people were on their mobile phones. Cannon decided to give Rich a call and provide him with a heads-up regarding the overall situation. As the phone rang, Cannon noticed Stone and Wingrew standing some distance away from the others. They were talking quietly, almost whispering.

"Yes, Mike?" Rich's voice.

Cannon took a second to realize that Telside had answered the call. He dropped his gaze away from the two men that he had begun to stare at and answered his assistant.

"Hi Rich, how are you?" he asked.

"To be honest Mike, not too well."

"Why?"

"Traffic snarl-ups on the motorway," Telside replied. "The snow's got heavier since I left you and we've been sent via detour along some A and B roads. Just south of Telford we ended up on the A41. I just pulled into some *Services* as you called. Lucky you didn't phone five minutes earlier I wouldn't have been able to answer."

Cannon was relieved that Telside was persevering in getting back to his stables, despite the snow. He knew that Rich would be sensible and responsible concerning the weather. He wouldn't try to drive if it was too dangerous.

"Oh, and I've let Michelle know that you'll be late," Telside continued, "it's the least I could do."

"Thanks, Rich," Cannon replied. "I'll give her a call myself after we hang up. I think it may be very late before I get away."

"Okay Mike, understood. Once I get to Stonefield, I'll get the horse settled, and hopefully, we can have a good look at him in the morning?"

Cannon agreed. It was hardly likely that he would be away from Cheshire until much later. He wasn't sure how Alton was choosing who she interviewed next but given the number of people to get through, Cannon could see himself waiting around until the early hours. He said his goodbyes to Telside then immediately called Michelle.

"I've been waiting for your call," she said almost immediately as she answered the phone. Mobile to mobile meant that she could see from the caller-ID who was phoning her.

"Yes, I'm sorry about that love," he said, "I presume you know what's going on?"

"Well Rich told me that someone had been killed, but he didn't give many details."

He wasn't sure what to say. Should he tell her all the details now or could it wait until he was home? He didn't want to worry her, so he said, "Yes, a member of the syndicate who I only met for the first time today."

"My God, Mike. What happened?"

Should he tell her or not?

"Murdered!" he said. Decision made, no need for subtlety, he thought.

"Murdered?"

"Yes…!"

"Are you okay?" she asked.

"Yes, I'm fine," he replied, "but I am likely to be very late. The police are here taking statements right now, but it's taking ages," he added. "I may even need to find a hotel up here if it gets too late and the snow gets worse."

He had no intention of doing so but he didn't want her to worry.

"Will you let me know?" she asked.

"Of course I will," he replied. "If I leave very late, I'll SMS you so that you know that I'm either on my way or that I've found a hotel or something to stay overnight in. I won't call as it could be very late."

She stayed silent for a few seconds. She realized how much she was missing him. Their relationship had grown even stronger over the past year. She felt that when he was away she was no longer whole. A part of her was missing. He could sense it.

He needed to do something about it….

"Be careful," she said eventually.

"I will. See you soon," he continued. "Love you."

"Love you too."

He was about to put down the phone when he heard her say, "Oh Mike before you go, I just wanted to let you know that Cassie called."

"Ahh, my lovely daughter. What did she want, money?" he asked, a smile on his face. Cassie was known to call whenever she needed something. Sometimes advice, but oftentimes money.

"No, she just wanted to shoot the breeze, have a chat."

"Did she say how her *internship* is going?" he asked. "The last time we spoke to her was what, about three months ago?"

"About that."

"And?"

"She just wanted to know how *you* were. How *we* were doing. Nothing much else."

Cannon thought about what Michelle had said. Something seemed strange. Normally he and his daughter would speak every fortnight. For the past few months however she had been unavailable at the normal day, and time, that they had set up over 12 months prior. He had initially found it odd but took it as her being busy, given her new job. She was now working at a law firm having completed her law degree and continuing towards her formal legal qualification by serving articles. She called it an internship, rather than an apprenticeship. In his eyes however, it was the latter.

"I need to give her a call myself. I'll do it tomorrow," he said, making a mental note.

He rang off after saying his goodbyes and stood silent for a minute. He noticed that Stone and Wingrew had separated from each other, no longer talking in whispers. Stone was talking to Harris, and Wingrew to Tony Clairy and Melanie Freed. The old lady looked tired, while Clairy was listening intently to what Wingrew was saying. Cannon noticed the glass of coke that Clairy was drinking. He watched as the man raised the glass to his lips finishing the contents in one swallow. All that sugar, Cannon thought.

He walked over to where Peter Brown was standing alone. He joined him in waiting their turn to be called into the interview room.

"So, Mr. Cannon," she said, "thank you for your statement. You can go now."

Cannon smiled at the Sergeant. She had already interviewed most of those that had waited patiently in the bar. Cannon was the penultimate person to be asked to provide what he had heard and seen. Only Stone was to come after him.

It was already past midnight and the door from the bar to the stairs that led to the exit had been left open after the others had left. Stone, being the last to be interviewed had been requested by Cummings, to accompany the Inspector, as he checked on how the SOCO's were proceeding with their investigation. Cummings did not want Stone to be left alone in the bar while Cannon was being interviewed by Alton, so he made the man shadow him, albeit from a distance. The indignity of Stone needing to follow in Cummings' footsteps for a while as the Inspector made his inquiries was not lost on him.

By the time Cummings had made his way to where the SOCO team was, they were just completing their work. The area in front of Block A had been of little use it seemed. The number of footprints in the snow had destroyed any chance of finding anything significant in terms of who had accessed the area. Before any of the formalities had been started, the taking of statements, Cannon had pointed out to Cummings the rear door to the Block and what he had witnessed when he had initially entered the building. Cummings had taken it on board and had asked Cannon to formalize it in his statement. In the meantime, Cummings had passed on the detail to the SOCO's for them to follow up and use as necessary.

The fork used to kill Punch had been removed and bagged for evidence, as was the straw near and around the body. By the time the SOCO's left, Cummings knew that every piece of evidence they believed was useable would have been removed.

"I assume I'll hear from you soon, then Sergeant?"

"When appropriate," she replied noncommittally.

Cannon sighed. "I do know how this works, you know."

Alton looked tired. Her eyes had dark shadows underneath them. It had been well over six hours since she had started the process of taking statements.

"Really?" she answered.

"Yes. You may not know but I was in the force, a DI for many years. Worked around the country."

"Is that so?" she replied without enthusiasm. "In which case," she continued, "you'll understand the next steps, won't you? Some good old-fashioned Detective work still needs to be done before we get to the point of drawing any conclusions. Any evidence we have will need to be consolidated, additional analysis will have to be done and everything correlated against these statements," she said with sarcasm and pointing towards the hand-written notes and other documents already signed by witnesses. She also pointed at the small tape recorder that she had used in the interviews to make her point.

"Yes, I do understand Sergeant. You and the Inspector have got a big job ahead," he replied. "However, given I was first at the scene, I think I may be able to help you more than the others....should you require it?" he added.

"I'm sure we'll consider your offer generously, Mr. Cannon, but I'll let the Inspector make that call should he decide to take you up on it."

Cannon looked at her again. What he had noticed during the statement taking, and he assumed the same applied to the others, was that his initial thought about her was confirmed. She was indeed very thorough. She had a no-nonsense approach to her job, and it was clear she didn't take fools lightly.

She wasn't what he would call a 'beauty', but she was pretty. She had a face, when not tired, that would generally reflect a softer side to her nature. It appeared that her job rarely gave her reason to smile, but he guessed that outside of her profession she would be a different person. Not radically, but at least more open, more accessible. She was around five feet seven, some would say a little plain and frumpy, though that would be unkind in Cannon's view. She had some sagging around her chin which only became prominent to him as she yawned. She had a slightly crooked nose that looked like a sporting injury of some sort, maybe a hockey ball he thought. Her skin was a warm colour, her eyes dark. Her mouth was downturned adding to the look of her being much harder than she really was. Whether she was acting that way, as part of the job, Cannon could only guess.

"No worries," he replied eventually, "just trying to help."

He looked at his watch as he stood up, his back creaking slightly. He stretched as he did so, his hands involuntarily reaching towards the ceiling. She watched him curiously, then asked, "Why did you leave?"

"The Force?"

"Yes."

"I'd had enough," he answered, a pang of guilt running through him. "I'd seen it all," he continued. "This," he motioned with his arm across the room, indicating the murder he had witnessed earlier. "I'd seen it too many times. Plus, it was getting to me, the things I was dealing with. The shit that I saw happening around me. After so many years I needed a circuit breaker. Something that would take away my thoughts from the ghosts that kept coming back to me. Those I had hoped to forget."

"And did you find one…?"

"Eventually," he replied. "My wife and my daughter."

Alton just nodded. A few seconds of silence passed between them before she added, "That helps."

"Yes it does, or indeed did, but it wasn't easy to break away."

She was curious. He noticed that she was beginning to soften, warm towards him. It was a sincere gesture on her part. He could tell. He had been there many times before and he could see through those that were just paying lip service, trying to pretend to be interested in others, in their humanity. He was beginning to like her.

"What happened?"

"My wife. She developed cancer. She died some years ago now."

"I'm sorry," she replied.

Cannon stayed stoic. He could never forget Sally, but he had Michelle in his life now. His sense of loss had diminished over time but whenever he talked about it, he still felt a little raw.

"Well, that's life, I guess," he continued. "We wanted a change and we found it down in Oxfordshire. We built a business over time, had some success and then…,"

"Shit happened?" she interjected, finishing the sentence for him.

"Yes," he replied. "And the ghosts that I thought had left, came back. Sometimes with a vengeance. Just when I thought they were gone."

"And now?" she asked.

"At times they come to see me," he acknowledged, "but not as bad as they used to do. I'm lucky now. I have a wonderful partner who is waiting for me at home. A daughter who has made me very proud and a great assistant who has been nothing short of incredible in helping me with setting up and running my stables."

She looked at him, her lips began forming the outline of a smile, but he noticed that she didn't follow through with it.

All business he thought to himself.

"So that would be Rich Telside?" she asked.

"My assistant? Yes."

"And as per your statement, you told him to leave. Go home?"

"Yes."

"Did you think that wise?"

Cannon realized where the conversation was going. It was becoming a direct inquiry, almost a test, a rehash of what he had already indicated had happened. Trying to find contradictions. He decided to put a stop to it. He wanted to get home. If she wanted to interview him again, then that should be done properly. He had given his statement as accurately as he could, now it was time to go.

"I think Sergeant, my reasoning and my actions have been made clear in my statement. I sent Rich on his way as I knew he had nothing to do with Mr. Punch's murder and that he needed to take the horse we had come to collect safely down to my stables. I did tell you in my statement that I thought it was best for him to do so, and that I would provide you with everything I know as to what happened here. I think I've done that."

Alton considered his answer. She knew that he was right. What she had heard from the other witnesses had already confirmed his story.

She thanked him for his cooperation and wished him a safe journey home, advising him that she or Cummings would be in touch as things developed. As he turned to leave the room, Cummings and Stone were returning. Cannon looked sympathetically at her. She had one final statement to take.

"Good luck," he said.

CHAPTER 4

"How are you doing?" he was asked.

"I guess I'm okay," came the somewhat terse reply.

"Well, if that's your attitude then maybe I should leave now?"

"No, please don't," he said, "I've not had the best of days."

Looking around, the visitor noticed how the part of the flat deemed to be a dining room was still full of used plates. Perhaps more than those used in a single day.

"What happened to the help?"

"She called in sick. Again!"

"When was she last here?"

"A few days ago. I think it was Monday."

"And it's now Thursday," the visitor replied disgustedly. "Maybe we need to get the council to find someone else?"

The man sitting on the couch didn't reply. The home help he needed had come and gone several times over the past eighteen months and he didn't want to get used to someone else right now. It was bad enough that he would need to find another suitable worker who was responsive and sensitive to his needs, let alone the poor dog having to accept another body into the home.

The visitor looked around again. The flat was musty, needed a vacuum, and dust had settled on the mantelpiece and on the small bookcase where a couple of cheap novels lay. They hadn't been touched for years, for obvious reasons. With the snow falling outside, as it had done on and off over recent days, opening windows and losing heat from the interior was not a good idea, especially given the occupants' infirmity. The visitor found the place oppressive. It needed a good clean, some air to freshen it up.

"How is *he* doing?" the visitor asked, ignoring the discomfort.

"The dog?"

"Yes, of course. The dog."

The man on the couch reached out to scrub the ears of his pet. Initially struggling to find him for a second, the visitor told the man where the dog was. A silent scold reflected on the dog owner's face and was aimed towards the visitor. The man always knew where his dog was. At least that was the message he was sending to his visitor. The animal, a sandy coloured Labrador, raised its head just as the man found it. Initially almost asleep but aware, the animals' training had kicked in, noting the small movement of its master towards him.

"He's fine, aren't you boy?"

The dog stood up slowly, the handle attached to a hard metal strap across the dog's shoulders tapping slightly against the seat of the couch. The man reached for the metal bar and using it as a guide levered himself up.

"Do you want some tea?" he asked.

The visitor looked around again before saying, "No thanks. I'd better be going."

"So soon?"

"Yes, I've got things to do, plus the drive."

The man felt the dog by his leg. Still holding the handle, he said, "Okay well thanks for coming, you know I always appreciate it."

The visitor looked around, taking in the room again, the small kitchen off to one side and the door into the single bedroom. It was always a relief to leave but there was a sense of sadness each time. *What could have been?* With one final look at the fading wallpaper, brown with white butterflies, goodbyes were said, and the visitor left.

Standing on the landing, outside the door, tears began to form in the visitors' eyes. If anybody asked, it was the cold wind that made the eyes weep. It whipped through the narrow gap between the three tower blocks making up the estate, swirling through the railings that stood atop the original brick wall that created a passageway or corridor along the flat frontages. The biting cold that had been kept at bay by the small three-bar electric heater inside the flat now stung the face of the visitor. While taking a brief pause to reflect on how life was unfair, the visitor noticed how the snow had turned to rain. Large drops began splashing on the forehead and face, bringing the visitor back to reality.

After a quick walk to the car, the visitor took one last look around, and with a slight flourish as if to say, *thank God I'm glad I don't live here,* they were gone.

CHAPTER 5

"I've had a look at his record again," Cannon said, "and I'm not sure why, but for some reason, it looks like Dominic has been struggling to work out what to do with the horse."

He was standing with Telside as the first lot of horses were returning from their exercises on the heath above Cannon's stables. The sound of the horses' hooves on the cement of the yard was comforting to him. Cannon, Telside, and the team of riders, jockeys, and staff heard the cacophony every single day. Steam was rising from the animals' bodies, condensed breath from those on the animals' backs, snorts, and gentle clicking of tongues adding to the mixture. The soft snow that had fallen overnight had supplemented that already on the ground and had been shovelled into piles against the walls of the stable buildings. This gave the horses a clear path through which to walk without the risk of injury. Care was taken to ensure that there were no accidents or injuries by a horse slipping on the ice that lay below the overnight dusting.

Telside was watching each of the eight horses that walked in circles in front of him. Cooling down was the official name of what they were doing but given the current temperature was just above freeing, the label seemed inadequate.

"Is there anything obvious?" Telside asked in response to Cannon's comments. "Wingrew is a good trainer, so it would be very unusual for him not to be able to get the best out of the horse."

"I know," Cannon replied, "it doesn't make sense."

Telside didn't want to ask the question but decided to ask it anyway. It was in his nature, and he knew Cannon would see it for what it was, a genuine concern.

"Do you think we've bought into a lemon?"

Cannon smiled at the reference. He associated it with cars rather than with a racehorse. Perhaps the word *nag* would have been more appropriate, he thought.

Trying to remain positive, Cannon replied, "No, I don't think he's a lemon, Rich. He's proved that to some degree already. The races he was successful in didn't happen by accident, he won them through a desire to win."

Telside nodded. They had both looked at the films and it was clear that the horse relished what he was doing. The question that needed answering was why had the horse run so poorly, in his last few races?

"Well, we know he doesn't have any conformation problems, he's reasonably fit, the scoping of his throat showed that there was no issue there, so what is it, Mike?"

"I'm not sure," Cannon replied. "His work is reasonably good."

"It was better today than yesterday," Telside replied, interrupting his boss, "but it still seems like the horse is holding something back."

"Some horses can be lazy in their work," Cannon replied, "as you well know, Rich."

"That's true but to me, it seems to be something in the horse's head."

"Like what? Any ideas?"

"I'm not sure, but as we agreed just now, it can't be fitness because when he ran those bad races he looked a million dollars. His blood was fine and everything about him seemed normal. We can only take Tim's comments at face value. We should check what he said to Wingrew and see if they tie in with how the horse ran."

Tim Prine was the regular jockey used by Wingrew and Stone. He was on a retainer with their stable. Having been a jockey for nearly 35 years and the Wingrew/Stone stable jockey for 16 his assessment of any horse he rode, in races or in training, was always sought. When he was asked by Wingrew how he felt about the poor runs that the horse had, he had told the trainer, *The horse is alright as an animal, but at this stage of his career he can't jump, and he can't race!*

Strong words but accurate in their sentiment.

What was bothering Cannon was the *why?*

Why had the horse suddenly lost its appetite to race properly?

What had changed between the previous season and the latest one?

Was it really something inside the horse's head that was impacting how it ran?

Cannon turned to walk away from the group of horses, his suede coat speckled with small snowflakes that had begun to drift down again. He decided he would take another look at the race videos that *Titan's Hand* was involved in and see if he could find a pattern.

"Rich?" he said, "I'm going to my office to have another look at the videos. Can you join me when you've finished with the second lot?"

"Sure, Mike. No problem at all. I should be there in just over an hour."

Cannon nodded, smiled, and then walked away towards his house that stood a relatively short walk away from the stable blocks and the cobbled yard. He knew that, as always, Rich would be efficient, thorough, and would be able to give him as accurate a report on each horse in the lot as anyone could.

Cannon was grateful that Telside was both an Assistant to him and a friend. An older friend and someone he could not do without. Over the years their relationship had grown stronger. Rich, a man of few words, except when necessary, was past retirement age now. In recent times Cannon had been giving it a lot of thought. What would he do when Telside retired? How could he replace someone with so much knowledge about the thoroughbred racehorse? How far into the future was that day? This year? The next?

He didn't want to contemplate any of the questions, but he knew that time was the conqueror. Some things were inevitable, and he hoped that when the time came he would be ready for it.

"I still don't get it," he said. "Just look at how well he won his races and then how badly he ran in these others."

They were sitting in Cannon's office, a mug of tea sat on either side of the desk close to the edge. Michelle had brought one to each of them just a few minutes after Telside had wandered into the house having returned from the second lot. He had told Cannon that he had a few things to discuss with him about the gallops once they had completed their review of the videos of *Titan's Hand's* races.

"He was well weighted, he was fit, and the jockey was riding him as he should!" Cannon said somewhat disappointingly, "it just doesn't make sense."

"Can we have another look-see?" Telside asked, "I'm assuming all the gear is the same?"

"You mean, the blinkers, tongue-tie, bits, even the type of shoes he was wearing?"

"Yes," Telside replied. "Was there…?"

"Anything different..?" Cannon interjected.

"Yes," Telside repeated. "Anything different between the wins and the losses?"

Cannon sat back in his seat, a high back Millberget swivel chair from IKEA that he and Michelle had battled to put together a few weeks previously. He still had a few aches and pains in his lower back from the effort.

"I can't see anything in particular," he replied. "From the Stewards' reports covering each of the runs *this* year, it seems the horse *lacked interest*. That ties in with jockey, Prine's view," he continued.

Telside just nodded. "Let's have another look, Mike, if you don't mind? There must be something that we are missing, if not then we really may well have bought into a lemon."

For the next 90 minutes, they reviewed the races that *Titan's Hand* had won and those that he had run badly in.

Wins at Stratford, Doncaster, and Worcester and good runs at Haydock and Uttoxeter showed the horses' potential.

Poor runs/losses at Kempton, Sandown, Carlisle, Huntingdon, and Taunton completed the horses' career to date.

"Well, that's the lot," Cannon said, stating the obvious after they had reviewed every race again. "I don't know how many more times we need to watch these races. At this stage, I'm starting to get a bit *google-eyed* with them. I think I know each race by heart now," he added.

"Ummm," Telside replied, but without commenting further.

Cannon looked at his Assistant. "What do *you* think, Rich?" he asked.

"Something was bothering the horse, Mike, but from what I can see, it seems to be more mental than anything else."

"Such as?"

"Fear, maybe?"

"I guess that's possible," Cannon replied, "but of what?"

"I'm not sure. It could be anything."

Cannon agreed. "Perhaps I'll give Wingrew a call later and see if he has any ideas, or knows when it first started?"

"I would definitely do that Mike. It may give us a clue as to why the horse has been such a disappointment."

"Okay, I will," Cannon confirmed. "Just as an aside though Rich, how did the horse do just now?"

"Well, that's one of the things I wanted to fill you in on."

"Go on."

Telside explained how *Titan's Hand* seemed to relish the work he had done that morning. He noted that in both the jump work and the three quarter gallops the horse seemed to enjoy stretching out, racing in pairs with another of Cannon's better horses, *Statue of Ramos*.

"Do you think his work was better because of how we structured it? Running with a better horse?"

"It could be, Mike," Telside replied, "or it could be the different environment from that he was used to at Stones place."

"What about his food? Had he eaten up this morning?"

"Apparently every last morsel," Rich responded with a smile. "Maybe we feed him better, and he appreciates it more?" he added, with a sense of cheekiness in his voice.

Cannon put a hand to his chin and frowned. He turned back to the screen that they had been watching.

"I don't know, Rich. Something seems odd. We'll just have to monitor the horse and see how he goes. I'll start to look at some options as to where to run him first. Wherever we do decide to race him we'll need to let the syndicate members know."

"All of 'em?"

"Well, we'll do it via Harris," Cannon replied, "that's his job to let the others know."

"Thank God for that," Telside said.

Cannon ignored the comment, deciding that for now, they had exhausted the subject of *Titan's Hand*. They would watch how the horse developed and they would decide where and when to take the animal to the races in due course.

"Anything else I should be aware of?" Cannon asked.

Telside gave him a rundown of all the horses that had raced together in the second lot. It appeared that with the season's hiatus from the bad weather coming to an end, the stable appeared to be improving with regards to the form of the various horses in the stable. Their times over measured distances were improving, and most, if not all of the horses in the stable were showing signs of their competitiveness.

"Excellent Rich," Cannon responded, "it could be the start of something big for us. Let's hope so, as we need it!"

They had finished dinner, but the washing-up had not yet been started. Some of the dishes and utensils still needed to be put into the dishwasher, while others lay in the sink waiting to be cleaned.

Cannon and Michelle sat quietly in the lounge. The TV was on but the sound was muted as usual.

Michelle was seated on one of the two couches and Cannon on the other. She was marking papers from school, a pile of them on her lap, others on the cushion next to her. Flashes of light danced from the TV as the screen changed from scene to scene.

"So, are you going to tell me?" he asked. "About your day."

"Do I have to?" she replied

"It's up to you."

"It's not been a good day, to be honest," she sighed, "we've had a few incidents."

"Oh," he answered, knowing that with regards to school, even a private one, an *incident* could mean anything. "Do you want to tell me about it?" He was trying to be sympathetic without being condescending. Their relationship was a good one. It was on a sound footing and was based on openness and honesty. Sometimes, however, when he asked the question about her day, he hoped that she was aware that he wasn't prying but was showing that he was interested. He wasn't sure why he had the doubt he did, perhaps it was the fact that he hadn't made the final commitment to her. They had been together for several years now and she had seen him through some difficult times, personally and professionally, particularly the years after Sally had died. She had filled that void.

Putting the papers aside, she sighed again, more deeply this time, before saying, "One of the pupils in my homeroom class has raised some allegations against one of the staff today and I spent hours in meetings with her, the Head and one of the school counsellors. It's a bloody nightmare."

"What sort of allegations?"

She looked at him sideways.

"Do you really want to know?"

"I guess it's just the policeman in me," he said, trying to lighten the conversation, "I can't help myself, seems like I can't forget..."

"Perhaps you need to accept that you're an ex-policeman," she replied, "ex..."

"Touche," he responded, putting his hands in the air, surrendering.

She smiled at his actions, deciding to provide a little more detail, but was wary about how far to take it.

"It was the usual...," she said, "bullying, unwanted advances..."

He took a few seconds before he replied. "Do you believe her?"

"They are just allegations at this stage, so we are treading carefully, but the Head has stood down the teacher and informed the Education authorities and the Police."

"What did the teacher say? How did he take being stood down?"

She looked at him quizzically again. "Mike, I think you need to get out more."

"Sorry?" he replied.

She hesitated for a second then said with emphasis, "The teacher is female. The student is also female. The *her* I was referring to earlier is a colleague, a friend."

"Bloody hell," he replied, "I'm sorry, I just thought...."

"You thought that it was a male teacher and a girl complainant, didn't you?"

"Yes, I...who is the teacher?"

"Cynthia Crowe."

"Cynthia?" he replied incredulously.

"Yes."

"I don't believe it."

"Neither do I, but we have to have it investigated, looked into."

"And how is she feeling, Cynthia?"

"Devastated, to be honest."

Cannon cast his mind back to when he last saw the teacher concerned. Cynthia Crowe, a Mathematics and Physics teacher. Highly respected within the school community. In her late thirties. An attractive woman. Serious, intelligent, no-nonsense, newly single. It had been at a school function celebrating the school's 120th anniversary. The school, a private and reasonably exclusive institution, was situated with a beautiful view over the northern Cotswolds. Located between Charlbury and Shipton-under-Wychwood, the city of Gloucester and ultimately the town of Cheltenham lay some distance away towards the West, on the other side of the fields that spread out in front of the school.

Cannon remembered having spoken with Cynthia for about twenty minutes as he and Michelle had circulated amongst those gathered for the occasion. He had been *dragged* around the room during the evening, at least that was how he had good-humouredly relayed it to Rich when they had taken the following days' gallops. He had met with Cynthia on several occasions previously, including having lunch with her and her now ex-husband a couple of times over the years. They had known little about racing, and he knew that they had no real interest in the game, but they had been very polite to him about it. He had her down as an academic, a teacher for life.

"Do you think there is any merit in the accusation?" he asked.

Michelle hesitated in her response. It was dangerous to assume anything in these matters, but she *did* have a view.

"To be honest, Mike, I have my doubts, but you of anyone would know that these things are not always clear cut.

He considered what she had said. It was true. One *never* really knew what was in the mind of another person, no matter how well you knew them.

"But you have an opinion?"

"Of course I do," she replied. "I think it's all nonsense, but we have to be careful as we don't know all the facts as yet."

Cannon nodded. He knew from his past life that what often appeared on the surface, wasn't always what was swimming underneath, especially when it came to relationships, Professional or otherwise.

"When you spoke with her what did she say? he asked.

"She was annoyed, frustrated, and very very unhappy."

"I'm not surprised. I know about being accused of something you didn't do and how it affects you."

He briefly thought back to when he was accused by the BHA of race-fixing. It wasn't true but he had needed to clear his name. It was a difficult time and one that he didn't want to be repeated. It had taken a toll on Michelle as well. He was glad that it wasn't him facing the accusations Cynthia Crowe did, but he knew it would again affect Michelle. He was afraid it would impact their relationship. The school academic community was very close, and they would support each other, but what would happen if Michelle was ever put in that position? Cannon didn't want to contemplate it. Eventually, he said, "I'm sure it will be fine. Cynthia struck me as someone who is *straight as a die* and I'd guess these accusations are no more than teenage angst, dangerous though they may be."

"You could be right Mike, but despite what *we* think, a process has to be gone through and yours truly may need to be part of it," she continued somewhat sadly.

"To be a character witness for Cynthia?"

"Yes, but also to provide her some moral support."

"I understand," he replied. "Where is she now, Cynthia?"

"I think she was planning to go to her family down in Cornwall. From memory, her brother and his wife have a B&B in a place called Hollywell Bay."

"I guess that may help?" he said contemplatively, "until the messy stuff begins. When do they intend to start looking into the detail?"

"It's started already."

Cannon was surprised.

"Yes, the Head was meeting with the school counsellor late this afternoon. The school board was expected to have a virtual meeting tonight and I think they want to have the pupil and her parents in for a meeting the day after tomorrow."

"Hardly seems sensible for Cynthia to get away doesn't it?"

"Maybe," she replied. "Perhaps a few days away will help though? Keep her mind off it?"

"Hardly! I'd guess she'd be thinking of nothing else," he responded, perhaps more forcefully than he wanted to.

Michelle nodded, accepting his point.

They sat for a moment with their thoughts, the TV continuing to show images that neither of them saw, nor acknowledged. Cannon picked up the remote that was sitting on a small table in front of him and turned the TV off.

It bought Michelle back from what she was thinking, where her mind had drifted off to. She was a schoolteacher, but one that was now called upon to address an issue she didn't want to. She was uncomfortable. Not because of the issue directly, but because it could have been her. She knew it was a difficult place to be, she knew the pupil concerned. It was this very issue that concerned her. School children in their mid-teens often see things, harbour things, believe that they are being set upon, and are required to comply with rules that they do not like, or think are unfair. Some will comply and some won't. Those that don't are often the ones that seek to lash out, make accusations, anything to get their own two minutes of fame. They don't always understand the consequences, the impact on others. Michelle however was extremely well aware of this.

"I'm glad you turned that off," she said, pointing at the screen, devoid of sound or colour.

"No problem," he responded. "There was only rubbish on it anyway, plus it's getting late," he added, slowly stretching his arms skywards and cracking his spine slightly. "I need to get up a little earlier tomorrow, Rich and I want to have another look at *Titan's Hand*."

"The new horse?"

"Yes, I have an idea about what's been going on. I want to see if I'm right."

"Do you think there is a problem with it?"

"I'm not sure," he answered, "but I do think that the horse is better than its

43

form suggests."

"Okay," she said, shrugging. "I'll leave that to you, Mike. That's something I can't help you with. I have my own problems to deal with."

Cannon realized from the tone of her voice that she was stressed, clearly upset about Cynthia Crowe but she was trying to hide it. It wasn't working as far as he was concerned. Though she had told him he was an *ex-*policeman, he still had his training, his gut-feel about people, and he could read them well. Sometimes overtly, sometimes covertly. Body language, facial expressions, tone of speaking were dead giveaways.

Michelle was showing all the signs of a lack of emotional support, something he hadn't expected from her. He knew that he was not always as attentive as he should be, *weren't all men?*

He stood up and walked over to where she was seated. She looked up at him, he appeared silhouetted in the light. His shadow from a six-foot-tall lampstand behind him seemed to drape across her.

"I'm sorry about Cynthia," he said. "Is there anything, I or we, can do in the interim?"

Michelle looked down at her hands, the papers now on the seat beside her, no longer in a neat bundle but stacked haphazardly across the cushion.

"I don't think so Mike," she answered. "I just hope that we can sort it out quickly. I'm concerned about the effect it will have on my other girls," she continued, "in addition as I said before, I have no idea how Cynthia will handle it."

He looked at her again, seeing a few traces of tears welling up in her eyes. He sat beside her, brushing away the papers onto the floor.

She went to pick them up, but he stopped her by putting his hand on her shoulder.

"Leave them," he asked, "at least give me a minute. There's something I need to say."

She looked at him quizzically, unsure where he was going.

He moved closer to her then put an arm around her shoulders. He smiled, their faces just a foot apart. She thought he was going to kiss her, his habit of kissing her forehead regularly was something she enjoyed each time he did it.

He felt her brace for the kiss.

"I think should get married," he said, without ceremony.

It wasn't what she had expected. She was taken aback, almost not believing what she had just heard.

"Sorry?" she said.

"Do I need to repeat myself?" he replied, a smile across his face.

"Are you serious?"

"Of course, I am," he retorted, "I've been thinking about it for a while."

"And you never said anything?"

He pondered her question before saying, "Well why would I?"

"Because if you were thinking about it, don't you think it would have been best to drop a hint maybe?"

"Perhaps," he admitted, "but then the surprise may have been lost."

"You're right there, Mike," she smiled, "it certainly is a surprise. In fact, given what we've been talking about, I'm flabbergasted."

"So do you?" he asked.

"Do I what?"

"Want to get married?"

She tilted her head, looking at him at a funny angle, then touched her lips with a finger in fake contemplation, teasing him. Suddenly her face lit up like a candle in a dark room and she wrapped an arm around his waist, burying her head in his chest.

She began crying, sobbing tears that were speckled with joy.

He reached down and kissed her lips, tasting the salt from her skin.

"I'll take that as a yes," he said, his heart beating inside his chest.

It hadn't been a hard decision. He knew that Sally would have approved. Michelle was good for him. She was also good for Cassie. Over the years Cassie and Michelle had grown very close. His daughter and now his future wife were the rocks that had allowed him a settled life, without them both, he wouldn't be able to do the things he did.

"Yes…" she said eventually… "yes, yes, yes!"

He felt a little overwhelmed himself. It had been a long time since he had been married. He knew there would be many things to do, arrange. The when? The where? The whom to invite to the wedding? He hoped that the making of arrangements wouldn't affect the stable. He still needed to focus. It was after all his livelihood. He had clients to keep happy, there were races to be run, staff to pay, vets to engage, and he remembered that he would likely need to meet with Cummings again about Fred Punch's murder. Thank God for Rich, he thought, the next few weeks and months were going to be hectic.

CHAPTER 6

The sun shone weakly through the grey cloud that slowly drifted in waves across the low hills of Shropshire. A cold wind continued to keep the temperature in single figures as the horses paraded in the ring at Ludlow racecourse. The past few weeks had been routine and difficult. The snow had eventually melted leaving deep puddles on the heath and Cannon had postponed training at times due to the uneven and dangerous conditions. The water had left the ground boggy with deep mud trails where training would normally have occurred. It wasn't ideal and Cannon and Telside knew that some horses would love the conditions and others wouldn't, but with advice from his farriers and vets, it was suggested to wait until the weather improved and only conduct training as necessary.

Cannon continued to watch *Titan's Hand* walk around the parade ring, while he and those connections of the other runners were likewise being observed by a small Thursday crowd that were spending a few minutes checking out the nine horses about to contest the third race of the day. The punters were looking for signs. Which trainer was looking confident, which horse looked on its toes? For Cannon, it was unusual to see the horses parade anti-clockwise. Parading this way as the horses now did, was a unique feature of the racecourse. Only Ludlow and Goodwood did it this way in the entire country.

As soon as the call to mount would be made, the spectators would be off to the warmth of the bar or the inside of the stands where the bookmakers would be waiting.

Titans' Hand was on the fourth line of betting and Cannon was a little surprised by this. He wasn't sure if the syndicate members were betting on the horse. He felt the horse needed the run before it reached its best. The interruption in training had meant that the miles he believed needed to be covered to get the horse fit had not happened. When he had called Harris as syndicate manager to let the members know that the horse was going to race, he advised him that the horse would take improvement from the run. He also let him know that given it was the first race since the new syndicate was formed, Cannon wanted to see what happened and how well or otherwise the horse would run, before making any decisions about the long term. There was a multitude of issues to consider, and Cannon had been specific with Harris. The course going, the weather, the racing gear to be used, the weight the horse was asked to carry compared to the other horses (the race was a handicap), the jockey onboard plus the usual requirement of luck were all contributing factors. The race distance at just over two miles was not an issue, as the horse had won over the distance in the past. It was everything else that mattered including attitude and fitness. *Titan's Hand* had been relatively easy to train. He had shown that he was a fighter. He had the will to win, but he also had his quirks. He seemed to have sensitive feet so he would be racing with concussion plates to lessen the impact each time he landed after a jump. Fortunately, being a hurdler the height of the *flights* that he was jumping over was much smaller, at three and a half feet, than those of a Steeplechaser. Hurdling was as much about speed as well as jumping.

When Cannon had called Wingrew regarding his initial impressions of the horse, Wingrew confirmed what Cannon had suspected about the horses' feet but hadn't added much more. Wingrew had said that he had been unable to work out what the horse needed to meet his potential. He, like Cannon, knew the horse had the ability, but he acknowledged that he couldn't find the key to be able to unlock the door. Cannon was surprised, given Wingrew was an extremely successful trainer, however sometimes one had to admit defeat. Sometimes a horse came along and no matter how hard you tried, no matter how much experience one had, it was just an impossible task to be able to get the best from the animal. As far as Wingrew was concerned, *Titan's Hand* was one such racehorse.

"What do you think Mike?" Harris asked. He was dressed for the weather. He wore a heavy coat over a thick blue jumper and grey corduroy trousers. A grey flat cap and a tartan scarf finished off his outfit. Gloved hands sat firmly in the coat pockets.

Cannon didn't respond immediately. There was something about the way the horse walked around that he wasn't sure about, and it bothered him. He parked the thought in his head.

"Sorry Brendon," he replied, "I wasn't listening. I just had a thought about something. Bit of daydreaming I'm afraid," he continued sheepishly.

Harris repeated the question.

"To be honest, as I said the other day when I suggested we run him today and then accepted for the race. I think he needs a bit more time to get him totally fit, but I want to see how he performs before I can make a real assessment."

"So, you don't think we should back him today?"

Cannon looked sideways at Harris. "That's up to you," he replied. "As a syndicate member and trainer, I want the horse to do well and as you know I think he has true potential, but I'd be a bit wary about giving my money away. At least today anyway."

Harris nodded. He wanted the syndicate to be successful as it would increase the potential of him to take on the leadership of other, larger, ones. He had been in the game for several years. Creating and managing syndicates was his living. Some had been successful, and some had not, leaving him carrying the can, the risk. His job was to buy, lease and sell racehorses, particularly those in National Hunt racing. He would then syndicate them, most times keeping a share for himself. When times were tough and horses didn't run, either through injury, form, weather, or other reasons, being the manager and part-owner was fraught with risk. Syndicate members could drop from view for a while, stop paying bills, sometimes never surface again and it was for such reasons that he needed the *Titan-H* syndicate to work. Things hadn't been going well in other ventures that he was involved in. Being retired he had ventured into housing developments in Spain. Initially, things had gone well, but slowly more and more money was needed to keep the projects afloat. Bank loans supported by mortgages over his house had provided a financial lifeline but the need to meet repayments while the project had stalled had put him in a precarious situation. Success on the racecourse, at least through some large bets were what Harris was searching for. He needed to be confident when he put his money down, Cannon was not giving him that feeling.

The call to mount was made just as the jockeys entered the ring. It appeared that they were staying in the weighing room until the last minute. They were keeping as warm as possible. The jockey booked to ride for Cannon was Tye Hanson-Richardson, known colloquially as *HR*. He was a journeyman rider. A weekday rider. Someone who seldom got a ride on a weekend. He had been a jockey for many years but was not the flashy type. When he was on a reasonable horse he usually got the job done. Sadly, the jobs he received were mostly *also-rans*. Not being part of a large stable like Tim Prine who rode for Wingrew and Stone, he made a living, but it wasn't a great one. Many people questioned how he could survive at all financially? Like many other jockeys in a similar situation there were always rumours about him and whether the horses he rode were being stopped or the races themselves were being fixed, Despite the best technology in the world helping the racing stewards watching every move made during a race, it was easy for a jockey to fall off at an obstacle or for a stirrup to be lost or even a saddle to slip. In tight finishes, a whip could be dropped, and a horse lose the race because of it. It was often better to lose a race than to win one and if there was money to be made by losing, then there was always someone willing to try and *make it.*

Cannon hadn't used HR previously, but he had seen him ride and he knew that the jockey had an affinity for the course. He had persuaded Harris to let HR take the mount believing that he had something to offer the jockey and he reminded him of it while he gave him the race instructions.

"Remember what I said HR," he stated, "I want you to stay mid-field with as much cover as you can get from the other runners, and then over the last 3 furlongs I want you to attack the lead as quickly as you can."

"Is the horse fit enough?" the jockey replied.

"We'll see," Cannon said. "To be honest I think he will likely run out of steam anyway, but I want to learn his best race pattern."

HR was disappointed. He was hoping for a win to boost his relationship with Cannon. Being his first ride, he wanted to create a good impression. Cannon noted the jockey's face drop.

"Don't worry," he said, "ride him how I asked and if you do well, I'll consider keeping you on him in the future. He's got potential this boy," he added nodding towards the horse as it was being brought to a halt by the stable-hand so that the jockey could mount. "It's possible that he could get into some good races," he continued. "If that happens, it could increase your profile and your earnings. Think about that," he added, hoping the message had gotten through. HR nodded, accepting a leg up from the trainer and landing comfortably in the saddle.

Cannon and Harris watched as the horse continued on, walking away from them, being led around the ring one more time. The colors of the new syndicate were unfamiliar to Cannon and its manager and took some getting used to, especially for Harris. A grey cap, a grey vest with red crossed stripes like an "X" on the front and back were totally foreign to the both of them. Only the roan colour of the horse was what they were used to. As the horses left for the track proper via a now open gate from the parade ring, the few remaining members of the public standing around moved away to find a spot to watch the race. Almost all sought shelter indoors. Cannon and Harris walked away together towards the owners' lounge. It was easily accessible now to both of them, the need for masks around the place a distant memory. No longer were wrist bands needed and social distancing required. Tables no longer had limits on them. Immunization from Covid-19 had made racing fun again, especially the social side. Despite there being few punters on the course, there were always enough owners to fill the O&T facilities.

They watched in disbelief and with disappointment. The race over eight hurdles should have been a relatively easy one for the horse. While *Titan's Hand* wasn't completely fit, as they both knew, he certainly appeared to be in much better shape than how the horse ultimately raced. Being an Open Handicap and weighted ten pounds below the top weight Cannon still expected a good race from his charge.

After the starter had called the nine runners together *Titan's Hand* had begun the race as expected. He had taken up a position mid-field and had cleared the first two hurdles in the straight easily. He had jumped them well, landing in third position as the runners left the stands behind them. Thereafter everything appeared to go wrong. Cannon watched through his binoculars as the horse seemed to go backward in the field of runners. The longer the race continued the further behind the leader the horse became. At one point it seemed that HR would pull the horse up, but he continued valiantly, urging the horse along. By the time the winner crossed the line, *Titan's Hand* had passed only two of the other runners who had almost come to a stop. He eventually finished in seventh position at least forty lengths behind the favourite who had romped home. Harris touched Cannon on the sleeve, resulting in the trainer lowering his binoculars and shaking his head.

"Any idea what went wrong Mike?" Harris asked.

"I'm not sure," Cannon replied, still staring through the window of the grandstand from where they had been watching the race. He was trying to see how the horse had pulled up, checking how the horse was moving while the jockey brought him back to the unsaddling enclosure.

"I'll have to check with HR. Find out what his view is, but something is bothering the horse, that's clear. I'll give you an update once I've spoken with him and have got the horse back home."

Harris nodded, like Cannon he was extremely disappointed. He watched as the trainer excused himself and disappeared out of the room. He would need to fill in the rest of the syndicate once Cannon had provided the necessary feedback. Privately he was beginning to have doubts as to whether they had made the right decision in moving *Titan's Hand* away from Wingrew.

CHAPTER 7

The drive back to Stonesfield was unpleasant. The traffic was slow due to an accident on the M5 just south of Worcester. Cannon had to take the A44 joining up again with the traffic from the highway East of Daylesford and North of Chipping Norton. What should have been a drive of just over two hours, took nearly three and a half. He had stayed until the end of the meeting, but not by choice, as *Titan's Hand* had left for home as soon as practically possible post his race. There had been other matters that Cannon had needed to follow up on. Post his discussion with HR, he had checked out the horse which had been dope tested after the race. The horse appeared fine. There was no sign of any heat in the legs and the horse didn't appear to have even broken a sweat during the race.

HR had advised that the horse had felt fine until they had moved out of the straight and then something appeared to go amiss. Cannon had given this some thought and was beginning to establish a theory in his mind.

Once the horse had been loaded into its trailer and had been driven out of the course to travel back home, Cannon had planned to follow shortly afterward once he had called Telside and let him know his view about the horse's run. Thereafter he had planned to say his goodbyes to Harris.

Unfortunately, before he had been able to get away, his phone had rung with a number that he was unfamiliar with. He had ignored it, letting the call divert to voicemail. He expected it to be a crank call but noticed that shortly after the call ended, a voicemail notification was received. After listening to the message, he had needed to call back to a different number as the voicemail requested. It was to Cummings.

"Thanks for returning the call," Cummings had said. "I need to see you tomorrow."

Cannon had asked the obvious question as to why, but he had been given nothing more than a brush-off by the Inspector.

They had finally agreed on a time for them to meet. Cummings had also requested a separate meeting with Rich. "To get his view on what had happened on the day of Punch's murder," Cummings had explained.

After the conversation, Cannon had sat alone in the member's bar to keep out of the cold. He didn't notice how quickly the next two races bypassed him. He spent a few minutes on the phone for a second time with Telside, letting him know that Cummings needed to see him the next day, thereafter he sat with his thoughts, thinking about Titan's *Hand's* race then recalling what had happened up in Cheshire. By the time Cannon had finished a cup of tea that he had ordered it was almost time for the last race.

Leaving the course so late in the day meant that he had met others leaving for home at the same time. While the traffic from the course was much lighter given it was a weekday meeting, he still had the same problem that most of the traffic did, in trying to turn into Bromfield Road from the racecourse exit. He eventually got away from the T-junction as the sky was starting to darken, the lights of the vehicles coming from the opposite direction blinding him at times. Dusk and the weak setting sun in the west, to his right, exacerbated his frustration about the day.

It was nearly eight o'clock before he drove into his yard. Along the way, he had called Michelle and let her know where he was. She said that she would make him dinner and make sure it was warm when he finally arrived home. He thanked her, then let her know about the meeting with Cummings the next day. In response, she said that she had a few things to talk to him about as well when he got back. He wasn't sure from the tone of her voice if it was something positive or otherwise. He would find out soon enough.

CHAPTER 8

After he had arrived home from Worcester, they had spoken very briefly about the day's events, then he had eaten before conducting his evening rounds of the stable. He had walked around the buildings, his torch illuminating the areas where the lighting in the yard could not reach. There were shadows from tree branches that danced in the breeze that had become stronger as the evening had progressed. At times they appeared to jump at him from out of nowhere. He was always wary as he walked around, his senses attuned to his environment. A few years previously he had been attacked by someone without a face and he had never forgotten the incident.

It had been very cold, the winter chill made worse by the prevailing wind. Clouds blanketed the sky, leaving no breaks but had been moving quickly. Rain had threatened. Cannon had hoped that it would stay away.

Once he had come back inside the house, tiredness seemed to hit him like a brick wall. He had apologized to Michelle, and they had agreed that it would be best for both of them to wait until the next day to talk about what was on her mind. Michelle had let him know that she had taken the day off so that she could take her mind off what was happening at school. He wasn't sure it was true but had decided not to say anything. He knew that she had a lot on her mind, just as he did, and she would tell him when she was ready.

"It will be sometime next week," she said.

It was the following morning. Cannon and Michelle were standing in the kitchen. She had her back against the sink and a cup of tea in her right hand, her left arm held across her waist. She looked protective. Cannon stood opposite her, leaning against a cupboard door.

"Did they give you any idea what they want you to do?" Cannon finally replied.

She looked at him, a frown upon her face. "They want me to give a character reference," she said

"For Cynthia."

"Yes. At the hearing."

"Next week?"

"Yes, next week, Wednesday morning at ten o'clock."

"Oh," he replied, "is this the formal meeting?"

"Yes, the HR department is coordinating the internal process. The police are going to talk to Cynthia tomorrow."

"My God," Cannon responded, "I know they have to take all these things seriously as it's now become a very big issue in schools hasn't it, sex offending?" he added, "But Cynthia...I still find it hard to believe."

"So do I," Michelle agreed.

"And the kid?"

"Samantha Prittly."

"What's she like?"

Michelle took a drink from her cup, then a second mouthful, finishing it before placing the empty mug in the sink. Cannon guessed she was considering her answer. "I guess you would call her...plain, quiet, but studious," she answered.

Cannon nodded his head, encouraging her to continue. "Vindictive?" he asked.

"No, quite the opposite. She's one of those girls that keeps a low profile, never acts up in class, never any trouble. Almost the ideal student to be honest. She's reasonably bright, above average academically, and gets on well with her peers."

"So, this *is* a surprise then?"

"Yes," she replied. "It's almost out of character for both of them, Samantha *and* Cynthia."

Cannon pondered what she had said. In his time as a Detective, he had been involved in several cases, resulting in the finding and arresting of various male sex offenders. Some men had raped and murdered, tortured, and disposed of victims in many different ways. The perpetrators had come from all walks of life, all levels of society, but in all his time he had never come across a woman offending in the same way that men were. Yes, there were women accomplices in some of the cases, but predominantly they were bit players in the actual crimes. There were exceptions, of course, Moira Hindley and the Moors murders in the sixties were an example. Male teachers were *some* of the perpetrators he came across who were caught conducting such crimes, but mostly the crime itself was done outside of the school environment. Their victims were, as a rule, not their own pupils or even kids from the school they taught at. Cannon wasn't naïve enough to think it didn't happen in his day, he just hadn't come across it personally. Perhaps given todays' grooming of victims, those guilty of such crimes, felt it was easier to get away with? Trying to be someone they are not? He didn't understand their logic, their thinking. They would get caught in the end. Sadly, with the internet and social media dominating many peoples' lives, cases like that of Jeffrey Epstein and the linkage to royalty, meant that exposure to every tiny detail, and the salaciousness that went with it, were often the catalyst of some people's journey into darkness. The thrill of things! Cannon knew that evil was often found in the most innocent of places and people. Nothing surprised him, yet to hear what Michelle was faced with, and it being so close to home, unsettled him.

"Do you have any views on the matter?" he asked eventually.

"I don't think it's true," she replied after giving it a few seconds' thought.

"Umm," he mumbled, "it's sad that the presumption of innocence until proven otherwise has been lost, isn't it?"

"Yes. It seems that all one has to do nowadays is make an accusation and the other party is guilty irrespective of the facts."

"The old adage of *where there's smoke.....?*" he proclaimed.

"Exactly."

For a few seconds, they looked at each other, saying nothing. Their eyes met. He felt sympathy for her. He could only guess what she was feeling inside. He took a few steps towards her then wrapped his arms around her shoulders pulling her closer to him. After what seemed like a lengthy silence, he stood back, telling her that things would work out and that she needn't worry about Cynthia Crowe, Samantha Prittly, or her pupils at the school.

"It could happen to me," she said suddenly. Her voice quivering.

"It could happen to *anyone*," he responded with a smile. "You just need to let the process take its course. If Cynthia is innocent, I'm sure the reason behind the accusation will come out."

"And if she *is* guilty?"

"Then the law will take its course."

"And what about us..?" she asked, "I think I'll be devastated at getting it wrong."

"Hey, steady on," he said. "I think you are getting ahead of yourself...as I said before, let the process take its course, and then we'll see how we feel then. We have enough on our plate as it is..."

"You're right, Mike," she conceded. "I'm sorry.."

He smiled.

"Nothing to be sorry about....however....?" he continued, leaving the sentence unfinished.

"However, what?" she asked.

"Well, there is the question of...."

"What?"

"Letting Cassie know about us getting married," he said sheepishly.

"Are we still...?"

He was surprised by her reply. He thought that it had been settled. He had asked the question and without any significant response, he had taken it as read.

"I thought..." he stammered.

"You thought that it was a done deal?"

"Isn't it what you want?"

"We....ll," she teased, her mouth and face changing into a mock gesture of uncertainty. She moved her hands back and forth in a shaking motion.

He knew then that she was leading him on. "You...you...," he said a huge smile across his face. He reached for her again.

"No," she said, turning away and laughing coquettishly, evading his grasp. "The groom needs to wait..."

She moved to the kitchen door and stopped, turning to face him.

"You needn't worry...about Cassie." she stated, "I've already spoken to her."

"When?" he asked

"Last night, when you were driving home."

"And?"

"She was happy...for both of us. She said she would call you today sometime."

For a second he was speechless.

"Bugger me," he said to himself finally as Michelle left the room.

Cummings and Alton arrived thirty minutes late. Cannon had been working in his office, considering which of his horses he could place into races in the next few weeks. There was still racing underway throughout the country, but some courses had needed to cancel or abandon their meetings due to bad weather. Some like Kelso, Newcastle, Carlisle had been badly affected by the elements. Fortunately, courses around the Midlands area and further South had been lucky, with the weather being slightly kinder to them. Cold didn't prevent racing, but waterlogged courses did.

Cannon was working through the options but was also concerned about what to do with *Titan's Hand*. After he and Michelle had finished talking, he had spoken with Telside about the horse. It seemed that *Titan's Hand* did not show any after-effects of his race from the previous day. Despite it being so poor a run, with the horse appearing not to have done anything more than a jog around the course, Cannon had been surprised to hear that the horse had eaten up well and had worked positively during the morning training.

"It's as if he had been out for a picnic run yesterday," Rich had said in his inimitable style.

Cannon had taken it on board, advising Telside that he had watched the videos of the horses' career runs once again. He had seen them so many times before, but now he had a theory. It was starting to take shape in his mind. He would test it when he next took the horse to the races.

He showed Cummings and Alton into his office, offering them refreshments which Michelle was happy to arrange.

Once they had sat down and gone through the civilities, Cannon asked the obvious question about how he could help.

"We wanted to let you know that we have made an arrest in the case of Mr. Punch's murder," Cummings advised.

"Oh," Cannon replied, somewhat surprised, "well I guess that's good? Are you at liberty to say who you have in custody?"

From his background, Cannon knew the answer to his question, but was interested to hear who the police had arrested and why it was necessary to come all the way down from Cheshire to tell him in person? A simple phone call would have sufficed.

Cummings smiled, knowing that Cannon was playing a bit of a game with him.

"You may be surprised," Cummings answered. "It's Dominic Wingrew!" Cummings watched for Cannon's reaction.

"I am surprised," Cannon replied. "How did you come to that conclusion? I must admit he isn't my main suspect."

The inspector smiled inwardly at Cannon's use of the specific words he did. "We went through all the statements," he said, "and taking yours as the most thorough and detailed, we checked it against those of the others. Each one corroborated your recall of events, so in investigating further we were able to narrow it down to Wingrew."

Cannon considered the reply but kept quiet.

"If you can remember the incident, Mr. Cannon? Of all those at the meeting that day, Mr. Harris and Mr. Brown were with you at the time of the murder? Loading the horse?."

"Yes, that's right."

"The Punch's had gone off themselves into the various stables. Sarah Walters had left the meeting early, to go to Newcastle. Melanie Freed had left to go home. Stone had gone off to his office and you mentioned in your statement that you saw Wingrew go into a stable block alone just as the meeting was getting underway. Is that right?"

"That's what I said in my statement, yes."

Cummings continued with his commentary. "You also said that when you were running towards the commotion, you saw Mr. Swiftman running behind you at one point and when you finally found Mary Punch sitting on the stable block floor, Tony Clairy and Cindy Higgins were apparently coming from different stable blocks to see what was going on."

"Yes, that's right, and Alex Stone came into the stable block from a back door."

Cummings nodded. "So that accounted for all the syndicate members."

"Yes, but what about the stable staff? Or even Stone for that matter?"

"Well, we managed to verify from the office staff that Mr. Stone had indeed been his office at the time the commotion started."

"And Wingrew?"

"Ahh…this is why we arrested him as our prime suspect. No one can account for his movements once he had left his stable staff meeting which was going on at the same time that the syndicate was meeting."

"Go on," Cannon said, his interest piqued.

"It seems Wingrew had left the syndicate session to meet with the stable team in preparation for evening stables. Once that had concluded, Wingrew, 'took a walk' according to him while the team was getting organized. The feed, blankets, and new bedding for each horse so I've been told."

"That all makes sense," Cannon replied, "it's what we all do."

"Hence why we were able to narrow the murder down to Wingrew."

Cannon wasn't so sure as it didn't fit with his own narrative. "What about Clairy and Higgins?" he asked.

"It seems they were together. They've provided alibis for each other."

"Convenient," Cannon replied somewhat sarcastically.

"Yes, that's true but we can't find any evidence to the contrary."

"It all seems a bit circumstantial Inspector, if I may say so. Is there any other evidence? CCTV, DNA, or anything else?"

"At this stage, no. The CCTV we were able to obtain shows Wingrew going into stable block C, but we can't find anything that shows him going into stable block A."

"Anything else?"

Cummings was a little embarrassed. "There is no DNA evidence either. Nothing on his clothes, nothing on the pitchfork relating to him."

Cannon commented and as he did so, Michelle came into the room with tea and biscuits. They thanked her and she left the room, closing the door behind her. Alton who had been quiet the entire time and had been writing notes as needed agreed to be 'Mother' and poured the tea for each of them. Once each had tasted the warm liquid, they continued with the conversation.

Cannon was a little disappointed with what he had been hearing. He thought Cummings would be much more thorough. "When did you arrest Wingrew?"

"The day before yesterday."

"Has he applied for bail?"

"Yes, the bail hearing will be tomorrow. I'll be there along with Sergeant Alton here. We'll be opposing it of course."

Cannon nodded. He didn't think that bail would be denied and he expected Wingrew to be out of custody and back at Stones' stables as soon as practically possible. He wondered what that BHA would make of it? Whether they would suspend Wingrew's license or not?

Cummings broke into Cannon's thoughts. "One other thing which you may not know but did give us something to add to our lines of inquiry about the

Punch's and Wingrew."

"What's that?" Cannon asked.

"They knew each other. Wingrew and Fred Punch."

"Really?" Cannon wasn't sure of the relevance to the murder but parked it in his memory.

"Yes," Alton jumped in, her first comment, apart from offering to pour the tea. "We've established that Wingrew suggested to Fred Punch that he and Mary, join your syndicate."

"For any specific reason?" Cannon asked.

Alton paused and looked towards Cummings who nodded imperceptibly for Alton to continue. "We think Fred Punch knew something about Wingrew."

"How do you know that?"

"Because Mary told us, in her statement."

Cannon was intrigued and simultaneously confused.

"So, you are suggesting that Wingrew asked the Punch's to join the *Titan's Hand* syndicate."

"Yes. He introduced them to Harris, it seems."

"For what reason?" Cannon asked

"We think it was to keep him close. To make sure that whatever Punch had over Wingrew, Wingrew would try to ensure that Punch kept quiet about it."

"Okay Inspector, I get your drift, but something doesn't make sense."

"What's that?"

"The horse and hence the syndicate of owners, including new ones like myself meant that the horse was being moved away from Stone and Wingrew, so I'm not sure how this would have kept Punch close."

"Agreed, we understand that now," Cummings replied. "And that's why we have come to see you in person."

"I wondered when we would get to that," Cannon said.

"No flies on you then, Mr. Cannon," Cummings said with a smile.

"Go on." Flattery wouldn't work on him, Cannon thought, nice though it was to receive it.

"We need your help." the Inspector said. "If as we suspect, Wingrew wins his bail application, we would like you to be our eyes and ears for a little while as we continue with our investigation."

"In what way?"

"Well, given the circumstances we suspect that Wingrew will continue training and will probably end up at some point with a few horses either in races that you, yourself, may have runners in. Or at least have runners racing at the same meeting."

"So?"

"We think that it would be useful if you could keep your ear close to the ground for us," Cummings replied, "to see if anyone else had heard on the grapevine, of what we think Punch knew about Wingrew."

Cannon reflected on this, about Wingrew and what he had been observing with *Titan's Hand* in his races. Was there something going on that would confirm his suspicions? He wasn't sure though how that would lead to murder. Maybe he had missed something?

"And if I do hear anything?"

"We would like to know about it."

Cannon nodded an understanding. "Can I say, Inspector, that from what I've heard so far, your case against Wingrew doesn't appear to be very strong? It appears as we said before, quite circumstantial. Unless there is more evidence *I* wouldn't be very confident of getting a conviction."

"Yes, we know that Mr. Cannon," Alton waded in, "that's why your help is needed. The more information we can get about Wingrew, his relationship with Fred Punch, the better."

"Okay," Cannon replied after a few seconds, "I'll see what I can find out. Though clearly there are no guarantees."

"Thank you, Mr. Cannon," Cummings said. "I....we, appreciate it. I'm sure your police force background will be very useful."

"That was a very long time ago Inspector," Cannon stated, "though I do admit, there are certain things that one never forgets."

"Noted," Cummings replied with a smile.

They paused for a moment to finish their tea, then Cannon said, "One last thing, if I may?"

"Yes?" the Inspector and Sergeant replied in unison.

"I assume you know that Wingrew may have his training license suspended, pending the initial hearing in court? If he does, then I'm not sure how much I can help given he nor his horses will be on any course. So other than me trying to tease out any rumours or chatter about him, from the other trainers, the chances of finding anything else will be slim."

"I understand, Mike," Cummings said, using Cannon's Christian name for the first time, "but whatever you can find out that's relevant, I'm sure will help us, no matter how insignificant it may seem."

"And as a heads up, concerning the position of BHA, we have done some research already," Alton said, referring to her notes. "We think that Wingrew's license won't be suspended until he is formally convicted. The BHA has advised that suspicion of murder is not grounds for suspending or even cancelling anything as yet. They advised us that the trainer has the right to be presumed innocent until the court deems otherwise."

"I guess that's true," Cannon replied, "it's how the system works."

"Precisely," Cummings concluded. "Now you can see why we need you, Mike."

The trio spoke for a short while on none descript matters. Cannon sharing a few anecdotes from his time in the police force. His position as DI and the reasons why he left the institution to become a racehorse trainer. The visitors listened intently. Amused, saddened, surprised.

By the time Cummings and Alton left, it was mid-afternoon. The sky was turning dark, low clouds threatened rain. It had been forecast but how much would fall, only time would tell.

Cannon waved one-handedly as Cummings reversed his unmarked car from the parking bay then drove out through the open gate onto the road, turning towards Woodstock. As he stood in the cold, he replayed the discussion he had just been through in his mind. He knew something was wrong but couldn't quite put his finger on it. He turned around and walked back into the warmth of the house.

CHAPTER 9

The man with no eyes had returned from his walk. He seldom left the flat but was feeling particularly down. He had struggled with the steps to the ground floor but had been helped by his companion, his golden Labrador. He had never seen the colour of his dog's fur, but it *was* golden. At one point some time back while out walking, a group of kids stopped him and teased him about his affliction. They were a group of four boys, riding bicycles, 14 and 15 years old he believed. They tried to tell him that his dog was a black Labrador. He ignored them. However, because of such incidents, the man had reduced the number of times he went out alone. When he had first moved into the place he used to walk quite regularly, counting steps as he did so. He memorized the numbers and this allowed him to gain a perspective and he was able to size things. He worked out how many steps to take to get to a lift, a stairwell, from the building to a roadside kerb. He slowly increased the area in which he walked. It was easy to do blocks. Walking right or left from the building's front entrance when he got to the road, he could then go right, then 3 lefts, and find his way back home. Or if he went left, he did the same thing by keeping right. Three rights and again he was back home. When he got more confident he walked even further. A guide dog and confidence were all he had needed. However, that was some time ago. Now he was less likely to leave the flat. Occasionally he did so, and it cheered him up taking away some of his negative feelings. His disappointment, frustration, and anger at what had happened to him.

After he had removed his coat, hat, and scarf, he fed the dog, giving it canned meat and kibble. He then filled up a bowl with fresh water. Once the dog had finished eating, it came from the kitchen to sit at his feet. The man would clean up the dog bowl once he had finished his call.

"Hello?" he said when the number he had dialled was answered. Hearing the familiar voice, he asked how the other person was.

"I'm okay," came the reply.

"I've been out for a walk," the blind man said proudly.

From the other end of the line, a sigh could be heard before the voice said, "I'm not sure that was a good idea. We've spoken about this before. It's dangerous."

"I know that, but I needed to get out. I've been stuck in here for ages and anyway, whenever anybody visits it's generally a short one. No one wants to walk with a blind man it seems. Even one who doesn't like to wear dark glasses or use a white stick!. It's only the dog that gives me away."

The voice on the phone agreed and apologized for being so forceful. It was his decision after all.

"Do you have any news?" the blind man asked.

"Not yet but we are working on it. We think the message is getting through," the voice said.

"That's good to hear."

"Yes. It is…"

A silence suddenly developed between them. They spoke every day. Sometimes there wasn't much to say from one day to the next and the call was very short.

"I'll let you go then," the blind man said.

"Okay. We'll talk again tomorrow?"

"Of course. I won't be leaving the house again. It's cold and the rain didn't help, although it had stopped before I went out. The pavement was a little bit slippery, and the dog wasn't too happy going through all the puddles."

"I could imagine so," the voice answered.

Without any additional words passing between them, the blind man put down the phone. He wished it hadn't come to this, but what choice did he have?" He hoped it would be over soon.

CHAPTER 10

She sat silently, listening to what was being said. It was difficult to listen to, to hear the accusations and she wasn't convinced they were true or accurate. When it was her turn to speak, Michelle hoped that she would be able to set the record straight. Make things clearer?

She knew Cynthia Crowe as well as anyone in the school. She knew that she was as straight as a die. She did everything a teacher should do...by the book.

Listening to Samantha Prittly say what she did about Cynthia, in front of her parents, a school counsellor, Michelle, and the Headmistress of the school was quite confronting. The session was an internal school meeting. Before the Head was ready to hand over the matter to the police to consider pressing charges it was important to hear more about what had been said and done and by whom concerning the allegations. Once the internal process was completed then the next step would be taken if necessary.

They were all squeezed into a small meeting room, all seven of them. They were almost sitting on top of each other. It had been decided not to use the staff room as it was much too public a locale during school time and the Head's office was deemed to be too supportive an environment of Cynthia. They had needed to find a neutral venue. The room they were now using was generally used by the teaching staff for private discussion or debates of a. Such meetings could be anything from sporting matters to complaints about facilities, workload, and curriculum plans. Today, however, the discussion was really about *sex*. At least that was the inference. The 'unwanted' advances that Cynthia was alleged to have made, were deemed to be of a sexual nature. As the discussion progressed the allegation needed to be substantiated, the Head had stated. Samantha was warned that as the nature of the complaints was serious, her allegation could not be frivolous.

Once the meeting was formally established and everyone was in agreement with the process, the Head invited the school Counsellor, Wendy Havers, to speak first.

"Well, Head," Havers began, "in my conversation with Samantha, it seems that two things are to be looked at here. Firstly, what was alleged to have been said in class...."

"It was *said in class*," Samantha jumped in, "*it was*...why does no one believe me?" she complained, an expression of annoyance and grief etched on her face. Tears were already building up in her eyes. At fifteen going on twenty, she was a girl who knew about herself, where she wanted to go in life, what career path to take, but perhaps unclear on her feelings or emotions. At least that was what Havers was hoping to highlight, given the opportunity.

As a female counsellor, she had been chosen ahead of one of her male colleagues to remove any potential gender bias or lack of empathy and understanding on Samantha's behalf.

Samantha's Father put his arm around his daughter. He was about to speak but the Head hushed him with a gentle hand movement, indicating his opportunity to comment would come eventually.

"Please continue Mrs. Lavers," the Head said, diplomatically ignoring the young girl's outburst.

"Thank you, Head. As I was saying, the alleged comments could be taken incorrectly, or even misconstrued if taken out of context."

"How so?" the Headmaster asked.

"Well, *see me after class*, could mean anything. It could be deemed threatening or even sinister, but as we discussed in the previous meeting when the allegations were first made, the evidence is less than clear," the Counsellor continued. "The position we took to suspend Mrs. Crowe was based on policy and was best for all until we could get Mr. and Mrs. Prittly in to hear what was being alleged. Ideally, today's meeting is to see if we can resolve things before we ask the police to investigate further or indeed need to advise the necessary authorities. That is part of the school and the Education Department's process, but taking them to the next step depends on *this* discussion."

The head nodded an understanding, then asked, "We have the phone messages as well?".

"Yes," Lavers replied. "Again, they need to be seen in context. On face value, they likewise can be misconstrued."

"Could you read them for us please?"

"Of course. I've given everyone a copy of each of them on the printout you received before the meeting, so I assume that you have all read them?"

Michelle and the Head nodded in unison, Mr. and Mrs. Prittly both shook their heads. Cynthia did not respond at all.

" 'Please can I see you after class', sent during school hours a few weeks ago. 'I desperately need to see you', sent a fortnight ago, 'Why have you ignored my request?' sent the day before the complaint was formally lodged with the school by Samantha. As you can see, these messages along with the alleged comments in class could be construed as bullying or indeed have an alternate meaning."

"Could be..?!" interrupted Barry Prittly, "what else *could they be*? This is getting ridiculous," he went on. Pointing his finger at the Head he continued with his accusations. "What type of school are you running here?" he asked, "I'm getting the impression that this....this...meeting is nothing but a whitewash, a way of...."

"Mr. Prittly!" the Head shouted, "may I remind you.." she continued rather more gently than her initial outburst, "...may I remind you that we are seeking to get to the bottom of these allegations, and in the spirit of fairness we cannot let our loyalties or emotions, prejudged or prejudice the findings. We, therefore, need to hear both sides of the issue before we jump to any conclusions," she added. "And with regards to the type of school that we are *running* as you called it? Well, we are running a successful school, a girls' school for boarders and day students and one that is the envy of the county and may I even say of the country. We do things well here. We treat our staff and our students fairly and we want only the best for the school community. So.." she continued with a gentle jibe. "...if this school is not good enough for you, we don't hold any authority over you. You can take Samantha out of the school at *any time*. We will of course be sad to lose her, as she is a good student, but that choice is *not ours,* it is yours and yours alone."

The Prittly's looked at each other. Mother, Father, and daughter. Sylvia Prittly spoke, breaking the silence. "I don't think we need to do anything just yet, let's see where this takes us before we make any rash decisions."

The Head nodded, "Very well," she said. "Mrs. Lavers, anything else?"

"The only thing I can say is that it is against policy for a teacher to contact students by phone, particularly via text, as messages of this type can be misread and as a consequence cause unnecessary concern. We always advise our teachers not to do this, even if the student doesn't respond to requests made personally in class."

"And that's the issue here?"

"Yes."

"Thank you, Mrs. Lavers," the Head replied. Turning to Cynthia, she said, "Mrs. Crowe, your view of things? I know we have discussed them before, but so that Mr. and Mrs. Prittly can hear them firsthand, and likewise Samantha, could you give us your view of what these phone messages and comments in class mean?"

Cynthia Crowe sat erect in her chair. On the table in front of her, she had her notes. Inwardly Michelle smiled. She knew her colleague to be both organized and meticulous. Cynthia cleared her throat, ensuring her voice would be as clear as it was in class. Despite the small room, she wanted everyone to hear what she had to say.

"Let me start by saying that I hope once we have had this discussion, the matter will go no further. I intend to make the meaning of my communication with Samantha here very clear, and with that, bring the matter to a resolution. My reputation as a teacher is important to me, and while I understand everyone's concerns, as I have said previously there was nothing untoward in what has occurred between myself and Samantha."

"So, you say!" said Barry Prittly, not able to contain himself.

"Mr. Prittly, we are not running a kangaroo court here," the Head stated, "so please let us continue without interruption....please! We will make a final decision about the next steps at the end of the meeting once we have heard from everyone."

Prittly nodded in acquiescence though his face seemed to suggest that he had different thoughts.

"Mrs. Crowe, please continue."

"Thank you, Headmistress. As I said before, my correspondence and requests to meet with Samantha were made in good faith and I hope that you will agree, were beyond reproach. In effect, they were intended to meet with her in private as I had noticed her becoming more withdrawn in class and her marks were beginning to drop. It was obvious that something was bothering her, and I was hoping to get to the bottom of why."

"Was there any reason why you didn't speak with her homeroom teacher first, to get an alternate view or to share your concerns," the Head asked, pointing towards Michelle, "or indeed speak with any of the school counsellors?"

"Yes, there was," Crowe replied, "I wanted to make sure that there was a reason to be concerned before I spoke to anyone else."

"Because...?"

"If there wasn't, then there was no need to waste anyone else's time. It was for this reason that I sent the texts. I had no joy from Samantha when I asked her to stay behind after class or indeed after school and I know I did the wrong thing by sending them, but I was concerned."

"Umm... but can you see how they could have been misunderstood?" the Head asked.

"Yes. I can."

"Okay..anything else?"

"No, not yet," Crowe replied. "However, I'd like to hear what Samantha has to say."

"I'm sure we all do, Mrs. Crowe....Samantha," she said in the quietest and calmest voice she could, to placate Barry Prittly, "is there anything you would like to say?"

Samantha Prittly looked down into her lap, her hands were folded together, resting there but nervously. She looked at her parents. She could see in their eyes both concern and fear for her. Turning to look at Cynthia, then Michelle, and finally at the Head, she began to explain her side of the story.

"A few weeks ago, a couple of the girls in my class started bullying me. I don't know why, but on social media, they started calling me dull, and a drip, then finally insinuated that I was a lesbian. That because I have no boyfriend, then I must be gay."

Samantha's parents suddenly sat up in their chairs. What they were hearing was news to them. As parents, they were extremely concerned to hear what was being said.

"Go on," the Head said, her voice expressing concern. What Barry Prittly had said earlier may well have been prophetic, but was not anything caused by the staff of the school. Samantha Prittly hesitated before continuing. "They, the girls concerned that is, began to say that they had heard that Mrs. Crowe was also gay. They even mentioned a few other teachers as well. So when I was asked to stay behind after class and I started to receive the texts, I began to panic. I started to think that what the girls were saying about Mrs. Crowe was true."

"So you saw a sexual connotation to the texts?"

"Yes. I did."

"Yet you didn't discuss it with anyone until you laid the complaint?"

"No."

"Not even your Homeroom teacher here?" again pointing to Michelle.

"No."

"Nor any of the school counsellors?"

"No!" the girl cried out.

"Excuse me Head, but how many times must my daughter say 'no' before you get it!" Barry Prittly said.

The Head took a deep breath. Barry Prittly was beginning to irritate her.

"Mr. Prittly," she advised, "we need to be clear about the events leading up to where we are today, as well as the process followed so far. If you could just let us get on with things without interruption, hopefully, we can conclude this meeting and resolve this matter sooner rather than later?"

Prittly stayed silent. Inside he was seething but through pats on his arm from his wife, he decided to stay quiet and see what happened next.

Before Samantha could continue, Michelle spoke for the first time asking her why she hadn't said anything to her as Homeroom teacher? It was known within the school community that raising issues or concerns about other teachers in a Homeroom environment was the starting point for any matters of pupil concern to needed to be looked into. A Homeroom teacher once told, had an obligation to follow up on *any* matter and then revert back to the student any findings. The whole point was to try to resolve the matter before things escalated out of control.

"I don't really know," Samantha said. "I guess I was confused by what the girls were saying and what Mrs. Crowe had asked of me."

"Can you now see that there was nothing behind the requests?" Michelle asked.

Samantha Prittly didn't reply. She bit her lip, no longer sure of herself. It was obvious to all in the room except perhaps her parents that what was implied, inferred, or thought by Samantha had indeed been misconstrued. Cynthia Crowe had no idea what was happening on social media between her pupil and the other girls, she only knew that Samantha had suddenly become withdrawn in her class and her marks were becoming poorer. She wanted to find out the reasoning but had been unsuccessful in doing so. It had taken until now for everything to come out, to be revealed.

"Can I ask who these other girls are?" the Head asked.

"I..I..I'm not sure I want to say," Samantha said.

"Because…?"

"For fear of reprisals…isn't it obvious?" Barry Prittly said.

"Mr. Prittly," the Head tutted, her patience growing thinner by the minute, "I am aware of the potential implications, but if we want to stop what is going on, the bullying of your daughter, and possibly others, we need to get to the bottom of it. We also can't have teachers being exposed to lies and innuendo resulting in the situation we currently find ourselves in," she went on. "It is pretty *obvious* to me," she added somewhat sarcastically, "that we need to stamp out what has been going on between Samantha and these other girls and we need to have a conversation with them so that they know what they have started. We are talking about your daughter's welfare as well as the reputation of one of my finest teachers *and* indeed of the school itself. It is therefore incumbent upon me, indeed all of us, to ensure that the school environment is safe and is not a place where bullying is tolerated…in any form."

Both the Prittly's nodded in unison, acknowledging what had been said. They smiled at their daughter, giving her moral support and expressing their concern for her.

"So, having heard what we have so far, could I ask Michelle, Samantha's homeroom teacher, to say a few words about what she knows of Mrs. Crowe?"

"You mean a kind of reference?" Sylvia Prittly asked.

"Yes," replied the Head.

"Oh.."

The floor was given to Michelle, who then provided her view of Cynthia Crowe's character. She explained how and when they had first met and how over the years they had become colleagues, friends, and how they had shared matters of a personal nature when Cynthia and her husband had divorced. Cynthia had no children and was a dedicated teacher. Michelle had said and indicated that she was confident that how Cynthia had acted was with the best intentions. She acknowledged that contacting Samantha by text with the words used was wrong and that she felt that it was a genuine mistake, nothing else.

Once she had completed her commentary, the Prittlys and Samantha were offered the chance to ask further questions. None were asked.

The Head then nodded, proclaiming that unless anyone objected, the meeting which had been recorded from the start was to be declared fair and impartial. She said that based on the evidence provided she believed that the matter was now effectively closed. As Head of the school, she concluded that it was clear that there was some detail that the meeting could not glean as true because Samantha was unwilling to disclose it. However, based on what Cynthia Crowe had explained to the meeting, the issue had come about through the misinterpretation by Samantha of Cynthia Crowe's good intentions. Samantha was then offered the chance to provide the girl's names who were bullying her on social media, but again she declined to do so. The Head suggested that the door remain open for her to approach Michelle in the first instance should the bullying continue, and the school would follow the matter up as per policy.

The Prittlys reluctantly accepted the findings of the meeting, but Barry Prittly was not completely happy. Before he left the meeting and after the recording of the conversations were stopped he said that he still expected the school to get to the bottom of the bullying going on. He felt the behaviour was rife.

"You may be right Mr. Prittly," the Head said, "though I doubt it is any better or worse than in any other school. It is the time we are living in. If Samantha doesn't wish to provide us names then it is difficult for us to take it any further. But having said that, as you heard, the door is always open to her to bring the detail to our attention. We *will* follow it up. You have my word," she said finally.

Reluctantly Barry Prittly shook the hand offered him. Sylvia Prittly was more accommodating. After they and Samantha had left the room, it was agreed that Cynthia would be suspended for two weeks from her duties for breaking school policy and for texting her pupil. She was taken to task for doing so and putting herself and the school at reputational risk. Cynthia accepted her punishment promising not to do anything '*so stupid*' in the future, but still intending to help any pupil who appeared to be ill at ease or struggling in her classes. She agreed that she would always discuss matters with Homeroom teachers first and if needed, with the school counselling team.

The Head accepted this and indicated that she would contact the necessary authorities advising them of the outcome of the meeting and would provide a transcript of the discussion. She expected that the matter would not be taken any further, but did not provide any guarantees. The Head added that given what was going on in the world, with the grooming of children, any contact outside of agreed confines was often seen as the thin edge of the wedge by authorities. Everyone was nervous, and with good reason, so anything of this ilk had the potential to blow up out of all proportion. It was why the rules and policies needed to be obeyed…religiously….to protect everyone.

The comments were seconded by Lavers and accepted by all.

The meeting then broke up, with the Head going back to her office.

Michelle, Lavers, and Cynthia Crowe stayed behind for a few minutes.

"Thank you for believing in me, both of you," Cynthia said, "and thanks for the support Michelle, your reference was well received."

Michelle smiled, "No problem," she said, "everything I said was true. You are a friend *and a caring and committed teacher*. No one should be subject to what you have been through especially when there was nothing to it."

"I concur," Lavers added, "though I must admit I was surprised that if anyone would have broken policy, you were the least likely one on the staff that I would have thought of."

"I know, I realize that now," Crowe said, "I was just worried for the girl. She withdrew so suddenly that I wasn't sure what was going on."

"Well, I guess we all learn..not only pupils but teachers too?"

"You are right," Crowe replied, "and for *not* learning, I need to take my punishment on the chin."

"Fortunately, it should go no further," Michelle said, "and at least that's a positive. Perhaps having a couple of weeks off will do you good?"

"Maybe, but I will give it a lot of thought. It's been an experience I never want to repeat."

"Understood," Michelle said. "Well, I must be getting back to my classes now. At least prepare for my next one which is straight after lunch," she advised.

The three women said their goodbyes. Michelle went off to her Homeroom, Lavers to her office, and Crowe to pick up her things from the teachers' staff room before leaving for home in the small village of Hailey, about eight miles away from the school.

CHAPTER 11

"I think we should tell the police," he said. "After all this is the second letter we've got."

"We can't do that," came the reply. "We need to find out who is sending them."

Wingrew stood up. Having been released on bail he was standing in Stones' office. The past forty-eight hours had been a nightmare for him. He had sat alone in a cell within the walls of the Chester Police station on Blacon Avenue whilst awaiting his bail hearing. He was extremely concerned. The new letter had detail within it that was no longer just inferred, as it had been in the first, but was far more accurate. It was too close to the bone.

"And how are we going to do that?" Wingrew asked. "This was delivered anonymously. There isn't even a stamp on it. The courier just dropped off the envelope with all the other stuff we received."

"I know," replied Stone, "I know…"

While getting Stone to acknowledge his concerns, Wingrew was still unhappy. He raised the issue of Punch's murder. "You know that wasn't me, don't you?"

"Of course I do," Stone said, "who do you think put up the bail money for you?"

"Don't think it isn't appreciated," the trainer replied, "but we need to find out who did it and why. If it's related to these letters, someone knows what's going on, and perhaps it's a warning. Perhaps someone is setting us up?"

"Possibly," Stone continued, "but we shouldn't panic. We need to be careful. If we do things properly, sensibly, we'll get out of this mess. Let's see if we can flush them out. If we can, then there is no need for anyone to be any the wiser, not the police, not the owners, anyone."

"Okay," Wingrew responded reluctantly, "tell me what you are thinking…"

CHAPTER 12

Cannon watched the horses run. He was particularly interested in seeing *Titan's Hand* race again. The gelding was scheduled to race at Haydock in a couple of days' time in another Open Handicap, over two and a quarter miles. In the meantime, the horse seemed to be enjoying his training. He was jumping well, just briefly touching the hurdles with his front legs, but was now much more efficient in his style, much better than he had been.

"I can see a lot of improvement," Cannon said to Telside. "I've got a feeling he may do well at Haydock. I think I'm starting to work him out," he continued, "but I must admit it's something that I would have thought someone like Wingrew should have been able to sort out just as easily."

"Perhaps he's had too many horses to be able to focus on this one?" Telside asked. Standing on the gallops they studied their small string of horses in the first lot. Eight horses at a time were all that they were normally able to handle. Cannon knew that Wingrew was responsible for at least six times as many horses as he had in his stable and that the Cheshire trainer would have relied on others to keep him informed of how they were doing, in training and in their races. Wingrew could not attend every race meeting whenever horses under his care ran. He had staff for that. Some were experienced and others less so. It was often a case that some staff were more observant about things and others less so. Those that weren't were ultimately let go. Some carried grudges with them, some even acted on them.

Cannon realized that with the move of *Titan's Hand* to himself, the syndicate, of which he was now part, expected more than what they had been able to get from Wingrew. Cannon also knew that with so many more horses in training, Wingrew would have more syndicates, more owners, to keep happy. He had struggled at times himself to keep a good horse in his stable. Owners were often fickle and sometimes moved their horses away on a whim, so he had sympathy for his rival trainer. Good facilities did not always guarantee good results, no matter how demanding the owners were.

"You may be right Rich," Cannon suggested, stamping his feet into the soft ground, then putting his binoculars to his eyes to watch the different pairings of horses complete their work. The weather had brightened up a little, but it was still cold. Their breath drifted into the air towards the pale blue of the morning sky, while steam from the horses mixed with that of the riders as they encouraged their mounts on. The jockey's exertions and expletives carried on the breeze that had replaced the showers and rain overnight.

The two men discussed the upcoming races that they had scheduled some of the stable to run in, now that the weather had improved, allowing racing to restart in some areas of the country. Cannon would take *Lightfingers* and *Chelsea Heights* to Market Rasen in Lincolnshire the following day and Telside agreed to take *Waking Man* and *TiedowntheLion* to Newton Abbot racecourse in Devon the day after. If things went according to plan, *Titan's Hand* would then be at Haydock Park two days later for the Saturday meeting.

"We have more chance with *Chelsea Heights* tomorrow in the three-mile chase than we have with *Lightfingers* in the two and a half mile novice, but hopefully there will be an improvement in attitude from *Lightfingers* in time? I think being two years younger he has much more potential than *Chelsea* if only we can keep his mind on the job."

"I think you are right," Telside replied. "Let's see when we take him out in the second lot whether things have improved since he was last on the heath. It's been a couple of days since he stretched his legs after his minor injury, that knock he got last time he was out. I think though he's a bit like *Titan's Hand,* he seems to have things going on inside his head that stops him from being a better racehorse."

Cannon nodded in agreement. As he watched the last part of the session slowly winding down, he pointed out *Waking Man* to Telside. "I think we may have a good one there," he said, stretching out a hand and indicating the horse being walked around in a circle. *Walking down* as it was called. "The owner has been very happy with what we've done with him so far. If he progresses through the grades, we may have another Cheltenham runner in a couple of years."

"Two wins from four starts, with a second and a fourth, isn't too bad a start to a career is it, Mike? No wonder the owner is pleased," Telside said smiling.

"It's a pity though that not all of the ones we get are so good. I hear you want to move on *Petty Thief?*"

"Yes, and likely *Wallpaper Sam* as well."

"A big call Mike. Losing two from the stable."

Cannon turned to face Telside. Both men knew that these things needed to be done. To survive in the business, genuine trainers needed to be somewhat ruthless. Keeping horses in work that had little chance of racecourse success was not always the best thing to do. The owners could become difficult, the animals themselves did not always enjoy the experience either. Routines, being locked in stables, racing, did not suit every racehorse. Those with minds that wandered or were aggressive generally didn't bring success and what most trainers were trying to do was to get the best out of their charges, but at the same time provide them with the best of care…food, shelter, and healthcare. Just as one would treat a human being. As in all industries, you could find those with ulterior motives, money being the predominant one, but successful stables had reputations to uphold. At times some made mistakes, did unusual and silly things, got themselves in the papers when they should have been keeping low. Gordon Elliott for example, the Irish trainer and a winner of the Grand National being banned for 12 months, some part suspended, for a photo that emerged of him sitting on a dead horse while he was talking on the phone. Elliott had accepted his mistake, took his punishment.

"I think it's best for everyone," Cannon replied eventually. "It makes space for another couple of horses as well. You never know, Rich," he said, "the next one could be a future champion?"

"Aye, true…you never know…"

Cannon could tell that Rich was looking a little tired. His comment seemed to come from a weary mouth and a body beginning to feel its age. He watched as his best friend, and his original mentor walked away, waving to the riders that time was up and that the session was over. Cannon noticed that Rich was hunched slightly, his back no longer ramrod straight. With Rich nearing seventy years old, Cannon was surprised how he had lasted as long as he had. Early morning rises into cold and wet weather at times was enough for any man, and Rich had been doing it for decades. Cannon was in awe of the man, but he needed him more than ever. A better horseman and a more reliable judge of what it took to survive in the game Cannon had never met.

Harris had organized a meeting via digital means. Zoom! Cannon had never used it before, and it took Michelle to set up the program for him. He had been used to FaceTime but with so many people in the syndicate, the new software was a much better option.

It was six pm. The only thing left to be done for the day was for Cannon to conduct his evening check of the stables. Through a partially open window in his study, despite the cold, he could hear some of the stable staff completing the few remaining tasks they had in bedding down the horses for the night. A breeze pushed its way through the small gap in the window opening. He was inclined to close it, but decided to leave it just for a little while longer. The day had been fresh but mostly clear and there was no rain predicted for the next 24 to 48 hours. The lack of cloud cover however would mean that temperatures would drop overnight and there was a possibility that there would be frost on the ground in the morning. Cannon never liked to see the grass on the heath being frozen. He always worried about the horse's legs, particularly those with a lesser confirmation. One slip and a horse could be damaged for life or at least be out of racing for a season or even longer. He hoped that Telside would be okay when he took the long journey down to Devon the next morning. It would be Rich and a stable hand, with Telside driving the horsebox. They would need to leave at around seven am at the latest, both runners having races later in the meeting at 3:15 pm and 3:45 pm. The problem with such a trip meant that they wouldn't be back until well after 8 p.m. It would be a long day and Cannon reminded himself of what he had noticed earlier that morning about Rich.

"Are we ready to start?" Harris's voice cut into his thoughts. Cannon pushed the button on the screen that Michelle had alerted him to so that he could speak to the others.

"Yes, I'm okay."

"Good," Harris replied. "Well, I think that's everyone, at least everyone that could make it."

Cannon could see some of the participants staring into their screens trying to see who was on the call and who wasn't.

Harris provided the answer. "Unfortunately, Alex and Sarah aren't able to be here and Mary, for obvious reasons is still too upset to dial in, so it is just the rest of us for now," he said. "Hopefully the others can join next time," he continued.

The heads on the screen all nodded, a couple commented at the same time resulting in just some of their words being heard, some were less than complementary.

The loudest objection was from Peter Brown. He complained as to the time of the meeting and the short notice he had been given to attend. It was impacting his routine on his farm.

Harris tried to placate the man, saying. "I'm sorry Peter if this call is inconvenient to you, but if you don't wish to attend then that's okay. I will always send you the minutes of the meeting by email afterward…as I do to all syndicate members."

"Aye that may be true," Brown said, "but given I'm new to this syndicate, I want to hear first-hand what Mr. Cannon has to say about the horse. After the last run, I'm not sure whether it's the horse or the trainer I need to look at more closely?"

The others on the screen could be seen smiling at Brown's statement. The horse had only been with Cannon for one run and within a very short time. They all knew that. It appeared that Brown was the only one with unrealistic expectations.

Harris, keen to get Cannon's view on where things were at, asked him about the upcoming race at Haydock.

"Well before I get to that, I'd just like to say that I hope Mary Punch is feeling somewhat better than when I last saw her, and I'd like to pass on my condolences again."

Harris said that he would minute the matter and pass on the collective best regards to Mary. He also asked the syndicate members if he could send some flowers on the syndicate's behalf, to be sent on the day the funeral was held? Fred Punch's body was still being kept at a mortuary in Warrington, pending release by the local coroner's office. It would remain there until the investigation into his death had been concluded. Everyone agreed to the proposal.

Cannon stayed quiet about his discussion with Cummings. He hadn't heard anything since the policeman's visit and wasn't sure how much the rest of the syndicate knew about Wingrew's arrest and subsequent release on bail. He didn't want to raise the matter as he wasn't convinced in his mind that Wingrew was the killer.

"Okay, back to business, Mike," Harris said. "Tell us about *Titan's Hand*. We know he is running on Saturday, up at Haydock, what are his chances like?"

"To be honest with you, Brendon, I think they are pretty good."

"That's great to hear," Harris replied. Nods of confirmation from the others could be seen on the screen. "Is there any reasoning behind your confidence?"

Cannon took his time in responding. "Let's just say, trainer's intuition," he said. "I don't want to give anything away, but we may have unlocked the key to him winning. Certainly, doing much better than last time," he added.

"I should think so," Brown interjected, "bloody horse cost me two hundred quid last time."

"As I often tell my owners, there are no guarantees in this game, so please be careful with your money. Remember I'm also a 20% stakeholder now so I want to ensure that when I feel the horse is right, I'll let you know."

"But you think the horse is right for the weekend?" Harris persisted.

"Yes I think so," Cannon replied.

"That's good enough for me then," replied Brown.

Cannon laughed. "As a good Yorkshireman I'd thought you would keep your money in your pocket, Peter, but I guess I was wrong?"

Brown didn't quite get the gentle dig, but most of the others did. Before the farmer was able to respond, Harris asked if anyone of the syndicate members planned to make the trip to the race? Tony Clairy and Mary Higgins said that they would come together, Brown was a definite and Swiftman likewise. Melanie Freed indicated that she would not attend due to a bout of flu that she was struggling with. Harris would be in attendance, but he doubted Stone would be, and he wasn't sure about Sarah Walters.

Cannon advised them that he would see them all in the parade ring once *Titan's Hand* race was called. He indicated that he may not have time to see them any earlier but agreed to meet them all in the owners' bar once the race had concluded. He would see what happened on the day.

Everyone appeared to be happy with the information that Cannon had imparted as they slowly dropped from view and out of the meeting. Once Cannon was sure the software had been shut down, he sat back in his chair.

He wasn't totally happy at being a stakeholder *and* the trainer of *Titan's Hand*. It was still new to him, and he found the exercise of justifying to the others that he was doing the right thing by them, and to the horse that he now part-owned, very difficult. How could he provide his co-owners anything other than his assessment of a horse's chances in a particular race? There were so many variables to consider on the day. As he had said, there were *'no guarantees'* but sadly where money was concerned there was often a lack of understanding. In some cases, that lack of reasonableness, the lack of tolerance, and particularly high expectations could turn into something far more evil. Murder, death, he had seen it too many times. He was feeling somewhat uncomfortable after the call. He shivered. As he reached over to close the window, the lights of Michelle's car crossed the threshold of the farm wall that surrounded the stables and the edge of the house that ran along the road from which she had come. Michelle brought the vehicle to a stop on the driveway. As she locked the car with a push of a button on the fob attached to her house key ring, she saw him peer through his window. Waving, he noticed her carrying a small box. He walked to the front door to greet her.

CHAPTER 13

She had read the email. It had arrived overnight, but she hadn't seen it until she had given herself the opportunity of sitting down for a few minutes. Sarah Walters sat in a black high-back chair. It was the only one in the shop. All the others were stools with small backrests. She had been busy all day, her feet were sore from the driving, and then the standing as she had walked around the city and ultimately into her shop. She had driven well over two hundred and twenty miles during a hectic afternoon, leaving her shop on Lowther Street in Carlisle at 1:30 pm and arriving at her Birmingham store just off Cannon Street just before six.

The dark and the cold had made her mood sombre, made worse with the understanding of what she had been heading into.

It had been an upsetting meeting. The store manager had been in an argument the previous day with a customer. Once she had been able to talk to the staff and establish the facts, Sarah had no choice but to let the store manager go. The issue with the customer was the straw that broke the camel's back. Sarah had long suspected that other things were going on at the shop. She found out very quickly that money was being stolen, and that product was being taken. Customers were also being encouraged to go to competitor businesses either through coercion or suggestion from the store manager. It appeared at face value that a friend of the store manager had started a rival business and it was recommended to customers by the store manager that the rival was both cheaper and provided better value for money than Sarah's business. This resulted in both revenues and patronage dropping.

Sarah was glad to be sitting on her own now. The remaining staff had all gone home, pledging their loyalty to her. She wasn't fully convinced but had no choice in accepting what was said to her. She would need to find a replacement manager as soon as possible, but she already had a plan. She would ask one of the store managers on the other side of town to look after both stores temporarily. It was not ideal, but she didn't want to spend more than a day or two at the Birmingham store as she needed to get down to Brighton to see someone. The visits there were very important to her, and she had let the individual down several times before.

As she sat with a cup of tea beside her, she began to read the email for a second time. She had become a member of the syndicate because she had always wanted to own a racehorse. Her business was doing well, but she baulked at the idea of being a sole owner of a thoroughbred. She liked to spread the risk, as she did with some of her shops. Some, not all, were partially owned by the store manager, along with Sarah. Once they had earned her trust, Sarah would relinquish up to 20% of the shares in a specific store. She always wanted overall control, but she knew that sometimes incentives were called for. *He* had made the suggestion, which she had then implemented. Likewise, when *He* had suggested that she should consider joining the *Titan's Hand* Syndicate she was cautious. Firstly, she looked into the horse's background, then who was training the horse. She checked into the races that it had run in before she had finally decided to take the plunge. She was therefore a little upset to find the horse being transferred to Mike Cannon's stables so soon after she had committed. Her demeanour at the initial meeting that she had attended (which she admitted to herself she had ended rather abruptly) was evidence of that. She had told *Him* of her annoyance the day after the meeting, the day after Fred Punch's murder.

"Well," she said out loud to herself, "Haydock isn't too far away from here, Maybe I should make the trip and give myself a break?" she continued. "It can only do me good."

As she contemplated the possibility, she thought she heard a noise just outside the front door of the shop. The door was locked, but with the lights being on she guessed that a customer may have assumed the place was still open and had tried the door handle. Sometimes the shop stayed open until 9 pm, particularly on a Thursday, but given the circumstances of the day she had closed the shop earlier than the advertised opening hours. If it wasn't a customer at the door she thought, then it could have been the wind. She decided to take the short walk to the entrance door. The door itself was fully covered over, using roman-blinds, the closed sign was correctly positioned and when she looked out into the street she couldn't see anything other than the pavement, the occasional person walking by and a few cars that drove along the street. Pieces of detritus, an empty crisp packet, and a paper coffee cup blew along the ground as a gust of wind took hold of them, tumbling them over and over.

Sarah sighed. She should have been on her way now, heading south as she had planned. Unfortunately, she would be staying in the city this evening. She still needed to book a room in a hotel, but she expected that she would have no trouble finding one. It wasn't the holiday season anymore, Christmas had long gone.

She returned to her chair and began to look at her calendar on her phone. However, before she had opened the *app* completely she felt the full force of a crowbar as it crashed across her shoulders from behind. The impact sent her spinning off the chair onto the tiled floor. Fractured ribs from the blow pierced her right lung leaving her no opportunity to scream or cry out. She had no oxygen on which to call due to her being winded, in pain, and in shock. She tried to roll onto her back, but the pain stopped her. She couldn't see who had assaulted her but in her mind, she thought that it must have been someone who had broken in. The noise she had heard! She tried again to see the owner of the shoes that danced around her prostrate body. Her face close to the floor tiles, she heard a grunt before the crowbar hit her again. Her skull shattered with the blows that rained down. She felt the first but was dead before the second, third and fourth left her face and head nothing more than a patchwork of flesh and blood.

The beating didn't stop until the attacker was convinced Sarah was dead. With the store's product having a strong smell, the toluene, the formaldehyde, the acetone, and other chemicals all providing their signature odour, the masked attacker knew what to do next. Turning off most of the store's lighting and making sure not to step on the sticky blood and fragments of skull and soft brain tissue oozing across the floor from beneath Sarah's body, the attacker emptied dozens of bottles of chemicals taken from a large shelf attached to a back wall of the store, onto Sarah's lifeless body. Then they continued to spread more of the liquid across the various tables and onto the floor, dropping each empty bottle from a gloved hand when done.

A strong stench from the spilled liquid began to drift through the air. The mask the attacker was wearing limited how much of it was breathed in, but they knew that if they waited too long, that they could be overwhelmed by the strength of the fumes themselves. It was time to go. So far no one in the street had any idea of what had occurred inside. The attacker checked the window at the back of the store through which they had entered. It was slightly ajar, just as they had left it. Turning towards the shop interior before exiting the window, the attacker threw a bottle filled with petrol and a lighted rag stuffed into its neck onto the tiled floor. The bottle exploded, glass fragments flying in multiple directions. Shrapnel. The liquid in the bottle ran like a small stream along the ground, slowly, inexorably, spreading fingers towards the dead owner. Within seconds Sarah's body was aflame, a whoosh-like sound rent the air as the fire took hold. The attacker leapt the few feet to the ground from the window and walked casually to where their car was parked. As the attacker turned the corner and onto the main street, a bright flash lit the darkness. The front windows of the nail bar exploded outwards into the street from the heat of the fire inside. Shards of glass were scattered onto the road, cars screeched to a halt in a vain attempt to protect them from being engulfed in a shower of flames. Pedestrians fell to the ground as a shockwave hit them as they walked along the pavement.

Inside the shop, fire consumed the contents. Sarah Walter's body was seared and scorched by the flames. The skin on her face started to melt. Fortunately, she would never feel any of it.

A car with stolen number plates and a masked driver drove away slowly and into the night.

CHAPTER 14

"How are feeling about tomorrow?" she asked.

"Pretty hopeful actually," Cannon replied. "I think we may have turned the corner with the horse, at least it seems that way on the gallops."

They had decided to go out for a drink and an early dinner. It had been tough over the past few days and weeks. The White Horse Inn in nearby Stonesfield would do the trick. A typical family-run pub was situated just on the corner of Pond Hill Road and The Ridings. The latter being relevant as to where the pub was placed – in the country, near a network of bridle paths. The early evening drinkers were enjoying themselves in the bar, while Cannon ate his Pork Ribs, and drank a pint of local IPA. Michelle had ordered salmon and a small gin and tonic. Occasional raucous laughter from the bar made it difficult for him to hear her at times, but it was as one would expect on a Friday night.

"I'm glad we came," she said having swallowed the last of the fish, "it's been a while since we went out *on the town.*"

He smiled at her, looking around at the other diners. Three tables in use other than themselves. Two occupied by elderly couples and the other a single man who was eating while reading a book.

"Hardly *on the town,*" he said, nodding towards the man sitting alone seemingly engrossed in his book, "but pleasant nonetheless. The food here is always good though," he added wiping his mouth and hands with the napkin provided, sticky sauce having been basted on the meat.

"You know what I mean," she replied in good humour. She was enjoying the occasion, something she believed they should do more often.

Cannon simply smiled. He was happy with where things were at in his life. Michelle meant everything to him. He felt content. Drinking the last of the beer he put the glass down on the table and asked her whether she wanted dessert?

"Coffee though," she answered after shaking her head briefly, "you?"

He hesitated. He was tempted to try some bread and butter putting that he had seen on the menu earlier, but he was also conscious that it could be a slippery slope for the evening. Pudding after such a large meal would likely mean that he would be fast asleep on the couch well before he should be, and he knew he had a few things to check around the stable in preparation for the long drive to Haydock the next day.

"I'm tempted, but I'd better not. I'll just have some tea."

"If you like, though we could make some at home," she answered, "if you would rather we go home now?"

"No, it's alright, I'm happy to stay for a while. I'm enjoying myself," he continued. "Anyway, there is something I wanted to ask you."

She looked at him curiously, trying to read his face. "What?"

Cannon looked at her, "I was thinking…..," suddenly his mobile phone which was inside his jacket pocket draped over the back of his chair, began to ring.

"I'll let it ring out and they can leave a message," he said, trying to ignore the sound.

The other diners looked at him, expressions ranging from disgust from one of the older couples, to another that seemed to be imploring him to answer and stop the incessant ringing. Feeling slightly embarrassed and with Michelle urging him to answer with a raising of an eyebrow, he fished the device from his pocket. He didn't recognize the number initially, but it seemed vaguely familiar. He had added the number to his contacts list, but had forgotten to insert a name other than the initials 'BHTH'. He stood up, mouthing 'sorry' to Michelle and saying "hello" into the phone almost simultaneously. He then walked out of the pub, leaving Michelle sitting at the table. He held a finger pressed firmly against his left ear as he tried to hear what the caller was saying.

Standing on the pavement outside the pub, he shivered as a cruel wind blew across the dark sky. Having left his jacket inside the pub, he felt exposed to the cold. He walked towards a corner of the building to get out of the breeze.

"Mr. Cannon, Mike!…Mike!" he could hear the caller say.

The signal reception was a little weak where he was standing compared to just twenty metres away. 'BHTH'? For a brief second, he was confused as to whose voice he could barely hear, then he realized who it was… 'BHTH'…Brendon Harris, Titan's Hand!

"Hi Brendon," he shouted, "can you hear me?"

A crackle was the only reply. "Let me call you back," he said into the mouthpiece, not sure if Harris could hear him. A garbled response was all he could hear in return. "Okay, give me two minutes," he replied, and he ended the call.

He walked back into the pub and explaining briefly to Michelle that he needed to call Harris back, he collected his jacket and walked out again, leaving Michelle to order a coffee for herself.

Cannon knew that he should have let Harris know that he would return his call once they had gotten back home. He realized after he was outside that he could have just sent a text advising Harris that he would call him within the hour, but that wasn't his style. Cannon was used to responding to calls almost immediately. His former life had been consumed with emergencies. Calls in the night that had required him to drive without hesitation to murder scenes. The horrors of sudden death and human depravity that had etched themselves in his mind. It was a long time ago but always close to the surface. Unexpected and disrupted calls like the one from Harris seemed to bring the memories back to life, without reason.

Standing where he could get the best reception, the strongest signal strength, three bars on his phone, he returned the call. Harris answered immediately, his voice now much clearer.

"Mike?" he asked. A strange thing to do when one thought about it, given he had called Cannon initially. "Mike?" he questioned again, "can you hear me?"

"Yes," Cannon replied, "loud and clear."

"Thank God."

Cannon was taken aback. Surely *Titan's Hand's* race the next day wasn't life and death?

Although Harris seemed agitated, Cannon assumed that he was calling about the horses' welfare and an insight into what to expect at Haydock, nothing more serious than that? He was wrong!

"Are you okay, Brendon?" he asked, "you seem a little upset. If it's about the horse well...."

Harris cut him off. "No, Mike," he interrupted, "It's not about the horse, at least not directly," he continued.

Cannon frowned. "Come again?"

"It's about Sarah."

Cannon's mind raced, *Sarah? Sarah?*

"Oh, Sarah Walters," he replied somewhat innocently, "Is she coming tomorrow?" He was suddenly reminded of the rather unsavoury encounter with her at the syndicate meeting up in Cheshire. The storming out and the throwing of business cards onto the table. He expected Harris to remind him to be courteous to her if she was attending the race meeting the next day.

There was a short pause before Harris replied, "She's dead!" he answered without ceremony.

"What?" Cannon replied instinctively, "Dead? How?" he asked, expecting something medical or at least an accident of sorts.

"Her body was found yesterday morning in one of her shops in Birmingham. It had been destroyed by fire. The police are still investigating the cause."

"Oh my God," Cannon said sympathetically, "that's shocking news."

"Yes," Harris said, "I just thought that I had better let you know before the police did. It seems a DCI Peters is somehow involved."

Cannon felt a shiver down his spine. His jacket was keeping him warm from the breeze, but he suddenly went cold. Intuition? It was as if he had known what Harris was about to say and he now realized that he shouldn't have taken the phone call. The four words that Harris had spoken, had resonated with him.... *"before the police did"*... A second death within the syndicate. He knew that the police would put two and two together and note the two deaths from within the same small group! Was there a link? They would obviously look into it, and it was possible that they would conclude that there *was* something behind the two deaths. Coincidence was not something the police believed in easily. Cannon knew that, and he knew that along with all the others in the syndicate he would be questioned again. Once the death of Walters was looked into more closely, and the body had been examined by the applicable Pathologist on behalf of the Coroner, the police would be advised of the cause of death. Then if deemed that the fire was an accident, a verdict of misadventure would likely be reached and that would be the sad end of the matter. But that was still to be determined. Cannon's initial reaction from his years of experience as a DI was that something didn't seem right. He could always be wrong of course, but given he was already looking into Wingrew's activities on behalf of Cummings, the death of another syndicate member so soon after the murder of Punch left him with a bad feeling. The death of Walters stirred something within him. He too didn't like coincidences. There may be nothing in it, but his mind was beginning to race. Was everyone in the syndicate at risk? If so, why? More importantly, from whom?

Cannon acknowledged Harris, thanking him for letting him know about Walters, then asked, "Do you want me to scratch the horse tomorrow? It's the least I can do…out of respect."

Harris gave Cannon's offer a few seconds' thought, before replying, "No. I think we need to press on. I haven't let anyone else know about poor Sarah and I think most of the members are attending tomorrow, so I don't want to spoil the day for them. We will just need to be circumspect if you don't mind until I find the appropriate time to let everyone know."

"That sounds eminently reasonable Brendon," Cannon replied. "I'll leave that to you then. Thanks for the heads up though, it is appreciated. And please accept my condolences again."

"Thank you," Harris replied before ringing off.

Cannon looked at the blank screen of his phone for a few seconds. He took a deep breath then exhaled slowly, the cool of the night turning his breath into a cloud of white. He turned to go back into the pub, but as he did so Michelle was coming out pushing against the weight of the heavy front door.

He held it open for her, she smiled then told him that she had paid the bill and unfortunately he would have to have tea at home.

Cannon smiled as she linked his arm.

"Come on," she said, "let's get to the car, it's really cold."

"You're so right," he answered, looking up at the deep black sky now clear of clouds, blown eastwards by a strengthening breeze. "I think we may have frost in the morning."

Looking at Cannon's face in the dim light of the street lamps, as they walked a hundred metres or so, to their car, Michelle said, "So are you going to tell me all about it?"

"The call?"

"Yes, of course…the call."

"Sure," he said, "once we are in the car."

"Good," she replied, unlinking herself from his arm and racing him over the last twenty metres. Once inside the vehicle, he turned on the heater and began the drive home. Over the short trip back to the stables, Cannon filled her in on his conversation with Harris. Both of them had completely forgotten that Cannon had wanted to ask Michelle a question just before Harris' call.

The death of Walters played on his mind.

He wasn't sure why, but he was extra vigilant. As Cannon conducted his final rounds of the stables before heading back inside and getting ready for bed, it seemed to him that every sound he heard had a sinister meaning. Creaks from stable doors seemed magnified in the chill of the night due to the cloudless sky. The wind with a bite that rattled through the trees created distorted shadows as Cannon's torch caressed the areas of blackness that the lighting attached to the stable buildings could not reach.

An occasional whinny or sneeze from within the stable block caused him to stop in his tracks. He was on edge and he couldn't quite understand why. He wasn't sure if his mind was playing tricks on him, but for some reason, he had an uneasy feeling, a premonition perhaps? The conversation with Harris bothered him even though nothing had been proven. Walter's death may well turn out to be an accident. Perhaps he was over-reacting as Michelle had said after he had shared with her the details of what he and Harris had discussed.

"Perhaps?" he had replied as they had chatted in the car. He wasn't convinced, but he had put on a brave face.

Once he had completed his inspection of the stables and had checked the horse-box ready to take *Titan's Hand* up to Haydock, he went back into the house. Michelle was no longer in the lounge, having gone off to the bedroom to get undressed. Cannon took his time locking the front and back doors of the house, something they seldom did, before double-checking for any open windows. He then headed off to bed. Tomorrow would be a long day.

He slept fitfully for a while, the ghosts of the past invading his dreams. As he struggled with them, he suddenly opened his eyes. He wasn't quite sure what had happened. He could feel Michelle next to him, her gentle breathing gave him comfort. So, what was it that was disturbing him? Had the dreams left a sound in his mind that he couldn't shake, or had he heard something else, something real? The clock on the bedside table told him that it was seven minutes past two. He lay quietly, eyes closed, trying to distinguish what was making the various sounds that he could hear. A scratch – the branch of a tree against the roof. An owl hooting. A slight moan – the wind. A thud…..

Cannon wasn't sure what it was. He slowly climbed out of bed, put on a dressing gown then opened the bedroom door and crept, keeping low, to his office, his eyes slowly adapting to the darkness. Once in his office, he kept down, inching towards the window. Once in position, he tilted the blinds slightly away from the window sill to peer through the glass. As he did so, he thought he saw a shape near his car. He looked again, unsure. Was he imagining things? He tried to see again, peering through the gap that he had created to get a better look…and he thought he saw movement. He was sure he was right. He slowly let the window blinds fall back into place and decided to go outside and see what was going on. As he turned towards the door, the light in the room came on, temporarily blinding him.

"Mike," Michelle asked, "what's going on? Why are you….?" she suddenly realized what was happening, but knew it was too late.

Cannon raced past her, heading towards the front door. He turned on the outside lights at the front of the house before venturing out into the cold. Armed with only a torch he immediately realized how ridiculous he looked. He shined the torch towards the car. Nothing! Taking a few steps closer he shone the light towards Michelle's car…again nothing. Michelle came to the door, he put a finger to his lips suggesting that she should stay quiet. He continued walking towards the cars, shining his torch in front of him, swinging the arc left and right, upwards and downwards. At the cars, he looked on the ground searching for footprints in the gravel. Nothing!

He felt foolish but he was sure that he had seen something or someone creating a shadow outside. Eventually, the cold drove him back inside the house. Had he dreamt it? He convinced himself that he hadn't, but he had no way of proving what he thought he had seen.

He realized that his actions had frightened Michelle and he tried to reassure her that there was nothing to worry about. That he had been dreaming. He took care to hold her in his arms as they tried to go back to sleep. Then without warning, the alarm went off. Five am! He wasn't sure how long he had slept for, but he felt that he had just completed twelve rounds of boxing.

CHAPTER 15

"So, it was definitely murder?" Detective Chief Inspector Chris Peters asked again.

"Yes, Inspector," the man wearing the previously white apron replied, "without the shadow of a doubt."

The body of Sarah Walters, or at least what was left of it, was in pieces. It lay in various bowls and dishes spread across a couple of small silver steel tables in one of the outsourced laboratories of the Midland Lab Services Group, used by the Coroner and Police for such investigations.

The blackened stumps of Sarah Walter's arms and legs were missing fingers and toes. The trunk of her body had shrivelled in the heat, internal organs slowly cooking, the flesh searing then partially evaporating.

"As you can see from the trachea, the throat," the Pathologist, Lynton Shaw advised, "there is no sign of scorching. She was dead before the fire started. The lungs were clear of the fumes and smoke of the fire. The only thing affecting them was the cigarettes she clearly liked to smoke. You can see the tar build up…here," he pointed at one of the bowls.

Peters had seen many autopsies and he never liked any of them. He looked quickly to where Shaw was pointing, then looked away again. He could never understand how some people could do the job of cutting up bodies every day, all day. Week in and week out. He looked at Shaw's previously white apron now covered in dark red blotches and smears.

Who went to work every day nicely dressed, and then allowed themselves to be covered in all sorts of various body residues, he thought? Notwithstanding his views, he was still thankful for such people. Without them, he could never do his job.

"Soooo….?"

"She was bludgeoned to death," Shaw advised. "You can see where the skull has caved in. The poor woman has been hit many many times with an iron bar or something similar."

"So, the skull didn't explode through the heat of the fire?"

"Not in this way, no," the Pathologist said, "look," he continued before pointing at the deceased's head that was sitting in another bowl. "As you can see here, there are quite a large number of impact points. The skull has been hit with a blunt instrument and the bone has fractured and in some places splintered. As you can see, the breaks in the bone are downwards, and inward, indicating a blow from above. In a fire, the heat would essentially boil the brain and if the skull *was* weakened in any way, it is possible for the bone to crack, but not like what we have here."

Shaw took a deep breath before taking another look at the skull and the melted face of the victim. "Yes, I can see that now. Would you know how long she would have been dead before the fire got to her?"

"Looking at the blood flows in the body, the state of the skin, I'd suggest no more than a few minutes. Maybe ten to fifteen."

"So short a time?" replied Peters.

"Yes."

"And what about at the site when you were there? Any potential DNA?"

"You mean from anyone else, other than the victim?" Shaw asked.

"Yes."

Shaw weighed up his response before saying. "Unfortunately not, Inspector. The fire destroyed nearly everything, including any possible DNA specimens. As you can imagine, there would have been many visitors to such an establishment, so trying to find one specific amount of DNA would be like looking for the proverbial needle.."

"In the haystack…?" the policeman chimed in.

"Exactly," Shaw confirmed "So, unfortunately, I can't help you there."

"Do you know who the lady is?"

Shaw smiled to himself. He always found it funny that the police wanted to ask him who a victim was. It was the job of the police to find that out. It was *his* job to find out how a victim died. However, in this case, it was easy to determine who she was.

"You're in luck there, Inspector. I think I can help you with that question."

Peters raised a surprised eyebrow.

"Over here," the Pathologist said, requesting Peters to take a few steps across the brightly lit room. From inside a small stainless-steel container, about the size of a shoebox that he carefully placed onto another table, Shaw lifted a lady's purse, blackened by heat, the leather twisted and curved around the zip.

With a gloved hand, he pulled out a driver's license, still readable despite the obvious damage.

"There you are, Inspector. *Sarah Walters*. You can see her address and her date of birth. She was 53," he said.

Peters looked closer. Shaw remained in possession of the license, holding it in his hand. The policeman knowing not to touch something that could potentially be used as evidence.

"How did this survive?" he asked.

"It's quite simple, to be honest," Shaw replied. "Most people think that a fire, such as that in the particular shop we are looking at here, would have destroyed everything within it, and that's generally the case. However, it would seem, luckily I might add, that in this case, the purse may have been close by or in the lady's hand when she was struck down."

"And?"

"Well, it appears to have fallen *under* her body and as a consequence was protected from the flames. Obviously, the heat had an effect, but the fire didn't get to the purse directly. It was melted *onto* her clothing which then stuck to the front of her body. The body was photographed in situ, and then my team bagged it and brought it here. It seems that somehow the melted plastic was missed because it wasn't easy to spot. I assume it was because everything was blackened? Somehow however it was not collated by the SOCO's and so it ended up here."

Peters looked at the license again. He would take up the oversight with the appropriate person later, the Head of the Scene of the Crime team.

"Anything else?" he asked.

"There are a few other cards in there, which may be useful to you. Credit and Bank Cards. Loyalty cards."

"Thanks. I believe we found a phone, but it was just a piece of scrap. I've spoken with our technical team, but they are not confident of getting anything from it directly. I think they are following up with BT and Vodafone."

Shaw nodded. Phone records were not his concern.

It was clear that Shaw had been able to provide Peters everything that he could. They had worked together previously, so Peters knew the drill, but he asked Shaw the same question that he always did.

"You'll let me know if you find anything else useful?" he said, knowing that Shaw's detailed report along with necessary photographs of the body, the purse, and its contents would be on his desk by first thing the next day, Saturday.

"Of course, Inspector," Shaw said, pointing towards the remains of Sarah Walters then turning back to Peters, and adding, "By the way, I know from initial reports that the fire was deliberately lit and I know I shouldn't get involved, but from me to you Chris, I hope you nail the bastard who did this, I really do!"

Peters looked Shaw in the eye. For a few seconds, he could see the emotion expressed by the Pathologist. It was unusual. There was sadness and anger on his face.

With purpose, Peters replied, "I will Lynton, I will!"

CHAPTER 16

Dominic Wingrew was standing in the parade ring. He was being interviewed by ITV Racing ahead of their broadcast which would start at 1 pm. He had arrived at Haydock, which was only a short trip from his stables, at just after 9:30 in the morning. He had four runners across the 6-race card and his team would be driving the horses to the course, expected to arrive by eleven. The horses then needed to be vetted, blood samples taken, and their micro chips read by the Stewards staff responsible for the meeting itself.

Wingrew was never comfortable in front of the cameras, certainly not when being asked about the chances of the various runners. He was much happier after each of his races when he could bask in the winners' spotlight, or disappear into the course stables when a horse didn't come up to public expectations.

"So how do you think you will go today Dominic? You have four runners, one in each of race, 1, 3, 5, and 6, the big one for the day being race 5," asked the Channel host, Simon Goldman.

Wingrew hesitated for a moment. He appeared to be considering the question, but he knew already what he would say. It was part of his routine, the planning of his responses before he was even asked the question.

"We have the favourites *EmailMeNow* in race 3 and *Bold Comment* in the big race, but in race 1 and 6, we'll just have to see how we go."

"That's *Wiredtothemoon*, in race 1 and *The Postman* in race 6?" Goldman asked.

"Yes. Both are between 12 and 15 to 1 currently," Wingrew said. "So, we'll see how they do."

"And in the big one, a horse you used to train, *Titan's Hand*?"

"Yes. He had some good runs for me over the two seasons I had him. I think he could be the main danger to *Bold Comment*."

"That's interesting," replied Goldman, a practiced smile on his face. He then thanked Wingrew and turned back to the TV camera, repeating what he had discussed with the trainer, before signing off the segment. It would be played just before the first race as the runners were in the parade ring.

Wingrew thanked Goldman and then left to go and find Stone who had planned to meet him in the Owners and Trainers bar.

As he walked away, he knew what would be happening in the various races. He had done exactly as Stone had requested. Has he had over the past year, throughout the Flat *and* the Jump seasons. He wasn't happy, but, *they* had no choice. Somebody knew what was going on, the letters they had received confirmed that, and it unsettled him. Combined with his arrest and bail over

Punch's murder, he had endured much better days. He knew though that he was innocent, and his lawyer had asserted that the police's evidence against him was weak, being circumstantial at best, however, his world was being turned upside down and he was feeling very uncomfortable.

He walked into the bar, which was already half full despite it being only 10:45. He would confirm the plan with Stone and then go to the course stables to ensure that the horses were all housed properly and were ready for the Vet.

Cannon had only brought two horses for the Haydock meeting. He had *Titan's Hand* and *Once and for All* running in race 2. The latter was a 3-mile chase. His runner was 3rd favourite at the start of the day, at 8 to 1. Cannon thought the horse had a reasonable chance given the opposition. The weather overnight had remained breezy but there had been no rain. Given the track was expected to dry out and the going change from being *very soft* to being just shy of *good*, so still a little bit soft, it was ideal for both his runners. This was particularly so for *Titan's Hand* who liked the sting out of the ground given the sensitivity of his feet.

Cannon's horses had arrived at little after midday, a little later than planned, due to the traffic. They were just in time to meet the requirement of having horses available to be tested and checked by the on-course Vets. Any later and *Once and for All* could have been scratched. Cannon had arrived just before 11 am and he had waited in the stables until his charges had been settled in.

As he walked towards the owners and trainers bar, he saw Brendon Harris just ahead of him, amongst the crowd. Despite the cool weather, a large attendance was expected. He could see groups of punters coming from every entrance heading towards the stands and the bookmakers. He called out to Harris who turned and greeted him. The smile on his face was less enthusiastic than normal, he was still upset by what had happened to Sarah Walters. Despite his concerns about how it would be received, he had finally decided to write an email to all the syndicate members about what had happened, that morning.

"Hello, Mike. How are you?" he asked.

The two men shook hands briefly, then continued walking through the crowd. Cannon took his time in responding to Harris's greeting. Keeping a sombre tone, he said, "I'm okay. I saw your mail earlier, so I need to ask you more importantly, how *you* are doing?"

"I must admit, I didn't sleep very well, to be honest. I really struggled with what I wanted to say in the email that I sent. I knew I had to do it, but it wasn't easy."

"I understand,"

"You know it was me who encouraged her to join?"

"No, I didn't know that," Cannon replied.

"It's a long story, but the short version is that I've known Sarah for quite a few years. My late wife was a regular client of hers, in Brighton, where we lived for a while. It was Sarah's second shop I think. Anyway, when my wife died a few years ago, Sarah's business had grown quite significantly throughout the country. Despite that, she was still able to come to Brighton on a fairly regular basis. When she heard about, Joan, my wife, she sent flowers and came to the funeral. I kept in touch with her and over time she expressed an interest in what I was doing. Finally, she decided to take me up on my suggestion."

"And the rest, as they say, his history," Cannon added.

"Yes. Though not a very happy ending is it?"

Cannon did not respond as the two men continued walking. They remained silent, each with their thoughts as they reached the Owners bar. Inside all the syndicate members, except Mary Punch, had congregated at a couple of tables that they had pulled together. It seemed that they were talking in hushed tones, but once Harris arrived and all the '*sorry to hear*' comments had been said and the commiserations shared, the mood improved. Cannon sat between Tony Clairy and Dick Swiftman. Cindy Higgins looked like she was being pestered by Peter Brown, and Melanie Freed decided to bend the ear of Harris. Alex Stone arrived a few minutes after Cannon and Harris, having left earlier with Wingrew to check on their runners.

"How do you think we'll do?" Clairy asked Cannon while taking a peek across the table at Brown.

"I think we have a good chance," Cannon replied. "The horse has been working well and I think we've been able to iron out a few chinks."

"What about the favourite, *Bold Comment*, trained by Dominic?" Swiftman asked.

"He's a good horse as well," Cannon replied, "so it should be a good race."

"But you're confident?" Clairy pushed the point.

"He'd better be," Brown shouted from across the table, "the last run was bloody poor. Useless in fact!"

Cannon ignored the comment. Turning back to Clairy he said, "I'm as pleased with the horse as I could be. He's got a great chance. Now we just have to wait and see."

Clairy and Swiftman nodded, while Brown shook his head then turned his attention to Higgins. Clairy watched, staring.

CHAPTER 17

As the day wore on, Wingrew's horses in races 1 and 3 ran as expected. The favourite failed in the third race and his outsider won the first race on the card. When asked about the winner in race 1 Wingrew expressed surprise. As regards race 3, he expressed disappointment. He pointed out that both horses were owned by Alex Stone and he was sure that Alex would have felt the same.

The parade ring was busy. Fourteen runners were declared for race 5, the main race of the day. It was an event of just over two miles and over eight obstacles – the hurdles. The day had grown brighter as predicted. The sky cleared, but the breeze had strengthened, drying out the course a little more than expected. Cannon's earlier runner in race two, *Once and for All*, had enjoyed the softer going, finishing a creditable third, just two lengths behind the winner. Cannon had been pleased with the run, so had his owners.

By the time the runners expected to be 'off' in the fifth race, the going would have likely improved to *good*. Cannon had decided that cushion plates would be needed to protect *Titan's Hands'* sensitive feet and he had advised the Stewards accordingly. An announcement had been made on course to the public just before the horse parading.

The syndicate members, excluding Stone, who had the favourite in the race, and was with Wingrew saddling up the horse, all gathered together in a group to watch *HR* mount up. Cannon had decided to keep the jockey on the horse, as he didn't think the bad run last time out, was the jockeys' fault. The colours of the grey cap, grey vest with red cross stripes like an *"X"* on the front were something that Cannon was not yet familiar with. He watched them shift and rustle on his jockeys' slim body as the breeze blew harder. He hoped that the track remained at *good*. If it went up to *firm* he believed the horse would *feel* its feet and would not perform as hoped. The race was expected to be run at a strong pace given that the track had improved. Cannon knew that the horse would be competitive whether the race was slowly run or not. He was mostly concerned about keeping the horse sound.

At the off, *Titan's Hand* began slowly, losing a few lengths as the field began the charge towards the first hurdle. The syndicate had moved to the Owners section of the main grandstand, but Cannon had decided to watch the race alone from within the restaurant at the top of the stand. Sometimes if the horses were on the far side of the track he liked to see what was going on by looking at the TV coverage. It gave him a better perspective.

By the time the race was three-quarters of the way through, with only two hurdles left to clear, the field was strung out. Upfront, *Titan's Hand* and *Bold Comment* were neck and neck about four lengths ahead of the third runner. Barring any mistake, Cannon felt that *Titan's Hand* would win. As they came towards the penultimate jump just as they entered the straight, the jockey on *Bold Comment* began to ride more aggressively than HR, who hardly moved on his mount. Despite the urging, the favourite did not respond. Cannon watched the duel through his binoculars. He noticed the rhythm of the jockey racing alongside HR. The contrast. HR had still not moved as *Titan's Hand* moved ahead, reaching the hurdle and a length ahead, before clearing it safely and landing two lengths ahead of his competitor. HR gave the horse a mild kick in the belly and a single whack on the rump with his whip. The horse responded magnificently, reaching the final hurdle five lengths ahead of his rival who was now fading badly. *Titan's Hand* cleared the final jump easily and increased the gap between him and the rest of the field. HR eased the horse down as he crossed the finish line at least 12 lengths ahead of the next horse. The favourite had faded over the last 300 metres, finishing a poor fourth, much to the disgust of its' backers. The *Titan's Hand* syndicate was in a celebratory mood, however, cheering well after the race had concluded.

Cannon walked down to where the syndicate members were assembled receiving pats on the back as he arrived.

"I need to go and meet him," he said, pointing to the track. The horse had begun the walk to the winners' enclosure and the jockey still needed to weigh out, before the all-clear and final declaration of winners would be made by the Stewards. To their celebratory cries of approval, they let Cannon leave, before realizing what Harris was urging them all to do. In their excitement, they had forgotten that they too, could all go to the winners' enclosure for the obligatory photo with the horse and the presentation of a small trophy. Clairy had a camera with him and began taking pictures of the horse being led in. A racehorse wasn't quite the wildlife he was used to taking photographs of, but being good at what he did, he promised to share his pictures with everyone in the group once he had the chance to review them.

After the short presentation and while Cannon was being interviewed by Simon Goldman for the TV, the syndicate members went off to the bar again to celebrate their win. It was obvious that some had bet quite heavily. Brown in particular, despite his reservations, had plunged 500 pounds on the horse to win. He was particularly happy now. Harris likewise had been confident in betting 100 pounds each way. The rest had been unsure, betting just a few pounds only, so that they had an interest in the result. The prize money for winning the race was 18000 pounds, so those that didn't win big by taking a gamble still benefited from the horse winning first prize. Cannon likewise was happy with the result. He had been confident that he would work out the horse's quirks eventually. He still wondered though why the obvious had not been uncovered by Wingrew. Racing the horse at Haydock and the way the horse ran proved his point.

At the stables he watched the groom wash the horse down, then once he was dried off, Cannon inspected the horse's legs for any damage. He also looked for any wear and tear on the horse's hooves. Once he was happy, Cannon asked the groom to walk the horse around on the grass in front of the stables. With only one race to go, the walking down area was less congested, with most of the earlier runners now on their way home, and the runners for the last race already heading towards the parade ring. *Titan's Hand* appeared sound and had recovered well from the race. He was ready to be boxed and driven home to Stonesfield. Cannon gave the go-ahead to the groom and the horse box driver to get on their way. Cannon would likely arrive home a short while after they did and he would check up on the horse again, as he would with *Once and for All*.

He made his way back to the bar. The moving back and forth from stables to the bars was very common for trainers. Sometimes it was a good experience and at other times less so. Owners could be cruel if their horse ran poorly as it often meant that bets were also lost, leaving a bad taste in the mouth. However, if a horse won.....!

On arrival at the bar, Cannon could see that the drinks were already flowing. Brown in particular was looking happy. He was standing with Harris. Clairy was standing, almost head to head with Higgins, in quiet conversation, both with drinks in their hand. Swiftman sat at a table with Melanie Freed.

Cheers erupted as he walked into the bar. He felt embarrassed but understood the excitement. All thoughts of poor Sarah Walters had been forgotten it seemed. At least for now. He was offered a drink, but Cannon declined, before finally accepting a soft drink. He had a long drive home. Over the next half hour, he was congratulated, again and again, Brown even conceding that his earlier outburst had been out of order. Cannon accepted the apology graciously. While he finished his drink, he watched the final race on the TV. Wingrew's runner, *The Postman*, had drifted out in the betting from 15's to 20 to 1, due in part to *Bold Comments* poor run, in race 5. The horse however bolted in, winning by 6 lengths. Cannon smiled at the trainers' interview. It had been an *odd day,* Wingrew had said, given the results of his four runners. Cannon knew what it felt like, he had experienced such results in the past.

CHAPTER 18

It was Monday morning, and cold rain had started late Sunday night. The staff of Sarah Walters' Birmingham city centre nail bar, which now no longer existed, were all seated in the reception area of the West Midlands police station in Lloyd House, on Snow Hill Queensway. It was an impressive building but seen as a bit of a fortress by the local community. It was not easy to get into and a challenge to get any support outside of it.

Four people were waiting. Three had been employed at the time of the fire, just a few short days ago and one, the Manager, had been sacked. All had been asked to make statements by the police. Peters had requested a Senior Sergeant from his squad to take statements about what had happened on the day the Manager was sacked and what, if anything, they knew about the fire.

CCTV footage from around the area had been obtained and Peters, much to the chagrin of his wife, had reviewed it during most of Sunday. The video obtained had shown a person of indeterminate looks, due to the clothes, beanie, and snood they wore, parking a car, an old Ford, about three streets away from the shop. Thereafter they are seen walking towards the store, before disappearing into an alley. Later as the storefront exploded, the figure could be seen walking away. It was obvious that the individual was the likely killer of Sarah Walters and had probably started the fire. However, while the figure appeared to look like a man, it wasn't that clear cut. Close-ups had revealed the type of jacket the figure was wearing (which was zipped up to the throat with the snood covering the lower part of the face) and the type of jeans and shoes being worn by the individual, but it was impossible to make out any features of the suspect. Peters had asked for the film to be forensically inspected. Initial feedback based on calculations made of the shoe size was that the figure was definitely a man. Unfortunately, that meant that all of the individuals sitting in the reception were unlikely to be the killer. Peters however kept an open mind, he hoped that somehow he would get a lead from their statements.

He reviewed the statements in detail, but nothing stood out that was of help. He threw the papers on his desk. The rain outside had gotten heavier, and the sky had darkened again. It was amazing how within a couple of days one's mood could be changed because of the weather or how an investigation was going. To add insult to injury he would normally take a short break about now and go and get himself one of his favourite coffees from the small coffee shop a short walk from the building. He would then take a walk giving himself time to think. But when it rained, as it did now, though he stayed inside. He had accordingly sent a junior officer to get his coffee for him.

The CCTV footage from around the city had not been able to help with identifying the driver of the car leaving the scene of the fire. The individual having kept their face covered until well beyond the city boundary. The suspect was clever enough not to stop at any service stations or even remove any face coverings while on the motorway either. Clearly, the person knew about cameras under bridges and along the road at various points. The last sighting they had, was of the car heading Southeast. The car appeared to leave the M25, east of Cheshunt and then disappearing into the Epping Forest. Whether the vehicle was heading towards Essex or somewhere else it would be difficult to know, but Peters guessed that they would find it somewhere in the woods near Chingford or Loughton.

A junior officer brought in the coffee and Peters thanked him, the man turned to leave the office when he was asked to send in another member of the team. When DI Sophia Drummond arrived, she knocked briefly on the open door and walked into the room. Peters asked her to sit down.

"What do you think?" he asked, pointing at the statements now sitting haphazardly on his desk.

"About the fire?"

"Yes, about the fire," he replied, more forcefully than he should have.

"Well from what we can gather, all the staff, and *ex-staff*, the manager who was fired, all have alibi's as to where they were around the time of the fire. So, we have no reason at this stage to think that any of them were involved."

"Is that an assumption?" Peters replied. He was getting a little frustrated. Having had his wife on his back for wasting their Sunday, he didn't need to be told something he had already worked out for himself. He looked at Drummond. He liked her and they worked well together. She was a shortish woman around 1.7 metres. She was always well-groomed. Her dark hair just below shoulder length framed a soft face with deep brown eyes and high cheekbones. If she had been another 15 centimetres taller she could easily have been a model. She was slim, walked well, and could charm the hind leg off a donkey. She had moved up to Birmingham a few years prior having spent most of her life in Dorset. Her strong West Country accent made her all the more interesting. At 32 she had done well for herself in what was still a male-dominated institution, even if the head Cop of the entire force was a woman.

"We've checked with those who the individual staff member said they were with, and they all seem to check out. So for that reason, I'd say, it's a *fact*.....Sir."

Peters smiled. He knew when she was being flippant. "Okay, so if it's not a staff member, do we have any ideas? Enemies? Ex associates?...maybe deals that have gone bad?"

"We are checking into that, Chris," she answered, using his Christian name. It was her way of calming him down. "I must say though, she did have a lot of people she dealt with throughout the country. With all her shops she must have made some people unhappy at various stages. As you can see from reading the statements she didn't seem to suffer fools lightly, and in fact, she seemed to have had a bit of a temper."

"Yes, I got that impression too," he answered. "I wonder if there was something that may have sparked this off. Something that could have happened recently? A break-up maybe? Boyfriend?"

Drummond waited for a few seconds before replying, "A break-up is hardly a reason for murder though is it, Sir?"

"Stranger things have happened," Peters replied, "and frankly as a woman I would have thought that you would be a bit more sensitive to what could happen if a relationship ever went bad. As you know, we men can be pigs at times," he added. "Violent one's at that."

"I know, Sir. That's why I never married."

"Or got too involved?" he asked.

"Exactly. Love 'em then leave 'em,'" she said, a cheeky smile on her face.

Peters smiled in return. He really *did* like her. She was a good officer, a good cop.

"Alright," he continued, "what else do we know about the car? The driver?"

"Not a lot," she answered. "We know that it was an old Ford Aspire, dark blue or black, and made in the 1990s. We also know that the number plate on the car was fake. There was no license disc on the windscreen, so we have no idea where it came from. If we find it, we could always check the engine number, but my guess is that it will likely have been filed off as will most of any other identifying features."

"Umm," Peters replied, "and we have no idea where it could be now then?"

"No."

"My gut feel is that we will find it dumped somewhere, probably torched."

"I think you're right, Sir. But what I still can't understand yet is the motive for someone like the lady concerned to be murdered by someone who then appears to drive nearly 200km immediately after killing her."

"Yes, that struck me as odd as well. It's almost as if the killer wanted to get as far away as possible from the crime scene, and as quickly as possible. Most often with cases like this, the perpetrator hangs around to see that their handiwork has been successful, especially if they are close to the individual."

"Which would suggest in this case, that the person concerned is not a family member or someone well known to the deceased?" she asked.

"That's very possible. I'm not sure of her family status or if she had any children, I'm still waiting on that information. I think she was divorced some years back, and her ex-husband died about three years ago."

"So, the killer may be someone she has had some dealings with? A competitor maybe?"

"Possibly, though again, competition in nail bars is highly unlikely to lead to murder, is it?" he said, reaching for his long-forgotten coffee that was now cold. He took a quick sip then called for the junior officer to take the drink and warm it up in the kitchen microwave. The carton disappeared only to return less than a minute later, steam billowing off the top of the brown liquid.

Drummond waited until the two of them were alone before asking, "Apart from her business dealings, did Mrs. Walters have any hobbies? Was she part of any club or society that could shed some light on anyone she dealt with regularly? Give us a more recent background? After all, we know where she lived. Bristol wasn't it?" she said.

"Yes," Peters replied, "on the way to your neck of the woods."

"Not really," she responded sarcastically, "...Sir."

Peters ignored her response.

"Shit," he said finally, "this case could become a bloody nightmare. With no obvious motive, yet! No clear suspect, other than the figure we think is a man in an old car that we can't find. A body that we were lucky to be able to identify, and no other leads. Jesus!"

They both looked at each other with a sense of foreboding. The team outside Peters' office would need to get on their bikes and find the car asap. They needed to get in touch with all the local forces across the entire country, especially in the South, and hope for a break.

If they didn't already have enough on their plate! Peters thought.

CHAPTER 19

The man with the dog put the packet of food away, his hands searching for the space in the top left-hand side of the cupboard where he could always find it. It would have been easier to have put it on a lower shelf, but Labradors were food-obsessed and he didn't want to leave it where the dog could potentially get access. Leaving the packet higher-up was the best solution. By the time the cupboard was closed and the packet of food safely away, the dog had eaten up ravenously. It was now drinking lavishly from the large water bowl on the kitchen floor.

The man walked clumsily into his lounge room. The TV was on, the sound off. He reached for the remote that always sat on the small table standing a few inches away from the left seat of his lounge settee. The man always listened to the 6 pm news, it was his lifeline to what was going on in the world. By the time he pushed the mute button, a story about a woman killed in a shop blaze on the preceding Friday, a few days earlier, was just concluding. He had no idea who the lady was, but he felt sorry for her. *What a way to die*, he thought. He was conscious of what fire could do, which was why he had no open fire himself. Not that he could have one in his flat anyway. Ever since his accident, he had been aware that for the rest of his life it would be an electric heater he would need the most during winter. Even gas-fired heating was not ideal. It was difficult to smell gas leaks and without eyes, he would not be able to notice if there *were* problems with a gas appliance.

He sat back to listen to the sports news, which was his main interest. The reporter was talking live from a place the man had once visited. As the reporter spoke, the blind mans' phone rang. It was a call he had expected. A little early perhaps but at least regular.

"How are you?" the man asked, once the caller had said who was calling.

"I'm fine."

"Any news?"

"No, we are still waiting."

The blind man didn't respond. He knew things would take time.

"How are *you* keeping?" the caller asked.

"About the same. Nothing much happens does it?" the blind man replied. "It's just me and the dog tonight."

The caller took the hint. "I think I can get up there soon, maybe in the next few days? I can pop in if you like?"

"That would be good," the blind man stated, "though don't go out of your way if you can't. Where are you off to anyway?" he added.

"I have a course to give up in Manchester, so it's sort of on my way. I may be able to stop by on the way up."

"That would be nice," the blind man said, now rubbing the back of his dog who had sauntered into the room and was standing by the man's leg.

"Okay, I'll see what I can do."

"That sounds good. I'll wait to hear from you then?"

"Yes…oh before I go, how are you doing for food?"

"I'm okay. The home help brought me a few things yesterday and said that they will do some shopping for me tomorrow."

There was a measure of understanding from down the phone. The caller seemed pleased. It meant that they didn't need to spend too long with the blind man when visiting. A short chat would be more than enough. Spending too long a time was depressing. Sadly, for the blind man, he knew what all his visitors were experiencing. He didn't begrudge them their feelings, he just wished that they would be honest with him. Having said that, they *were* trying to get him the support he needed. He just hoped it wouldn't take too much longer. The plan they had was working, it just needed the others to come to the party.

The call ended and the blind man pushed the mute button again. The news was over. The *One-Show* was just about to start. The weather had turned bad, the rain continuing to bounce off his windows. He was fortunate that he couldn't see the extent of it, however, his acute hearing gave him a sense of what was happening outside his closed curtains. He would be glad when he could eventually get away from the place. He hoped the rain would stop soon.

CHAPTER 20

'That was a really good win on Saturday, Mike," Telside said, as he and Cannon walked back to Cannon's car, which was parked on the soft grass a short walk from the circuit where their horses were being exercised.

"I agree Rich," Cannon replied as he climbed into the driver's seat. Telside stood at the door as Cannon wound down the window. "I think we've worked out how to run *Titan's Hand*, plus *Once and for All* ran a great race as well, didn't he?"

"Yes, he did Mike. I was pleasantly surprised with *his* run."

Cannon nodded then started the engine. Telside tapped the top of the vehicle, standing back as his boss drove away. Telside would see that the horses and their riders got safely back to the stables. Cannon in the meantime would start his paperwork concerning those horses he wanted to declare to run in upcoming events.

The morning had gone well. The rain had eventually stopped overnight, and the sky was slowly clearing. The horses seemed to be enjoying what Cannon had set each of them to do. Their work was good, and Telside and he were extremely pleased with how the stable was performing. Their race form was improving. *Titan's Hand* had shown his true self in his last race. Cannon now knew why, and he intended to take full advantage of it. He had already mapped out a plan for the horse. It was too late for this year, but he hoped that if the horse stayed sound over the summer and into the early winter, he would try for the Champion Hurdle at Cheltenham, the following March. That was almost 14 months away. At nearly 200,000 pounds to the winner, and nearly 75,000 for coming second, it was good prizemoney. Even coming in fifth in the race, netted around 10,000 pounds. While it was a long way off, Cannon was keen to try.

After he had left the bar at Haydock on Saturday, Cannon had called Harris as he drove home to let him know his thoughts. Harris was enthusiastic though a little cautious about telling the rest of the syndicate about the plan. He wanted them to enjoy the success of Haydock but not get too far ahead of themselves. The thought that two syndicate members had died in relatively bizarre circumstances still concerned Harris as much as it did Cannon. As the Manager, he had never experienced anything like what had happened to date. It made him particularly uneasy. Until the horse was moved to Cannon, things had been going relatively well. *Titan's Hand* had not always performed as expected, but the original syndicate members understood that horses could not win every race they participated in. With Stone originally owning 75% of the horse it was he who carried the biggest risk. Now at 30%, he was in the minority. It was this change that meant the rest of the syndicate had been able to outvote Stone and move the horse to Cannon, notwithstanding Cannon's willingness to train the horse and buy into it. Harris wasn't sure if they had made the right decision. He kept the thought to himself, but his main regret now was encouraging Sarah Walters to buy a share in the horse at the time the syndicate was originally established. He had similarly encouraged her to keep her share when the syndicate composition changed. She had wanted out, but Harris insisted she stay in. They had been friends for years and Harris felt that she would benefit from the horse being moved to Cannon's stables. He had faith in the new trainer and the run on Saturday proved it. Whilst it wasn't the most important issue in his life, success did make things easier for him. He hoped that the police could get to the bottom of what had happened to Sarah. Likewise, he was hoping for answers to the death of Fred Punch. He knew of Wingrew's arrest and subsequent release on bail and he doubted that Wingrew was the killer of Punch. He had no evidence himself as to whether Wingrew was guilty or not, but he was sure the man was innocent. Whatever else Wingrew was part of was of no concern to him. He had shared some of his thoughts with Cannon.

CHAPTER 21

The abandoned car was found by a group of ramblers who had been walking along the pathway next to the River Lee, close to the William Girling reservoir. It was only a short distance from the town of Enfield. The car lay half-submerged, its back half pointing upwards like a duck's backside when it dives under water searching for food. It had been in the river for a few days and the brown muddy water had flooded the inside of the cabin. Silt had built up around the windscreen and the windows, the upholstery on the front seats was soaked and had curled and crumpled from the river's flow as it washed through deliberately left open windows. The back seats of the car were wet but the top halves were relatively unscathed. Whoever had driven the vehicle towards the river from the bank had been brave. To dump the car into the water, they had used a small boat ramp standing alongside the river as a launchpad. Car tracks were evident in the grass and soil leading towards the wooden structure. Unfortunately, with the recent heavy rains, any footprints left in the soil, around the immediate vicinity of the riverbank, were only partially useful. The area had been contaminated by the group of walkers who had found the car. While the ramblers had worn hiking shoes, it was clear that the driver of the vehicle did not. However, as Peters would attest later, the evidence gathered at the scene was only of limited use. The individual who had dumped the car had known what they were doing. The spot itself was quiet and it was a long way from Birmingham. Peters believed that when the car was first discovered the local Police force had not reacted to the find as he would have liked. As there was no evidence of foul play with regards to its' dumping, they responded as if it was just another vehicle stolen by joyriders who eventually decided to dump it in the river for fun. It was only later once Peters' request for information about the car that he had been put onto the PNC (Police National Computer) database was noticed by the Essex Police, that some action was taken. However, as some parts of the forest area are the Metropolitan Police's responsibility and others are those of the local police, there was some confusion as to who was handling the matter of the theft and the dumping of the vehicle. It took a couple of days before Peters was contacted and advised that the car had been located.

"Bloody Hell," Peters said to no one in particular as he put down the phone. He was exasperated. He already had plenty on his plate and he knew he wasn't alone. The team outside had several cases that they were working on and Peters needed them to get results. Once a crime was solved it didn't let anyone off the hook immediately. There were always *add-ons* as he called them. Paperwork! Briefs to prepare. Court appearances to get ready for.

Evidence to lead.

The team heard his cry of frustration but they decided to keep their heads down. Eventually, they heard Peters call out for Drummond. It was just like any other day she thought. A call from the boss, and she went running. She knew it was the same for her male colleagues but the way she was summoned into Peters' office grated on her. She knew she should say something to him as he was a fair man, but there never seemed to be a good time. *One day*, she thought.

"Yes, Sir?" she inquired as she walked into the office. It was just after lunch and it looked to her that Peters had already drunk a few coffees during the morning. His desk was clear except for one coffee carton, that was still giving off steam from the hot liquid, but inside a wire basket next to his desk there were three large paper cups standing head to toe. She wasn't sure how he managed it, as it seemed to her that the amount of coffee he drank did not affect him.

"They found the car," he said, matter-of-factly while pointing to a two-page document he had been reading.

"Where?" she replied, sitting down and brushing a hand across her jacket. She never wore anything other than respectable clothes when she was at work. Dark trouser suits, light blouses, practical heels. They gave an impression of someone in control of herself and she liked that.

"Essex….down South…," he added, unnecessarily.

"Burnt out?" she enquired.

"Dumped," he replied, "in a bloody river."

"Have they got it out yet?"

"As far as I know, no. I've just got off the phone after I read that brief. There is not much in the report, unfortunately," he continued.

Drummond picked up the document but didn't look at it. She placed it on her lap with the intent of perusing it later.

"It seems the car has been in the water for a couple of days now," he continued.

"How do they know that?"

"According to the unit down in Essex, it's because of the recent rains that we've been having. They said that the local walking clubs normally pass that way when they go rambling. With all the rain about a lot of them didn't bother for a few days," he explained. "It seems that there is a bit of a regular get-together of hikers or walkers in the area every day, but with the heavy rains, they abandoned their walks for a couple of days until it stopped. The car could have been there since the same day as the fire, which is what I suspect, however, because no one saw it until this morning, it could have also been dumped overnight. Personally, I think it was gotten rid of as soon as possible."

"And there are no cameras in the area?"

"Only those around the motorway exits."

"And?" she asked

"Well, the car didn't go that way. That's something we know for sure. It left the motorway well before getting anywhere near the place it was found. The driver must have used some other route to get into the woods."

"Which means the driver knows the area?"

"Maybe."

"Which would also suggest that he used another car to get away from the river," Drummond said. "Did they find anything else?"

"Such as?"

"The clothes? An obvious disguise don't you think?"

"Not that I'm aware," Peters replied, "from what they've reported, all they found was the car. The false plates were still attached, barely it seems, but there was nothing else inside."

"And in the immediate vicinity?"

"You mean tyre tracks, etcetera?"

"Yes…the obvious..," she responded cynically.

"Nothing!" he answered, his frustration clear.

Drummond suddenly stood. She knew that he needed some space, some air. It was one of her *virtues* and something for which he was always grateful. "Let me make a few phone calls," she said. "I'll see what I can find out. It looks like you need a few minutes to yourself," she added.

Peters smiled. She was right. It seemed that anyone who went up in rank particularly those on the front line, not the political appointees, nearly always faced the stresses and strains of expectation. Burnout was an occupational hazard and Drummond could see it in him. They had worked together for too long for him to fail and he needed her like a building needs a lightning rod. If things began to get stormy, humid, or hot and he found himself challenged then she would be the circuit breaker for him. His relationship with her was purely platonic. He loved his wife and children, but Drummond kept him grounded at work. As she left his office, he reached for the coffee cup. The drink was cold, but he swallowed it anyway.

CHAPTER 22

The Lamb and Flag, a small pub on Hailey Road would have been difficult to find if it hadn't been for the satnav device. Situated on the B4022 it was a twenty-minute drive from Cannon's stables and surrounded by open countryside. The Limestone coloured building with the thatched roof provided a homely setting against the cold weather outside. There were three rooms, each with a log fire that enhanced the atmosphere expected by the particular customers. There was a bar for the early drinkers, a small snug for those that wanted a quiet drink and lunch, and a smaller room where tea and cake were more suitably served.

Michelle and Cynthia Crowe sat together, their tea now finished. Only a few crumbs from the sandwiches they had shared, were left on the plates that sat on the table between them.

"How are you holding up, now?" Michelle asked. The two women had agreed to catch up a week after the hearing held at school, Michelle calling Cynthia the previous day and suggesting that they meet mid-afternoon once she had finished class for the day. She had a shorter day every second week when sports and other extra-curricular activities were taken by the students. Sometimes Michelle was required to be available if needed and at other times, like today, when some of her students were given time off to study for their upcoming practice GCE exams, she did not. Cynthia likewise would normally have been undertaking supervising duties or doing other school-related work. Occasionally, if lucky, she would also have had a few hours off. As it stood, she was still on her enforced break.

On arrival, Michelle had noted that Cynthia seemed a little unwell. She appeared to have lost weight and her eyes were framed with dark rings. Her hair was not combed as neatly as normal and had begun to grow out in places. Her clothes still suggested that she took pride in what she wore but Michelle felt that they were hiding what was going on inside her friend's mind. Almost like a cloak. She had tried to make light of things initially but soon got the sense that Cynthia was struggling.

"I'm okay," Cynthia ultimately replied, but somewhat tentatively, "yes…I'm okay," she repeated.

Michelle looked into her friend's face before replying. She had noticed that Cynthia was gently turning her hands over and over, her fingers intertwining then parting before again lacing themselves together. It was an action that had continued throughout their conversation.

Michelle leant forward, touching her friend briefly on the arm. It was a sign of comfort and support.

"You know you're not the first, don't you?" she said.

"And I'm sure I won't be the last..." Cynthia added, looking down at her hands.

"Exactly. It seems to be the trend now, isn't it? It's as if you can't look at anyone, speak to anyone, or even smile at anyone without them getting offended. It's a joke in my opinion," she added, "but it's made worse by everyone jumping to conclusions without the facts. A quick click of the camera on a mobile phone, the immediate uploading of a photo to some social media platform, and before you know it, a teacher is suddenly in trouble."

Cynthia stared at Michelle. She hadn't seen her as fired up before like she was now. She was about to say so when Michelle continued. "As you know Cynthia, I love my job and I wouldn't want to do anything else, but when I see bad things happen to good people, I really get annoyed."

"I know," Cynthia said, "and I appreciate your concern. I'm sure I'll get over it soon, but I just need to get my head back into gear."

"Because..?"

Cynthia picked up her cup of tea then realizing that it was empty placed it back onto the saucer. Her hesitation in responding was noticeable. Michelle understood that where her friend was mentally, was not a good place. Despite the attempt to hide her feelings, Michelle could sense that Cynthia was struggling with what had happened to her. This despite it being clear that she was an innocent victim of a child's game.

"I think the whole thing has dented my confidence," Cynthia stated. "I mean I'm a grown woman, I've had experiences, but...but...this has been a whole new chapter that I never thought would happen to me."

"And it's over now," Michelle added sympathetically. "It's over."

"Is it?"

Michelle sighed inwardly. "Yes, it is...it's time to move on, to get back to work the week after next and put it all behind you."

There was a silence between the two friends before Cynthia said. "Do you think they'll change the policy?"

Michelle had hoped that Cynthia had heard what she had said and had taken her comments on board. Sadly, it appeared not.

"Look, whatever they do, it *doesn't* matter anymore," she continued, "you are a good person, a good teacher, and it's over now. A policy change about texting, no matter how clear, or even adding rules about talking with the kids won't easily change anything. Things happen, kids can be mean, to each other, to their parents, to us. Claims like those made by Samantha Prittly will keep on happening. We just need to be aware, be resilient and do the right thing. That's all anyone can ask. Of me and you."

Cynthia was surprised by Michelle's passion for the issue. She hadn't heard her friend speak so strongly on the matter before, but she knew that it was something that every teacher across the country likely felt. Yes, there were always those who would denigrate the profession. Some teachers did break the rules. Some did it because they felt that they could get away with it. Some because they were just bad people. Cynthia knew that she was a good person, a good teacher. Hearing it again from Michelle helped.

"Thank you," she said, "you've been a great help, and you are right. I know it will be difficult looking Samantha in the eye again when I next take her for class, but I'm sure I'll survive," she added, a tiny smile on her lips.

"And I'll make sure that I have a chat with her, one-on-one before you get back. I saw her yesterday in my home room class and she seemed okay, but I'll take her to one side when I can and see how she is going herself. See what she is thinking. From what I heard from Mrs. Lavers, it *seems* like Samantha has accepted the outcome of the meeting and has gotten over it already. I'll test it with her just to check and then I can let you know," she added empathetically.

"That would be good," Cynthia responded, sitting up straight in her chair, appearing a little happier.

"It's my pleasure," Michelle said, hoping that what she was seeing outwardly, was what was going on inside Cynthia's mind, "Oh, and if you need to chat, just give me a call or just pop around anytime. I'm here for you," she added, reaching over and giving her friend a peck on the cheek.

Cynthia smiled again, Michelle seeing it as a good sign.

On the short drive home, Michelle recalled the discussion. She wasn't sure why, but she still had concerns about Cynthia's mindset.

CHAPTER 23

Cannon was worried. He was beginning to have doubts, and it wasn't about getting married again, although for some reason the subject had seemed to have disappeared from their recent conversations. His concern was more to do with what he thought he had seen in the yard. He was aware that he could have been jumping at shadows, but he doubted it. He had been a policeman far too long, and he believed that his powers of observation had not yet dimmed, despite getting older. He likened it to what he had to observe with his horses. How they reacted to things both on and off the track. It was not easy but he had slowly observed their behaviours, noted their quirks, understood their needs. It was the same with human beings. He had learnt what they could do. In times of stress, when angry, when drunk, how they could lie, and how they would react when the world was against them. He had also learnt to trust his instinct, his gut, and he currently had a knot in his stomach. He knew something was going on concerning the *Titan's Hand* syndicate, but he had no real clue what it was or where it was leading. He had only just begun to form the basis of an idea, and he was still working on proving it to himself. The inability to confirm it yet was however eating away at him. What he believed had happened the other night, the mysterious movement that he thought he had seen, was making matters worse.

He was back in his office, Michelle was still not back from lunch. Having concluded his nominations for some upcoming race meetings, and only having a single runner at Hereford the next day, which he would not attend but would watch on TV, he decided to make a call.

"Cummings," the voice said, once he had been connected via the internal switchboard.

"Hello, Inspector, it's Mike Cannon here."

Cummings greeted Cannon in response, apologizing for not being in touch.

"That's okay," Cannon replied, "I understand. A policeman's work is never really done is it?" he went on, noting how a bastardized line from the *Pirates of Penzance* came to him so easily. It had been used on him many times in the past and he cringed a little when he used it himself.

"Precisely....," Cummings agreed, somewhat bemused. "Anyway, Mike, as I said, I'm sorry for not having called you in the past week or so, but things have been pretty hectic around here."

Cannon ignored the excuse asking, "What's the story with Wingrew at the moment? I saw him the other day at Haydock and he just seemed to be getting on with things. He didn't seem worried at all, at least outwardly."

There was no immediate response from Cummings, so Cannon continued, saying, "I did keep my eyes open as you asked, and I must admit there was nothing obvious going on, that I could see."

The Inspector seemed disappointed, and Cannon could tell that something had happened by the lack of response. While he had relayed an observation about the trainer, he had held back on his own thoughts about where things were at. He wanted to hear what Cummings was prepared to share with him. It was a former Detectives instinct and it proved correct.

"We've dropped all charges against Wingrew," Cummings finally advised.

Cannon realized that the decision must have been made quickly, so asked the obvious question, expecting that the forthcoming answer was the reason why Wingrew *had* been so accessible at Haydock.

"Simply put, Mike, a *lack of evidence.*"

"Other than circumstantial?" Cannon replied.

"Yes. We went hard trying to find something tangible, but we came up with nothing. Paula…Sergeant Alton, and some of my team, have spent most of their time since the day of the murder, right up until a couple of days ago, trying to find anything that we could take to the CPS to support a conviction. But we couldn't. Nothing stacked up. At least as far as Wingrew is concerned."

"So back to square one then?"

"Yes, I'm afraid so…"

Cannon considered what had been said. Based on their previous conversation when Cummings had asked him to *keep an eye on* Wingrew, it was now obvious to Cannon that unless something came out of left-field, the police had nothing at all on the trainer. He decided to throw Cummings a bone and see if he picked it up. He wondered if it was the right thing to do as he was no longer a policeman, though in his mind he often thought that he had never stopped being one. As he had mused on many occasions, the job, the life he had previously led, had never really left him. He in turn had never really left it. He believed that the Inspector was good at his job and he admired his attitude, but would he see that the advice from someone so experienced as Cannon was good advice, or would he just ignore it? Cannon knew that Cummings would be wary. Not every cop was straight, but Cannon liked Cummings and believed that he, like himself, would have wanted to be given a break in any case that they were working on. He hoped Cummings would see it that way. Cannon had a theory about Wingrew. He didn't believe the man was a killer and he intimated it.

"If it's any consolation," he said, "I believe you've done the right thing."

"You think so?"

"Yes, though I guess the powers that be, aren't happy?"

"Not only that, but neither is Alex Stone. He complained about how we disrupted his yard and potentially embarrassed him."

"Well, he *is* a personality and he did play for his country. He's always been seen as a wealthy man and I remember when his place in Cheshire was being built. He got quite a lot of publicity and a lot of stick about it because of the cost of the development, the investment he was making. I think it cost about three million pounds."

Cummings whistled through his teeth in response.

Cannon added, "As I'm sure you would know Inspector, wealthy people are often targeted by the press, so when something like Wingrew's arrest gets air time, who knows what impact it could have on Stones' yard. There is a lot of blue-blood horse flesh stabled there."

"True," Cummings replied. "I didn't realize it immediately, but it is obvious that Stone and Wingrew are completely joined at the hip."

"They are," Cannon replied, a sudden thought passing through his mind. "I expect that Stone may try and give you a hard time in the short term, but he'll get over it eventually, especially if you find the killer."

"You are probably right Mike, but he doesn't concern me. I've dealt with a lot worse in the past."

"I'm sure you have, Inspector, and I'm sure you don't need me to tell you what to do about it, so I won't. But I would like to ask you something else." The tone of Cannon's voice intrigued Cummings. "Go on," he replied, trying to sound nonchalant, though keen to hear what Cannon wanted to say.

"Birmingham...."

"What about it?" Cummings replied.

Cannon took his time. He was framing a thought and he needed Cummings to give it serious consideration. He could hear the Inspector breathing on the line. Cannon's sense of theatre often gave him an advantage, and he decided to use it now.

"Did you hear about the fire there a couple of days ago? In a nail bar? It was on the news and was reported on various websites, the BBC, ITV, and others."

"Well, I did see a little bit about it, but I haven't given it any thought. How is it relevant to what we are talking about?"

"The owner, the lady who was killed. She was there the day Punch was murdered. She was part of the syndicate."

"Who was that then?" Cummings asked. Cannon could hear him shuffling some papers, then tapping away at a keyboard.

As he was doing so, Cannon mentioned the name, "Sarah Walters. The lady who left early...before Punch's murder."

Cannon could sense Cummings taking on board what he had said. The Inspector stayed quiet. Cannon gave him time to respond knowing that Cummings needed to process what he was getting at.

"You think they are connected?" Cummings replied eventually.

"Do you believe in coincidence?"

Cannon's sarcasm was not lost on the Inspector. "Maybe...perhaps I need to think about it a little?"

Cannon shrugged. He had offered the man a bone. He wanted a tidbit in return. "I'll leave that with you then….but can I ask a favour?"

"Sure."

"Could I ask you to give DCI Peters of the West Midlands branch a call, and ask him his view of the Birmingham case?"

"Because….?"

"Because….well let's put it this way," Cannon said. "I think someone has been sneaking around my yard over the past couple of days, and I have no idea who it is or why."

"And you think it's related to this fire up in Birmingham?"

"No, I think it's related to the horse that I have recently taken on, *Titans' Hand*," Cannon replied, "Well, to be more precise I think it has something to do with the syndicate, and unfortunately, I've bought into it myself. I think something is going on and I'm worried as to where it could lead."

"Are you suggesting that the lady…Sarah Walters, was murdered?"

"I don't know, but I have a view. I was hoping that you could find out from Peters."

"I'm not sure he would like me interfering in his case, Mike, no matter what the reason."

"I thought you might say that, and I can understand your reluctance, but all I'm asking for is to find out what happened to Mrs. Walters. If it was an accident, or not?"

Cummings considered what Cannon had asked. He realized that letting Cannon know about Sarah Walters, and what had happened to her, would hopefully mean that Cannon would continue helping him in return. A *quid-pro-quo*, concerning the Punch murder. He still needed Cannon's help. If it was true that there were two deaths from within the same group of people, both dying under suspicious circumstances, then it could mean that there was potentially a killer amongst them.

Cannon had no idea as to the cause of the fire that Sarah Walters had died in, but he was following his gut instinct. When he thought about someone sneaking around his stables, he felt inside that he was on the right track. He believed that what he saw the other night was not a figment of his imagination and somehow it was related to the Titan-H syndicate. What he needed was affirmation and knowing if Sarah Walters had died through anything other than an accident would tell him one way or the other.

"Alright, let me come back to you," Cummings said eventually, but reluctantly. "I guess one favour deserves another, doesn't it?" he continued. I was his own subtle reference to Cannon's continued agreement to keep him informed of anything he could find out about the Wingrew. "This must remain between you and me though, Mike. No one else needs to know, right?"

"Absolutely," Cannon replied.

"Very well, I'll get back to you as soon as I can."

"Sounds good."

Cannon was just about to put the phone down when Cummings said, "Mike...take care. Stay safe. If someone is messing around your place, get the local police involved. Don't try to be a hero, it's not worth the risk."

"Will do, Inspector. You'll have no arguments from me."

Both men knew that Cannon was lying. Cummings let the reply go straight through to the keeper. As a final comment, he asked, "CCTV, do you have any?"

"Yes, and it's working, but when I looked at it the other morning, there was no sign of anyone."

"Could it have been an animal that created the shadow? I assume you have spotlights on during the night?"

"Yes, we do. They turn off around midnight, but the CCTV is always on."

"Maybe it was a fox?" Cummings suggested.

"Maybe...," Cannon echoed, "but in any case, I think I need to be more aware, more alert. At least until I'm happy that nobody is sniffing around."

Cummings agreed, then ended the call. Cannon slowly put down his phone. He turned to his computer to check on some of the upcoming race meetings that would suit the plans he had made for some of his horses. He decided to continue racing *Titan's Hand* at least until the early Spring. After that, the horse would be put away until the Autumn.

In trying to find a suitable meeting, the best and most lucrative option available was a grade 3 handicap hurdle on the 2nd day of the Grand National Festival at Aintree in April, still several weeks away.

Cannon shivered. The last time he was at Aintree, he had nearly won the Grand National. Nearly was not good enough for him, however. *Titan's Hand* was a hurdler, not a steeplechaser so if he wanted to win the *National (his dream),* he would need to find another horse. That may take a while, he thought.

If all went well, Cannon had planned to guide *Titan's Hand* to a Champion Hurdle to be held at Cheltenham late the following winter. "Aintree it is then," he said to himself, before completing all the details on the applicable e-forms, of the horses he hoped to enter into the festival.

CHAPTER 24

Wingrew stood at the door to one of the best steeplechasers in the yard. He was extremely lucky to have the animals that he had in his stables. Being a champion trainer, he had been blessed to be able to race many extremely talented horses over the years. Block B was where the best of the animals were housed. He watched as the groom continued with his work, brushing down a magnificent grey horse, *Salt of the Earth*. The horse was aptly named. Now eight years old and at the height of his powers, the horse remained statue-still, enjoying the attention it was receiving. A superstar of the track, he had won over 600,000 pounds during his career to date and was expected to be one of the favourites for the Melling Chase to be run over two miles, four furlongs at Aintree. The horse had run second in the Ryanair Chase during the Cheltenham Festival only a few weeks prior, just missing out by a head. Wingrew believed the horse was more suited to the Aintree fences and was now rock-hard fit. The sad thing about it though was that he knew the horse wouldn't win. Owned by Stone, the instructions had been given already.

"He looks good," he said to the groom.

"Aye," the young man brushing the horse replied, "he's ready, Mr. Wingrew. He could probably jump the Manchester Ship canal if you'd let him, the way he's going at the moment."

Wingrew nodded. He couldn't doubt the observation made by the groom. The horse was jumping out of his skin on the training track. The poor jockey who took him for his exercises needing to restrain the horse at times for being too exuberant, too keen to attack the fences.

Wingrew turned away, beginning to walk through the stable block towards the rear exit. He nodded at those grooms who acknowledged him as he walked. Some of the horses turned their heads, watching him, seeming to understand who he was. Occasionally he rubbed a hand along a face that had leaned out over the half-door of one of the stables, sometimes clicking his tongue he would offer a sugar cube to the occupant. There were millions of pounds worth of horse-flesh in Block B alone and Wingrew was feeling the pressure. While Stone was happy with what Wingrew was doing, many other owners were not. He was worried about his reputation. He was worried that someone knew what was going on. The letters they had received were becoming more demanding. Stones' idea hadn't produced any results and Wingrew was convinced that it wouldn't. Stone had told him to stay the course, but he was beginning to doubt the man. As he reached the rear exit, Stone came through it, almost knocking him over.

"We need to talk," Stone said, looking flustered. Wingrew noticed that the man was dressed casually, which was unusual. Normally Stone wore designer jeans and branded polo shirts with expensive jerseys or jackets, whenever he was around the stables. It was an image that he had fostered over the years. Living on the property in a house with six bedrooms but remaining single had perpetuated the playboy image and that suited him. Today, however, he wore tracksuit bottoms, admittedly those of his former club, a white t-shirt, and a grey top. It looked like he had been running but hadn't yet showered or changed. It was obvious to Wingrew that something serious had occurred that had prevented Stone from following his normal routine of dressing properly before being *seen* around the stables.

Not having showered as yet made it obvious that there was something on his mind.

Wingrew nodded silently, and they left the Block through the back exit. They did not speak again until they were safely inside Stone's house, two hundred yards away from Block A.

The house was extremely modern inside. Large acrylic canvases along with smaller oil and water colour paintings covered the walls of the hallway leading into a large open plan lounge area. The room furnishings were tasteful soft greys and blues. Easy cushions were scattered on several couches and silver throws were spread across the backs of two easy chairs. The walls were painted a warm white and a large screen TV was adorned one end of the room. Polished oak flooring and occasional rugs completed the room which faced towards a large pool in a private garden. The entire wall, one of triple glazed glass. A fire provided heat in the modern setting. It was situated below the TV in an open firepit and fueled by gas. Stone walked over to a small creamy white table, about 45 by 30 centimeters wide, standing alongside the back wall. On the table was a telephone base unit and handset. The latter was small, discrete, and about half the size of the latest iPhone.

Without hesitation, Stone pressed a couple of buttons on the handset and a voice escaped from the speaker of the base unit. As the person began to speak, Stone increased the volume.

"I'm leaving you this message, Mr. Stone," the voice said, in a fake Scots accent. It was obvious that the person was pretending to be a Scot in an attempt to hide the sound of their own voice. "It's a message for you to think about…" the individual continued, before again stopping suddenly and leaving an uncomfortable silence for a few more seconds. Wingrew looked at Stone who put a finger to his lips indicating that he should just listen. "I know what you are doing, and I know why…." A further pause, and then…. "I can let the authorities know and I can inform your other owners if you want me to, *or* we can make a deal……I'm assuming you have already read the letters I sent? If so, some of the detail in those letters will confirm to you that I am not joking. So, the question is…deal or bust....Mr. Stone...think about it... I'll be in touch." With that, the call ended as quickly as it had begun.

Wingrew looked at Stone, not knowing what to say. Eventually, he said, "What do you think?"

"Well, I don't think he's a Scot, that's for sure."

"He?"

"Yes, it's obviously a man. Can't you tell?"

"I thought so too, but nowadays with all sorts of technology available to change or distort a voice, it could just as easily be a woman."

"I suppose so," agreed Stone, "but what do you think about the threat?"

"I was just about to ask you the same thing," Wingrew said sitting down in one of the casual chairs. Stone remained standing, his baggy tracksuit pants seeming incongruous in the luxurious setting.

Stone was hoping Wingrew would be more responsive, having more enthusiasm to resolve things. If their plan ever came out publicly it would destroy the trainer's career and they would both end up in jail.

"I think it's real," Stone replied, "as I told you when I got the first letter. The thing that bothers me though, is how do they know? And what is it that they want? What does doing a deal, actually mean? Can we even trust them, whoever they are?"

He looked at Wingrew and was starting to get annoyed. He needed the trainer to continue to do what he was doing. He needed to keep on following instructions, stay focused and most of all, stay calm. Stone believed that if he did so, Wingrew and he could be out of the mess within six months. If, everything went their way.

"Your plan isn't working, Alex, " Wingrew said. "Since this started we haven't been able to flush anyone out yet, have we? Staying quiet, stalling, and not acting on the letters, hoping it would all go away, has achieved nothing, hasn't it?"

"That's where you are wrong," Stone responded angrily. "We've managed to get whoever it is, to keep coming back to us and wanting to make a deal. Their very words!"

"So what?"

Stone walked across the room, keeping his back to Wingrew. He stopped behind one of the couches and turned towards his trainer. "That call," he said, indicating the phone, "means that whoever it is, is desperate."

"How do you draw that conclusion?"

"If they really wanted to do what they say they would do, they would have acted upon it by now, and because of that it means we have other options."

"Like what?"

"To go along with them."

"I don't understand Alex. If that's your thinking why didn't you do that earlier? How does going along with them *now*, help?" Wingrew asked.

"Once we know who they are, then we'll get our *friends* involved."

Wingrew stood up. "Are you mad Alex? The last thing we want is another death associated with the stable. I've already been through hell after I was arrested and taken into custody. I don't want to go through that again. Plus, I *don't* want any blood on my hands!" he shouted.

Stone became angrier. The normally friendly disposition that he worked hard to maintain in public rapidly disappearing, like a breeze dispersing mist over a river. His face began to redden, and his hands opened and closed into fists. "Keep your voice down!" he said, "It's because of talking out of turn that we are in this mess in the first place."

Wingrew reacted, not willing to take a step back. "Now don't go there Alex, not for one minute. We...you, are in this mess because of what you *did*. *I'm* in this because I tried to help you get out of it."

"Though not without any benefits, Dom..... if I may say so," Stone replied sarcastically.

Wingrew looked at Stone, then stared at the floor for a few seconds. He realized that there was no point in arguing and he raised his hands in surrender. "Okay, okay," he replied, "calm down, calm down," he repeated. "If you want to go down the path of using your friends to solve this, then that's up to you, but I'm telling you, Alex, that I won't have anything to do with it. You can count me out on that one."

Stone smiled enigmatically. He knew that Wingrew would soon change his tune. If it meant that the trainer would be able to continue to do what he did every day, then Stone knew that Wingrew would soon acquiesce. He knew what motivated the man. He knew how to exploit the trainers' weaknesses. Status and success on the racecourse were what the trainer wanted. Stone had given him that opportunity. In return, all he asked for was loyalty. Sometimes that loyalty could be stretched but it was never to be lost or broken.

"We'll see," Stone said eventually.

After a few seconds of reflection, Wingrew asked, "So what now, Alex?" as he pointed towards the telephone.

"It's obvious isn't it?"

"Is it? I thought you just....."

"Indicated that we need to go along with what the caller said?" Stone interrupted.

"Yes..er, no... I thought you were talking about getting your friends involved. Isn't that what you intend to do, or am I confused?"

"He said he wants to do a deal," Stone replied, ignoring Wingrew and referencing the caller. "So until we hear from them again, we just need to wait.. there's nothing else that we can do."

Wingrew looked at his boss. He wasn't convinced about what he was hearing but decided to stay quiet. His recent arrest was still playing on his mind. Having been charged with murder, then being bailed before finally having the charges dropped, he didn't wish to go through it again. What Stone had said, still worried him. It was possible that that the voice recording that he had just heard could lead to further deaths.

CHAPTER 25

"Are you able to shed any light on what happened?" Cummings asked of Peters. He knew that he could have gone the long way around, following internal procedures, and requested the information about the fire that way. However, to get a speedier answer, he decided to call Peters directly. He knew it was a bit forward, unusual, and he wanted to maintain a good relationship with his senior officer, especially one in a different jurisdiction. He knew that it was a gamble to be so direct as most Detectives protected their turf with a passion. He was hoping that if he offered a future favour, in return for the information that he was seeking, he would get what he needed without too much hassle.

"Is there a reason why you are so interested?" Peters replied cautiously.

Cummings could sense that he was on shifting ground. Cooperation only happened when both parties benefitted and as far as Peters knew, there was nothing in it for him, yet, in sharing any information about the nail-bar fire. He had looked up Cummings on the internal database and saw that he was much younger than himself. He had a good track record of solving cases and he had been recommended for several citations over his career. Peters had been in the Force at least 12 years longer and was perhaps a little more cynical about life than his colleague was. At least he had Drummond to keep him grounded, especially when he was angry or frustrated, he thought. She was able to calm him down when necessary, which ensured that he went home to his wife without all the baggage and stresses of the day.

"To be honest with you Sir, it's less about why I'm interested in what happened versus whether we can help each other."

"Go on."

"Well, I'm investigating a murder up here in Cheshire, where a man was killed on Alex Stones' property. It was quite a bizarre…."

"Alex Stone, the ex-footballer?" Peters interrupted.

"Yes, the very same."

"Right….so…?"

Cummings realized that Peters was now engaged. The name *Stone* having caught his attention.

"As I indicated, the murder itself was quite bizarre and we didn't go public about it because we believe it was executed by someone working at the property. However, after we made an initial arrest the story got out pretty quickly."

"Ah yes, I recall seeing something about it on the TV. You arrested the trainer…what's his name…?" Peters asked, trying to drag the name up from his memory.

"Wingrew, Dominic Wingrew," Cummings said.

"That's right, Wingrew," Peters acknowledged. "So where are things at now then?" he added.

"We had to let him go. Dropped all charges."

Peters realized how embarrassing this could have been for Cummings, but he knew that it happened every single day. Sometimes the guilty were able to get away with things because of a lack of evidence. It didn't mean the person hadn't committed the crime, it just meant that it couldn't be proven. It could be very frustrating and Peters sympathized with Cummings. "So the investigation continues?" he asked.

"Yes, and that is why I called."

"I'm not sure I understand how I can help you, but if you want to know, the fire in Birmingham was deliberately lit and there was a victim…"

"Sarah Walters.." Cummings interjected.

"Yes. That's right."

"She was murdered?'

"Yes.."

"So that's the link," Cummings replied, expressing his thoughts out loud.

"The link?"

"Yes…it was the reason for the call. You see the person killed up here, a guy called Fred Punch was part of a syndicate."

"What…drugs?"

"No, a racing syndicate. Horse racing," Cummings added for clarity. "Sarah Walters was also part of the syndicate."

"Coincidental?"

"No, we don't think so?"

"We?"

Cummings realized it was now time to explain. "I've been working with another member of the syndicate that owns the horse, the new trainer."

"Oh yes?" Peters queried, waiting to hear more detail. He had yet to fully understand where Cummings was taking the conversation.

"The 'we', are just the trainer and myself. He's an ex-cop by the name of Mike Cannon, a former DI from Oxfordshire. It was he that suggested that I ask you about Sarah Walters."

"Could I ask why?"

"Because I still think that Wingrew is somehow linked to the murder of Fred Punch, and I asked Cannon to keep an eye on him for me whenever they cross paths at race meetings. I thought he would be in a good position to find out if there were any rumours about Wingrew floating around the traps. Possibly establish a motive for Punch's murder. Cannon however seems to think that the murder of Sarah Walters, now that you have confirmed that it wasn't an accident, could mean that the killings of both, have something to do with the syndicate itself."

Peters thought about what he had been told, before asking, "And you think that there is merit in this…this theory?"

"Yes, I do. As Cannon said to me, he doesn't believe in coincidences like this, and to be frank, Sir, neither do I."

"That makes three of us then," Peters joked.

"That's good….Sir," Cummings added.

"Call me Chris," the Senior Officer said, feeling a lot better now that he understood what was behind Cummings' call. He could sense that what was being told to him, could be of use.

"Done… Chris," Cummings replied.

"Good. So now that I know what this is all about, let me add a little more colour to the mystery," Peters said. "With regards to the fire and the murder of Mrs. Walters, we know that the likely perpetrator left the scene in a car that we thought was black, but now know was dark blue."

"How do you know the exact color?"

"Because the car was found near Enfield dumped in a river. It was confirmed as a dark blue."

"That's a long way from Birmingham."

"That's right," affirmed Peters, "a bloody long way."

"And did you find anything else?"

"Unfortunately bugger-all of any use."

Cummings could sense Peters' disappointment and frustration. "Anything useful picked up from the motorway cameras between Birmingham and Enfield. Any CCTV from the Services? Or anywhere else?"

"Not much, certainly nothing we can easily use. Whoever it was, man or woman took great care to hide their face as well."

"What do the experts say?" Cummings asked, referring to the specialist teams in the force that used video to try and determine the height, size, and sex of individuals.

"They'll keep trying, but what we have so far is very limited. The car itself has provided very little DNA evidence. Even with more, we may not have anything to compare it against anyway."

"Sounds like we are both in a similar situation then….Chris?" Cummings replied.

"Yes, you're right. But at least we have a possible link, though there is no obvious motive that I can see. Who would want to murder both victims and why?"

"Maybe Cannon is right though? Perhaps something *is* going on within the syndicate, but I'll be buggered if I know what."

"I presume everyone gave a statement at the time of Fred Punch's murder?"

"Yes, it was from those, the detail collected, that we narrowed the killing down to Wingrew."

"But I guess it was all circumstantial."

"Unfortunately, yes it was. That's where Cannon came in."

"Ah yes, Mr. Cannon. I think I'll need to interview him myself," Peters stated.

Cummings suddenly realized where such an interview could lead. Peters could potentially take over the Punch investigation, combine the two murders. It bothered him. He had thought that the call he was making would not affect his involvement in the case. It was *his* case and he wasn't willing to give it up. The information shared by Peters made the investigation all the more real now, it now had another angle to it that needed to be followed up. The death of Punch was no longer an isolated incident. The death of Sarah Walters confirmed it. There was the potential for something big to happen. Big cases were like gold to Detectives. They could make a career. Unfortunately for Cummings, he was the junior of the two officers, and even though he was good, thorough, he couldn't demand that he lead the investigation. He waited for Peters to speak and when he finally did so, he asked, "So how was this Fred Punch killed?"

"He was run through with a pitchfork," Cummings said.

"Ouch...ugly!"

"Yes, not a pretty sight."

"Umm...and you have no other suspects?"

"Not at this stage...but we are monitoring Wingrew as I said before. To my mind, he definitely has something to do with it."

"Okay well, I'll leave that one with you."

Cummings acknowledged the reply by saying nothing, allowing Peters to continue. "Look, Tim," Peters said, using the junior officer's name, "as an FYI, I don't want to take over any investigation that you are running. That's your patch and not mine. In the spirit of cooperation, which can often be a misnomer in our circles as I'm sure you would know, let's see if we can work together on this. Is that a reasonable position?"

Cummings thought for a few seconds about what had been said. He had been surprised by Peters' comments. "Yes, that sounds good," he replied, not quite believing true cooperation would ensue. His experience in the past told him that, but he was always prepared to be proven wrong.

"Great," Peters replied, "I'll give Cannon a call and see if I can set up a time to see him or at least have a chat. He sounds like he still has a nose for policing."

Cummings grunted a confirmation down the phone. He would let Cannon know what he had found out. It would be off the record but Cummings believed that he owed Cannon for continuing to check on Wingrew for him. He was about to put the phone down when he realized something that he needed to share with Peters.

"Oh, just a quick one," he said.

"Yes?" Peters responded.

"Cannon....he believes that there may be someone lurking around his property. He thinks he saw someone hiding in the shadows the other night."

"Umm.... did he ask for any protection?"

"Not as far as I know, but it was something that was worrying him. I told him to contact the local police if he was worried."

"Which I'm sure he appreciated?" Peters replied, somewhat sarcastically.

"Yes. I told him not to be a hero, but I'm not sure he was listening."

"He sounds like a typical ex-cop," Peters laughed. "I'll call him asap and see if I can help."

"Okay. Thanks for the chat, I'll wait to hear from you if anything comes from your follow-ups on the fire, the car, or with regards to Cannon. In the meantime, I have the Punch matter plus plenty of other work to be going on with."

"Don't we all?" Peters replied, "Don't we all?"

CHAPTER 26

Their lovemaking had been loud and aggressive at times. Beforehand he had taken lots of photographs of her. She had posed for him willingly, despite the flaws. It had once been her profession and the camera liked her. It wasn't the first time that they had slept together. Every time they met it was all about the sex, nothing more. Ever since they had first been introduced she had fancied him. He, a former athlete, who still had a reasonably good body, despite how he now treated it. She an ex-model with her scars.

They enjoyed the taste of each other and being able to experiment. They did not hold back, and nothing was off-limits. Neither had any sexual hang-ups.

When they had finished, they both lay exhausted on the bed, looking up at the ceiling of the hotel room that they were using. It was on her route to Manchester and its surrounding areas. She had a number of GP's to see there, but that would be tomorrow.

Tony Clairy smiled to himself. He had done well, bedding someone as willing as Cindy. It had been a long time since he had met someone like her. In the past, he took advantage of being a footballer. Travelling around the country and playing at a level that kept him and his team in the spotlight, allowed him the freedom of meeting women and girls who were willing to share a one-night-stand with him. Since his retirement and the setting up of his photography business, his sex life had been erratic. He had been in a steady relationship, but due to working away on assignments for various magazines and not being at home for long periods, his partner had ultimately left him. That had been well over two years ago. He had met several willing partners at various times since, but they had been transient, and the result had been less than satisfying. He felt that he was missing out, that opportunities were passing him by. That was until now. Now it was full-on. Regular and exciting, and best of all, without commitment.

Cindy rolled over onto her side, pulling the sheet over her shoulders. She didn't need him to hug her, she didn't need comforting. What they had together was an agreement. A transaction. No obligation. For her, it was all about the fun, the excitement. She began to doze. The afternoon was already turning dark. It was still bitterly cold. Winter had not yet released its grip and Spring still seemed very far away. She had nowhere to go once he left, and she had booked the room for the night anyway. She knew that when she awoke, he would be gone.

As she slowly drifted off to sleep, she mused on the fact that being part of the *Titan-H* syndicate, had provided her with much more than she had expected. Meeting Clairy was one example and getting a financial return after the horses' win at Haydock, was even better.

She had been reluctant to become part of it initially, but her ex-lover had insisted, even offering to pay her share. She had rejected his offer. She didn't want to be obligated to anyone.

Life had changed quite dramatically for her over the past few years. The accident had left her with the surgeons' knife marks that no one could see. She kept them covered up. She hid those on her body unless she was comfortable to have others see them, such as Clairy.

Showing the scars on the outside was much easier than letting others become aware of those she was carrying inside.

Melanie Freed picked up the photograph of her late husband in the silver frame. She smiled at the picture. It normally stood on the mantel just above the fireplace of the home where she had lived for forty-two years. She and her husband, Wilfred, had spent nearly thirty-six of them together. The picture itself had been taken while Wilfred had been serving in the RAF during the first Gulf War in 1991, nearly thirty years before. He had been involved in Operation Desert storm flying several sorties into Iraq, dropping multiple bombs on the Iraqi forces.

Wilfred had died of leukemia in 2015 he was only 59.

He had been a Leicester City supporter all his life. He never saw his beloved team win the Premier League. They did so the year after he passed away.

She looked again at his picture. Melanie had always loved horse racing. Being from Lincolnshire, she had often gone with Wilfred to the annual point-to-point races at Brocklesby Park, an event she had first been to as a child with her parents. It was her passion, but one he didn't care for. Football was his game. She never went with him, as she disliked all the noise and the bad language. Wilfred had been very circumspect with his money and when he died he had left Melanie with a significant amount in his will. Along with the house had made sure that she was very comfortable in her dotage. Being in a good position financially, she had found buying into the Titan's-Hand syndicate was one of several things that she had been able to arrange quite easily. It was something she had always wanted to do but had never dared to do while Wilfred was alive. She had waited for several years until the right thing had come along. Needing no persuading once the syndicate had been pitched to her, she was very glad that she had invested in it.

She kissed the photograph softly and placed it carefully back onto the cool marble. She turned on her heels and walked into the kitchen. It was time for tea.

CHAPTER 27

Brendon Harris was a worried man. The death of Fred Punch and Sarah Walters was making life more difficult for him. While he was the Manager of the Titan's Hand Syndicate, he was also the financial Underwriter. Mary Punch had let him know the previous day that she no longer wanted to be part of the group. The murder of her husband making it too painful for her to continue any association. He had now received a call from Sarah Walters' solicitor advising him that she had left specific instructions with him in the event of her sudden death. These stated, amongst other things, that her share in any club, membership, or syndicate was to be immediately liquidated and the proceeds placed into her Estate.

The solicitor had advised Harris that while her death was being investigated, Sarah Walters' assets, both those of a personal nature and those relating to her business dealings would be placed in Trust until Probate. Her will would only be acted upon once the coroner in Birmingham had given his approval to do so. However, the liquidation of her share in the Titan-H syndicate was thus being requested. Harris had acknowledged the request and the fourteen days within which to provide the proceeds from the sale.

It was this latter requirement that concerned him. Under the contract signed by all the current syndicate members, the terms stated that should any person or syndicate group wish to leave the syndicate, then apart from a 14-day notice period, the share concerned would be acquired by the Underwriter in the first instance. If other members of the syndicate wished to acquire the share or a portion thereof, they could apply to do so. If none of the existing members wished to buy any additional shares within 28 days of them becoming available, then the Underwriter could offer the share to another party outside of the current membership, should he wish to do so.

The problem for Harris was that he didn't have the money to buy back the share of Walters and Punch. At 10% between the two of them, the shares were worth around 7000 pounds. The problem was that Harris had already extended himself beyond his means. When he had bought his original share of 10%, he had hoped for a quick return to pay off his mounting debts. Debts predominantly consisting of monies owed to banks. He had mortgaged his house in Christchurch on the south coast in order to fund a gambling habit, which was underpinned by his need to be sociable. After his wife died a few years earlier from a thrombosis he had decided to blow the children's inheritance. In his grief, he had wanted to make of best of his final years. He went on exotic holidays and began living the high life. He had bought into the syndicate at the very beginning, and he had enjoyed rubbing shoulders with the likes of Stone and the others. He saw them as being successful people and he had been able to pretend that he was too. The initial success of the horse had given him a reason to become bolder than he would normally have been comfortable with. His bets on the horse had grown larger over time. When the horse started to run poorly, he had lost more money than he would have liked. Ultimately he found himself owing several bookmakers substantial sums. Being a man who liked to give the impression that he was in control, he kept his fears to himself, however, it was he who had persuaded Stone to have the horse moved to another trainer. He was hoping that the change would improve the horses' success on the track. It had been him who had suggested Cannon as the alternate trainer. His hope was that if Cannon could get the horse to run to its potential again, then perhaps he could recoup his losses and pay off his debts before things had gotten irredeemably out of control. He was initially surprised that Stone and Wingrew had agreed to the move but was grateful that they had. He had a suspicion as to why they had agreed so readily and he had decided to follow up on it.

After he had put down the phone on Walters' solicitor, he called 'Dick' Swiftman. He was hoping to get him to buy the shares of Punch and Walters. While Harris knew that he should offer them to all shareholders, he also knew that Stone, in particular, would not be interested (having already reduced his share down to 30%) and he doubted that the new members would be willing to increase their shareholdings so soon after buying into the syndicate. If he could get a commitment from Swiftman, then he could arrange a back-to-back transfer of the shares without any of the others querying his actions.

"Why would I do that?" Swiftman asked once he understood why Harris had called him.

Harris tried to charm the man, placate him. "Because with a new trainer in Cannon, the horse seems to have a new lease of life, and I'd have thought that it would be something you would want to take advantage of?"

"What about the others? Swiftman replied, "And what about you Brendon, why haven't you decided to buy them?"

"I have my reasons," Harris replied somewhat coyly.

"Well, to be honest, I have no interest in increasing my stake at this stage. What I have currently is good enough for me."

"Are you sure Dick? You've been in the *T.H.* syndicate since day one. I would have thought that getting a bigger piece of the pie would be right up your alley?"

Swiftman laughed. "Look Brendon," he said, "times are tough right now for most people, myself included. Running my building business takes a lot of blood, sweat, and tears. It's not like it used to be and it's not as easy to make money as before. I appreciate you thinking of me, but I've got my mind on other things right now." he added. "So, I'll need to politely decline."

Harris tutted and told Swiftman that he may regret his decision, but once he realized that Swiftman had made his final position clear, he put down the phone. Harris thought for a moment and then in desperation, he decided to call Peter Brown.

CHAPTER 28

"Just as an FYI Rich, I've had a call from an Inspector Peters from the West Midlands police and he's coming down here tomorrow to see me."

They were standing on the top steps of a relatively empty stand at Hereford racecourse. The mid-week meeting bringing a crowd of no more than a couple of hundred spectators to the races. Both men hoped that the two-hour drive from the stables to the track would be worth it. It was one of the closer racecourses to Stonesfield and Cannon and Telside had decided to send three runners to the races to take advantage of the better weather being experienced over recent days. The rain had stopped, and a weak sun and a stronger wind had started to dry out the sodden track. So much so that the Stewards had declared the previous day that if there was no more rain overnight, then the track going would be declared as 'good'. Cannon was happy to hear on arrival that the Stewards had been spot on with their assessment.

Telside didn't respond. Instead, he lifted his binoculars to his eyes and surveyed the track and the now full reservoir situated in the middle of the course. He could sense the irony, especially given the recent weather. The dam had been completed in 2019 to ensure that there was sufficient water available to keep the turf in the best condition it could be. Now there was too much of the damn stuff. If it hadn't been for the rain stopping it was likely that the days' events would have been cancelled, due to the course being waterlogged. As it was, the course looked in magnificent order and the first race had shown no ill effects on the runners. The track had held together well, and it was perfect for the likes of Cannon's runners, *Spiral Code* and *Be Inspired* both of whom were running in the next race, a three and a half mile Chase that was just about to start.

"Is that in connection with the lady who died in that fire?" Telside asked eventually, still staring through the eye pieces.

"Yes," Cannon replied, lowering his binoculars down to his chest. "As I mentioned on the way here, there is something about the *Titan's Hand* syndicate that really worries me."

"But you have a theory?"

"Yes. I've been thinking about it ever since the poor lady died, but it's just a theory Rich," Cannon replied. "Until I've spoken with the Inspector I'm just guessing."

Rich smiled, lowering the binoculars and turning to stare into Cannon's face. They had known each other now for nearly 15 years. Telside was heading towards retirement age as each day passed, yet he doubted that he ever would. Likewise, when he looked at his boss, he knew that the man would never stop being a cop. It was in the man's blood. Cannon would always say that he had moved on, and to all intent and purposes, that was true. He was a racehorse trainer and a good one at that. But inside he couldn't let go of his past. The symbiotic relationship between Cannon and Telside allowed each of them to do the things that they were good at. They supported each other. They were more than lead Trainer and Assistant.

Standing in the shadow of the stand, the fresh breeze tugged at their coats. Rich pulled the scarf at his throat slightly tighter using a gloved hand. Cannon pulled the edges of his coat together. It was a habit that he had and one he could not explain. No matter how cold or breezy the weather, he rarely buttoned up his coat, preferring just to hold the two edges in his hand.

Over the PA system, the race-caller began his pre-race announcements, talking about the runners and the status of the race betting.

Cannon noticed some of the few punters on track, gathered around a handful of bookmaker stands adjacent to the winning post. He wondered how those still operating a position on the course were making a living. Most gambling and betting today was done online. He thought that even one bookmaker on track would struggle to make a living, let alone five.

Cannon searched for the colours of his jockey as he looked across towards the starting position of the race. Being a race of endurance, the horses would be completing more than two circuits of the track. He hoped that by the time the field of twelve runners went past where he and Rich were now standing, that both his runners had gotten themselves into a good position, roughly around mid-field and that both had settled into a good rhythm.

Suddenly the race-caller announced that the field of runners appeared ready and were walking up to the start in a good line. A start was imminent.

"Good luck," Rich said.

Cannon nodded. Neither of their two runners was in the top three or four of betting and both men had limited expectations about their success. The plan for both runners was to get them race fit after injuries and the enforced break from racing due to the weather. Giving a horse a *run* was nothing new. The owners of both horses had been told of the long-term plan for each, and it was one of the reasons why there was no representative of either horse on course. Most owners had day jobs and couldn't always afford to be off work to watch their horses run, especially when the contest wasn't what one would call, a big race. Today's contest had total prize money of just over twelve thousand pounds for its class of race. The winner would receive seven thousand. Most owners would watch the race on TV if they even decided to watch the race at all.

As the field reached Cannon and Telside for the first time after running three-quarters of a mile, it had already begun to string out. The two runners upfront had started a fight for the lead resulting in an unnecessarily fast pace. There had been one faller so far, a runner that failed to clear the first fence.

The two men watched as *Spiral Code* and *Be Inspired* raced in sixth and ninth place respectively, around twelve lengths covering the entire field. Cannon looked at each horse, in turn, to see how each was going. *Spiral Codes'* jockey was dressed in a red and white striped top with a blue cap. A young conditional jockey sitting atop *Be Inspired* wore a lime green jacket, with a full yellow circle, like the sun, in the middle. On his racing helmet, he wore a lime green cover. Both runners appeared to be travelling well.

The order of the race barely changed over the next few fences. The field passed the finishing post for the penultimate time and then the real race began. The voice of the race caller began to rise in pitch as the leading pair increased the pace. Within a few hundred metres, however, both began to feel the effects of their earlier exertions. At the next fence, six from home, one of the two leaders mistimed its jump, crashing to the ground on the landing side of the obstacle. The other cleared the obstacle but stumbled on landing, the jockey almost falling but somehow finding his way back into the saddle. The horse lost his place as the rest of the field cleared the fence in single file.

The new leaders continued racing towards the next fence, however, one of the runners at the rear of the field was pulled up. *Spiral Code* found itself in third place and *Be Inspired* just a length behind in fourth.

"We're in with a chance here," Telside said.

Cannon nodded but didn't reply. He was impressed with how both his runners were travelling. They were still in the hunt and there was just a half-mile left to race. As the field jumped the next fence the runner in second hit the birch hard and catapulted over it. The jockey hit the ground, instantly curling himself into a ball to prevent further injury from the other runners still to clear the fence.

Unfortunately, *Spiral Code* was one of them. Being in third place, the horse found itself with nowhere to go. As it landed on the other side of the jump its off-fore hoof landed on the leg of the fallen jockey. This unbalanced the horse and jockey, and the horse fell to the ground, the jockey sliding from the saddle onto the turf.

"Damn!" Cannon shouted as he noticed his horse fall. Telside carried on watching as the balance of the runners continued with the race.

Cannon knew that a fall was part of racing, but he always worried about horse and rider whenever it happened. His last words to the jockey each time he sent out a runner were always the same, "come back safely." As the words resonated inside him, he hoped that in *Spiral Codes'* case, the horse and jockey were uninjured, especially when he saw the ambulance that always followed the runners in every race, stop at the fence.

Telside made a comment which brought Cannon back from his ruminating.

"The young lad is doing well," he said.

Cannon looked up the straight as the horses headed towards the finish line. With one jump remaining and several horses spread across the track, it was difficult to get a perspective of which horse was leading. The race caller was screaming with excitement as four horses approached the final fence, almost line abreast. Cannon's gaze turned to the large screen near the finishing post. He noticed that the leading horse was under a hard ride and was beginning to wobble as the journey began to take its toll. The jockey doing all he could to get his mount over the final obstacle. The other three jockeys, including that of *Be Inspired*, were vigorously encouraging their mounts onwards. The favourite appeared to be going the best of the four runners, with the rest of the field still some way behind, and a few dropping out of the race entirely.

At the last, the leading horse barely made it over before being passed by two of the other runners, the fourth horse falling. Of the two horses in front, the favourite began to draw clear of the second on the run-in to the finish line. The conditional jockey on *Be Inspired* did all he could to try and close the gap but eventually decided to ease down his mount and let him cross the line a gallant second, some nine lengths behind the winner.

"Bloody Oath!" Telside said, "Second, Mike…second. What a great ride by the young boy. Second..," he repeated happily, "at 25 to 1!"

Cannon was pleased. "Come on," he said, "let's go and lead him in then."

As they walked together down the empty stand and towards the winners' enclosures, Cannon's phone rang. It was the owner of *Be Inspired* who had been watching the race at home on the TV. The man was extremely pleased and told Cannon that he had bet 50 pounds on the horse for a place, so he had won over 360 pounds. When added that to the prize money for coming second, the man had done very well, and he thanked Cannon profusely. Cannon recommended to the owner that perhaps he should make a donation to the young jockey, still a 7lb (3.5kg) claimer. The young lad had only won two races in his career so far, but Cannon had no hesitation in putting the boy up on the horse. He had used him previously on occasion to ride work for him. He had seen that the boy had a good seat, was well balanced, and had followed instructions perfectly. He had accordingly decided to put the youngster onto *Be Inspired* to give him more experience. The horse had needed the run anyway and he wasn't expected to do too much in the race. Cannon himself was pleasantly surprised at the result and made a mental note to keep the young boy in mind for the future. While he was apprenticed to another trainer, Alan Pike, Cannon would use him as often as he could, especially in handicap races where the claim would come in useful.

After all the formalities were completed and the jockeys weighed out properly Cannon let his groom take *Be Inspired* back to the course stables to be hosed down and dried off before being loaded into the horse box for the drive home. *Spiral Code* had not suffered any obvious ill effects from his fall and had been led around the parade ring post-race with the rest of the runners. Cannon and Telside had watched carefully to see if there was any change in the walking action of the horse which could indicate that the horse had picked up an injury, but they could not see any. It was a pity the horse had come down when he did in the race, but as the jockey had relayed afterward, the horse was travelling well, and it was *"just one of those things."*

Both Telside and Cannon knew that a fall was part of racing and at times luck often played a part, but it was still disappointing when it happened.

Thankfully though, both horse and rider had returned without injury, and for that, Cannon was grateful.

The rest of the day seemed to pass by slowly. The third of their runners was in the fifth and penultimate race of the day. By the time the race was run the light was beginning to fade and what little warmth there had been in the day, disappeared with the coming sunset. Cannon was pleased that he didn't have a runner in the last. With the gloom descending upon the track, he was surprised that the Stewards would allow the race to be run. As it was, his runner, *Purple Smoke*, ran extremely poorly in its race. The horse had started as the second favourite in the two-mile hurdle but had jumped badly, crashing through most of the fences and ultimately ending up injuring itself. The horse crossed the line 7th of eight runners. Cannon and Telside were both disappointed and confused as to why the horse had run so badly. They would need to look at the race again the following day, but the jockey did advise that it appeared that the horse appeared to be favouring a leg in running. Changing its lead leg at times when it got to the hurdles. Cannon thanked the jockey for the feedback.

On the trip home to Stonesfield, Cannon let Telside drive while he called the owners of *Spiral Code* and *Purple Smoke*, giving them his view of what had happened to each of the horses in their respective races. By the time he had finished his last conversation, they were only 30 minutes away from home. The horse box carrying the runners from the day's events was likely to arrive at the stables at least forty-five minutes after they reached home and had driven into the driveway.

"I hope you will join Michelle and me for something to eat?" Cannon asked as the headlights from oncoming cars lit up the inside of their car.

"I'd be happy to Mike," Telside replied. "Would you just give my missus a call and let her know that I'll be home afterwards?"

Cannon responded in the affirmative and made the call which was gratefully received by Telside's wife.

"Thank you," he said after Cannon had finished.

"No problem at all, Rich," suddenly realizing that he should call home himself and let Michelle know that Rich was joining them for dinner.

"How far away are you?" she asked, once he had told her of the arrangement he had made.

"About twenty minutes."

"Okay," she said, "I'll add one more to the table."

Cannon laughed and rang off.

"She's a good 'un," Telside said after Cannon had put his mobile back inside his coat pocket.

"Yes, she is Rich," Cannon replied, "yes she is. I'm a very lucky man."

Telside looked briefly at his friend, before turning his eyes back to the road. The darkness of the interior was again briefly lit by the lights of the oncoming cars. Cannon's face illuminated for brief periods before darkening again as each car passed them by, travelling in the opposite direction.

The two men continued to talk about the results of the races, feeling that it had been a reasonable day overall. The stand-out was the second place achieved by *Be Inspired*.

"An appropriate name?" Cannon suggested.

Telside changed the subject at one point, asking about any wedding plans that Cannon and Michelle had possibly made, but Cannon told him that since he had asked Michelle to marry him, they hadn't had much chance to discuss it. He told Telside about the issue that Michelle had been dealing with at school. He didn't mention any names as nobody other than those involved needed to know, not even Telside. He did however talk about what had happened and where things now appeared to stand. Telside nodded an understanding.

As they entered the stable yard after almost two hours of driving, turning off the small country road and onto the cobbled driveway, Cannon had completely forgotten about the visit of Peters the following day. His mind was on upcoming races and the weeks ahead leading up to Aintree. He failed to see the figure hiding in the shadows, watching as he and Telside got out of the car, and entered the house.

CHAPTER 29

The blind man knew that the technology existed which would allow him to hear any email messages that he received. The problem though, was that he only had a basic mobile phone. It was several years old already and had no smartphone functionality. He was predominantly reliant on his home phone answering machine where people would leave him messages if he was unable to answer a call straight away. He sat on the chair next to a small hallway table and pushed the play button, a soft beeping noise having advised him that someone had left a message.

"Hi, it's me," the message began, "I just wanted to say that I am sorry that I haven't been able to visit you this week, but something came up."

The blind man patted the dog sitting on the floor at his feet. "Always the same," he said to himself, "something always comes up, doesn't it boy?"

"….but I just wanted you to know that I was right. I've been watching them." There was a short break before the voice recording continued. "I'm sure that my plan will work and then we'll soon have you out of there. We'll have enough money to get you the proper care you deserve….anyway, I've got to go now, but I'll be in touch as soon as I can."

With that, the message stopped. The man sat in silence for a few seconds. The only sound was that of a small carriage clock that sat beside the phone. The man wound it up every night before he went to bed. The ticking was soft, but the man had acute hearing which somehow had improved since he had lost his sight. The clock chimed each hour, and he used the sound to determine when to close his curtains each night. He seldom listened to the TV, preferring instead to listen to some music or the radio playing on a small hi-fi in which he could stack some CDs. if he wanted to. He never knew which CDs he was putting into the machine, but it didn't matter. He had a collection, compiled years before his blindness, so whatever he put on to play was alright with him. Likewise, whether the curtains were open or not didn't make any real difference to him. Nonetheless, he religiously followed a routine to open and close them using the chimes of the clock as a guide. It helped if he ever had visitors as it was better for them that there was natural light in the place.

He stood up from the chair and slowly found his way to the kitchen, counting steps in his mind to get to the kettle and then across to the kitchen sink to fill it up.

As he waited for the water to boil, he thought about the message he had just listened to. The promise that he had been made was genuine, heartfelt, but it was taking way too long. He had been living in the flat for several years now. It was a horrible place. Small, musty, and at times damp, particularly in the winter when the heavy rain caused the damp to rise. He was glad that he couldn't see the patches that stained the wallpaper, but he could feel it whenever he touched the walls.

The promise! The promise of getting him out of the place was all that was keeping him going. It should have been fulfilled a while ago, but all he could do was wait. He wasn't sure how long his patience could last. Resentment was growing inside him. It had been *years* now and his frustration was mounting.

CHAPTER 30

"Are we still on then?" he called, a smile across his face.

He was standing in the bathroom and was about to brush his teeth. Michelle was already sitting up in bed, the papers she had been reading now spread across the duvet cover. She couldn't see him, her mind had been elsewhere when he asked the question. She had been looking at a document which the Head had issued that afternoon. It was a draft school policy document issued to all staff for comment. It covered bullying, unnecessary sexual and other inappropriate advances, sexting, contacting students by phone, and a number of related topics.

"What do mean?" she called back, slightly aggrieved that he had interrupted her reading.

Cannon walked out of the bathroom, a toothbrush in his mouth. He was still fully dressed having just completed a walk around the yard. Rich had left for home over an hour and a half ago. After dinner, Cannon had seen Telside to his car, which he had left parked in the driveway all day and watched as he drove off through the gate and onto the road to Woodstock. Then he had helped Michelle with the clearing of the dining room table. As she had stacked the dishwasher, he had gone out, on his final rounds for the night. Since the incident, just over a week before, when he thought that he had seen somebody outside his window, it had set off something inside which compelled him to take a walk around the property each night before going to bed. He wasn't sure what he was looking for, but he had always followed his gut, his instinct. Sometimes it had been proven wrong, and he had taken it on the chin when it had been, however, he wanted to be safe rather than sorry.

Removing the toothbrush, despite a mouthful of paste, he playfully garbled a response back to her.

"Go and finish what you are doing!" Michelle said, waving him away before reaching again for her papers.

Cannon laughed, then turned and walked back towards the bathroom. He finished brushing his teeth, then spat into the basin bowl and rinsed the toothpaste away. He dried his face and walked back into the bedroom.

"I just wanted to ask if….?" Cannon didn't finish what he wanted to say. As he stood by the bed beginning to unbutton his shirt, the bedroom windows exploded inwardly. The sound of glass breaking, shattering, invaded their ears. Instinctively, he dived onto the bed to protect Michelle from the flying glass, covering his head with his hands. For a few brief seconds, but which seemed so much longer, they lay together in silence, not sure what had happened. Slowly, tenuously, Cannon stood up. He listened for any sound that would indicate if there was anybody outside the window, but he could only hear the wind. The curtains to the room billowed inwardly, glass pieces occasionally dropping onto the carpet as they flapped haphazardly.

"What happened?" Michelle asked, trying to calm herself.

"I'm not sure," Cannon replied quietly. "Are you okay?" he whispered. He then held a finger to his lips and waved an arm in a downwards direction indicating to Michelle to remain still. He took a step towards the window. He wanted to get outside as soon as possible but was wary that somebody could be on the other side of the curtain and the now thoroughly destroyed picture window. He crept across the few feet to the left side of the curtain, lifting it away from the window. He knew that with the light on in the bedroom, whoever was outside the room had an advantage over him. He had no night vision, but they would have him in silhouette. As he peered into the darkness his peripheral vision noted two bricks tied together with black straps and a buckle of sorts lying on the bedroom floor. Through the shattered window he could only see the dark of night. The window had a huge, jagged hole situated in the middle of it. The glass had cracks and lines like ice on a spider's web right throughout the remaining glass. The cold streaming through the hole caused him to shiver.

Moving away from the window, glass crunching under his feet and into the carpet, Cannon ran as quickly as he could towards the front door. He heard the frightened call of Michelle telling him to be careful, letting him know that she was going to call the police.

Before he got to the door he made a quick detour to grab the torch that he had used a short time earlier on his rounds and that he had left on his office desk. Once outside, he ran towards the bedroom window shining the torch all around the immediate vicinity. Directly below the window were a few pieces of glass that had been pushed outwardly by the billowing curtains, but as the area was paved there was no sign of anybody having been there. No footprints, no markings.

He turned around scanning the area but could see nothing. His torch illuminated the stable buildings, the feed barn, the cars parked in front of his office window. The night lights on all the stable buildings shone as they should have done, but they gave away no secrets. There was no one around. Whoever had thrown the bricks through the window had disappeared into the blackness of night.

Once Cannon had finished walking around the yard and was satisfied that there was no one around, he went back inside the house. He had been outside for over 30 minutes. As he had been dressed, and full of adrenalin, he had not been aware of the cold. By the time he walked back into the house through the front door, which Michelle had sensibly closed and locked until he had knocked upon it, he was shivering.

Michelle had made him a hot drink and he took the mug in both hands.

"Nothing!" he said. "I couldn't see anybody or find anything out of the ordinary out there," he added angrily. "Hopefully with more light, we'll get a better look in the morning?"

He looked at the time on his watch. It was just after midnight.

"I haven't touched anything in the bedroom, just so you know," Michelle said hesitantly, still unsettled, "but what's this all about, Mike?"

"I don't know," he sighed, "I really don't know."

He looked at her with concern. She was dressed in a light blue housecoat and wore soft pumps on her feet. Putting his drink down, he put his arms around her. "But I will find out," he said.

He could feel her shivering from the shock. He held her closer. He felt tired. It had been a long day. His mind was working overtime. She snuggled further into his chest. "I'm scared, Mike," she said quietly.

He caressed her hair with his hand. As he closed his eyes from tiredness he heard the sound of a car entering the yard. He opened his eyes again and noticed the flashing blue lights which lit up the house and would highlight the extent of the broken bedroom window.

CHAPTER 31

"It would have been good to meet under less auspicious circumstances," Peters said, sitting at the dining room table inside the house. Next to him was DI Sophia Drummond. Cannon thought it an overkill of Detective resources, given his own experience, but decided to keep quiet about it.

"I concur, Inspector," Cannon replied. "I'm sure you'll agree that when you called this morning, we didn't expect what happened to us last night to be on the agenda did we?"

Peters noted the subtle anger in Cannon's voice. Normally Cannon was very calm, level-headed, but what had occurred only 12 hours previously was still upsetting him. His planned conversation with Michelle, interrupted by the attack, had not been able to take place and the subject was *still* up in the air. It added to his frustration. The attempt to scare him off by throwing bricks through his windows had made him angrier. Cannon believed that the damage done to the window was an attempt to intimidate him. He knew it had something to do with the Titan-H syndicate and he said so to Peters.

"And you believe this why?"

"Because," Cannon responded vaguely.

"Hardly convincing, Mr. Cannon."

"Look Inspector, I know you are looking for some rationality behind my comments, and I understand that, but sometimes you have to go with your gut. In this case, that's what I'm doing."

Peters nodded then looked at Drummond who kept a straight face, hiding her thoughts.

Peters decided to be direct. On the trip down from the Midlands, he and Drummond had discussed the approach that they wanted to take with Cannon. He had been a cop for a long time, and they felt the best way to engage with him was not to be pedantic or beat around the bush. They had found out a little about him, and they knew that he had been good at his job. This made them a little wary.

"One of my colleagues, Inspector Tim Cummings who is investigating a murder up in Cheshire, that I'm told you are aware of, said that you wanted to know about a lady who had died in a fire. A fire that happened a week or so ago, up in Birmingham....why was that Mr. Cannon?" Peters asked, after an unnecessarily dramatic pause.

Cannon noted the lack of subtlety behind the question. It was clearly asked with suspicious intent. Cannon knew the trick and was disappointed that Peters felt the need to use it. It was as if Cannon himself was a suspect at starting the fire. Fortunately, Cummings had let him know, *off the record*, that Sarah Walters had indeed been murdered, so Cannon was prepared for the question.

"I believe the answer to that Inspector, is a coincidence."

"I'm sorry?" Peters replied.

"Coincidence," Cannon repeated. "Something that I'm sure you are well aware of Inspector."

"Carry on...."

"It's something that I found in my days in the Force that always disturbed me," Cannon continued, trying not to sound condescending. "With regards to Sarah Walters, I was informed of her death by Brendon Harris who was a friend of hers I believe. He called me about it the night before the Haydock Park race meeting a week or so ago. After he told me about Sarah, we discussed whether to run a syndicated horse that I am training that was to run that day. We finally agreed to race the horse...it was a difficult decision I might add, but as he is the Manager of the syndicate, I went along with him. After his phone call, it struck me as odd that two people, both part of a recently expanded racing syndicate, were murdered. Don't you agree?"

"About the coincidence?"

"Yes. Don't *you* think it strange that two people from the same group are murdered within a few days of each other? I certainly do."

Peters and Drummond both nodded.

"Add to that, what happened here last night, and I think that you would concur that there is something odd going on."

Peters wanted to hear more. Cannon's argument was compelling but hardly definitive. "So, this all started when you became part of this....this syndicate?"

"Well, it *actually* started the very day the syndicate formally met for the first time. Up in Cheshire."

Cannon knew that Peters and Cummings had spoken about the murders, and Cummings had been generous in his sharing of information. He had been careful in what he had said to Cannon but had provided him with enough detail to ensure that Cannon would continue to help him, by keeping an eye on Wingrew. Cummings still believed that Wingrew had murdered Fred Punch but did not have enough evidence to prove it.

"Yes, I heard what happened up there," Peters said.

"So, you will understand why I was curious about Sarah Walters?"

Peters did not respond. Cannon likewise remained silent. The old game about who blinked first. After a few seconds, Drummond interjected, "Concerning the syndicate members Mr. Cannon, Tim Cummings has provided us with a list of names and our team is following up with each of them regarding their movements on the evening that Sarah Walters was killed. Could you tell us where you were that night?"

Cannon smiled to himself. He knew that as with the murder of Punch, everyone who was at Stones' place on the day of his murder, was being looked at with suspicion. Nothing was ever ruled out completely until a conviction was finalized, despite Wingrew being the main suspect. Likewise, Cannon knew that Peters would be keeping an open mind about what happened in Birmingham until the culprit was caught and charged. Indeed, by asking about what had happened there, Cannon had potentially created a rod for his own back. The police would ask themselves 'why' he was inquiring.

Yet perversely, in some strange and complicated way, the incident overnight may well have helped him. It had the mark of someone trying to scare him off and hopefully, the police saw it that way. He was also a victim himself, surely not a suspect?

"I was here in Stonesfield," he said finally.

"Can you verify that?"

"Of course, my partner and my assistant would be glad to give a statement confirming it."

Drummond nodded. So far their investigation into the fire in Birmingham had produced very little to go on. The car found near Enfield had not yet revealed anything of note, though Peters expected to find that the car had been stolen sometime in the past, and likely resprayed from its original colour. The police were still working through the DVLA database but had not yet been able to find the owner yet.

"Thank you, Mr. Cannon, we will certainly follow that up," Drummond replied.

"Tell me what happened last night, Mr. Cannon," Peters said, "and why you think it is related to the two murders."

Cannon relayed in detail the events of the previous evening. He added that the local police had responded to Michelle's 999 call and had taken away the bricks used in the attack, along with straps that bound them together. Despite the lateness of the hour, the police had inspected the area outside the house immediately adjacent to the window as well as the wider surroundings. Due to the limitations of their torches, they had not been able to find any footprints of use in the area nor any around the stables or barn. Cannon would have preferred that they came back this morning, but they had insisted on conducting their investigation while it was still dark. Their logic being 'immediacy'. Cannon was disappointed and angry and had not been surprised at the result of the search. He knew that with the number of riders, stablehands, Telside, himself, and even Michelle walking around the place, there were footprints of all types on the grass and in those areas of dirt and mud. It would have been impossible to distinguish or separate one footprint from another, and particularly to find an odd one. The police had finally concluded that as there was no one injured or directly attacked, it couldn't be ruled out that what had happened, was nothing more than pure vandalism. Cannon had considered arguing the point with the two Constables, but he had decided against it. They had told him that they would record the incident, and would file his statement for future reference, but suggested to Cannon to contact his insurance company to see if they would pay for the damage. In the meantime, they advised him that it was okay for Michelle and himself to clean up the shattered glass and arrange for a glazier to replace the window. Michelle in desperation had already contacted a local tradesman before she had left for school that morning. He was expected mid-afternoon.

Once Cannon had finished his story, Peters asked. "So, you told me what happened last night, but do you have any idea who would have done this or even why?"

Cannon wasn't sure how much Peters knew about Cummings' request for him to keep an eye on Wingrew, so he was a little coy in his response.

"To be honest Inspector, I'm not sure who would have done it, but I have a suspicion as to why."

"And that is?"

"As I said previously, to try and intimidate me."

"In which case, someone thinks you know something about....?"

"About who murdered Fred Punch...!"

"And not about Mrs. Walters?"

"Of course not, Inspector. I have no idea who would have done that. All I know is that whoever killed Punch had something to do with the death of Sarah Walters."

"Okay, so that begs the question, Mr. Cannon...or can I call you Mike?" he asked. "I guess we are all friends here, are we not?" Peters continued, holding his arms out wide, theatrically, looking around the room.

Cannon remained quiet. He knew what was coming.

"Do you have a view?" Peters eventually asked.

"About who killed Punch?"

"Yes."

"No, I don't Inspector," he replied. "If I did I would have shared it with Inspector Cummings....Tim," Cannon added somewhat unnecessarily, but artfully letting Peters know that he had picked up on the 'we are all friends here' comment.

Peters felt a little letdown. He had hoped that Cannon would have been able to shed more light. That he had something to offer that would enable them to take things to the next level. What little they had so far was of limited use. The car, the CCTV pictures, even the body and the charred remains of the store in Birmingham had given them few clues as to the perpetrator of the murder of Walters. He realized that without a break it was going to be a long investigation. The possibility of not finding the guilty person was still something they may have to deal with. Cases like this one could well be trumped by another. It had the potential to remain unsolved. Coincidence and a gut feeling were one thing, but proving someone guilty of a crime and getting a conviction was something else.

As they drove away, Peters asked Drummond for her thoughts. After she had done so, Peters replied that he agreed with her summation but added that he didn't think that Cannon had shared everything with them. That he had held something back. She asked him what he thought that was. His reply, "I think he knows who killed Punch and I believe he intends to find out if the same person also killed Walters. Whoever that is made the mistake of smashing his window last night. That act of intimidation has galvanized him, and he is clearly very angry."

Drummond thought about what Peters had said. As they turned onto the motorway to head back North she commented, "Well at least there is one good thing to come out of the conversation."

"What's that?"

"We can rule him out of starting the fire."

"Yes, that's true," Peters answered, "I agree. Let's just hope nothing happens to anyone else in that syndicate though. Two deaths are enough. You can imagine what would happen if there were more!"

CHAPTER 32

Wingrew was about to leave for Leicester. He had four runners for the day, spread across the six-race card. He had checked the nominations and acceptances for the day and was pleased to see that Cannon had no runners at all at the meeting. It wasn't a surprise. Wingrew's stables contained at least eight times as many horses as those of Cannon. It was this quantity of horses-in-training that allowed Wingrew and Stone to do what they were doing. Any lesser number would have made it much more difficult.

As he departed his office on his way to his car, his mobile phone rang. He had just finished talking to a number of his assistants with whom he had left instructions concerning some of his horses that required walking, swimming, and other forms of management for injuries sustained in recent weeks. Some of the horses were being nursed back to health before resuming training, while others were convalescing and needed little more than rest and an occasional walk. It was a skill to stay abreast of each animal and Wingrew was good at his job. He looked at the name on the screen of his mobile and knew that he needed to answer it.

"Hello, Alex, what's up?"

"They've been in touch," Stone replied.

Wingrew was walking down the single flight of stairs from his office. He passed one of the staff, a work rider who was heading upwards. Wingrew remained quiet as they passed each other, just nodding to the young man. He didn't want to say anything at all until he was out of earshot and inside his car.

"Give me a second," he requested. Stone waited, staying silent until he heard a car door slam.

"Are you there?" Stone asked.

Wingrew held the phone to his ear as his car started. He waited for the phone to connect to the hands-free system before replying in the affirmative.

"Okay, good," Stone said. "As I told you," he continued, "they've been in touch, and they've told me what they want."

"Which his?"

"Two hundred and fifty thousand pounds."

"What?! A quarter of a mill?" Wingrew replied. "What the hell for?"

"He said, *to keep quiet.*"

"Is this all on a recording Alex?' A tape of sorts?" Wingrew asked, turning his car out of the grounds and onto the B-road that ran alongside the property. In ten minutes, he would be on the motorway, heading South.

"Yes, it's on the voicemail of my phone," Stone affirmed.

"Well, maybe it's time to call in the police now? It's getting crazy now and what we're faced with is bleeding extortion!"

"Extortion, blackmail….does it matter?" Stone answered. "Whatever it is, we need to sort it out before anyone else knows."

"I don't like it, Alex," Wingrew replied. "How do we know if we pay anything to this…this person, he doesn't just go to the police anyway? Worse still, to the BHA?"

"We don't," Stone replied, "that's why I need to get *my friends* involved."

"No!" Wingrew replied. "No, Alex," he said, pleading. "Please...not yet. Let's see if we can sort this out ourselves. If you don't want to engage the police, then fine, but we should try and resolve it without any violence. We are almost there after all. Perhaps a few more months? If things go our way it will all be over sooner rather than later."

"I'm not so sure," Stone replied. "To be honest I'm wondering if it will ever be over. Unless…."

Wingrew could sense Stone wavering. It was strange given Stone was the architect of the plan. Initially, Wingrew had been reluctant but had finally succumbed to the idea. Not being happy about it but accepting of it eventually. If it worked, it would set him up for life, as long as nothing came out publicly, and it had been working until the calls started. Somehow the caller had found out what was going on. Somehow….?

"Don't be stupid Alex. We don't need them…please no more talk about your *friends*. Tell me about the message," he said, trying to refocus the conversation. As he spoke, he turned his car off Holmes Chapel Road, East of Middlewich, and onto the M6 motorway. The traffic was heavy. Supermarket trucks, multiple delivery vans, various tankers carrying fuels and milk, along with a continuous stream of cars seemed to fill all three lanes of the road as Wingrew slid his vehicle in-between a small car and an SUV.

"Well apart from the money, they confirmed they know what we are doing."

"How did they do that?"

"By leaving a few examples. The voice, the lousy Scots impersonator, used Haydock as an example, but said they had quite a few more."

"Shit!" Wingrew exploded. Given what he was hearing, he could see his career disappearing before his eyes.

"Exactly. Can you see why we now need some help?" Stone asked.

Wingrew thought about things for a minute. Stone began to get impatient. "Dom...Dominic…are you still there?"

"Yes, I'm here Alex….I was just contemplating something…tell me," he continued, "how do they expect to get this money from us?"

"I think they want it in cash."

"In cash?" Wingrew laughed. "Are these people stupid?"

"No, I don't they are. I think they are quite clever," Stone replied. "If you think about it, anything electronic can be traced. Cash, unless it's marked, is very difficult to trace. I doubt it's even possible."

"But it's also very difficult to carry. To hide. Even to get hold of easily. How are they expecting us to get it to them?"

"They didn't say," Stone said. "Just that they've told us what they want, and that they will be in touch to confirm that we've got the money."

"And then?"

"Then they will tell us where to drop it off."

Wingrew moved his car into the fast lane. He was beginning to get impatient. His mood was growing dark. "And do we get any guarantees?"

"For their silence?"

"Yes. How do we know if we pay them anything at all that they will *keep quiet?* Honour their commitment in return?"

"We don't …yet," Stone replied. He too was beginning to get frustrated by the whole saga, He would be happy to hand the problem over to his 'friends' and let them sort it out for him. However, until Wingrew agreed, it would be difficult.

"Christ!," he heard Wingrew say.

"I'm not sure *He* is going to help," Stone said, sardonically. "I'm pretty sure divine intervention will be the very last thing we can expect."

Ignoring Stones' comments, the trainer asked, "So they said nothing at all about timing? When they want an answer from us?"

"No, they did say, and that's how I know that they are more aware of what we have been doing than we think." Stone said.

"How?"

"They want us to nominate, accept and run one of our horses in the next ten days. If we do that, then it will tell them that we are willing to do a deal."

"Which horse is that then?" Wingrew asked, pushing down on the accelerator in his frustration. The car had now reached seventy-five miles per hour.

"*Ready to Commit,*" Stone said.

Wingrew smiled to himself. "You have to give them some credit to come up with that," he responded.

"Exactly."

"So, if we do what they want…" Wingrew said, tooting his car horn at a driver in a small van just ahead of him, seeking him to move out of the way so that he could overtake, "what then?"

"The message was quite simple. Run the horse. Try to win, and afterward, they will be in touch."

"And then we'll just roll over?"

Stone got angry with Wingrew. "No, we bloody well won't!" he responded aggressively. "At that point, it will be up to them to give us a commitment. We get an agreement on their silence, or we keep the money, and we'll take our chances."

The trainer wasn't so sure about taking a chance but also wasn't happy just to lie down and be taken advantage of. His reputation was important to him. His livelihood was training horses. He had done what he had, to help out his boss. It was too late now, but he was buggered that some unknown individual would be allowed to kill off his career. Since the calls had started some months prior he had been trying to work out who the caller could be.

"And you still have no idea who the bastard is?" Wingrew asked.

"None whatsoever," Stone replied.

"Fuck!"

"You can say that again," Stone said

Wingrew didn't. He just put his foot down harder on his accelerator. He told Stone that he would call him on his way back from Leicester, and they rang off. They had agreed on their strategy for the day, and they hoped that things went according to plan. If so it would bring them ever closer to their objective. It was going to be difficult, and they still needed to be careful. It was supposed to be just the two of them that knew. Somehow, someone else had found out what was going on. The two men understood that not every race worked out as they would like. Sometimes a result went against them, and they just had to accept it. Any failure meant that the target was pushed out.

Before Wingrew knew it, he was doing ninety miles an hour. He suddenly realized his stupidity and quickly slowed down to the speed limit of seventy. He was still frustrated, but at least the sun was shining, albeit weakly. The partially cloudy sky was a welcome sight after the recent cold, wet spell that had gripped the country. Rain was again expected later, but by then the meeting may be over. He moved into the middle lane, keeping his speed at a steady seventy.

CHAPTER 33

Peter Brown stood at the door to his barn.

The afternoon had passed by quickly and the sun was heading towards the horizon. He had been busy and was hoping that the cold front heading his way would stay away until he was back inside his house. The cloud building in the East suggested that rain would arrive shortly. He had spent the past couple of days treating his entire flock to protect them from an outbreak of coccidiosis on the neighbouring farm. The illness if it wasn't protected against, could wipe out his entire sheep herd if he wasn't careful. The treatment itself was fairly easy to administer, a single dose of a readily available, off-the-shelf product containing toltrazuril. It just needed to be administered. Unfortunately, it was all down to him.

Brown's major concern was if the disease got into his flock of nearly 500. His total farm was roughly 240 acres in size, small by international standards, but much bigger than that of his neighbour, Jack Tennyson. It was the lack of care for his animals, by *the man next door,* as he called him, that had made Brown extremely concerned. Tennyson and Brown had been involved in several arguments over the past year, and it was clear that Tennyson was struggling to keep his farm afloat. Both men were farming with the same intention, to enjoy the rural lifestyle, but Brown could see that Tennyson was losing the battle. The man had been drinking heavily for years but in recent times it had been getting much worse. Tennyson could be seen at Whitehouses' pub on the London Road, South of Retford, way too often in Browns' eyes.

Brown put it down to stress caused by financial worries. Raising sheep for meat was not as lucrative as it used to be, but that didn't mean one ignored how to treat the animals for disease. The potential to cause him huge financial loss had made Brown angrier than he usually was, and he had challenged Tennyson on several occasions to *'get himself right'*. Brown's wife had tried to get him to be less vocal, but she had been unsuccessful. She had tried to pour cold water on the fire between the two men, but it only irritated Brown further. He told her one day that he didn't want her messing in a *man's* business.

Eventually, as the stoush escalated, Brown took it upon himself to rip out some of Tennyson's fences from a field where some alpacas were kept. The fence separated Tennyson's land from a road that ran across the top of the field. Tennyson was unaware of this until nearly two weeks later when he found that the animals had strayed, and he had lost them for good. Once Tennyson had established that Brown was the culprit, the feud between them quickly escalated. Initially, there were simple acts of vandalism, such as the damaging of tyres on Brown's car, and the pouring of sugar into a tractors' diesel tank. The sugar itself did not prevent the engine on the tractor from running but in time it clogged up the fuel filters. On another occasion, Tennyson poured a pint of water into the fuel tank of another of Browns' tractors and this resulted in significant damage to the engine. Brown had never been able to prove that Tennyson was the culprit, but he did not doubt it in his own mind. As a result of the ongoing arguments and the tit-for-tat exchanges, Tennyson had on several occasions threatened to take Brown 'out for good'. It was a threat that Brown took seriously, and he reported the comment to the local police. Unfortunately, the police did not take it as seriously and suggested that the two men try to resolve their dispute. They confirmed that they would intervene if things got too far out of hand, agreeing to visit the properties of the two men in due course to try and understand what was going on between them. Sadly, to date, that had not happened.

Recently, however, Brown had become more concerned about Tennysons' behaviour as his neighbour began to act even more erratically. Only a couple of days prior Tennyson had arrived at Brown's house, knocked at the door, and when Brown answered, took a huge swipe at him with a baseball bat. Fortunately, Brown was quick enough to close the door on the man, but he had heard and felt the thud and cracking of the wood as the door took the full force of Tennyson's attack.

Brown had no idea as to the reason for this latest outburst of anger, but he had felt the need to once again bring in the police. They had advised him that due to personnel shortages they would only be at Browns' house the next morning. He was still waiting a week later.

Facing the open barn, Brown began to close its large wooden doors. He had driven both of his larger tractors inside the building, in order to protect them from another possible childish, but vicious, attack. In addition, he was worried about the supplies of drench, feed, and chemicals that he had acquired recently. He knew that Tennyson was unlikely to be able to buy anything similar for his farm, as the man had little money, other than for alcohol. It was not impossible, that the man would decide to steal some of the farm supplies from his neighbour if he desperately needed them. Brown closed the door, dropped the large latch into its slot, and began to secure everything with a warehouse padlock. He had bought it that morning at the local ToolStation outlet in Retford, just off Hallcroft Road. As he began to unlock the new padlock he was suddenly hit with a force that flung him forward, his head smashing against the door. As he fell to the ground, frothy blood began pouring from his mouth, his eyes remained wide open, staring, indicating a sense of disbelief at what had happened to him. The arrow fired from a crossbow had been travelling at over 300 feet per second and had pierced his heart and left lung, exiting the front of his chest by about 6 inches, its sharp tip covered in a red mass of sinew, flesh, and blood.

As if in slow motion, Brown dropped to the ground, the padlock falling from his now lifeless hand. In the gap between a group of small out-houses that faced the barn doors, the figure packed the crossbow into a canvas bag. After looking down at the grassless ground where the figure had stood waiting for Brown to come into view, the figure walked a short distance to a nearby group of trees. Breaking a branch with a significant amount of leaves on it, approximately 4 feet long, the figure returned to the area to brush away any sign of footprints. The figure then ensured that a grassy area behind the small buildings that had been walked on while finding the best position in which to hide was likewise brushed vigorously with the tree branch. This disturbed the area significantly enough to erase any trace of the route used to ambush Brown.

Fortunately for the figure, the rain that was expected to arrive would likely begin within the hour, hopefully wiping away any further signs or evidence of anyone ever having been in that particular place. The figure once satisfied with its work, crossed over the fence, the border of the two properties, from that of Brown and into that of Tennyson.

CHAPTER 34

"Can I pop in and see you?" she asked.

"Of course," Michelle said, "anytime you like. How about after school sometime in the next couple of days? You can come to the house, and we can talk in private."

"That sounds good," Cynthia Crowe replied.

Michelle covered the mouthpiece of the phone, as Cannon walked into the lounge wondering who she was talking to. She mouthed the name 'Cynthia' and he nodded in response. Deciding it was best to leave her to talk, he turned on his heel and walked out of the room towards the kitchen.

"I did speak with the Head as I said I would," Michelle continued, "and she is looking forward to having you back."

Cynthia seemed grateful, her voice in response indicating as such.

"Thank you so much, Michelle. You really are a friend."

"It's no problem at all. It was nothing. I'm sure you would have done the same for me."

Michelle found it interesting, yet pleasing, that their friendship had developed so quickly. Prior to recent events, they had been more colleagues, now, however, it seemed that they were the best of friends and somehow it felt as if they had been for years.

For a second there was a pause and Michelle sensed a change in Cynthia. Almost as if a light switch had been turned off. Her voice seemed somewhat different.

"Can I ask you something?" she said.

"Of course. What is it?"

"What do I do?" she said, after a few seconds hesitation.

"What do you mean?"

"What do I do when I'm faced with Samantha Prittly and her friends again? When I have to teach them in my class? I'm not sure I can do it, Michelle."

She began to sob. Michelle was confused. When they had last met it seemed that Cynthia had gotten over the incident even though she had originally stated that her confidence had been shattered. Michelle had hoped that her support and that of the school teaching community would have meant that Cynthia knew that she had nothing to be afraid of. Was that why she had called and asked to come and see her?

"Are you okay Cynthia?" Michelle asked down the line.

The sobs continued, getting louder. Michelle repeated her concern, trying to help. Cynthia could be heard blowing her nose, her crying slowing, then stopping almost as quickly as it started.

"I'm sorry, Michelle," she said eventually, "I'm not sure what came over me. It just happened. I thought I was stronger than this, but clearly, I'm not."

"Maybe you could speak with Wendy....before you go in?" Michelle suggested, referring to the school Counsellor involved in the hearing with the Prittly family. "Perhaps she can provide some guidance?"

Cynthia did not respond immediately. Michelle sensed that her friend was thinking about it.

"Maybe…," Cynthia replied tentatively, "but I'd still like to have a chat with you first…face to face. I think I need it," she added, almost pleading.

Michelle was happy to oblige. "That's fine…as I said…anytime you like."

"Thank you so much, Michelle. That's really kind of you. I'll come over in the next couple of days. Would somewhere around 7:30 work for you? Will Mike be okay with it, do you think? I won't be putting you out, will I? Tell me if I am…"

All the questions were asked in rapid succession. Almost fired off like bullets from a gun. Michelle could sense that Cynthia was beginning to feel stressed again. "Cynthia…Cynthia…relax…it will be fine," she said, breaking into the questioning and hoping that her friend was listening.

Silence ensued. Finally, Cynthia apologized for being so pushy, for being so needy. Michelle told her that everything was fine, and they agreed to get together at the house over the next three or four days. It would give Cynthia the necessary time afterward to get herself organized before getting back to school. Her mental state hopefully would be more settled.

"How are you feeling?" Cannon asked.

"I must admit I am a bit concerned about Cynthia, but I did tell her that I'm happy to support her as long as she needs it."

He looked at her. "I meant concerning what happened the other night. The window…"

"Oh," she replied, "that!"

"Yes…that." he echoed.

She looked at him, reading his face. They were sitting at the dining room table where she had found him after her call with Cynthia. He had been reading the Racing Post when she entered the room. He noticed that she was frowning.

"I'm sorry, Mike. I was just contemplating what Cynthia and I had just discussed. I thought that was what you meant."

Cannon smiled. "That's okay," he said softly, " it's just that being the second night after the attack, I'm a bit on edge and I was wondering how you are feeling."

"Well…last night I didn't sleep very well even with the window fixed. I kept waking up. In fact, after you left for the first lot, I was even more scared, despite knowing that there were lots of staff around the place by then."

"Which is why I'm asking," Cannon replied. "I don't want to scare you even more, but I had a look at the CCTV, and I couldn't see anything or anyone on it. Nothing at all."

"Are the things even working then?" she asked.

He took a sip from his cup of tea, before replying. The fact that nothing was recorded of anyone in the yard able to throw the bricks through their bedroom window was a major concern to him. It was making him jumpy, nervous. He had been attacked years ago in the same area before any CCTV was installed and had expected that by installing the system such incidents were a thing of the past. Now however as there was no vision of an intruder on the recording unit, on the hard drive itself, it increased his nervousness. He had checked the machine and it was working 100%, yet nothing! He was worried that the lack of anything concrete about who had been outside, undetected, was going to upset Michelle more than she already was.

He wanted to talk to her about something else but wasn't sure if he should.

"Yes it is working," he said, finally answering her question, "so something else must have happened."

"Any ideas?"

"At this stage, no," he said hesitatingly. "Unfortunately, the camera was not pointing towards the area where I think they came from. If it was, then the movement of the individual would have been picked up by the motion detectors. The damn things are focused more on the stables and the barn and are not facing towards our bedroom window. They are positioned correctly as intended," he lied, not wishing to scare her, "I don't think we ever expected anything to happen as it did the other night."

"Do you think the Police are right? That it was vandals?"

Cannon didn't want to answer her question directly. He had worked out in his mind where the culprit had come from, how they had entered the property unseen and it made him extremely wary. It was clear that whoever it was, had other intentions. The problem he needed to understand, was why? He believed the attack was connected to the Titan-H syndicate, but he could not work out who the perpetrator could be. The police had dismissed his suspicions as he had no evidence to back up his theory. In their eyes, the entire incident was one of vandalism.

"I'm not convinced," he replied finally, "but I have nothing to back it up with, other than gut feel."

"Which is why the police have dismissed your theory?"

"Yes, but let me share with you my thoughts," he continued. "I think that whoever it was, got into the farm by climbing over the wall that runs alongside the road next to the outer wall of the house. It's the closest point to our bedroom window and as I said before, there are no cameras pointed at the house."

"But what about the parking spaces just in front of your office window, isn't there a camera pointed towards that area?" she asked.

"Yes there is and that's what bothers me. Remember the other night when I thought I saw someone outside?"

"Yes."

"Well, you'll recall that when I checked, the CCTV didn't pick up anything at all either."

Michelle nodded, then suddenly shivered, wrapping both arms around her waist as if she was hugging herself. It was warm inside the house, yet she felt cold. Cannon could see that she was beginning to feel frightened again. He wanted to reassure her that she had nothing to worry about. He wanted her to be aware of the situation, but not panic.

"Look," he said, standing up and taking her by the shoulders, looking directly into her eyes. "I'm sure it will be okay, love. We just need to keep an eye on things. If somebody is hanging around I'm pretty confident we'll catch them sooner rather than later. I've had Rich and one of the lads move a couple of the cameras and have had them pointed to face the house," he explained. "In addition, I'm thinking of getting a night watchman, a security guard if you like, for a couple of weeks as a backup. He can keep an eye on things overnight as extra protection. Not that we need it," he said smiling.

Michelle seemed to relax a little. Cannon thought that she had accepted his suggestion, but was surprised when she asked, "What about the car?"

"Sorry?" he said

"The car? How did the individual get here? To throw the bricks?" Cannon looked at her quizzically as she continued with her questions. It was clear to him that she had thought things through herself, much as he had done. Again, he did not want to answer her, but he realized that he had no choice. She was a smart woman.

"I think they must have stopped down the road somewhere and walked. We didn't hear a car that night, did we?"

"No."

"So, they must have parked some ways away so as not to have the sound of the cars' engine arouse suspicion, especially if they had stopped right outside the house. The road is only on the other side of the house outer wall."

"So, they carried the bricks?"

"I guess so, yes."

"Odd, isn't it?" she said.

"Yes, but I suppose with it being dark and with very few cars on the road so late at night, it was a calculated risk."

"Which means they were serious."

Cannon could not argue with her logic. He understood where she was going with her questions. She had proved to herself that the incident was much more than vandalism. She also wanted him to know that while she appreciated him trying to assure her that everything would be okay, she knew that somehow things had taken a turn for the worse. Until matters were resolved, both of them would need to remain vigilant.

"Yes," he said finally, "You are right. We need to be careful until I can get to the bottom of it."

She seemed placated, though he doubted she was as calm and settled as she appeared. He realized that they had forgotten about their discussion of Cynthia Crowe, and he was glad that they had. He also realized that it was the wrong time to raise the matter that he wanted to talk to her about.

It could wait until the morning.

CHAPTER 35

"It won't be long now," the caller said, "I'm making good progress and have issued an ultimatum."

"That's good," replied the blind man, his landline phone held firmly to his right ear, "but don't take too long, I'm not sure I can stand much more."

He balanced a cup of tea on his knee, his dog was lying at his feet on the untidy carpet, bits of fluff and dog hairs spread across its surface. The home help lady had been sick for a couple of days and had not been in to clean for him. The weather had not been helpful either. He could hear the wind blowing fiercely outside, rattling the junk that lay on the balconies that some flats had accumulated and dumped there. Strong gusts caused windows to buckle and empty tin cans and pages from discarded newspapers raced along the external walkways. Overnight, heavy rain had fallen, and he could smell the damp that was seeping into the walls that faced towards the West. It was a typical early April day, and he was feeling the cold. The small two-bar electric heater didn't give out enough heat to warm the entire flat and he was scared to put on the gas heater due to the cost.

"How long will it take?" he asked, somewhat desperately. He knew he needed to be patient as this was his last chance, but it was a long time coming and he wasn't even sure that it would work. "As I said just now, I don't think I can take too much more. It's so cold in here. The bloody winter never seems to end."

"I understand," the caller said, "but you just need to trust me. I *will* sort this out for you…and soon, I promise."

The blind man sighed, knowing that he had no answer. He was in the hands of others. He appreciated what was being done on his behalf but was frustrated that it had come to this. He needed people to fight for him and he had hoped that the matter could have been resolved years ago. The fact that it hadn't and that some people, those involved, had made a good life for themselves without bearing the consequences of their actions still annoyed him. Life wasn't always fair, but it wasn't meant to be unjust either.

"I'm sorry but I need to go now," the caller said, breaking into the blind mans' thoughts, "I'll call again tomorrow. Just be patient…just a little while longer."

"No!" the blind man replied, "call me when you have news, a result!"

The caller was surprised at the response. It seemed vitriolic and unnecessary. The blind man continued with his tirade. "I'm sick and tired of hearing, *be patient, it won't be long,* I just want an outcome. One way or the other!" As he said this, the cup on his knee flew off and spilled the warm liquid onto the carpet just missing the dog. The animal jumped up quickly, thinking something had happened to its' master, or that he had been injured so it turned to check on him as its' training demanded. As it did so its paws squelched through the sodden carpet.

"Shit!" the blind man called out, dropping the phone onto the cushion beside him. The man realized that the dog had reacted, his immediate thought was that the warm liquid had spilled on his companion. He checked to see that the dog was uninjured. "It's okay boy," he whispered, as the dog nuzzled against him, checking selflessly on its owner, "I'm fine," he said, rubbing the animal's head to settle him down. Once the dog was comfortable, it stood silently next to the mans' legs, remaining vigilant and attentive. The blind man searched for the phone, finding it at the second attempt, in a corner of the couch. He put the receiver to his ear.

The line was quiet. He said "hello?" into the mouthpiece but there was no response from the caller. He could hear breathing on the other end of the line and repeated his "hello?".

"Are you finished?" the voice said, somewhat brusquely.

"Yes….I'm okay and fortunately, the dog is too. I'm sorry I got upset, but I hope you understand why?"

The caller visualized the scene. Having visited many times, the caller was glad to of not been able to visit recently. It was a sad state of affairs, however. The caller knew that the blind man did not deserve to be stuck living in that area of the country. The crime, the domestic violence, the verbal abuse, and the squalor in some parts were becoming too much for the man and it was understandable.

"I get it," the caller said eventually, "I really do. Just remember though, the thing being done…. is for you. For you!"

Feeling somewhat chastised the blind man apologized. The caller accepted the apology and told the blind man that he would only call again once he had better news. A result. The caller then rang off. The blind man listened to the click as he was disconnected. He sat back in his chair, rubbed the dog's head, and began to weep.

CHAPTER 36

Cannon had looked again at the results of the race meetings from the previous day. Some of them surprised him, but that was what racing was all about. Things didn't always work out in the way one expected.

He was about to depart for Southwell, just over 2 hours' drive away. He had memories of the course being attacked only recently. A group of people who were opposed to jump-racing burned down a couple of fences as part of their campaign. It was an attempt to intimidate the course owners and the industry. Fortunately, despite being closed for a period while the police investigated, the Nottingham course had survived. Support from the BHA and a local brewery, a major sponsor of the courses' annual beer festival held every December, had ensured that it was now back in business.

He picked up his binoculars, car, and house keys and walked towards the front door, as he reached it, the home phone began to ring. He looked at his watch. The first race was at 1:10 pm. It was now 9:50 am. Fortunately, he only had two runners for the day, but he wanted to be there to watch both of them compete. If he left now, he expected to be at the course and inside the course stables with his runners by 12:15 pm. That would be enough time to check on their well-being before their events. His first runner, *On Eggshells*, was racing in the second event of the day, a Handicap Hurdle over 2 miles, and his second runner *Statue of Ramos*, one of his better horses and a training companion of *Titan's Hand,* was running in a Handicap Chase over 3 miles in race four, carrying top weight.

He wasn't sure if he should answer the phone or not. If it was Michelle and he didn't answer it, then she would call him on his mobile. If it was someone else like a crank call then it would be a waste of his time. Those in his contacts list knew to call him on the mobile in the first instance. They were guaranteed to be able to leave him a message if he was unable to answer, so whoever was calling on the home phone probably expected him to be there and didn't have his mobile number, or if they did, they weren't used to calling him. He hesitated before eventually walking over to the phone, picking it up on the sixth or seventh ring.

"Hello?" he said, not wanting to answer by using his name.

"Oh…hello…I'm sorry, I was about to put the phone down. Is that Mr. Cannon? Mike Cannon?" It was a man's voice.

"Yes, it is," he replied, somewhat cautiously. "Who is this please?"

"My name is Philips, Sergeant John Philips of the Nottinghamshire Police. I'm calling on behalf of my boss, Inspector Ann Walker who has asked me to give you a call."

"Oh yes?" Cannon responded warily. *Nottinghamshire Police?* he thought, wondering why they were calling him. He was about to head in their direction. Was the call coincidental? Something he was never comfortable with.

"Yes, Sir." Philips said, "We were wondering if you were coming to the races today? Up to Southwell? We see you have a couple of runners there."

Cannon found it odd that the police were calling him knowing about his runners at Southwell, but he explained to Philips that he was just about to leave to get to the course and needed to get going otherwise he would be late.

"That's no problem, Sir. In fact, that works perfectly."

"I beg your pardon, Sergeant? I'm a little confused. Do you want to tell me what this is all about?"

Philips didn't hesitate and was quite forthcoming. "My boss," he said for the second time, "would like to speak with you about something, and thought it was a good idea to meet with you face-to-face at Southwell if you were going to be there. Rather than she and I drive all the way down to Oxfordshire."

"Could you tell me about what?"

Philips seemed a little coy, a little reluctant to disclose anything on the phone.

Cannon looked again at his watch and saw that it was now just before 10 am. He wanted to get on his way so repeated his question.

"Well Sir," said the Sergeant, "it relates to a murder."

Cannon immediately thought about Sarah Walters, but that investigation was with DCI Peters of the West Midlands police, so why was the Notts Police calling him? Was there a breakthrough? Had something popped up in Nottinghamshire?

"Is this to do with the Sarah Walters case?" he asked. "Is DCI Peters across this?"

Philips was aware of who Peters was, answering, "Umm…I believe DCI Peters and Inspector Walker have been in touch, so yes Sir, I assume he is aware of the case. However, the reason for the meeting is not about *that* matter."

"So, if not Sarah Walters? What are we talking about?" Cannon asked

For a second there was no reply until Philips said, "The unlawful killing of a Mr. Peter Brown."

Cannon left the yard in a hurry as he hated being late. Philips had shared a few details about why the police needed to talk with him, and they had agreed on a time and a place to meet at Southwell racecourse. The apparent murder of Brown had shocked Cannon. As soon as he could, he had called Michelle, pulling her out of class. He didn't want to alarm her, but he felt he needed to let her know about Brown. Unfortunately, he had no detail other than what Sergeant Philips had told him.

"I'm pretty damn sure that what I suspected all along, is now true," he had said. "These murders are all somehow related to the Titan-H syndicate."

"So, what do you need me to do?" Michelle had asked.

He didn't have an answer for her, only saying, "Nothing specifically. I just need you to be aware of anything strange you may see around the place. In other words, just keep your eyes peeled, especially if I'm away at the races or Rich and I are up on the heath."

Michelle had taken on board everything he had said and had smiled at his attempt at being protective of her. Keeping her eyes peeled for something odd going on, when there were so many people moving into and out of the stables, walking into the barn and across the yard at all times of the day, was not going to be easy. Most of the time she was at school anyway, so she wasn't sure where he was coming from. Anyway, she could look after herself. He still had that old-fashioned notion about himself which seemed almost caveman-like. *A man protects the woman.* Perhaps that was what had made him a good cop?

She had smiled inwardly, happy that he took the position that he did, and she loved him for it, despite him being completely *wrong.*

"Okay, darling," she had replied, adding the word of endearment she had seldom used before.

Cannon had sensed that she was teasing him. "I'm bloody serious, Michelle!" he had exclaimed. "If I'm right, then this is the *third* murder of a syndicate member. If you add what happened to us the other night into the mix, you can bet your bottom dollar that it's likely that we, or someone else, could be the next victim, and I'm damned if it is going to be anyone from my family."

"Including you, I hope," she had said.

"Yes, and it's no laughing matter. We've both been through it once before and we know what it's like," he had said, "but never again!" he had pronounced vehemently.

From his tone, she knew that he was more much serious than usual, and she had acknowledged his concerns. Once she had promised to be careful, they had said their goodbyes and he had continued on his way up the M1.

After calling Rich and giving him the same message as he had given Michelle, he felt a little better, though he was concerned about Rich. His assistant wasn't too far from retirement age. The man was in his Sixties yet was as fit a fiddle. Not fit enough though to take on someone intent on murder. He thought again of poor Fred Punch and seeing the body, run through with the pitchfork. He had seen many bodies and had attended many murder scenes in his life, but some stuck in his memory more than others. The death of Punch had been added to those that stood out. His mind began to work overtime as he tried to put the pieces together of a very bizarre puzzle. He wasn't having much luck as something was missing. In his past life at a crime scene concerning a murder, he would be looking for a motive, a means, and an opportunity. From what he knew of the deaths so far, he already knew how Punch and Walters died. Philips had let slip about Brown, so Cannon considered that his killer had the wherewithal, the ability, the time, to carry out the crime, so the opportunity itself had existed. What was missing was the motive. For most of the way, he had spent the majority of his time on the phone, talking with Michelle and then with Rich. As he drove along, aware of the traffic but not concentrating as much as he should have, the various road signs advising drivers of exit lanes, directions etcetera came in and out of view. He didn't really notice them as he knew the road well. Travelling to watch his horses run at various meetings and at different racecourses meant that he racked up the miles along much of the same roads. He knew the stretch of road that he was on like the back of his hand. His subconscious mind noticed what his eyes did not, suddenly however the motive for the murders hit him like a ton of bricks.

What he didn't know however was *who* had the motive.

Cannon had called Cummings, but he had not been able to get hold of him. He left a message for the policeman to call him back, but by the time he reached the course, he had still not heard from the young Inspector. It was later than he had hoped when he finally walked into the course stables and caught up with his groom. It was 12:30 pm, the first race was only 40 minutes away. His charge, *On Eggshells*, was acting exactly as her name suggested. She was calm, laidback, and watched as Cannon moved around her. He began the saddling-up process, checking her legs for any heat, and started to fit the bridle and reins. She did not require any headgear, so wore no blinkers, earmuffs, or winkers. The earlier formalities required about the horse had all been completed and she had been declared fit and ready to run.

"How's she been?" he asked the young groom.

"She travelled up well, Sir, and she's been on her best behaviour all morning," replied the young man, beginning to brush down the horse to get her coat as smooth as possible. His name was Ray Brollo and he was a relatively new hire. Rich was responsible for taking on the support staff and Cannon had heard good things about the boy. He was about 17 years old, just over 1.6 metres tall, and weighed approximately 60 kilograms. Cannon thought the boy would blow away in a strong breeze but remembered what

Rich had told him once. *"The boy has good hands and a great seat."*
Cannon had watched the boy ride work on several horses and had been impressed with the way he had handled them.

"That's good to hear," he said. "By the way, Ray, I've noticed how well you ride work, do you want to be a jockey in the future?" he asked, anticipating the answer.

"Yes I do, Sir...though as you can see I'm too big for the flat," he said sheepishly, "But the jumps have always been my preference anyway."

Cannon liked the lad and the way he went about treating the horse. He had never taken on an apprentice or a conditional jockey (as they were called in National Hunt racing) since he had started training. It suddenly struck him that he had seen many good riders move on from his stables because they had no opportunity of a long-term job with him. He knew that the job of a work rider could be a short one, and many liked the transient lifestyle. The moving from stable to stable to get different experiences was not so bad for young people, he thought, however, his personal development and success over the years, made him think that perhaps it was time to consider taking on an apprentice. He parked the idea for now, but he knew that Ray Brollo would be a good candidate.

Once he was happy that the horse was properly saddled up, he watched as Brollo led the mare out of the stable for her race. The first race on the card had just finished, the race callers excited voice having been silenced into announcing the result to the on-course crowd, which had grown quite significantly in size for a Friday meeting.

The mare had a lovely walking action and seemed to personify her name. She seemed to know that she was *On Eggshells* by name and *On Eggshells* by nature. It had amused Telside and himself when Cannon had welcomed her into his yard for the very first time. She seemed to fit her owners as well, who were also very quiet. They were a retired couple, Jean and Henry Young. They both loved their racing and they met Cannon in the parade ring, shaking his hand and smiling. They seemed very happy to see him and they both joked about needing to wear heavy clothing to keep warm and dry. Cannon liked them and they were right. It was cold and rain clouds still threatened to send squalls of rain their way. Despite the weather, his owners were in a buoyant mood, and they appeared to take life less seriously than most other people that Cannon knew. They were smiling, holding hands, and giggling in the way that young lovers did. Jean, short and round, was from Cardiff, and Henry, bald, medium height with a ruddy complexion, was from Bath where he had lived all his life. He had been taken to Chepstow racecourse, amongst others, on many occasions as a teenager, which is where his love of the sport had started.

"How do you think she'll do?" Henry Young asked. Cannon had mixed views about her. She was a lovely animal but not the bravest or the fastest.

She was at the right level but how she went in a race, depended on the day. He noted that she was only fourth in the betting in the small field of just seven runners, but the Youngs' had so much positivity about them that they always believed their horse would win irrespective. In her career so far, the horse had won twice and finished third once out of eighteen starts under National Hunt rules. Before taking to the jumps, she had only won once on the flat out of thirteen races.

"I think she'll do her best," Cannon replied diplomatically. "She's as fit as she can be and the track will suit her, it's just a matter of whether she runs up to expectations."

"That's good enough for us," Jean said, and she grabbed her husband by the hand, telling Cannon that they would see him in the 'O&T' as she called the Owners and Trainers bar, "after the race."

Cannon watched them walk away then turned to see the jockeys for the race enter the parade ring. He had not heard the bell ring. As *On Eggshells* continued to walk around the ring, the outside rails now scattered with spectators, Simon Pullman tapped his racing helmet with his whip acknowledging the trainer. He and Cannon shook hands. Pullman was a good jockey and had ridden for Cannon several times before. He was a lightweight jockey so he could ride those horses lower down in the weights in Handicap races. *On Eggshells* was carrying the lowest weight of the seven runners so a jockey like Pullman was a good asset to have. He stood in his all-pink racing colours, a pink cap, and a pink jacket, awaiting his instructions from Cannon. He had not ridden *On Eggshells* before.

"I think just ride her as she feels," Cannon said. "She will have no problem with the distance and her jumping is as well as can be expected. The only thing to be aware of is not to get too far back on her, as she is a bit one-paced and she takes a while to wind up."

"Sure, no problem," Pullman replied. "How far does she travel in a sprint?" he asked.

"She can do about 350 metres, maybe a little more before she gives in. So if you ask her for more she'll likely fade," Cannon replied, meaning that the horse could run at her top speed for a little less than a quarter of a mile. "I think if you let her go at the two-furlong pole that will be her maximum., but don't push her until then."

"Got it," Pullman answered.

A few seconds later a call came out from the Clerk of the course for the jockeys to mount. Cannon and Pullman walked over to where Ray Brollo had stopped with the horse, and Cannon helped his jockey up into the saddle. He tapped the horse on the rump, wished the jockey the best of luck and to come back safely, and then stood and watched as young Brollo began to lead the horse on towards the gate that the runners used to walk down to the course proper. The spectators began to disperse, heading for the stands, the food courts, trackside, or to the betting ring.

As Cannon walked out of the parade ring on his way to the stand, his mobile phone began to ring. Fishing the device from his inside coat pocket, he looked for a name on the screen, but it only indicated a number. Initially, he didn't recognize it and was wary of answering, until he suddenly realized it was a number from Chester. Cummings!

Cannon answered, asking Cummings to hold on for a minute. The noise around him and the lack of privacy made it very difficult to have a conversation.

Having found a less crowded spot near the empty winner's enclosure, directly behind the weighing room, Cannon told Cummings that he was now able to talk.

"You called me," Cummings said, "I got the message, so I'm returning the favour."

There was no need to stand on ceremony, so Cannon said, "Have you heard about Peter Brown?"

"What about him?"

By the response, Cannon knew that the answer to his question had been given. "Clearly not," he replied, trying not to sound too sarcastic.

"Why? What's happened?"

"He's dead."

"Dead?" answered Cummings.

"Murdered, it seems."

"Oh my God! How do you know this?" It was a genuine query, and it was clear that the police in Nottingham had not yet connected the dots completely.

"I received a call from a Sergeant Philips a couple of hours ago, just as I was about to leave home for Southwell, where I am now. He was from the Nottinghamshire police, and he told me that the Detective appointed to run the case is someone called Ann Walker. Do you know her?"

"No, I don't think so," Cummings said.

"Well, apparently she called DCI Peters after picking up something on the PNC database about the murder of Sarah Walters and the link to the Titan-H syndicate. It seems that when they interviewed Browns' wife, who found the poor man, she must have mentioned the syndicate and what had happened to Walters. I'd guess that it didn't take too long for them to make the connection."

"So, they called you?"

"Well, the Sergeant said that after Walker had called Peters, she had felt it necessary to talk with me. I think Peters believes that I know more than I let on."

"And do you?"

"No," Cannon replied. "Until Philips called me I had no idea about Brown."

Cummings stayed quiet. It was clear he was thinking. Cannon could hear the race caller beginning to announce that the next race was due to start in two minutes. He made a suggestion to Cummings.

"Look, I'm not trying to tell you how to do your job and I know that Peters outranks you, but maybe between the two of you and this Inspector Walker, you need to have a collective *chat* and determine which of you is going to lead this investigation?"

"Mike, you know that happens anyway. I'm sure in this case it will be no different."

"Okay, well I'll leave it to you then, Tim!" Cannon said somewhat angrily, and deliberately using the young Inspectors' Christian name. He hadn't planned on telling Cummings about the attack on his house but decided that it may be in his interest to do so, especially given Cummings last remark, which appeared to be one of dismissal. Cannon knew about co-operation across the various County forces, and it wasn't always as harmonious as some would have one believe.

"Did Peters tell you about the bricks thrown through my window the other night?" he asked.

Cummings was stunned. "No," he said eventually. "The last I heard was when you told me about seeing someone creeping around your yard."

"Well Tim, that proves my point, doesn't it? Three deaths, an attack on my place, and yet another officer I'm being asked to meet with. Does anybody really know what's going on?" Cannon said somewhat disparagingly. "To be frank I'm not even sure why I'm meeting with this other Inspector."

"I understand. I suggest you see what she wants and why she feels it necessary to talk to you."

"And then?"

"Leave that to me," Cummings replied. "I'll come back to you."

Cannon acknowledged the comment and cut the conversation, pushing the red off button on his iPhone.

As he did so, he heard the race caller shout "...and they're off."

"Can I get you a drink?" Henry Young asked, a big smile creasing his narrow face. His bald head gleamed in the overhead lights of the Owners and Trainers bar. It was hot and bright within the room, a stark contrast to the increasing darkness outside that was encroaching from the East.

Cannon declined, asking for fresh orange juice instead. He told Young that he was driving, and the older man nodded his understanding. The reality however was that Cannon didn't take a drink because he wanted to be on his game when he met with Philips and Walker after the fifth race.

A wind had whipped up, blowing across the racetrack. Rain was coming soon brought by the wind. Empty burger papers and coffee cups from the food court littered the lawns. A couple of men wearing yellow jackets chased after the discarded items before they were blown onto the track, catching up with the litter after conducting a wild dance as the papers swirled in the breeze. The men had long spiky poles with which to pick up the rubbish and disposed of it in black plastic bags that they carried with them.

Cannon accepted the orange juice that Young proffered and then both of them along with Jean Young toasted each other as well as *On Eggshells*. The horse had run particularly well, finishing a creditable second, some three lengths behind the winner. The Youngs were absolutely delighted with the result and told Cannon so.

"I'm very pleased as well," Cannon said, before eventually leaving the couple to enjoy themselves. He needed to get *Statue of Ramos* ready for the next race.

Having gone through the process of saddling the horse for race four, he had watched *Statue of Ramos,* a huge jet-black gelding, walk around the parade ring. He had stood under an umbrella that he had borrowed from the Youngs who were still celebrating their 'success' in the O&T bar. As the dark clouds had rolled in after the third race, he knew that the rain would soon follow, so he quickly sought out his owners having seen them earlier well prepared for the day. The Youngs had been glad to help, telling Cannon that they only expected to leave after the fifth race anyway, so they would watch race four from the O&T bar. They had wished him and the horse well and Cannon had thanked them again. He would have been happy to have all owners be like the Youngs, but he knew realistically that some people were often like their horses. Friendly, and happy one day, then stubborn, belligerent, and downright dangerous the next.

The owner of *Statue of Ramos* was a little like that. A businessman from Ipswich who now lived on the South Coast. He had made his money in the Import and Export game, but in recent times due to Brexit, he had been more interested in the impact of all the rule changes on his business, than anything else. With the ongoing issues and complex rules of dealing with the EU states, the mans' main focus was on addressing how to navigate through them. Accordingly, he had less time for his horses, of which he had a number. *Statue of Ramos* was one of them and a good one at that.

It was a pity that the man couldn't attend the meeting, Cannon had thought, as the horse, carrying the top weight of 75 kg, had romped home in the driving rain by nearly 15 lengths. That, over the 3-mile chase course!

Cannon was pleased, as not only did the win cement his view about the gelding, but it also confirmed in his own mind the quality of *Titan's Hand*. The two horses trained together regularly, and Cannon believed that the *Titan* was the better of the pair. With what he had seen, he believed that if there were no injuries, *Titan's Hand* would do very well at the upcoming Aintree meeting.

He had decided to return the umbrella to the Youngs, once all the formalities from race four had been concluded. The jockey, Brian Mariner, had been extremely impressed with *Statue of Ramos* and had asked Cannon immediately after the race whether he could ride the horse again, at his next outing. Cannon had looked at the man who was rain-soaked, mud-spattered, and a little breathless from his exertions, but still smiling. They had stood under a gazebo while the horse was being unsaddled in the number one stall. Cannon had said that he would speak with the owner and that it would depend on where the horse ran next and the weight that he would be allocated. Moving to a higher grade or class would likely result in the horse being allocated a lower weight and the question that would need answering was whether Mariner could make that weight. The jockey had nodded and understood the situation but repeated his request anyway. Cannon had nodded and said he would let the little man know, in due course.

Eventually, after returning the umbrella to the Youngs, he had said his goodbyes and had run through the still pouring rain, past the weighing room, and through a door that led into the backside of the main stand. He had then walked up the stairs to the Seasons Restaurant, which overlooked the course. Cannon was then shown to the table that he had booked and where he had arranged to meet with Inspector Walker and her Sergeant. He had texted Philips with the details, the policemen had given his mobile phone number that morning during their conversation before Cannon had left for the course.

The restaurant had been relatively quiet all day and at its height had only been one-third full. It was now less than a quarter, the place being vacated as the day wore on. The people still in attendance were those with an interest in the final two races. Some were staring through the gloom and the rain that continued to fall outside. They would be lucky to see much of the race given the conditions and Cannon thought that they would be able to see much more by watching one of the many TV screens situated on various walls throughout the restaurant. He turned in his chair to look at one of the monitors just as the fifth race was about the start.

CHAPTER 37

"Thank you for agreeing to meet with us, Mr. Cannon," Inspector Ann Walker had said, "and my apologies for the state we're in and for being late."

She had introduced herself and Sergeant Philips and Cannon had stood to hold out his hand. Both of the policemen were extremely wet. Their clothes had almost lost their colour, the rain having darkened them as it seeped into the material. Water fell from their heads and ran in small rivulets down the side of their faces, falling onto their shoulders and down necks. It was adding insult to injury. They had driven all the way to meet Cannon and ended up getting soaked to boot. They would hardly be in the best of moods.

Cannon had suggested that before they settled down to talk, that they try to find them something with which to dry themselves. Cannon had asked the restaurant staff whether they had any towels for the policemen to use. A junior of the restaurant staff was sent off to try and find them one.

While they all waited, they made small talk, discussing the bad weather, the racecourse layout, and Cannon's earlier race success. Walker said that she knew very little about racing, especially jumps racing.

"Oh, I always take part in the sweep for the Grand National each year," she said, "and I do the same with the Derby as well, but I've never got the winner and I actually have no idea who is running half of the time."

Cannon looked at her. She was tall, about 1 metre eighty-three. In her late thirties, he estimated. Slim, dark blond hair (now even darker with the rain) green eyes, and quite high cheekbones. Her nose suited her face and somehow made it softer. Her smile was genuine, and he noticed how straight and white her teeth were. He wasn't sure if an Inspectors' salary would cover the cost of the dental work, but he had an idea that someone else had paid to have some expensive work done. As she moved her hand to brush away a strand of hair that had stuck to her face, he noticed two rings on her wedding finger.

Philips was also tall. A centimetre or two more than Walker, and he was very broad. He had a bull-like build. His shoulders, arms, and legs gave the impression that he was a rugby player. His ears had cauliflower markings on the tops. Probably the man played *Union,* Cannon thought. He was younger than Walker, in his early thirties, Cannon guessed. The man had short brown hair, receding slightly at the front, brown eyes, and a guaranteed broken nose. He still had most of his teeth which one seldom saw in a rugby player nowadays though he kept his lips quite close together as if he was wearing a mouthguard. Eventually, the towels arrived and after thanking the staff who had brought them, the two visitors dried themselves off as best they could.

"I hope that helps a little?" Cannon asked after the towels had been collected by one of the waiters. "You must be cold. Are you sure you wouldn't like something warm to drink before we start?" he asked, indicating the still falling rain hitting the outside of the window. He could just about see the six runners jogging down to the start for the last race. Inwardly he was glad his races had finished when they had. He hoped that his staff driving the horsebox back his stables would be driving carefully on the roads. He suspected the motorways would be very busy and quite slippery given all the rain that had fallen so far.

"I'm sure we are fine now, Mr. Cannon," Walker said looking to Philips who nodded in agreement, "and thank you again for arranging the towels."

Cannon smiled before asking again about a drink.

Philips requested a coffee and Cannon decided to join him. He called a young waiter and ordered for them both. He asked Walker if she was sure that she didn't want anything. She looked at both men, then changed her mind. She ordered tea.

Once the drinks arrived, Walker turned businesslike providing Cannon with the background as to why they wanted to meet with him.

"And you think I can help?"

"Let me put it this way, Mr. Cannon. We think that given your discussion with Chris Peters, err .... DCI Peters, recently, that it's possible that the murder I am investigating is somehow linked to the one that he is looking into."

"Possible? Not probably?" Cannon asked.

"Well, we don't have any definitive evidence as yet," she replied, "But we do have another lead and just between the three of us *girls*," she said leaning forward as if sharing a personal secret, "it has resulted in us questioning a neighbour of Mr. Brown with whom he recently had several disputes. However, until we have concluded questioning the man and been able to rule him out of our inquiries, what we have is two separate deaths, both of which have been established as *unusual*."

"You mean *two* murders."

Walker seemed a little uncomfortable with Cannon's words, so she responded by saying, "Allegedly."

"Okay. So relative to these *alleged* murders, how can I help?" Cannon asked again.

While he waited for her response, he drank some of his coffee. He noticed that Philips did the same but that he drank the whole cup in one go, putting the empty container back onto the saucer. Walker had not touched her tea yet.

"Well, notwithstanding our ongoing investigations on the other lead that I mentioned, I am keen to understand your part in the Titan's Hand syndicate." She looked at Philips for confirmation of the correct name. He nodded imperceptibly his affirmation.

"My part?"

"Yes,"

Cannon was a little bemused at her words, answering, "Well I'm a small stakeholder plus I'm the trainer of the horse. I took over from Dominic Wingrew and have raced the horse a few times. Apart from that, I don't know what else I can tell you."

"What are your thoughts about the syndicate members?"

"Sorry?"

"The membership. What do you think about them?"

Cannon thought for a second. "Well, they are an eclectic bunch, I can say that," he answered.

"Is that all?"

"Look Inspector, I'm not sure what you are suggesting, and I'm still unsure as to why you wanted to talk with me."

Cannon *did* know, but he wanted Walker to be open with him. He had played the same game himself many times in the past, but as a civilian, he found it difficult to dance around the issue. He preferred that she got on with asking him what she needed to.

"DCI Peters told me that you and he have recently met.....at your property?"

Cannon confirmed her question. "He also told me that you met to discuss the recent death of a lady in Birmingham, another syndicate member, that you believe is linked to an earlier incident that occurred in Cheshire?"

Cannon nodded again, allowing her to continue her questioning. "DCI Peters indicated that you have a theory that the two murders were related. He mentioned to me that you, yourself, were subject to a recent attack, which you *also* believe has something to do with being part of the syndicate. Is that right?"

"Yes."

"And now," she continued with some flourish, "now...we have a third death. All of whom were syndicate members."

"Correct," Cannon replied. "And with regards to the first murder, did you know that Dominic Wingrew was initially arrested as a suspect?"

"Yes, I did. Though he was subsequently released I believe?"

"That's my understanding."

"And there we have the problem, Mr. Cannon. We have three deaths and no real suspects."

"None at all?" Cannon asked, surprised at her admission.

"I think it fair to say that with three deaths in three different localities, the problem we have, is of any substantive evidence."

"Which is why the charge against Wingrew was dropped."

"I'm not really at liberty to say, but…."

"Cummings…sorry, Inspector Cummings told me about the dropping of the charges against Wingrew," Cannon interrupted.

She was about to query him about his comment, but before she could speak, he said, "He needed my help to keep an eye on Wingrew for him, so he was a little more forthcoming about the situation."

Philips looked at Walker, perhaps thinking about whether what Cannon had shared, meant that some internal policy or protocol had been breached. Before he could say anything, Walker answered it for him by suggesting to Cannon, that the agreement Cummings had made with him, was reasonable. No damage had been done.

"So, if we cut to the chase, Mr. Cannon, it seems to me that you have nothing additional to tell me about the Brown mur…err…killing?" she said, correcting herself.

"No."

"And you have no theory to offer me?"

"Not yet."

Walker seized on his reply. "Why…not yet?"

"Because, like you, I need to find evidence to prove *my* theory…" he teased.

Philips seemed a little agitated and he spoke for the first time in a while, raising his voice as he did so. Cannon thought that the man was trying to use his bulk to 'stand over' him.

"Do you realize that it is an offence to withhold information from the police, Mr. Cannon? Anything you know that could be pertinent to the case that we are investigating should be provided to us without delay."

"I understand that Sergeant, I wasn't born yesterday," Cannon replied. "I've probably investigated more crimes than you have had hot-dinners, if I may say so! However, concerning what happened to Peter Brown, I have no idea at all as to the circumstances of his death."

There was a deafening silence between the two men for a few seconds. Cannon stared at Philips, who stared back. The sounds of the last stages of the final race of the day, and the shouts of the connections in the room at one of the TV screens, began to echo throughout the almost empty restaurant. Cannon felt a movement under the table, perhaps a foot kicking a leg? Whatever it was, Philips suddenly offered an apology for his comments, which Cannon accepted without reciprocating. The man had annoyed him.

Cannon concluded that he wouldn't hear the last of Sergeant Philips. The investigation into the death of Brown was likely to lead to further discussions with all of the syndicate members, not just Cannon.

It was obvious that Walker had hoped for more from the conversation but the meeting between them ended with Walker stating that they would be in touch soon. The whole thing was a non-event. Cannon watched them leave, the entire meeting being unsatisfactory from both sides. He had been the beneficiary from the conversation as he had some more detail about what had happened to Brown. In return, Walker and Philips received no benefit at all from their discussion, as far as he could see. He still wasn't sure why they had wanted to meet with him in person when they could have talked with him on the phone? When he replayed the discussion in his mind, he concluded that they suspected that he knew more than he was letting on about the murders, *and they were right*. As Philips had said, if he didn't provide anything he knew freely to the police then he could be *requested* to do so. He didn't expect it to get to that stage, and he also didn't want anyone else to get hurt just because he hadn't shared what he thought was going on. However, he hadn't yet been able to connect all the dots and he was still unsure who had been sneaking around his yard and had attacked the house. That was still a mystery and one he felt desperate to solve.

CHAPTER 38

"Here's the letter," Stone advised. "It's got no markings on it, other than my name." He was holding the paper by its edges using his fingertips. He placed it face-up on the bar counter in the visitor's centre, for Wingrew to see. It was just after seven pm. Outside it had been dark for well over two hours and the lights from the building created square and oblong patterns on the ground.

There was just the two of them in the building.

"How did it get here, how was it delivered?" Wingrew asked.

"I don't know, to be honest, I think it was just dropped off. From what I understand from the girls at reception they said an Uber driver delivered it. By Hand!"

"Who the hell are these people, Alex?" Wingrew said in exasperation, "Do you have no idea at all?"

"How could I?" Stone said, annoyed at Wingrew's inference, "nothing's changed has it? This is the first I've heard from them since the voicemail."

"And the girls just accepted the delivery?."

"Of course they did. That's what they do, don't they? It's their job. They are receptionists! They don't get into detail when the post or parcels are delivered, they just accept them, sign for them and say thank you! That's all we pay them for."

Wingrew knew that Stone was right. Even the CCTV of the Uber driver wouldn't help them. He also guessed that while they may be able to identify the car the person used to deliver the letter, Uber themselves would be unlikely to tell them who the driver was. Not only were there privacy matters, but it was also possible that the car had multiple drivers in any 24-hour period.

Unless…

The trainer dismissed the notion he was considering. Stone had *friends*, but he was reluctant to suggest to his boss that they be used, especially after rejecting the idea previously. A motorbike gang running drugs, smuggling illegal immigrants into the country, bringing in cigarettes to cheat the taxman, and involved in all sorts of other illegal activities were not the type of people he wanted to get involved with. What he and Stone were doing was bad enough.

He looked at the letter on the bar. It was filled with typed information that both of them knew was correct. The implication was obvious.

"I think we need to run the horse," Wingrew said.

"*Ready to Commit?*" Stone asked

"Yes…"

"I'm not sure we should," Stone replied. "Given the success, we had at Leicester, we're almost there!. We just need Aintree to work for us."

Wingrew looked at his boss. "That's a hell of a call, Alex. It could work out the total opposite, and what then?"

"It could, but maybe, just maybe, it's a chance worth taking."

"A bloody big chance. I'd say."

"I know but if we could delay these bastards," he spat, indicating the piece of paper on the bar, "then maybe we won't have to pay them anything."

"How do you work that out?"

"If Aintree comes off, we can just ignore them."

Wingrew pointed out the obvious problem with what Stone was saying.

"Alex, *even if* Aintree comes off, which will be great, don't you see that these people, whoever they are, still have all this information?"

"Of course, I do. So what?"

"Well, they can still use it. As much as it concerns us now, it will concern us even more later, if we don't address it! Irrespective of what happens in Liverpool."

"Ahh, that's where you are wrong, Dom."

"I'm confused then," Wingrew said. "Explain it to me."

Stone took his time before saying. "We are so close now. Aintree is the answer. If that all works, we'll be back to where we need to be two months before the deadline. So, if we can put these…these….sons of bitches off until then, I believe I'll be able to handle things after that."

"I know what you're thinking Alex, but as I said before, I don't want anything to do with that."

Stone looked at his trainer smugly and knew that Wingrew would go along with whatever he decided. Wingrew had no choice, and they both knew it. They were in the mess together, the details on the page in front of them confirmed it. "My plan is this," he continued. "We'll pretend to go along with it. We'll run the horse and then will wait to hear from them."

"And then?" Wingrew asked, afraid to hear the answer.

"We'll delay anything they ask for about payment until after Aintree. If Aintree works then…" he let the sentence slide.

"What happens if they decide to go to the authorities beforehand?"

"They won't," Stone responded, "they won't. They have too much to lose plus what's on this page is their word against ours."

"I'm not so sure about that Alex. And I wouldn't be so bold to suggest that this is all they have. If I were them, I would be keeping something in my back pocket. Just in case."

Stone looked askance at Wingrew. "You sound like you know who they are?"

"I wish I did, as I would end this nightmare right now if I could. Remember it's my career, my reputation we are…"

"..talking about," Stone interrupted. "Yes, I know. But remember it's also our livelihood and in all probability our freedom as well. So, let's be clear, resolving this quietly will be a win-win for both of us."

"I understand," Wingrew conceded.

"So that's why, despite Aintree, I'm making the call."

"As back-up?"

"As security…"

Wingrew nodded. He knew when he was beaten and when he had no choice. He looked his boss in the eye, then said quietly, "I'll nominate *Ready to Commit* at Market Rasen for next week. It's just four days before the Grand National Festival starts. It should give us the time we need."

"Perfect," Stone replied, picking the letter up from off the counter and scrunched it into a ball using both hands. "I'll show these bastards!" he said, angrily throwing it against the wall behind the bar, watching it bounce off and fall onto the floor.

CHAPTER 39

"We need to find out from everybody in the syndicate, their movements around the time of the Brown killing," Peters said, "then we can try and correlate with those details we have, of where everyone was, at the time that Walters was murdered."

He was on a 'Zoom' hookup with Cummings, Walker, and their respective Sergeants. It was just after 10 am, the session having been initiated by Cummings. The collective belief was that Cannon was right in his thinking that the murders had something to do with the Titan-H syndicate, but no one yet had the answer, why.

After the meeting at Southwell with Walker and Philips, Cannon had phoned Cummings and given him feedback. He had told him that he was disappointed with the conversation, and he had expressed his frustration.

"They wanted to meet with me face-to-face but when they did, they had nothing to say," he had complained, "it was a complete waste of time."

"Did they not tell you anything at all?"

"Only about Browns' neighbour, who was a possible suspect."

"And that's it?"

"Yes." Cannon had thought about what to say to Cummings before he had contacted him. He had anticipated the way the conversation was likely to unfold, telling him, "The only other thing is that they think I know more than I let on."

"And do you?" Cummings had asked.

"Let me put it this way," he had said, "I'm certain that Dom Wingrew is involved somehow, but I'm not convinced he's a killer."

"You told me that before," Cummings had replied, "that's nothing new."

"I agree, but I think I know the reason why the murders are happening."

"Why?"

"I need to find out a little more and then I'll be able to tell you."

"You mean you know now, but you don't want to share it?" Cummings had said, becoming irritated himself.

"No. It means that I think I have an idea about what is going on, but so far it's just my guess."

Cummings was more than displeased. Cannon was not helping, and he realized it. In an attempt to keep the Inspector on his side, Cannon had said cryptically "The only thing I can say at this stage, is to take a look at road signs."

***

Cummings watched the other faces on the screen of his laptop. He was sitting in his office and Paula Alton had squeezed herself next to him so that she could be seen by the laptop camera. Ownership of the case was still a bone of contention, each jurisdiction still believing that the murder they were investigating took precedence over the others.

"How do we coordinate that then?" he asked, referring to Peters' request to coordinate the movements of the syndicate members. He suspected that his case, that of Punch, was being pushed to one side, seen as the lesser of the three being looked into. Peters was all about focusing on Walters and Brown.

"What do you mean?" Peters queried.

"Well, there are a lot of people in the various locations that we will need to interview. Let me see here…" he continued as Alton passed him a list of names concerning the Punch investigation, "…we have the following people that we need to get hold of. Alex Stone, Brendon Harris, the Manager of the syndicate, Richard Swiftman, Mary Punch, Cindy Higgins, Melanie Freed, Tony Clairy and Cannon himself."

"And what about Dominic Wingrew?" Peters asked, his voice a metallic sound as it exited the laptop speaker. "Isn't he your prime suspect for the Punch killing?"

"He was," Cummings replied, "but in my recent discussion with Cannon, he raised some doubts about him being the murderer. Doubts which now make sense to me."

Peters nodded, not happy about the extent of Cannon's involvement, his influence over where the investigations were going. However, he knew that Cummings had found him useful and decided to let things ride for now.

"In addition," Cummings said, "we have not been able to find anything to support the circumstantial evidence we have so far. In fact, we don't even have a motive," he added disappointingly.

"Well, if not Wingrew, then who?" Peters complained.

"I don't know.."

"All the more reason why we need to coordinate our efforts," Walker jumped in. While they all acknowledged Walker's comments, it appeared that they were at a stalemate regarding the next steps. Not an unusual position when linked crimes crossed multiple police force boundaries. Each wanted to protect their ownership of a specific investigation.

"Do these people see each other outside of the syndicate?" Peters asked.

"From what we can gather," Cummings replied, "Harris, Swiftman, and Stone, have known each other for quite a while, as they were the original members of the syndicate, along with Sarah Walters. With regards to the others, it seems not."

"So, let's get them all in for questioning. Surely someone knows something?" Peters ordered, finally pulling rank.

For the next fifteen minutes, they worked out a plan of who would interview whom and when. They would reconvene in 10 days at the latest, earlier if warranted. In the interim, they agreed to share intelligence, though they all knew it would be offered like a dripping tap, steady but irritatingly slow. Turfs were being protected. After much discussion, it was agreed how the findings would be collated and cross-checked. Their respective staff would review each and any anomalies would be followed up. In addition, they agreed that until the matter was resolved, Peters being the Senior officer would also act as liaison with Superintendent Barrow, the Head of the West Midlands Police. Barrow had been given the task of coordinating all communication with her counterparts across the other jurisdictions.

CHAPTER 40

They were extremely happy with the way *Statue of Ramos* had pulled up. It was two days after the race at Southwell and the horse had not skipped a beat since. The owner had been delighted, calling Cannon the previous day, thanking him for his efforts and congratulating him on his success.

Since the race, the gelding had eaten everything put in front of him and despite Cannon requesting his work rider to take it easy, they watched as the horse almost pulled the poor boys' arms from his sockets.

"It seems he wants to give *Titan* a run for his money," Telside said, as the two horses galloped side by side on the damp heath grass. Over the past thirty-six hours, there had been little rain and only a gentle breeze. It was still grey, but the morning sun was threatening to breach the gloom in places. The prevailing cloud had kept the frost away for which Cannon was eternally grateful. Despite being the start of Spring, it did not mean that it was going to be much warmer than what they had endured in recent months. The vagaries of the weather Gods could still see temperatures at or below freezing overnight if they so decreed.

"I think you're right, Rich," Cannon replied, "the win the other day was too easy for him. He seems to know how well he did. Probably made him a bit arrogant."

Telside laughed. They both knew that *Titan's Hand* was the better horse but were pleased that his racing partner was giving him a run for his money. Cannon planned to get more miles into the *Titan's* legs in readiness for Aintree. While *Titan* was the faster horse, being a hurdler, the *Statue*, as they now called him, was the bravest of the two. His courage over the larger fences was undeniable.

It was an interesting dichotomy. A fast horse over the smaller fences that he could potentially run through at times, versus a slower horse with a big heart that jumped over much bigger obstacles. The question for all trainers was working out which horse suited which type of event.

Overall, the morning had gone extremely well. All the horses in the yard appeared to be doing as expected. With the official National Hunt season fast coming to an end, some of Cannon's charges would be going off to various farms for a well-earned rest soon, while others would be off to Ireland to continue racing under the watchful eye of Sam Mitchell, who had a training property close to the Punchestown racetrack. The remainder would stay *in work* and compete at some of the summer meetings.

The challenge for all small stables was to ensure that they were able to stay afloat. Horse racing was a sport and a business. One big win could mean the difference between continuing to grow as a stable or abject failure, no matter how well the yard was managed. Cannon knew that he needed his horses to win. It was just the same with the bigger stables. Success on the track was paramount.

"Have you set a date yet?" Telside said, his soft lilt interrupting Cannon's musings.

"What? Oh sorry, Rich, I was just thinking of something. What did you say?"

Telside repeated his question.

"No, we haven't. In fact, every time I try and raise the subject, something gets in the way."

Rich chuckled. "I'm beginning to think you've changed your mind," he said.

"Hardly, I was hoping to get it done as soon as possible after the season finished."

"Get it done?" the older man replied, "that's not very romantic is it, Mike?."

Cannon laughed. "You are right Rich, but you know what I mean."

Telside clapped his boss on the back. "Well, if I were you, I'd also *get it done,* but quickly. I'm sure Michelle won't be happy waiting too much longer."

Cannon nodded. He knew he needed to get things sorted. He hadn't even spoken with Cassie, his daughter, since he proposed to Michelle. He knew that Cassie was busy pursuing her legal career and that she had her own life to lead, but he had hoped that a call to congratulate him would have happened already. Was it because Michelle would be replacing her mother? That Sally was somehow being usurped? He believed that Cassie knew that he would never forget her mother, but sometimes things changed. Attitudes changed. He would call his daughter as soon as he could.

With training now over, Cannon left Rich to get the work-riders feedback on the feel of their mounts and he drove back to his yard. The trip only took a few minutes. As he opened the car door, his mobile phone rang. It was Michelle.

He looked at his watch, noticing that it was just after 10 am. It was the school period change over time.

"Hi," he said, "I was just thinking of you. There's something we need to talk about."

"That's fine, Mike, but can it wait until tonight?"

"Sure. No problem," he replied feeling a little deflated. After he had spoken with Rich, he had wanted to finally get to talk to her about the next steps. He realized though that she normally didn't call him during the day unless it was necessary, so he knew that now wasn't the time to take it things any further. "What's up?" he asked.

"Nothing serious, if that's what you mean. I just wanted to let you know that I'll be a little late home tonight. Probably around seven?"

"Okay..." he replied. "Something going on?"

He could hear the excitement in her voice when she answered. "One of the girls… a colleague, a teacher.… Simone Welbeck has announced that she has got engaged to her partner, but in addition, he has been offered a job in the US. He's a physician and he's taken a job at the John Hopkins Hospital in Baltimore."

"I hope he's got his indemnity insurance sorted out?" Cannon responded jokingly, knowing the impact of litigation in the U.S. could be devastating to any good doctor.

"Mike!" she replied, "be serious….!"

He stayed quiet, accepting her admonishment. He waited for her to continue.

"Anyway, the reason for the call is that we are going to have a quick celebratory drink and a few nibbles with her in the staff room. It shouldn't take too long, so as I expect I should be home for dinner, although we might be eating a little lighter tonight. I thought I'd call you now rather than at lunchtime just so you know."

Cannon had no issue, just reminding her not to drink too much as she would be driving home in the dark.

"I promise. It will only be the one. I don't want to be pulled up for drink driving," she said.

They finished the call. Cannon got out of his car and walked into the house. By the time he was working on his spreadsheets, checking the various nominations and acceptances for upcoming events he had forgotten about his conversation with Rich. His focus was on what was left of the season. The finale being *Titan's Hand* run in Liverpool. Something about the festival was eating at him. He called up the various acceptances for the three days, then printed out the details of each race. At least he could see the runners. The jockey details were still scant, but he could also see the various trainers. He had some horses himself having been nominated and accepted to run during the festival. He looked again to see if the detail matched with what he had expected to see. What he saw, confirmed his thinking.

CHAPTER 41

"It's on," the visitor confirmed, "they have done what we asked."

"How do you know?" the blind man asked. "How do you know they will stick it, that it's not a trick?'"

The visitor was both sympathetic and slightly annoyed. It was understandable that the blind man was cynical as it had taken a long time to get to this point, however, he needed to have some faith.

"I think we have too much information about what has been going on for them to do anything foolish," the visitor said, "and if they felt that they had nothing to answer for, they would have just ignored my voice mail and the detailed information I sent them."

"I hope you were careful?"

"Of course, I was. Why do you think otherwise?" the visitor asked watching the blind man's face.

"I don't."

The conversation between the two seemed strained. The tone was almost antagonistic. The wait was nearly over. They were so close now. Both wanted this to end. The blind man could hear his dog panting a little. He needed water and the blind man knew that the bowl was empty. He would fill it once his guest had gone.

The dog had enjoyed the attention it had received earlier. Now however it again lay at the feet of its owner. It appeared to be asleep but every time the blind man moved a leg or sat forward, the dog would open its eyes, alert, ready to serve.

The visitor remained silent and turned to a companion, a stranger, who was sitting on a chair opposite the blind man. It was the first time the two of them had come together to see the blind man.

The stranger's head moved quickly but subtly, left and right. An indication to the other that they need not say anymore. The stranger indicated that it was almost time for them to leave, being slightly uncomfortable in the flat and saddened by what they saw. The environment was a lot worse than had been expected. Apart from the wallpaper now yellowed with time, it was beginning to peel and small bulges like bubbles could be seen where joins met. The damp patches in the corners of the room were almost black, and the stains on the carpet from where food and drink had been dropped or spilled exacerbated the feeling of helplessness that the blind man must have felt at times.

The blind man waited for the visitor to speak again. As he did so, he lifted a half-full cup of tea that he had been resting on his stomach, to his lips. The stranger watched as some of it dribbled down the mans' chin and onto his cardigan. The blind man could sense the tension between the two visitors. He knew that to visit him was always a challenge, that people had their own lives to lead, and they were always busy. He was thankful for all the help he received, whether it was from the visitor, or the home help provided by the council. However, he had always felt that he was the forgotten one and that he deserved more. He knew that time moved on and peoples' memory was short. Short-term memories were driven by selfishness, a me-too culture, and immediate gratification. All traits, in his mind, that had gotten him to the point of despair. Sadly, it was a reliance on the failings of others and not their success that would provide him with what was his due.

Eventually, the visitor broke the ice that had formed between the two of them.

"I expect that this will all be over within the next few weeks."

"I hope so."

"Do you have any idea where you would like to go?"

The answer was immediate. "Spain!"

"Spain? Why there? You don't know anybody there! And what about the dog? What about us....?" the visitor asked incredulously.

The blind man responded with a passion in his voice. His commentary moving in its simplicity. "You do know that if I hadn't lost my sight, I would have been able to see lots of places? Places across the globe..."

"Yes."

"Well because I can't do that anymore, I just want to *feel* them," he said, his voice soft, yet clear. "I want to feel the warmth of the sun on my face. I want to taste the food. I want to hear the voices...voices I should have heard years ago. Voices, sounds, smells and yes....even the sights if this...." he pointed to his face, to his sightless eyes, "...if these....had not failed me. I was on track to experience it all...and...." His voice trailed off.

The visitor knew why the blind man had said what he had and was sympathetic. The visitor had always been supportive, ever since the incident had happened. The visitor had empathy for the blind man but could never feel what the blind man felt. The visitor understood what was wanted and had hope that it could be delivered. Ten years was a very long time.

CHAPTER 42

The car turned into the yard, the headlights flashing across the side of the stable before turning ninety degrees to face the house. The beams shone into Cannon's darkened study, illuminating the inside.

He was in the kitchen, and he heard the car's tyres on the driveway. He looked at the clock on the wall above the door. It was just before 7 pm. *Good timing,* he thought. He had considered making some dinner for the both of them but wasn't sure how hungry Michelle would be, so he put the salmon he had taken out from the fridge, back onto the shelf. As he stirred the tea he had started to make, he expected to hear the car door slam and Michelle to walk through the door. He picked up the sugar bowl he had used and opened the pantry door. As he did so, he heard a scream, then a second one. He reacted instantly, dropping the bowl onto the floor as he exited the kitchen and ran towards the front door. Pulling the door open he saw the lights of the car were still on, their beams still shining into his study. The drivers' side door of the car was still wide open. Slumped on the ground, half-hidden by the open door, he saw the dark outline, a silhouette of a woman. "Michelle!" he shouted, running the twenty metres between them without a thought.

Just as he reached the prostrate body lying in the dark shadow created by the open car door, he saw movement out of the corner of his eye. A figure dressed totally in black, first running, then slowing slightly, about to climb up and over the perimeter wall that bordered the road to Woodstock. He found himself in two minds, help Michelle or chase the figure and try and catch them? He took a few steps in the direction of the fleeing figure. Now he was on the passenger side of the car, still unsure what to do. In the split second that he made the decision, he saw the figure leap from the top of the five-foot wall onto the other side. He knew that it was useless to try and catch up with the individual as he expected that a vehicle was probably nearby that would be used to get away with. He suddenly heard a groan. *Michelle!* he thought, she was more important now, everything else was irrelevant at this stage.....he could always look at the CCTV footage.

He rushed around the rear of the car and as he was about to kneel and check on Michelle, he realized that in the chaos, the individual was now moving, attempting to stand, but it wasn't Michelle or her car at all. Another groan, almost guttural rent the air. Cannon was breathing hard, his breath like steam. He knelt down looking to see who the woman was. As he tried to help her to her feet, using his forearms under her armpits, he felt blood on her neck, sticky and warm. The woman groaned again, and he decided to get her to sit in the car seat, legs on the paving. She was in a bad way. Cannon surmised that whoever had struck her, must have used something metallic, as she had been knocked temporarily unconscious. Who was she? He felt for his phone, looking to turn on the in-built torch. He wanted to see how badly injured she was, before moving her inside the house. As the torchlight hit her face, a car turned rapidly into the yard, tyres screeching, headlights on full beam blinding Cannon as the vehicle drove at speed, stopping just a few feet from him. With his phone in his right hand, he lifted the left to shield his eyes, trying to see the driver of the new car. The engine still running, the occupant opened the driver's side door, "Mike!"

A woman's voice. Michelle! Unsure what was going on, he turned to see who was sitting in the other car. The woman, now illuminated by the lights from Michelle's car, had her eyes closed, her head lolled from side to side. Cannon could now see her properly. Blood matted her hair which smeared the headrests. He could see that she was in a bad way. He recognized who she was. *Cynthia Crowe!* Michelle ran over to the open car door as Cannon bent over to ask Cynthia if she knew where she was. He received a garbled response. He knew that she was suffering from concussion, in addition to the open wound on her head and obvious blood loss. Michelle screamed. "Oh my God, Cynthia!"

Cannon took charge. "Call 999," he said. "Get an ambulance and the Police here. Quick!"

Michelle used Cannon's mobile to make the call as she ran into the house. She was looking for towels to help stem the bleeding. When she came out Cannon was helping Cynthia to her feet. She had regained some of her balance and was speaking more lucidly. He helped her to stand, then told Michelle to wrap the towels around the back of Cynthia's neck and use a second to cover the top of the head. He wanted to put pressure on the wound to stop the bleeding, but he knew that stitches and other treatment were likely needed. Cannon stood to Cynthia's right side and put his arm around her waist and Michelle put Cynthia's left arm over her right shoulder. Between the two of them, they managed to get Cynthia into the house and out of the cold air, sitting her down at the dining room table. Michelle ran into the kitchen filling a bowl with hot water. She added some disinfectant and found a clean towel that she thought would be useful to clean up the wound on Cynthia's head. At least it would be something while they waited for the ambulance to arrive.

On her return to the dining room, she looked at Cynthia who was still somewhat confused. Michelle placed the bowl on the table then soaked the towel in the water, dabbing Cynthia's head gently. Blood smeared the white cotton as it continued to seep out from the gash.

"What the hell happened, Mike?!" Michelle asked. It was the first time they had spoken properly since the initial confusion.

"To be honest, I don't know. I heard a scream then ran outside to see what was going on. At first, I thought it was you lying on the ground, and ….."

"Did you see anyone?" she interrupted, looking at Cynthia and slowly peeling away the towel from the top of her head.

"Well, I saw someone, yes, but I have no idea who. Why?"

"Because whoever it was, I nearly ran them over just now. As I came up the road someone was running in the opposite direction heading towards the T-junction," she said. "Thirty seconds before that, I thought I saw a car parked on the grass by the side of the road. It seemed a bit odd, given the time of night, but I didn't think too much of it. It was only when I had to take action to evade hitting the individual running towards me, which I immediately thought was odd, given they were dressed in dark clothes, that I put two and two together….It struck me that it could be the same person who smashed our windows."

"Did you get a look at them?" Cannon asked.

"No. I just saw the figure."

"Man or woman?"

"I have no idea Mike, it was too quick."

Cannon nodded. He had asked her more in hope than anything else.

Turning to Cynthia he asked, "Did you see who attacked you, Cynthia?"

"No," Cynthia answered. Her voice was slow and drawn out, but clear.

"Nothing at all?"

"No," she repeated. "I was hit from behind. As I got out of the car…I didn't see a thing."

Cannon suddenly realized something. He was afraid to say it, but it needed to be said. "Can I ask what made you come here tonight?"

Cynthia winced as her wound was continuing to be bathed. She pointed her eyes in Michelle's direction. "I wanted to see Michelle, as I wanted to get her advice. She said I could visit at any time, and I thought that by seven o'clock she would be home."

Michelle looked at Cannon sadly. "And because of the little celebration we had at school tonight, I was much later than normal….," she said.

Cannon realized the implication. "It should have been you," he said, looking at her.

"What do you mean?" Michelle asked.

"This!" he pointed at Cynthia's head, the blood on the towel, and Cynthia's clothes. "This…this was intended to be you. It's a case of mistaken identity. Cynthia was in the wrong place at the wrong time."

Michelle reacted with an intake of breath. "God!" she said, slowly realizing the implication. Understanding what Cannon was suggesting, slowly seeped into her consciousness. She stared at him. She was scared. Her eyes were wide with fear.

Cannon didn't want to show her how worried he was, but unfortunately, his face gave it away. He thought he knew what was going on, but now he wasn't so sure. She began to tremble. He could see her shiver. He reached out to reassure her just as red and blue lights lit up the room.

The ambulance carrying Cynthia Crowe had left for the John Radcliffe Hospital just 10 miles away. She had been assessed by a paramedic who determined that she would need X-rays to see if her skull had been broken. They had managed to stem the bleeding and had been able to clean some of the blood from her neck and throat but had suggested that she would be better treated in hospital concerning the rest of her injuries. She had been given morphine for the pain and was treated for shock. The last comment by the paramedic to Michelle and Cannon before the ambulance doors were closed and Cynthia was driven away was that she had been very lucky. The blow to her head was more of a glancing blow rather than one directly from above. If it had been the latter, then she could have been killed.

The police, two men, a Constable and a Senior Constable, had arrived a few minutes after the ambulance and Cannon had given his statement while Cynthia was being attended to. Michelle had remained by his side, holding his hand tightly. He could feel the pressure in her grip.

"And you didn't see anything else?" the Senior of the two policemen asked.

"No," Cannon advised. "As I said in my statement, it was all over very quickly. All I saw or thought I saw, was a dark figure climbing over the wall. You have Michelle's, err, my partner, err fiancés statement as well," he added. "She like me saw someone, but we have no idea who…or even why they attacked Mrs. Crowe."

"Umm…I understand something else happened here the other day?"

"Yes," Cannon replied stoically, but without further comment. He looked at his watch. It was now close to 9:30 and they hadn't eaten yet, even if it was going to be a light dinner. He was starting to feel tired…and he could see Michelle was flagging as well. He hoped that the policemen would go soon. He wanted to think about what had happened. He knew that they had been lucky. Whoever had attacked Cynthia, had done so thinking it was Michelle. Cannon thought about the two cars. They were different makes and models but in the dark, it was possible to confuse them, especially with the headlight beams being the first thing one would see coming through the gate. Requiring the element of surprise would mean that the attacker would need to be quick in deciding to leave their hiding place and expose themselves out in the open.

"Do you have any CCTV here, Sir?" the Constable asked, looking at his boss, seeking acceptance for jumping in with a question.

"Yes, I do. I am happy to share it with you, but I haven't looked at it yet. The recorder is in the tack room, so we'll need to take a *quick* walk over there," Cannon replied.

The Senior officer sensed the tiredness in Cannon's voice. He looked at the two of them and could sense how they were feeling. "Okay, Mr. Cannon, I think we have all we need for now. It's pretty reasonable to suggest that what happened tonight would appear to be an escalation from what occurred the other night. Accordingly, I would suggest that you keep all your doors locked and possibly leave another light on the outside."

"What about some police protection?" Michelle suddenly asked, "surely what happened earlier would indicate that this person is intent on harming us, killing us maybe?" Her last few words were too much for her and she began to cry. It was no surprise, just pure pent-up emotion that needed a release.

Cannon put his arm around her, telling her that they would be okay.

The policemen waited until Michelle had regained some composure. The Senior stated that he would ask back at the 'station' whether they could provide someone to protect the yard for a couple of nights. It was unlikely given the resources available but indicated that they may be able to have a patrol car drive past the area every hour or so during the night. If there were any cars parked in places that they should not be, they would investigate them accordingly.

The officers waited for a reply but seeing how disappointed Michelle looked at the idea, they received the lukewarm response they had dreaded. There was a short silence. Cannon wanted the policemen to feel uncomfortable. Finally, it was suggested by the Senior Constable, that he and Cannon, walk across to the tack room to quickly view the CCTV vision. There they could make a copy for the police to take away with them and they would see if they were able to analyze it offsite, if warranted. It was agreed between them that the junior Constable would remain with Michelle. Cannon checked with Michelle whether she was okay with the suggestion. She nodded in agreement, thinly smiling an apology for her outburst.

Cannon suggested that he and the policeman look at the CCTV footage from around a quarter to seven through to around ten past the hour. When the recording began the first thing the policeman advised was for Cannon to replace the system he had. The quality of the recording was not great. The system itself only recorded in black and white, even during full daylight.

"You need a system that records in colour and at better resolution," he said. "In black and white it is very difficult to get the detail we need. We have no idea of the colour of the clothing the person is wearing for example or even things like the colour of their hair."

Cannon nodded. He didn't want to raise his own experiences from the past when all that existed on the few CCTV systems in existence were monochrome recordings. In his day it was all about proper policing, hard work, and focus. Not like today, he thought, where there was disappointment when the solution to a crime was not put on a plate. He stayed quiet, wanting the whole episode over.

They watched the recording mostly in real-time, speeding up the vision on occasion and pausing it if they thought that they could see movement. The areas they focused on were of the camera facing towards the house front door and another that had an angled shot of the car parking area. As they watched Cannon could see that something was wrong. The vision from both cameras showed no activity at all. Even at the time of the attack at just after seven, there was no recording of any cars arriving, nor indeed any movement of a figure anywhere.

"Is this thing working?"

"Of course it is, Constable," Cannon responded somewhat angrily, "you can see that the other cameras have recorded activity at the same time as those we have just looked at," he said, pointing at the clock on the other camera recordings.

"Well, as you can see, Mr. Cannon, there is nothing here is there?"

Cannon could not believe what was being pointed out to him. He was flummoxed. Why was the system not recording anything in these important areas? He considered looking at the recording a further 15 minutes earlier than the start time that they had started from but decided not to bother. He wanted to get back to Michelle. He resigned himself to what he had seen so far, and he shrugged his shoulders in defeat. He made a copy of the recording, and the two men waited as the system wrote the data onto a CD. Once the CD writer had completed its' work, Cannon ejected the disk and passed it over to the Policeman.

The promise was that the disc would be passed over to a forensic scientist to examine the footage. Hopefully, if there was anything useful that they could glean from the footage, then they would come back to Cannon.

Fifteen minutes later, the police car turned out of the yard heading back to the station.

"How are you feeling?" Cannon asked.

Michelle looked pale in the kitchen light, and it was clear that she was still shaken up. It was now after 10:30 pm and despite the late hour, he began making them some cup-a-soups. They had decided that it was too late to eat anything heavy so he hoped that the soup along with some crackers would be light enough.

Sleep would be difficult for both of them. He suspected that neither would be able to relax with any degree of comfort, but he was trying to keep a brave face.

"I'm okay," she replied, her voice thin and unusually weedy.

"What about you? And also, what about poor Cynthia? How is she? We need to find out, Mike we…"

"Hey, hey," he said, "take it easy, love. I'm sure Cynthia will be fine, she's in the best hands now," he added reassuringly. "We'll give the hospital a call in the morning to check up on her if that helps?"

Michelle agreed. She knew that he was right, and she told him so.

Cannon smiled, but inside, his mind was reeling. Why was there no vision of the attack on Cynthia? How was it possible that nothing was recorded when the cameras were all working? He was confounded and he needed to think about it. It would be a long night.

CHAPTER 43

After a fitful night, they awoke almost simultaneously as the clock alarm broke the silence. It was 5:30 am. They had been able to turn off the light just before midnight. She had held him tightly, her head snuggled into his shoulder, her left arm across his chest as he lay on his back.

As they opened their eyes, the darkness outside made it seem that they had hardly slept at all. Sunrise was still another twenty minutes or so away and it would only start to get light enough to see anything in the next forty-five minutes. He switched on the lamp on the table next to his side of the bed.

"I don't want to get up," she said.

"Me neither," he replied softly, "but I guess we have no choice do we?"

"Not really," she replied.

He sensed that she was still a little upset from the events of the previous evening. He lay still for a few seconds. During the night he had dreamt. His dreams were often of ghosts from his past but this time they were not. He couldn't recall what he had been dreaming of, so he asked Michelle if she had dreamt at all. She replied that she hadn't. He acknowledged her before he suddenly had a thought. In all the *excitement* during the previous evening, no one asked the question why Cynthia was in the yard in the first place?

"Because I asked her to," Michelle replied.

"What? To come last night?"

"No. It was an open invitation. We had agreed she could just pop over if she wanted to talk."

He turned to look into her face. "As I said last night, it was the wrong time, wrong place. I wasn't aware of your arrangement. but to my mind, it's clear that the attack was meant for you."

"How do you know that?" she answered.

"It's obvious isn't it?" he replied. "If it was meant for her, why wait until she came here? Why not find somewhere else? Her place for example?"

"I guess so," Michelle answered after a few seconds, grabbing hold of his hand.

He kissed her on the cheek, then he said something that nearly floored her.

"Or.....I could be wrong....Could it be something to do with the Samantha Prittly matter, do you think?

"Do you mean the father?"

"I'm not sure," he replied, "how did you assess the man?"

"Well, he was very angry…"

"And *you* were supportive of Cynthia?"

"Yes."

"Umm," he responded, "I think we had better let the police know. He certainly had a motive to attack you, but at the same time it could also mean that I'm completely wrong about last night. Maybe you *are* both targets?" he continued, his voice highlighting his concern. "Perhaps what I was thinking originally could be totally off track. Perhaps I've been looking at things the wrong way?"

Despite both their concerns, Michelle headed off to school. Cannon had meanwhile left the house to meet with Telside to take the first lot at just after 6:30. Michelle had said that she would call the hospital from her car to check on Cynthia's condition. It would be a little later in the morning than she would have liked, only at 8 o'clock. However, she had decided not to call too early, knowing that the staff were likely to be busy with the shift changeover, which she knew ran from around seven in the morning, for an hour or so. She also said that she would advise the Head at school about what had happened, sharing the theory about Sam Prittly's Father. Michelle knew that the Head would be shocked to hear about the attack on Cynthia, and Michelle would be at pains to explain that she was only providing a theory. She wanted to reiterate the point that the Police would be the final arbiter of anyone's guilt. Evidence was necessary, not speculation.

"I don't think the Police will be of too much help," Telside said, "they don't have enough resources to put a copper on every doorstep anymore as you know, Mike. Unless whoever attacked the poor lady left a clue, I'd guess finding out who did it will be by pure luck rather than by design."

"I couldn't agree with you more, Rich," Cannon replied disappointedly. "I'm just thankful that it wasn't Michelle."

Cannon's mind wasn't totally on his work. He was feeling the cold, which was unusual for him. He clapped his hands together as a pair of his charges ran from right to left in front of the two men. Both horses cleared the hurdle with ease, the riders urging their mounts to increase their pace as they ran on to the next one. They were following instructions, both horses expected to race in the next two weeks. Cannon wanted to get speed into them. He knew they jumped well, and both had stamina. What he needed now was the capability to sprint when required. As both horses reached the small jump one of the two took off late, hitting the obstacle with its front legs. Both horse and rider somersaulted in the air, cartwheeling 180 degrees before smashing into the ground.

"Fuck!" Cannon shouted, beginning a sprint towards the still immobile horse and rider. "Stop the rest!" he called to Telside who was already 15 metres behind him. Telside knew what Cannon meant. He wanted the others to cease riding, cease exercising their mounts. "And call for an ambulance!"

Cannon continued his run, the soft ground gripping at his feet. He could feel himself slowing. He was no longer as fit as he used to be. His heart hammered in his mouth. "Christ, no, no!" he shouted, desperate to see the rider and horse get to their feet. He was thirty metres away from the jump when he saw the horse stand up shakily. "Thank God," he said out loud. The horse had probably been winded. He would check on it once the horse was caught. In the meantime, he needed to know about the rider. He ran as hard as he could over the final ten yards, running around the wings of the jump, finding the rider still on the ground.

"Please, please, please," he cried out, "please be alright." He was about to pick up the riders' hand and feel for a pulse when a couple of other riders and their mounts arrived at the scene.

"Is he okay?" one of them asked.

"I don't know," Cannon replied, kneeling down, hoping to put his ear to the mans' mouth. Hoping to hear that the rider was still breathing.

"Look at the helmet, Mr. Cannon, and the way he's lying," one of the other riders said, "it looks like there is something wrong with his neck."

Cannon looked again, afraid of what he might see. Unfortunately, his greatest fears were realized. He could see that the rider was dead. It looked now that he had been speared headfirst into the ground, his helmet smashed inwards on impact. The poor boy had no chance. It was Ray Brollo. Tears began to well up in Cannon's eyes. It was the first fatality he had experienced on his training ground. He wiped his face with a muddy hand, telling the riders to take their mounts back to the stables. He also asked them to chase up Telside and tell him to hurry up with the ambulance. He would stay with the body. "Also get Rich to call the police!" he shouted, disconsolately, as the riders turned to leave. Once he was alone, he cradled the young boy in his arms. The boy with whom he had spoken to only a few days before about becoming a jockey. Cannon wept. It would be another ghost for him to live with. Another death that he would never forget.

CHAPTER 44

"I suspect there will need to a workplace Health and Safety investigation?" the man said.

Cannon nodded. He was still feeling numb. The ambulance door was being closed on the young boy by the driver, the body had been loaded onto a gurney and covered with a sheet from head to toe, before being lifted inside the vehicle.

The paramedic looked at Cannon sadly. He had seen so many deaths and injuries during his time with the NHS and while he was used to seeing a body and people dealing with grief, he never really got used to it. Fortunately, the man thought, he wasn't someone who drank, as he knew that if he had gone down that route he would likely have been dead himself by now. His wife and children kept him sane. They did not know how much he needed them, as he never really told them how he truly felt. However, without their support, he would not have survived a week in the role let alone the six years he had served to date.

With the rear door shut, the paramedic placed a hand on Cannon's shoulder, wished him well, then climbed into the ambulance. As the vehicle slowly pulled away down the heath, Cannon watched in silence as the yellow and black box slowly disappeared from view.

Standing alone, Cannon looked around at the vast grassland that he and his team used for the training of his horses. He saw the cold obstacles and the flattened grass, the churned-up soil and the grey sky merging in the distance with the long winding trail that his horses walked along every morning before and after exercising. He sighed audibly. His greatest joy was also the source of his saddest pain. He had lost a young man. Yes, it was an accident, and these did happen in racing, but when they did it was devastating. Today it was the boy, tomorrow it could be a horse. Whenever they happened, he felt the loss in precisely the same way.

Ghosts....

"I'm not sure we should race again until after the boys' funeral," Cannon said. "What do *you* think, Rich?"

He was standing at the door of the tack room, and it was the day after Ray Brollo's accident. Telside was sitting on a chair, his feet on top of the desk he used for his paperwork. It seemed almost incongruous that life could carry on as normal when there was so much sadness around. To some degree, it was fortunate that up until now, Cannon had never lost an employee. But now that he had, he was struggling to make sense of what to do. He needed Telside's view, his counsel, regarding the steps he should take. The atmosphere within the ranks of the track riders was understandably sombre. They had lost a friend, a colleague and it played on their minds. It could have been any one of them. It was the risk that each of them took every day. They all knew it, and they all accepted it. It was part of their job.

"I think we need to be respectful and practical, Mike," Telside replied. "We should honour the young boy's life, show his family that we care, provide them all the support that we can, and then move on. You've got Aintree coming up shortly as well, and there is a ghost there that is still to put to bed," he continued, referring to the death of a former owner who a few years earlier had stopped his own horse and Cannon from winning the Grand National.

Cannon looked at his Assistant. He could hear the compassion, sense the empathy in Telside's words. He waited for the older man to speak again. Cannon needed to hear more. He needed to know that what he was feeling was normal, natural.

"I'd guess you are in a bit of a funk right now Mike?" Telside continued, "am I right?"

Cannon nodded, a tight-lipped smile crossing his mouth. He wanted to acknowledge Richs' observation of his feelings, of Rich being correct in his assessment. Telside clicked his tongue, removed his feet from the desk, and stood up. He brushed himself down with his hands and then half sat on the desk again, resting his arms over one leg, one foot on the floor, the other on the chair he had just vacated. "Look," he said, "I don't want to make light of what happened, and as you know I never will, but it's not the first death we have ever experienced is it?"

"It's the first employee I've ever lost, Rich," Cannon replied hastily, "you can hardly…"

Telside put up a hand, stopping Cannon from continuing with his response. He wanted Cannon to know that he should not take everything on himself. That he wasn't responsible for what had occurred. That accidents do happen. "Mike. I'm not suggesting anything. I know that you understand that these young *men and women*, do what they do because they *love it*. It's their livelihood as much as it is *yours*. They live to ride, to be with the horses and they live to be the best jockeys that they can be."

"I accept that Rich, but…"

"But nothing, Mike," Telside replied forcefully, his intent on making his point clear. "You do a great job, Mike. You look after your staff, the horses, your owners, my God you've looked after me ever since we started working together. I don't know anyone in *this game*, who is as caring or as compassionate as you are, so I think you need to take stock and accept what happened as a life lesson. Shit happens sometimes and we may not like it, but it's a smell that hangs around occasionally!"

"Are you finished?"

Telside seemed a little embarrassed. He had said what he felt, and he was well within his right to do so. He looked down at his hands, not wanting to look into Cannon's face. He thought that maybe he had said too much, that he had possibly overstepped the mark. He waited for Cannon to reply. With a brief cough, Cannon said. "You are right you know, Rich. I've seen many deaths in my time. Wives, daughters...husbands, lovers, kids....even my own bride, but to see one so young who had trust in me, it's hard, it's...."

"I know Mike," interjected Telside, standing up and offering his hand, "but we all need to move on. You can't stand still, you've promised too many people, including Michelle, Cassie, and Sally not to..."

At the sound of Sally's name, Cannon realized that Telside was right. He had lost his wife, but she would never be forgotten. Likewise, he would never forget Ray Brollo. The young jockey would join the faces that came to visit him at times. Some who visited brought a smile to his face, Ray Brollo would be one such visitor...

Something inside him took away the negatives he was feeling. Somehow Telside had found the key to unlock his guilt. Cannon knew that he had to take the next step. It needed to be one going forwards not backward.

"I think you are right, Rich.....we carry on..."

CHAPTER 45

It was just after eight in the evening. Michelle had just returned from the hospital having spent an hour visiting her colleague and friend.

"How is Cynthia doing?" he called from the kitchen.

"She's improving slowly," Michelle replied, as she removed her coat in the hallway before entering the room. "The doctors have told me that she was very lucky. She could have suffered brain damage at the very least, if not have been killed. The blow she received was enough to kill her if it had been straight to the head, but whatever it was that was used to hit her, ended up slamming into her shoulder blades first then glancing onto the back of her skull."

Cannon nodded. He knew from experience that Cynthia Crowe was indeed a very lucky lady.

"Are you hungry?" he asked, offering to make her something. He expected she would be starving but he knew that sometimes fear tightened the gut and took away any sense of needing to eat.

"No, I'm fine," she replied. "Maybe some tea though?"

Cannon added water to the kettle, turned it on, and then found a cup for her. He inserted a tea bag, a small dash of milk but no sugar. As the kettle boiled he finished his own dinner of cottage pie and vegetables, all of which had been premade by her and had been kept frozen in the freezer.

As she drank the warm liquid, they sat in silence for a few minutes in the kitchen just enjoying being together. Eventually, she said, "How are you feeling now, Mike?"

"I'm okay," he replied, almost nonchalantly, casually. She sensed a little bit of bravado about him. almost as if a barrier had been put up. It seemed odd given what had happened over the past twenty-four hours.

"Are you sure?" she asked. Her sense of worry for him being very evident.

"Yes, I'm fine."

"I'm concerned about you," she added.

He turned towards her. "I guess I'm concerned as well," he replied, "for you…."

She touched his face, gently caressing his skin. He closed his eyes. He enjoyed the sensation.

"You know, it could have been you in that hospital," he said.

"I realize that," she answered. "I think somebody up there must have been looking out for me."

He noted how her eyes moved upward when she said, *up there*. He knew she had said the words almost flippantly, but he was grateful to whoever it was that had indeed been looking out for her.

"I'm not sure how I would have coped if it had been you that was attacked," he continued, "and I'm still trying to work out why."

"And you are still worried about that poor boy as well?"

Cannon shirked at the mention of Ray Brollo's accident.

"I'm sorry," she said, "I didn't mean…"

"I know…it's just…"

"Too close to home?" she replied.

"Not only that," he answered, "it's personal…and that's what's bothering me. I've accepted what happened to Ray, but what could have happened to you still concerns me a lot," he said.

Cannon explained to her about his conversation with Telside and how he had rationalized what had happened on the heath. She understood where he was coming from. "Did you find out why there is nothing on the CCTV recorder concerning Cynthia?" she asked.

"Not yet," he replied, "but I have made some enquiries."

"What do the police think?" she asked.

"I haven't had any feedback from them yet, but they do have a copy of the CCTV footage. I'm not sure what they will find, but we'll just have to wait and see."

Michelle smiled softly. She knew that he was thinking about other things. It was obvious to her that he was pursuing his own thoughts about what had happened in the yard. However, he wasn't yet sharing what he was thinking. She decided to change the subject. "I spoke with Cassie on the way back from the hospital," she said.

"Oh?"

"Yes. I told her that she needs to call you. That it's been too long since you both had a chat."

"And what did she say?"

"She agreed."

"Did she say when?" Cannon commented.

"No, but I suspect it should be in the next day or so."

Cannon just nodded. *Kids*, he thought, realizing as he did so that his daughter was now well into her mid-twenties. She was no longer a child. She was a grown woman, ploughing her own furrow, chasing her own career. As he lost himself in thought, his mind drifted to what he had wanted to discuss with Michelle a few days prior. "The other day, when the window was smashed. I wanted to ask you whether you still wanted to get married," he said. "It seems since I first mentioned it, that we haven't had time to talk, so given the opportunity I…."

She looked at him with mild surprise, then put a finger to her lips and *shushed* him. She had also wanted to discuss their personal matters but had not been able to find a suitable time. Recent events had seemed to conspire against them. "As I said, I've been speaking to Cassie," she added, "and we thought it best to sort things out between us, rather than burden you."

"And what did you decide?" he asked inquisitively.

"That it was still a good idea," she answered teasingly.

"Was there going to be any different conclusion?" he asked in mock surprise.

"There could have been…" she answered.

Cannon realized that he was being teased. "Okay, so what do we do next?" he asked, his naivety about weddings being very real. When he married Sally, all the arrangements were made by her and her family. Cannon had limited input, which equated to none at all. That suited him at the time.

Michelle decided to fill him in on what she and Cassie had discussed so far. It appeared to him that a lot had been said between the two of them already and his concern about Cassie being upset that Michelle was a replacement for Sally was unfounded.

"So, to reiterate?" he asked, "and for my own sanity, we *are* still on?"

"Yes!" Michelle replied.

"And it will be sometime in the Summer?"

"Yes…in around 16 weeks," she replied, with extreme confidence.

"Ahh.."

"So, you're no longer worried?"

"No, now that we've sorted that out, I'll relax a little," he replied, a smile on his face. "I think I'll survive…for now…" he replied.

When they went to sleep a few hours later, he wasn't sure whether he should be more anxious about the wedding, and less so about the happenings with the *Titan-H* syndicate, or vice versa. Either way, there were things outside of his control that were beginning to make him nervous.

CHAPTER 46

Cannon thanked the caller again. What he expected could be the case would be checked, then confirmed. He didn't know the technology behind it, but he thought that it could be done. As a consequence, he needed to call Peters. He picked up the phone and asked for the Detective.

"Hello, Mr. Cannon, how are you?"

"I'm okay…considering…." Cannon replied, "unfortunately it's been a rough couple of days," he added, without offering any additional detail.

"Well, if its' been worse than mine then you've really had a bad time."

Cannon did not want to discuss the merits of policing. He had been in the job for years and he knew what Peters was likely referring to. However, that was all in the past…or was it…?

"I wanted to see if you had managed to get anywhere yet?" Cannon asked, "Specifically in relation to Peter Brown."

"Mr. Cannon, you know I can't disclose any information about an ongoing investigation, no matter what the circumstances are …."

"So, do you have any suspect at all?" Cannon interrupted.

"I'm not at liberty to say."

"Which would indicate that you have none," Cannon replied, emphatically.

"I wouldn't say that's true Mr. Cannon, it's just that…"

"You can't tell me…yes I know."

"I'm glad we've cleared that up then," Peters replied.

Cannon was annoyed. He wanted to help Peters and he believed that he had something to offer, but he seemed to be facing a brick wall. "Look Inspector, there are a couple of things I need to get off my chest and in doing so, hopefully, they will help you, Walker, and Cummings in your investigation…*if* you are willing to listen."

Peters heard the directness in Cannon's voice. He was about to respond but decided to hold his tongue. If Cannon had something else he wanted to share about the Brown or Walters case then he was happy to hear it.

"Go ahead," he said.

"Firstly, as I've said all along, I believe the deaths of Fred Punch, Sarah Walters, and Fred Brown are all linked."

"Yes, I know. But so far there is no evidence to that effect." Peters countered.

"Perhaps not yet, but I think I can prove it."

"How?"

"I'll need a little longer before I can do that, but I will give you some information that may be of use to you," Cannon continued, "and if it proves to be correct then I hope it will be the final piece of the puzzle."

"And what are you expecting me to do with this information?"

"Verify it, confirm it."

Peters stayed quiet. He was thinking. As he contemplated what Cannon had said, he recalled his conversation with DI Drummond about Cannon knowing more than he was telling.

Cannon began to explain his theory, asking Peters to check some detail for him.

"So, if you can follow that up for me, then I think I can put the pieces together," Cannon said, trying to sound as contrite as he could be and hoping Peters took the bait.

"Hang on a minute, Mr....Mike, what you have just told me doesn't prove anything. In fact, we already know most of it. What I'm failing to see is anything tangible that ties the three murders together."

"It's as I told you," Cannon replied, " All of them are linked...to the *Titan-H* syndicate."

"So you say.....and yet you have no real proof of this?"

"Not yet, but can I ask you a question?" Cannon responded.

"Yes, of course."

"If I hadn't given you the information I have, would you have anything else to tie these murders to?"

"As I said before, I'm not..."

"..at liberty to tell me. Yes I know...but I can guess that everyone you have spoken to in the syndicate as to where they were when Walters and Brown were killed, can provide an alibi?"

Peters remained quiet. While his own team and those of Cummings and Walker were still checking the movements and whereabouts of the syndicate members, so far they had drawn a blank. In addition, Peters had told his team to look at other possibilities. There were so many questions that needed answering. Was there someone out there with another motive for killing Walters? Could the fire have nothing to do with the syndicate, and even if a syndicate member was involved, what was the motive? Likewise, why was Brown killed? There was no obvious benefit to the syndicate or any of its members. While Browns' neighbour had been questioned and released, could Browns' death have been due to a local dispute? These were all possibilities that were being looked at, but progress was slow. So far they had not been able to extract any concrete evidence from the arrow used to kill Brown, nor the wrecked car that was used to get away from the Birmingham fire. Once-off murders were always the most difficult to solve. Sometimes luck could play a part, sometimes the answer was obvious, sometimes time moved on, people moved on, resources were reassigned, and the case remained unresolved, put in the *too hard* basket.

"I'll tell you what, Mr. Cannon," Peters eventually replied, his tone expressing some reluctance, "let me check the information you have provided, and I'll get back to you as soon as I can. In the meantime, can I suggest that you remain vigilant around your property, and I will contact your local station and ask them to increase the patrols in your area. Is that reasonable?"

Cannon knew that what was being offered was the best that Peters could do under the circumstances, so he thanked him accordingly. He put down the phone with a slight smile. What he needed to be checked was now with Peters. If Cannon was right and Peters confirmed it, then the last piece of the puzzle would fall into place.

CHAPTER 47

Ready to Commit had fallen at Market Rasen during the second race, the owner had been on course and was extremely disappointed. After the race itself, the horse was checked for any injuries and was found to be lame in the off foreleg, which Wingrew believed was the reason why the horse had run so disappointingly. Before the race, there was no sign of anything amiss and the jockey had only felt a change in the horse's running action just after the start. He had been in two minds as to whether to pull out of the event but had persevered. At the very next obstacle, they had crashed to the floor, making the decision a moot point. Fortunately, neither horse nor rider suffered any injury, the jockey only needing to swallow his pride regarding his horsemanship and decision making.

"It looks like your stable is somewhat out of form," Ian Night, the owner of *Ready to Commit*, noted, to Wingrew. They were standing together watching the horse cool down after the race, a slight limp the give-away to the on-course Vets' diagnosis of lameness.

"I wouldn't say that Ian," Wingrew replied, "It's more that we've had a bit of a bad run. It can happen you know."

Night smiled uncomfortably. The trainer knew what was coming. He had seen it many times before. Had heard the pretext.

"Well, I'm sorry to do this, but I think I need to move the horse," Night said softly. It was a message that he wanted to send but found the process difficult. A man of few words, softly spoken but passionate about his horse. He was a life-long jumps racing supporter, a one-horse-at-a-time owner, and the backbone of the industry. A retiree who travelled the country to watch his horse, come rain or shine. A man of reasonable means now enjoying the fruits of his years of labour.

Wingrew never took the removal of a horse from his stables personally. It was an owners' right to do what he wanted. However, he reflected on Nights' comments and knew that the owner wasn't aware why results didn't always go the way they were expected to go. If only they did....

"I understand Ian, though I would prefer to keep him with me."

Night stayed quiet. He continued to watch the horse, steam still rising from the animal which evaporated in the cool air.

"Do you know where you want to place him?" Wingrew asked eventually.

"I've been in touch with Colin Faulk down in Worcester," Night replied. "He said he was happy to take him as he's had a few horses move on himself."

The normal merry go round, Wingrew thought. "He's a good trainer," he acknowledged.

"Thanks. I think so too," Night replied.

"Do you know when?"

"As soon as practically possible, if that's okay?" Night added, feeling slightly embarrassed.

"Of course," Wingrew replied, sighing inwardly, "once the horse is back in Cheshire I'll make arrangements. He'll need a bit of treatment beforehand though, but he should be sound again soon if he is managed properly."

Night thanked Wingrew again for his understanding, then walked away towards the main stand and the warmth within it. His horse was led away to be washed, dried, and driven back to Wingrew's stables.

The trainer looked around him as the few spectators on course leant against the parade-ring fence waiting for the runners in the next race to appear.

He muttered to himself under his breath. The effect of what Stone had gotten them into was hard to take. He hoped that it would be over soon. Losing a horse was one thing, losing one's liberty was something he didn't want to think about.

"I'm on my way," Wingrew shouted into his hands-free phone. He had just left the car park having readied himself for the nearly three-hour journey back to Cheshire. The day had improved after the first couple of races. What he and Stone had hoped for had occurred. In the remaining four races, Stones' three runners had run successfully for him.

"A good outcome today," Stones' voice emitted from the speaker inside the car.

"Yes, it brings us a step closer, thank God," Wingrew answered, turning the vehicle onto Caistor Road after filling up with fuel and then heading towards the M180 just north of Scawby.

"Were there any questions? The Stewards okay?"

"No, nothing at all…"

"That's good. It certainly helps. I think we're on track …."

"I should hope so!" Wingrew replied, surprising himself at the forceful nature of his response. "I can't keep hiding from it, Alex….we lost another today," he added.

Stone maintained a sense of calmness. He needed Wingrew to do the same.

"I know it's been tough, Dom, but just hold on for a little bit longer," he said. "We've just got to get through Liverpool, and it will be over."

"We hope!"

"Well if not, then we carry on…we…I…still have until June."

"I don't think I can last 'til then. We've got to resolve it as soon as we can."

"Understood Dom," Stone replied, trying to sound positive.

The darkness that Wingrew was driving through seemed less threatening than the hole that they were trying to fill and the elephant in the room that they had still not yet spoken about. The loss of Nights' horse brought Wingrew back to the real reason he had travelled all the way to Lincolnshire. The threat of exposure and the need to address the challenge they faced still persisted. They did not know if running *Ready to Commit* at Market Rasen was going to result in an approach from anyone, but so far there had been nothing. Wingrew had not seen anything out of the ordinary while on the course. They still had no clue who their tormentor was.

"Did anyone get in contact?" Stone asked.

"No, nothing at all."

"I suppose that's a good thing then?"

"Yes, I guess so, though I'm surprised that it's been so quiet."

"Let's hope it stays that way." Stone replied, before wishing Wingrew a safe trip and dropping off the call.

The road works on the M62 just West of Rochdale had slowed him down. He had been driving for over two-and-a-quarter hours already, and he still had another hour to go. A cold pie from a Marks and Spencer outlet at the Birch Service station between junction 18 and 19 was the best that he could do for dinner, to ease the hunger pangs. He had eaten it in the car as he drove, crumbs were scattered across his lap and onto the floor of his footwell. The remnants of an over-priced coffee sat in a paper cup between the two seats. He reached for it then realized the cup was almost empty. He drank the cold dregs and put the cup down just as his phone rang.

On the screen of his media system, he could see that it was Stone calling.

"What's up, Alex? Everything okay?"

"Where are you?" Stone asked with purpose. There was something in his voice that made Wingrew sit up. The metallic nature of it seemed to galvanize him into an immediate reply.

"I'm just coming up to the Thornham interchange. Why?"

"Are you able to pull over?"

Wingrew looked in his rear-view mirror. The road was busy, but he could always stop on the hard shoulder. "I can if you give me a minute," he replied. "What's going on anyway?" he added.

"I've just had a call," Stone said.

"About?"

"Aintree...."

Wingrew was confused, "Aintree?" he queried. "What do you mean?"

Stone asked Wingrew to tell him once he had stopped the car. Once he had done so, Stone carried on. "I received a call as I told you. It was a recording... from our unknown *friends*. It was a message using that same Scots accent and someone played it over the line when I answered."

"Did you get the chance to ask anything?"

"No."

"So, what did it say?" Wingrew enquired.

Stone seemed to hesitate. Things were coming to a head much quicker than he was hoping. "The message made two points. The first one was essentially a statement to.....*look inside the boot*. The second was, *follow the comments, follow the instructions....*"

"I'm not with you Alex. Which boot?" Wingrew replied. He was starting to feel very nervous. It seemed like walls were closing in on him.

"*Your* car boot."

"What?!! You're telling me that someone....."

"Yes, that's what the message said...."

"Okay. Just give me a minute. Stay on the line, don't drop off. I'll be back shortly."

Stone heard Wingrew open and close the car door, then waited in the silence until the trainer returned. In less than a minute Wingrew was back on the line.

"It's a box," he said, "in my bloody boot! How the hell did that happen?" he said out loud, angrily.

"Is there anything in it?"

"I don't know...I haven't opened it yet."

"How heavy is it? What does it look like?"

Wingrew turned on the interior light of the car. "It's just a square white box. It looks like a CD box, to be honest, you know the ones you can buy anywhere."

"Is it heavy? Can you sense anything inside?" Stone asked.

Wingrew gently shook the box. There was no sound. "It's very light," he said. "I'm not sure if there is anything inside, but I tell you what Alex, I'm extremely pissed off....and scared shitless. How the fuck did.....?"

"Don't worry about that right now," Stone replied. "It's obvious that we need to act..."

"To do what Alex? These bastards have been inside my car boot. They've been watching us, and we have no idea who they are. I could be sitting with a bomb in my hands...."

Stone wanted his trainer to focus, saying, "Dom. Dom. If it's so light then I doubt that it's a bomb. Remember they want money. Exploding a bomb is not the best way to stay in the background, is it? So, open the box....let's see what instructions are in there...."

Wingrew placed the box down on the passenger seat and slowly lifted the box lid. As he did so, a party popper elicited a short sharp bang, sending confetti all over the inside of the car.

Stone heard the clap of the small toy, then the voice of Wingrew swearing.

"What happened Dom? Are you okay?"

Wingrew growled. He noticed a small piece of string sellotaped to the lid of the box, the other end to the party popper that had been stuck to the bottom. By opening the lid, the crude joke had been set off. Inside the box, there were also two pieces of paper, now covered with brightly coloured confetti. One of the pieces had the word BANG, printed on it, the other a series of typed dot point sentences under the heading, INSTRUCTIONS.

"Yes. I'm okay," Wingrew said finally, brushing off more detritus into the footwell. He looked at the page with several dot points on it. The detail took up half of the single A4 piece of paper. Having conducted a very quick read through he said, "They've issued a final ultimatum."

"For when?"

"The penultimate day of the Aintree festival."

"Fuck!" Stone said, angry at what he was hearing. "That's the last thing we need," he added.

"Yes, plus they've upped the ante."

"What? What do you mean?"

"They want 300,000 pounds now. It says here in these *Instructions* that we have been stalling and that they know that Aintree is how we intend to get out of the mess we are in. It also claims that they have been watching our every move and that if we don't give them what they want by the Friday of the festival, then they will disclose everything they know."

"I still think they are bluffing," Stone said.

Wingrew wasn't convinced. He was still worried that somehow his boot was broken into and that he had no idea as to how. What else had they done, he thought?

"Okay, we can discuss it when I get back, but from what I can see the instructions they have written down here are extremely thorough. I'm not sure that you can be so sure that they aren't serious," the trainer said.

"In the back of a car?" Stone queried. "They want us to leave 300 thousand pounds in the boot of a car?" he repeated.

"That's what it says," Wingrew replied, "on Topham Chase day. The day before the National."

Stone rubbed his chin. "We can't do this, Dominic. We need the results to go our way. If we pay these people we are almost dead meat. We can't afford to miss out on our biggest payday. We need to somehow delay this. If we get what we need from the festival then it's all over. These people can just go to hell," he added, flicking the page of instructions onto the floor.

Wingrew picked up the paper, placing it back on the table that separated them. They were sitting in the bar area inside the visitor's centre. Outside the crisp, dark night, suggested a morning frost. The clear sky indicating no immediate threat of rain. It was close to 10:30 pm.

Stone looked at the instructions again. "I think we need some help," he said, and despite the late hour, he dialled a number from his mobile phone.

CHAPTER 48

The day had dawned cool, but the sun had quickly burnt off the slight frost. The sky was a clear blue and Cannon had been pleased with the work of his charges. The team of riders had been very positive despite the sad death of one of their own. Ray Brollo had been remembered with a minutes' silence before exercise began. The first string of the morning had lined up in a single row, side by side as the sun rose behind them. Telside videoed the scene and both he and Cannon were moved by what they saw. The snorts and slight movement of the horses in the quiet stillness of the Oxfordshire countryside typified what horse racing was all about. It wasn't just money. There was a sense of camaraderie as well as competitiveness. In the early quiet of the morning, a life lost was remembered.

Cannon put the phone down. The call from Peters had confirmed what he had suspected and while it still did not prove anything, it gave him enough to work with. It was just after midday. He knew he needed to call Harris.

"Hi Brendon, how are you doing?" he asked when the phone was answered. It sounded like Harris was outside, in a street somewhere, walking. Given the weather, Cannon was not surprised.

"Hi Mike, how are you?"

"I'm fine Brendon, thanks for asking. I just wanted to check with you about *Titan's Hand* and Aintree."

"Oh yes, are we good to go?"

"Well, the horse is in fine form and has been doing well since his last race, so yes everything is going to plan."

"That's excellent news…" Harris replied enthusiastically. "I knew moving him to you was the right move."

Cannon accepted the flattery but wanted to get back to the real reason for the call. "Look, Brendon, I just wanted to check something with you," he said.

"Sure, what is it?" Harris replied.

Cannon wanted to be careful with his words. What had happened to three members of the syndicate had been tragic and he found it difficult trying to sound upbeat while he was still feeling the rawness of their deaths. With the police still struggling to find answers and then piling the accident on the heath and the attack on Cynthia Crowe on top, the Aintree meeting was almost inconsequential. Yet, it was Cannon's job and life carried on.

"I wanted to make sure that everyone is going to Liverpool on Friday?" he asked.

"As far as I can tell, yes everyone has accepted my invitation, except Mary Punch," Harris replied, "she's still traumatized apparently. She came back to me immediately saying, no." Cannon had seen the email to all the syndicate members from Harris asking them if they would like to attend the meeting? Harris had sent it the day after acceptances for the race had closed.

"And you have a room?"

"Yes, I managed to book one at the Mercure, St Helens for a small get-together afterward. Hopefully, we will be celebrating a win. What do you think?"

Cannon smiled. It was just like Harris. As manager of the syndicate, he was the eternal optimist. "Let's cross our fingers," he replied.

"And everything else," Harris joked.

Cannon laughed out loud, before asking, "And on the day itself?"

"Ahh...this is where I think we've done well. As owners, we have owner access obviously, but I've also booked us into the Princess Royal restaurant so that we have a table to sit at for the day."

"Wow, that will cost a pretty penny," Cannon stated.

"It does, but we don't often get the chance to enjoy a day like this, so I thought the syndicate could do with something to break the drought of bad luck we have suffered recently."

Bad luck? Cannon thought...

Having got the information he needed, Cannon thanked Harris for his time and said that he was looking forward to seeing everyone at the festival. It was just a few days away. Cannon hoped that nothing else went wrong before then.

"It couldn't have been Samantha Prittly's dad that attacked Cynthia," Michelle said, "he's away, overseas."

She had just walked in through the door and wanted to let him know almost immediately. She had been in such a rush to do so, that she hadn't even removed her coat.

"I know," he replied. He had just walked from his study into the hallway to greet her. He had seen her drive into the yard, her headlights on, but the beam was not set on high. Sunset was just a few minutes later each day and Michelle was home a little earlier than normal. He guessed that she had left the school as quickly as she could, to tell him about Barry Prittly.

"What? You know...?"

"Yes."

She was speechless. She stared at him for a second, almost deflated. "And you never told me?"

"I didn't know until......" he responded somewhat sheepishly.

"But you do now...?" she interrupted.

"Yes."

"Because…??" she enquired, her hands on her hips, suggesting that she was slightly aggrieved.

"I received the answer only an hour or two ago."

She looked at him trying to assess what he was thinking. He was keeping a straight face. "Do you know where he is?" she asked eventually, removing her coat and dropping it onto the back of a chair. She moved past him, heading to the kitchen. He could sense her tensing. He followed her, answering, "No, I don't."

"He's in Norway. He and his wife Sylvia, they left over a week ago."

"That's good to know," he replied almost offhandedly, placatory.

Cannon realized his mistake. He had come across as condescending, flippant, and she reacted to it. "Mike, if you knew that the Prittly's weren't involved in the attack on Cynthia, you should have told me earlier!"

He put his hands up in surrender, "I'm sorry, but as I said, I didn't know until just a couple of hours ago."

"But you had an idea?"

"Yes, I did," he conceded, "but I wasn't sure. Plus, I didn't want to say something and then be proven wrong. I wanted to get a better idea first."

Michelle stared at him. She had endured a difficult day at school. The staff and students had somehow been made aware of the reason why Cynthia Crowe was away from school. As a consequence, rumours had begun to fly. Samantha Prittly's parents' names were doing the rounds as suspects and Michelle had had to look Samantha in the eye during homeroom class. It had been an uncomfortable feeling. Michelle had eventually taken Samantha to one side in an attempt to re-establish a positive relationship with her student. It was during their conversation that she had learnt about Mr. and Mrs. Prittly being out of the country. As she stood in front of Cannon, the silence and tension between them slowly dissipated. "So do you know *who* it was then that attacked Cynthia?" she queried.

"No…not yet."

"But you have an idea?"

"Yes…."

He told her.

CHAPTER 49

"You need to be careful," the blind man said into the mouthpiece of his landline handset, "I suspect that they may try to set a trap for you." He was standing at the single window in the small bedroom. It was the only bedroom in the flat. It was said to be a double, but if he had put a double bed in the room, then he would have no space for storage. As it was, the single bed and two-door wardrobe more or less filled the entire room. He could feel the cool of the glass pane on his face, before a brief ray of sunlight flittered across it for a second or two. A blind man may not be able to see but he can sense, touch, smell, hear. From outside, beyond the window, he could hear kids shouting and laughing, a ball bouncing on the concrete playground that the council was supposed to maintain but seldom did. The swings and slides, the roundabouts, and whirly wheels were all broken. Now the place was more of an impromptu soccer pitch than anything else. He couldn't wait to get away.....memories.

The voice on the other end of the phone was confident. "Don't worry, everything is under control. Only a few more days...."

"You're taking a big risk you know."

"I know, but we've come so far, haven't we? If I didn't remain totally anonymous to them, then it would be easy to get caught. This way, I think we'll be safe. We can't do transfers into bank accounts, and they could easily mark banknotes. Anything like that can be traced," the voice said.

"But can't *anything* be traced?"

"To some degree, yes, but this is the best way...and I still have all the information. It's my protection."

"I suppose so," the blind man said. He was reliant on others and so far their plan was working. Turning away from the window he slowly moved out of the room, towards his favourite chair. The dog was lying on the carpet. It opened its' eyes as its' master felt for the arm of the chair. It stood up, yawned, and once he was seated, settled down at his feet. "I was trying to think of an alternative myself, but I can't," he continued, speaking directly into the mouthpiece. "Cash is way too bulky, and you don't want to leave a digital trail do you?"

"No, plus what I want from them will be easy to move."

The blind man was beginning to feel more positive. He had been living in his own private hell for way too long. His nightmare would soon end. He thanked his caller for letting him know what was going on and as they said their goodbyes, the caller promised to collect the blind man on the coming Saturday.

On the day of the Grand National, while millions would be watching and listening on TV, radio, and throughout the world, the blind man hoped to be celebrating his freedom. He didn't care about the winner of the great race.

CHAPTER 50

Both men were standing in Stable Block A. It was here that Fred Punch was killed and for which Wingrew had been arrested. Since the evening of the initial statement taking and the inquiries from the police about their movements a week or so prior, they had not heard anything since about the murder of Fred Punch. Both were unsure if it was a good or bad thing about the murder, their main focus had been on protecting themselves from their own problems. If Punch hadn't been killed, then they may not have found themselves in the situation they were now in. As it was, things were coming to a head. With the *Titan-H* syndicate members all getting together on Topham Chase day, Stone had high hopes that his *friends* would be able to resolve the issue once and for all on the day. He had made the call and much to Wingrew's chagrin *they* had answered it. Stone was meeting with them in his office later that afternoon. Wingrew was not invited, and he was glad of it. With only a few days left before the day itself, time was running out. Would it also run out for them as well? Wingrew was worried. Stone was angry. Being inside the Stable Block they could now speak freely. The previous evening they hadn't considered what the instructions they had been presented with had really meant. It was only in the cold light of day that they realized the significance of what was being asked.

"Kruger Rands? Gold, fucking, Kruger Rands!?"

"That's what the instructions state," Wingrew replied, "they've even listed several bullion dealers in Liverpool where you can buy them."

"The bastards!" Stone exclaimed. His anger and frustration rising again as it had done the previous evening. "How the hell…?"

"It's very clever…," Wingrew said, before being cut off by his boss.

"Clever! Clever!" Stone repeated animatedly, "it's *too* bloody clever by half," he said. "I didn't see this coming. These…these….fuck!" Stone slammed his hand against the wall. He turned in disgust, walking away from Wingrew, then turning and walking back towards him, a finger pointed in Wingrew's direction. "When my *friends* get hold of these people, they are going to wish they never started this," he said. "God…Kruger Rands!"

Wingrew could tell how exasperated Stone was. In his own mind, he knew how close they were to a resolution of their problems, and how much they both had to lose. Being so close yet now sitting with the threat of exposure made for poor bedfellows. He wasn't happy with Stone's solution, but he was coming around to the idea.

"300 pieces at one ounce a piece," he said, "that's about eight and a half kilograms, 18 pounds in old money. That's easy to carry isn't it?"

"Too bloody easy," Stone replied. "And at a *Grand* a pop, that's 300K easily."

"All to be left in the boot of a car," Wingrew noted. His admiration for the simplicity of the request evident.

Stone was not so embracing. "Over my dead body…" he said.

"What options do we have?" the trainer asked, listening for any of his staff coming into the barn. Over time he had come to suspect that a similar conversation such as the one they were having now, had gotten them into the situation they were facing. Walls had ears. Staff were not always as loyal as they should be. Speaking out of turn. Being overheard, was the likely source of their problem, however, the worst part they still faced was not knowing who they were dealing with. "What happens if we don't deliver Alex? The last thing I want is to go to jail. Surely we need to act as if we intend to comply with the instructions, whether we like it or not?"

Stone looked at Wingrew. He smiled. "I'll get the coins," he said, "but I'm not going to part with them. I have an idea. If it works, by the time the Topham Chase comes around on Friday, we'll have made enough money to settle our debt….and the coins in the back of that car will be safely back in our hands. We just need to keep on doing what we have been…and my friends will take care of the rest, " he said ominously.

CHAPTER 51

Cannon was watching the market. *Titan's Hand* was third in the betting for the main hurdle race of the day, while *Statue of Ramos* was on the sixth line for the Topham Chase itself. The festival was to start the next day. He looked through the program, checking the various races. He wanted to check which trainers were running which horses during the festival. He only had three runners across the three days, his third horse being a relatively young horse called *Thunderstruck* which Cannon had been slowly taking along. The horse was talented but had been prone to choking down, sometimes called *swallowing its tongue*, when it was racing. Cannon has worked with his Vet and after surgery had allowed the horse time to come right. It had been a long process, but the horse had improved over time to the extent that he had decided to run the horse in a Grade 3 hurdle race on the third and final day of the festival. The horse wasn't even mentioned in the betting, as he had not raced for well over a year, but Cannon hoped that the experience in front of a large crowd would help with the horses' confidence. He had high hopes for the gelding as long as he could keep the horse healthy and sound.

Concentrating on his work, his back to the door, and making notes, he didn't hear Telside walk into his study.

"We're about to get going, Mike," Telside said, making Cannon jump slightly. "Is there anything you need from me before I go?"

"Oh, err, sorry Rich, what did you say?"

Telside smiled. He knew that Cannon had several balls in the air that he was juggling, and he was sympathetic towards him. To be faced with the inquiry about Ray Brollo, the attack on Cynthia Crowe and the house, future wedding plans and then trying to do his job for his owners, no wonder his boss could be distracted. Telside also knew that Cannon was extremely worried about the lack of progress by the police regarding the syndicate member deaths. "I said, we are about to leave...me and the lads."

With three horses to transport, Rich and two stable-hands, along with the drivers needed to get on their way to the Aintree course as soon as they could. Traffic in the area would be extremely busy and they wanted the horses to be relaxed before their races. It would be a four-hour trip given all the road closures around the track and the road works along the way. Stabling the horses over two nights, or three as was the case for *Thunderstruck,* was expensive but Cannon believed it was worth it. *Titan's Hand* and *Statue of Ramos* would be driven back to Stonesfield after their races on Friday, *Thunderstruck* would be driven back in the second box on Saturday evening.

"Is everything in place? Do you have all you need? Course-passes? Hotel details?" Cannon asked. "Are the horses settled? How are they looking?"

Telside laughed out loud, he could tell that Cannon was feeling the pressure. He suggested a circuit breaker. "Everything's in order Mike. Just take it easy. Why don't you phone Cassie?" he asked, "have a chat...."

Cannon thought about it for a second, then stood up from his chair, arched his back, and pushed his hands into his sides. Sitting at his desk for the whole morning was making him stiff. "Maybe I'll give her a call later," he replied.

Telside nodded. "Okay...I'll leave that up to you..." he left the implication hanging in the air. Cannon sensed what Telside was suggesting but didn't react. He knew he and Cassie should be talking more, but he was leaving that to Michelle for now. Their relationship was growing closer, and he was pleased. It was what he wanted. He knew however that he needed to work on his relationship with Cassie as well. He parked Telside's suggestion for now. He would follow it up when he could.

"Okay, well, drive carefully, and I'll see you tomorrow night," he said, holding out his hand. The two men shook hands. For a small stable, the Grand National meeting was a significant event. The last time Cannon had attended the meeting it had proven disastrous, he hoped that this time it would be more successful, even if his three horses didn't win anything. He always wanted his charges to come back safely. It was his personal mantra.

As Telside left his study, Cannon had a bad feeling in his stomach. There was a lot to be won and lost over the next few days and he was certain that somehow things were coming to a head, not necessarily in a positive way.

He found himself standing alone in his study lost in thought when he heard the rumble of the two-horse boxes start up and slowly begin to head towards the yard's gate. He walked out of the house into the cool of the late morning. The day was partly cloudy, with the watery sun just about to head into its downward arc, the soft blue sky belying the still long night to come. It would be almost dark by the time the small flotilla reached the Northwest. Cannon had intended to give Telside and the others a wave, but he was too late. The back of the second horse box, its brake lights shining, was all he got to see as it turned onto the road leading away from the yard. He suddenly felt cold. He was alone. The sound of engines, the crunch of tyres on gravel and tarmac slowly faded. He turned to walk back into the house, as he did so, he could hear the phone ringing.

"If you are right," Peters said, "we'll be making an arrest, but I must warn you, Mike, that we'll need more than you have provided so far."

"I understand Inspector," Cannon replied, "will you be there?"

"Yes, and DI Cummings will be in attendance as well."

"What about Walker?"

"No, she has a few other matters to attend to, as well as continuing to follow up some leads in connection with the Brown killing."

"Leads?" replied Cannon, somewhat suspiciously. He knew that the police used jargon to pretend that they were doing something about a crime, but they were often not. He guessed this was the case now. If they did have a lead then they would not need him to do what he had suggested.

"Well yes," Peters replied, "there are other possibilities you know. Brown wasn't the most popular farmer in the region. He seems to have created quite a number of enemies for himself, not least of which, some of his neighbours."

Cannon remained quiet. He didn't wish to comment. He had his own view about Brown, and why he had been killed. Time would tell if he was right. Noting the silence between them, Peters continued. "Inspector Walker is also aware that you and Sergeant Philips didn't hit it off too well when you met. So, based on what you proposed to us, she agreed to take a step back and allow me and my team to work with you....on her behalf."

"That's very kind of her," Cannon replied sarcastically. He was pleased that he wouldn't have Philips to contend with over the next few days. He was happy with Cummings, however, and would tolerate Peters. He wasn't sure why he was feeling so cynical, but he suspected that potentially losing Michelle had made him realize how fragile life is. The ghost of Ray Brollo.......

Still feeling slightly bitter, Cannon rang off. He would see Cummings and Peters in Liverpool in just over 48 hours.

They were standing at the bar in the Fox and Barrel, near Cotebrook. A white stone-washed pub in the country. A Freehouse, which was also recognized in the good food guide, and had been for several years. It was just before 5 pm.

"A nice place," Lachie Drew said, "I've never been here before." He took a gulp of his *Sly Mr. Fox*, draught ale, finishing half a pint in a single swallow. He complimented the maker of the beer with a smack of his lips and a sudden belch. Stone seemed a little embarrassed as a few of the lady customers in the bar looked towards the giant of a man who stood over him.

Stone was well known and a regular at the pub. Being easily recognized in the area any attempt at being discreet was difficult for him when Drew acted the way he did. Perhaps he should have expected it, but Stone had been hopeful that a Thursday afternoon meeting out in the country would have been easier to get away with than it now appeared to be.

"Should we go and sit down by the fire?" Stone asked, pointing to a *snug* that was empty, likely waiting for the evening crowd.

"Whatever," Drew replied, picking up his glass, drinking the last of the amber liquid, and ordering another from the barman. "We'll be over there," he pointed, "put it on Mr. Stones' tab," he added. Stone led the way taking his glass, a barely touched serve of neat whisky, with him.

Once they were seated, and the beer had been delivered, Stone told Drew what he needed, what his problem was. The large man listened intently. As Stone spoke he looked Drew up and down. He was a man of around 196 centimetres tall, approximately in his mid-thirties, with a huge bull neck, bald, and with hands that looked like saucers. Just below the collar of the white polo neck shirt that he was wearing, Stone could see a series of tattoos. He guessed that there were more across the man's body, but he didn't want to speculate. Drew also wore a long shiny leather coat that nearly touched the floor when he was standing, dark blue denim jeans, and sensible black shoes.

"What do you think?" Stones asked once he had finished what he wanted to say. He had been careful not to give too much away. What he needed was for his tormentors to be caught. He didn't need them to be injured or worse. He had heeded Wingrew's comments. He also didn't want to let Drew know that a car boot with 300K worth of Kruger Rands inside it, was what he needed protecting.

"And that's all you want? Nothing else?"

"That's right, nothing other than I explained."

"Why not?" Drew asked.

"As I said, these people are trying to extort money from me, and I just want them dealt with."

"Why didn't you just get the police involved?" A sensible question.

Stone had been ready for it and replied without hesitation. "Because I want to keep my name out of it. If you start going public, then people start to pry. Even the police look for things that are not there. They go digging in places you don't want them to go," he lied, "and before you know it, someone else tries the same thing."

Drew stared into Stones' eyes. He was dubious. He had heard the lies many times before. Stone didn't flinch.

"Why?" he asked

"Why what?"

"Why is someone trying to get money from you?"

"To be honest, it's none of your business, but if you must know I think it's a former employee, a disgruntled employee who just wants payback." Another lie.

"Umm…." Drew answered with a non-judgemental response.

"So, is that a yes? You'll take the…the work?"

"Ten thousand." Drew said suddenly, "upfront."

"And for that, you'll…?"

"Deliver you a present…"

"Alive?" he asked, leaning forward so that he could whisper.

"Yes, if you want."

"And if I don't want?" Stone asked, inquisitively, but aware of his discussion with Wingrew.

"That would be Fifty Thousand….per person," Drew answered, noting the expression on Stone's face. "There is a lot more to do in the *latter* scenario, but I won't go into detail," he added, "just that it does involve a number of others and each needs to be paid."

Stone nodded his understanding. He knew that the second option was always available to him, but he didn't want to go down that route yet. It would be a measure of last resort. With luck, the next three days would deliver all they would need. He and Wingrew had runners in thirteen races over the festival. By Sunday they could be out of the mess they were in. If Drew could deliver what he promised and the 300K remained safe, he expected that whoever was trying to rip him off could be *persuaded* to drop what they had been doing and he could settle what he owed himself. It would mean that he and Wingrew would be free of any future obligations. They would be home safe. The nightmare would be over. He agreed to the Ten Thousand and took an option on the Fifty Thousand. The two men then discussed how payment would be made.

CHAPTER 52

The day began brightly. Aintree racecourse was bathed in sunlight from early morning. Dew had settled on the track, the drops of water sparkled in the early morning sun. Some of the runners for the first day of the festival were being exercised, some for subsequent days had already concluded their work. Telside had just finished giving all of Cannon's runners a quick blowout. The horses were being washed down before returning to their stalls for the rest of the day. Telside's mobile phone rang. "Hi Mike," he answered, "are you on your way?"

"Yes, I just thought that I would let you know that I'm in the car, and I wanted to thank you for last night. It was good to hear that you arrived without any problems."

"No worries, Mike. I hope I was able to give you some peace of mind."

"Well in relation to getting there, you did. Absolutely."

Telside chuckled. "Well, if I can give you more good news, the *Titan*, the *Statue*, and *Thunderstruck* have done really well this morning. They seem to have settled in well overnight and ate up everything we gave them."

"That's good to hear," Cannon replied. "I guess we just need to wait now."

"Yep…though it will be interesting to see how the day goes. The weather is expected to get cooler, and some rain is expected during the day. It may affect the going if it sets in later."

"I'd be happy if it softens up a bit. It can only help with the *Titans'* feet, because if it dries out during tomorrow that could affect his chances."

"I think more rain is expected tomorrow actually," Telside replied, "in fact, it could rain every day from what I can tell. It's amazing how quickly the weather changes up here," he added.

Cannon smiled to himself. "Yes, it's always a challenge up there. The weather can be very fickle sometimes. Anyway, I'll see you soon, Rich," he said. "Have a good day and take care. Enjoy the racing." He turned off the hands-free phone and began to concentrate on the road.

The three hours plus drive would give him plenty of time to ensure that he got his mind right. There was so much to unravel, and he needed to ensure that he had everything clear in his own mind.

He would call Michelle when he arrived in Liverpool. In the meantime, he decided that he would call Cassie. Apart from wanting to hear how she was, he had an important favour he needed to ask of her. He would put the radio on when he had the chance, to listen to the broadcast from Aintree.

"The *Instructions* stated that they would tell us which car to use, do we know which one yet?" Wingrew asked.

"No," Stone replied. "But they had better hurry up and tell us."

"Do you have the coins?"

"Yes, I do, and the bags. They are in my office."

It was just after 10 a.m. and Wingrew was calling from the Aintree racecourse. The crowds were already beginning to roll in. Cars, buses, and the larger horse boxes of trainers whose stables were closer to the track could be heard around the area. Horns screeched, people shouted and the hustle of the organizers, on-course announcers, and those with concession stands all added to the general cacophony of sound. Had Wingrew not been in the relative quiet of the stabling area, then it would have been very difficult for Stone to hear him. He had a busy day ahead and a crucial one too. If their plans were to work, Stone needed to do make the right investments and Wingrew needed to get the right results. Over the next 3 days, both their futures depended upon it. The difference between their success and failure would come down to the risks they were prepared to take. In addition, many questions still needed answering. Who was it behind the voice on the phone messages? How much did they really know about the situation that he and Stone were trying to get out of? Would they stay quiet after the payoff?

"When do you expect to get here?" the trainer asked, "as ITV have asked for an interview between the first and second race, at around 2 o'clock, and I've got runners in the first, third, fourth, and seventh," he continued. "Two of which are yours..."

"I know," Stone replied, "I hope to be there around 12:30 but I just need to do the *necessaries* first," he said, deliberately being vague.

Wingrew knew what Stone meant. They had managed to work themselves into a position of relative safety without anyone suspecting....at least they had until the threat of exposure had surfaced. If only they could get through the festival and not lose the coins, then he would be happy. Wingrew still didn't like the idea of Stones' friends being involved, but they had come so far......

Tomorrow would be a make-or-break day... get through that successfully and they could both enjoy the Saturday. Stone had a runner in the National itself, but Wingrew didn't believe the horse could win. It would be a step too far to hope that it could. The prize money itself would have helped in part to solve their problem, but sometimes it was better to look elsewhere for a solution...and they had.

They met in the O&T bar. It was crowded, but Stones' profile gave him an advantage in being served by the barmen. They were now standing at a cocktail table, various people nodded at him as they pushed by. Shoulders knocked into shoulders and occasionally a drink was spilled. Suits recently cleaned and pressed, dresses new and recycled, shoes newly polished were all on show. The noise made talking almost impossible. Several TVs throughout the facility showed what was happening around the course, on free-to-air TV as well as the on-course betting status. Wingrew had suggested that they caught up before he needed to disappear for the day. He was meeting the other owners of his runners in races one and four, Stone being the owner of the horses racing in the other two races. Wingrew stood as close as he could to his boss, "Any news?" he asked, his mouth as close as possible to Stones' ear.

"Yes, a voice mail on my mobile. They used an untraceable land line, number withheld. They called when I was between the car park and the course entrance." Stone was almost shouting. A negative. Fortunately, however, with all the noise it was impossible to overhear what he was saying. A positive.

Wingrew frowned. "Do you think someone was watching you?" he asked.

"I'm not sure, maybe, but the message was clear," Stone replied, "but let's not worry about that now. We can discuss it tonight, back at home. For now, I need to coordinate everything with our friends. Let's get through today first. We've got the four races to navigate before tomorrow. I'll see you in the parade ring for race three."

Cannon listened to the races as he drove. There was a mixture of results. Some seemed quite surprising, but some were as he would have expected. Still, it was the festival, and anything could happen.

By the end of the days racing, Stone was getting nervous. Both his horses had done much better than he and Wingrew had expected. One of them had won its' race and the other ran a creditable third in its' particular event.

He had been back at his stables by at least an hour before Wingrew's car pulled up in the visitor's car park. As Wingrew alighted from his seat, Stone came out of the building. The lights inside shone through the blinds adorning the windows, and dark shadows danced on the driveway as Stone was silhouetted against the building behind him.

"Do you know that today cost me Sixty-grand!" he shouted. His anger was obvious as he walked with purpose towards Wingrew.

The trainer stood still. He had expected the tirade and now he was getting it. Even in the greyness of a single spotlight that shone downwards on the other side of Wingrew's car, he could see that Stone's face was ruddy with aggression. Fortunately for them both, there was no one else around in the immediate vicinity. The returning horses were being offloaded at the back of the different stable blocks, so the two men had the parking area to themselves.

"I think we should go inside," Wingrew said, taking Stone by the arm and turning him around, aiming him back towards the door, through which he had come. Stone shrugged himself free. "Sixty Grand!" he repeated, "Sixty!" Wingrew knew why Stone was feeling the way he was, and the trainer accepted the criticism. The plan they had agreed upon was supposed to make the next day less risky. If they had achieved their goal for the day, as they had hoped, the remaining half a million they needed could have been made over the next day or so. Now that they had lost today's investment, without any return, keeping hold of the 300K in gold coins was an absolute must. If they lost that as well, then they were dead…..both of them.

"So, what do we do now?" Wingrew asked.

Stone rubbed his face with both hands. He needed to think clearly. "I've been thinking about it while I've been waiting," he said, "I think I have a solution."

"Which is…?"

"There are two things we need," Stone stated, his anger slowly abating. "Firstly, we need to set a trap so that my friends can take care of our mysterious caller and…."

"What did they say….the caller?" Wingrew interrupted.

"I'll get to that in a minute. The other thing we need to do is to *win* the Topham."

"What?" Wingrew exclaimed. "Are you mad Alex? You can't just *win* a race like that. You of all people know how racing works. There are *no* guarantees…ever, in racing. Plus, the Topham is over the National fences which makes it even more of a challenge."

"Of course I know that," Stone answered, "but with the prize money and a couple of well-placed bets, we can clean up…and we won't have to rely on the National itself. If we win the race, we're home!"

Wingrew was not convinced. "Your horse *Old Yella* is at 18 to 1 currently and there are twenty-five-odd runners, in the race…"

"I know, but do you think he can win?"

"I suppose he could, yes of course, but so can many others…he can do the distance alright, but there are some good horses in the field."

"Okay…just leave that to me," Stone replied, "let me work on it."

Wingrew stayed quiet. He waited for Stone to continue. It seemed to Wingrew that his boss had somehow lost the plot. He had no idea what he was thinking.

"Now, re the other matter…," Stone sat down on one of two visitors' chairs, an Executive chair stood vacant on the other side of a large desk. They were in Wingrew's office. It was extremely well appointed as one would expect for such a senior trainer. The office size was approximately four metres by four metres, and on the walls were framed photographs of some great horses winning big races. Wingrew had never won the Grand National. He had been runner-up twice, but he had won the Champion Hurdle at Cheltenham. He had also missed out in the Cheltenham Gold Cup, finishing third once and then almost winning with the same runner, *Robin Hood,* who fell at the last when leading the race, a few years later. He knew how difficult it was to win races…it was easier to lose…

"What about it?" Wingrew asked.

"I've spoken with my friend. They will be looking out for us tomorrow. All we need to do now is pretend to deliver what our mystery man wants."

"The coins?"

"Yes. Split equally in the two rucksacks."

"And stored in which car?"

"Funnily enough….yours," Stone said, a surprising lilt to his voice.

"Mine?" Wingrew responded.

"Yes…funny that isn't it, Dom?"

"I'm not sure what you mean Alex," Wingrew replied, sinking into his chair, opposite Stone. He felt embarrassed. The heat of emotion reflecting on his face.

"I don't mean anything by it," Stone replied, his eyes narrowing slightly. "I just find it interesting, that's all."

"Me too. Maybe it's because they know my car? Having been able to get into the boot before?"

"Maybe," Stone retorted. "Let's see what happens tomorrow, shall we?"

Wingrew nodded. He tried to see into Stone's eyes, to guess what the man was thinking. Stone maintained a straight face. Wingrew looked at his watch.

"I need to go and check on the horses," he said, standing up again. "Those that ran today and especially those for tomorrow."

Stone stood up likewise, "I'll speak to you again in the morning then?" he said, staring at the back of his trainer, as Wingrew left the room.

They were staying at the Park Hotel on Dunningsbridge Road just a mile from the racecourse. Cannon and Telside were sitting in a small lounge area. It was just before 9 pm and they had enjoyed dinner together in the dining room. Cannon had called Michelle to let her know of his safe arrival and had followed up his earlier call with a second one to Cassie.

"Two in one day, Dad," she had said, "how special is this?" she joked.

"I suppose *very* special," he had replied.

They had spent a few minutes on the phone, Cannon telling her what he needed from her. She had been surprised but was happy to comply.

The noise from the bar was slowly receding. The patrons had been told to keep the noise down and that the bar would be closing at 10 pm. Some of those staying at the hotel had decided to go drinking elsewhere. Others had gone off to their rooms and a few had decided to prop up the place until closing time.

"Do you want a coffee?" Cannon asked Telside.

"No thanks Mike, I think I'll go to bed, it's a big day tomorrow. I want to be up bright and early for you so that we can get to the track. Both the *Titan* and the *Statue* will hopefully do us proud don't you think?"

"I hope so, Rich. They are both ready. If they can replicate their last runs, they could do very well."

"Are you concerned about the Topham? The *Statue* has never seen those types of fences before."

"That's true, but he's a brave horse. He should be able to cope, after all, they only have to jump them once, not like in the National." Cannon thought again of the last time he was at Aintree. The horse he had trained, *RockGod,* was on its way to win the race until its' owner had strayed onto the track in a bizarre attempt to stop it......

"I think you are right, Mike. If Brian Mariner uses his head and rides the race tactically, then there is no reason why the horse shouldn't do well, despite the good quality field."

Cannon smiled. He knew that Rich had done his homework on the other runners. They knew that there were about six or seven other horses that were the potential winners. However, if things went their way, then they could be celebrating by the same time tomorrow.

Cannon was more hopeful that *Titan's Hand* would do the better of the two horses, but time, as with anything, would tell.

In addition, time would also reveal who had been killing the members of the Titan-H syndicate...and more importantly, why?

CHAPTER 53

"I'm on the course now," the voice said. The blind man could hear a babble of voices in the background. "It is still early, so I haven't yet seen *him*, but I did notice that the trainer is here already," the voice continued.

The blind man was both nervous and excited saying, "You need to be careful, I'm not sure it will be as easy as you think. They may set a trap."

"Yes I'm aware of that," the voice replied, "that's why I have been watching their every move. If I see them do anything suspicious I'll let him know."

"Then they'll know you are at the track!"

"That's true, but he doesn't know who he's dealing with, so I could be standing right beside him, and he wouldn't have a clue that it was me."

"If you say so," replied the blind man. He felt his dog at his feet. Soon he would be out of the flat and he and his dog would have a better place to live. He couldn't wait to be free of the shackles of living in such a poor environment. Tomorrow he would be collected. He would stay with the caller until his new place was ready. He tempered his anticipation.

The rain that had fallen overnight had stopped a few hours before. It was breezy now, and it was cool. It wasn't a drying wind and there seemed to be moisture in the air. It was expected that the track would be yielding. A good surface for those horses that liked to race through mud. Rain was expected again later in the day.

Wingrew had left his car where he had been told to. As he departed the parking area and headed into the course proper, he hadn't noticed anyone paying particular attention to himself or his car. He didn't even know if Stones' friends were in place yet or not. As he had entered through the gates the volume of people arriving early for the day was suddenly evident. A mass of humanity was already wandering around the various enclosures. Wingrew was glad he had access to areas that many others did not, but he was beginning to worry that with so many people around, it would be difficult for Stone's friends to follow anyone through the mass of humanity. He wasn't convinced that Stones' trap would work, but he had no choice other than to take things on trust. In addition, he had concerns about Stone and his comment related to the Topham. His boss had not said anything to him about what he was going to do, to try and win the race. He certainly couldn't try and bribe his way to victory. Nowadays there was too much for a jockey to lose if they did take a *bung*. Also, he couldn't see how Stone could influence other trainers not to try and win the race either. Every one of them had their specific owners to answer to. He was reminded that *Old*

Yella was now at 20 to 1 in the betting. The horse had drifted overnight from the 18 to 1 chance that it had been originally. There were at least four horses higher up in the betting, one of which was *Statue of Ramos,* the Mike Cannon horse, and it had firmed into 8 to 1 in the betting.

Thinking of the other horses in the race, reminded Wingrew that Stone had a further interest in the day, that of his ex-charge, *Titan's Hand,* who was running in the main hurdle race of the day. That race was number seven of eight, the Topham, being race six.

Cummings and Peters met Cannon behind the Lord Sefton stand. There were plenty of people on track, but most were congregating between the Queen Mothers' stand and the parade ring. Cannon advised the two policemen that he had asked Harris to ensure that all the syndicate members would be attending the function at the Mercure, St. Helens straight after the race meeting. Cannon had originally anticipated revealing what he knew about what was going on, at the course itself, when everyone would be in the Princess Royal restaurant for most of the day, but he had decided against it due to the public nature of the place. In addition, because the Topham was the race immediately preceding the main hurdle race, he would have found it difficult to be with his horses as well as with the syndicate members. His priority was always with his charges first and foremost.

"So, I'll see you at the hotel?" he said.

Peters nodded. Cannon had given them an overview of his thinking, He knew what he was sharing was still circumstantial and that he was speculating somewhat, but it was enough for both Detectives to agree to stay on course and to keep an eye on the various Titan-H syndicate members throughout the day. Both policemen had acknowledged that they would need help to do so and had enlisted a small army of police, both uniform and plain clothes. Cummings had been instrumental in making the arrangements. Being local he knew which strings to pull and with the promise of an imminent arrest made to the Chief Constable in connection with the Punch killing, he had been given the resources they needed.

Lachie Drew had arranged for four men in addition to himself to keep an eye on Dominic Wingrew's car. He had provided them a photograph of the trainer by forwarding a text that Stone had sent to him. Drew was happy that he hadn't needed to meet Stone on the morning of the Topham. He had been given entrance tickets the night before the race meeting and had left them at a local club house for the other four men to collect at their leisure. Stone had also provided details in the text of Wingrew's car. It included a photograph plus the registration number. All the four men needed to do was stay as close as they could to the vehicle during the day and only allow the trainer access to it. Should anyone else attempt to open the car or the boot then the men were to intercept them and take them to a private place where Drew would meet them. He didn't need to know where the individual would be taken, but he would receive the details when necessary by text, and he would meet them there, in due course.

Drew was curious as to what was in the car boot, but his curiosity was tempered by his commitment to do the job that he was paid to do. He didn't believe in the old-fashioned notion of *honour amongst thieves*, but he did enjoy his freedom. Incarceration was not for him, so he kept a wide berth, where possible, from anything that would directly implicate him in anything nefarious. He was even wary of everything electronic, so he disposed of all smartphones as soon as a specific job had been completed. He knew that a digital footprint was dangerous, so he covered his tracks as soon as he could.

Harris had been sitting alone at the table for at least half an hour. The *sun was already over the yardarm* somewhere, so he had already finished his first scotch by the time Dick Swiftman arrived. The two men shook hands and began to talk about the day ahead. As they did so, both men took turns to gaze through the restaurant window at the gathering crowd, quickly growing in size.

"It's going to be a big day," Swiftman noted, "I believe it's a sell-out."

Harris agreed, "Let's hope it's a big day for us too. I'm really looking forward to *our* race. I understand that Mike is pretty confident with our chances."

"I see his other horse in the Topham has also firmed in the betting," Swiftman said, "what do you think he can do in that one?"

"I'm not sure, but I see that Alex has a horse, *Old Yella*, in the race as well."

"Umm…," Swiftman replied, "not to mention the others, the rest of the field, twenty-three of them to be precise. It will be tough to choose a winner."

Harris said nothing but knew that no matter what horse was running they each had to face the Grand National fences and while they were no longer as daunting as the old obstacles used to be, they certainly created a challenge for every runner. He picked up one of the race cards that dotted the table and opened it at the first race of the day. It was still nearly ninety minutes away. He was about to ask Swiftman which of the runners he fancied for the race when a group of people walked through the restaurant door, their voices causing both men to turn and see who the people were. They noticed Cindy Higgins and Harris waved to her to attract her attention. She responded with a wave of her own, then began walking towards them. Within seconds Tony Clairy walked through the door, just a few metres behind her. Before each had greeted the other, Melanie Freed had appeared, alone, at the entrance. As she looked around, a large group of women, obviously on a hen's weekend, came through the door and gobbled her up, pushing past her, heading towards another table already half-filled with six other women. Harris stood and excusing himself from the table, walked towards the old woman. As he got closer to her, she recognized him and smiled, taking a couple of steps towards him. He smiled in return and reaching her, they shook hands and he thanked her for coming.

"I wouldn't have missed it for the world," she said.

"First time?" he asked, as he led her to the table.

"Yes," she answered, before arriving at the table, greeting the others, and taking a seat.

The table had two empty seats remaining, both of which would be taken shortly. One was for Cannon, the other for Stone.

Alex Stone had used his celebrity status to gain access to several jockeys who were arriving for the meeting. He had focused on those who he felt were riding horses that could win the Topham Chase. He knew that all of them were aware of his runner, and he asked them subtly about their rides for the day. He asked about their views of the course, their view of his own horse's chances in the Topham, and then left each one of them with an understanding of his desire to win the race. He also left them with the thought that he didn't expect any of his other runners throughout the day to challenge for the major prize in their respective races. The meaning was very clear.

He was very careful however to ensure that none of the riders would be able to suggest or prove that he was asking them to lose a race, but his inference was undoubted. He smiled throughout the various exchanges almost making the entire conversation seem like a joke, a wish on his part that his horse would do well in the main race of the day.

Knowing that some of the jockeys were aligned to large stables and other large owners like himself, he knew that most were incorruptible….he then decided to talk with some of the jockeys on those horses with a lesser chance in the Topham. If they could ride interference, then…..

Cannon had left Telside and the rest of his team with the two horses safely ensconced in the stables, awaiting their respective races. He arrived at the Princess Royal restaurant to find that he was the last person to make their presence felt. He apologized to everyone for his tardiness and for being late, but it was soon forgotten as he found himself being bombarded with questions about *Titan's Hand* and the horse's chances in the upcoming race. Cannon gave his best assessment, noting that the rain overnight had improved things for his runner.

"His feet have always been a problem for him, but the softer ground can only do him good," he said.

"Do you think he will win?" Swiftman asked.

"I'm hopeful," Cannon replied, "but as I've said before, there are no guarantees."

"But you're confident?" Stone asked, his interest obvious. The others noticed it too. Before Cannon could respond, Harris said, "How much are you wanting to bet, Alex?"

Stone looked at Cannon. He needed a big win. He didn't want anyone to know just how desperate he was, so he tempered his response. "Just a hundred or so," he replied, looking into Cannon's face. Cannon didn't flinch.

"At 7 to 1," Harris said, "that would be a good bet."

All the others around the table agreed. Stone nodded as well, thinking that if Cannon was so confident in the horse, then he wouldn't be betting just a hundred, he would be betting a few thousand. Twenty thousand to be precise. He needed to take home half a million from the day, as the *old* way wasn't going to help today. That was too difficult to arrange this time. But, if *Titan's Hand* could win and if Stone could win on the Topham plus save his Kruger Rands from being *stolen*, then he could get out of the mess that had plagued him for the past year. He had sought a way out, had asked for six months and he had been given the extension. That extension was due to expire in less than sixty days. The next two days were going to be, make or break.

CHAPTER 54

The earlier races had proved to be a mixed bag of results, and so far not a single favourite had won its race. The form guide had been of no use at all in giving spectators, pundits, and punters any idea as to which horse to put their money on. Stone had taken Cannon at his word and had placed a significant bet with his bookmaker. He had called the man on a private number from his mobile while standing with Wingrew as they had watched their own horse parade ahead of race three. The bet he had made was for *Titan's Hand* to win. He had been given odds of 13 to 2. He had bet Twenty Thousand pounds. If the horse won, he stood to collect 150 thousand pounds in total, inclusive of his own stake. That in itself would go some way to close the gap on the amount he needed. The outcome of race three itself, for which Stones' horse had been the second favourite had given him a boost. The horse had run sixth in a field of eleven runners.

Stone and Wingrew were standing together in the saddling enclosure prior to the Topham Chase. Cannon and Telside were already in the parade ring with *Statue of Ramos*, having saddled up the horse and taken him there a few minutes earlier.

"Have you heard from your friends, yet?" Wingrew asked.

"I made a call earlier, just before the start of the last race, but so far nobody has shown any interest in the car," Stone replied.

"Do you think they will?"

"I'll be surprised if they didn't. Why go to all the trouble of making the demands, if they had no intention of going through with it?"

Wingrew agreed. "I would assume then that they will make some form of attempt in the next hour or so? If they don't, how will they know that we won't be leaving ourselves? Their opportunity to move in will almost certainly have gone."

Stone nodded. He was anxious to get the day over with. If things went according to plan, they could be home and dry by tonight, and the function that Harris had arranged for the evening could be one that they could relax at. "Let's get *Old Yella* into the ring," he said, watching as the horse was led around by his groom.

Wingrew made a small motion with his hand towards the groom and the horse was taken towards the parade ring.

Stone and Wingrew walked together behind the horse. "We have to win this," Stone said, "I'm banking on it."

The trainer looked at his boss. He wasn't confident and the price being quoted by the bookmakers was indicative of the way the betting market felt about their horse. *Old Yella* was now being quoted at 25 to 1. "I hope you have saved your money?" Wingrew said as they stepped into the enclosure. The place was packed with owners, trainers, and officials. Around the edge of the ring, people were standing five deep, a mass of humanity crammed together, full of *experts,* first-timers, and those on the course just for the experience, social or otherwise. Away to the west of the track, clouds were beginning to gather. The foibles of the weather from across the Atlantic and the Irish Sea were beginning to make their presence felt. Dark clouds were looming. The temperature, already cool, was beginning to drop.

Wingrew pointed towards the coming rain. He could sense it on the breeze that had started to strengthen. "If we're lucky, the race will be over by the time it gets here," he said, "but I think the next one will cop it."

"Which can only be good for us," Stone said. "*Titan's Hand* enjoys the mud. Remember his feet?"

Wingrew barely responded. He knew exactly how good the horse was, and when best to run him. Giving the horse away had not been his choice.

A bell suddenly sounded and the jockeys for the race slowly made their way to meet the owners, get their instructions, (which most would ignore), and then climb aboard their mounts. The sight of twenty-five horses, as they circled the parade ring, the brightness of the jockey's silks, and the spring blossoms on some of the trees dotted around the course, made for a spectacular rainbow of colour. The Topham Chase was the highlight of the day for punters. If only the rain would hold off.

Cannon watched through his binoculars as the horses made their way to the start. *Statue of Ramos* had drifted slightly in the betting, but Cannon was still confident. When the horse had paraded, his black coat gleaming in the slowly disappearing sunlight, he had exuded health and fitness. The horse knew why he was at the racecourse, and he seemed to enjoy intimidating the other runners. His huge frame made some of the other runners look small. The favourite, *Its-easy-to-be-me,* had also eased slightly in betting, the extent of the coming rain was the unknown factor affecting where punters were placing their money. The course was already soft and if the rain arrived within the next few minutes it could have a significant impact on the outcome. Some of the horses milled around at the first fence, the jockeys having taken them there to see what lay ahead. Away into the *country,* as the National course was described, a row of intimidating fences stretched out into the distance. The crowd in the stands began to stir as the starter called for the jockeys to take their places, lining up in a single row across the track. Cannon looked again for his owners' colours, checking where Brian Mariner, the jockey, had managed to place the horse. Cannon was pleased, the horse was on the outside, away from the bunch that would likely charge for the inside in a mass of equine and human bodies.

"Do you think Jack is watching?" Telside asked, standing beside Cannon and likewise looking for the colours of their owner down in Ipswich, Jack Swendells. Being a Friday, it was likely that the businessman was stuck behind a desk or in a meeting and unable to follow his horse.

"I'm not sure," Cannon replied, "he did say though that he would try to get to a TV if he could." Telside responded with an "okay," before adding, "Here comes the rain, Mike...perfect for *Titan*."

Cannon lowered his binoculars and smiled. With the increasing moisture on the track, the odds for *Titan's Hand* would soon start to tumble.

The Topham Chase turned into a race of three runners, until the last two furlongs. As expected, those runners who loved a soft and wet surface dominated the others. Before reaching the penultimate fence, Stone's runner, *Old Yella,* had capitulated and ultimately ended up finishing eighth. The loss of the winner's purse was tempered by Stone's astute betting. He was disappointed, but he knew that racing provided no guarantees and as he had done for months he had made alternate investments. He would let Wingrew know later what the return on his investment was. He had known all along that he couldn't really influence the various jockeys he had spoken with, to get them to *pull* their horse or try and bring other horses down by interfering with them, but he *had* tried. Some of the jockeys did appear to take heed of what he had asked, and he was in their debt. He would settle with them in due course. His main focus, however, was still the next race. He had faith in *Titan's Hand,* and he believed that the horse was the meal ticket he needed to get out of his mess.

As the Topham Chase reached its concluding stages, *Statue of Ramos* and an outsider at 40 to 1, named *Winds of Change* battled together in lockstep up the Aintree straight, reaching the final furlong after having raced for over a mile with no more than a head between them.

The crowd roared as the spectacle unfolded before them, the 50,000 plus spectators packed onto the course cheered, screamed, cajoled the two horses as both raced towards the finish line. Cannon watched on the big screen as the jockeys pushed their mounts forward with all the energy they could muster. Tired legs ploughed through the soft grass and mud as the rain lashed down. The jockey's colours were no longer bright but were dull, wet, and covered in the black earth thrown up from the track.

The horses' heads bobbed up and down almost in unison as the finish line edged ever closer. The on-course commentator screeched as his voice reached fever pitch. "It's *Statue of Ramos,* just ahead of *Winds of Change*," he called, "now *Winds of Change* is fighting back. Only 100 yards to go, it's the *Statue*...the *Statue*....50 yards...it's the *Statue* by a nose, *Winds of Change* is coming again.....Oh my goodness, I can't call it!" he shouted, "A photo, it's a photo finish…wow what a race!"

As the cheering died down, applause rang out, the racegoers showing their appreciation for what they had just witnessed. All eyes turned towards the big screen that replayed the finish.

"What do you think?" Cannon asked Telside, as they tried to make their way through the crowd and get to their runner who was returning to scale. Both horse and jockey were soaked through from the heavy rain that was now falling. Cannon was in front of Telside as they moved between the heaving throng that was buzzing in anticipation as they waited for the official result to be announced.

"I think he just missed," Telside said to Cannon's back, who was now a few yards ahead of him. Within seconds of Telside's comment, a huge roar went up from the crowd as the result was posted onto the large screen facing the main stand. The announcer let those on course know, "The official result from race 6, the Topham Chase is, First, number 16, *Winds of Change*, Second….

Both Cannon and Telside were disappointed, but the horse had done its best and the jockey had given everything, including a great ride. Aintree had not been a particularly successful hunting ground for Cannon. He hoped that *Titan's Hand* could change all that.

CHAPTER 55

"Any movement?" Stone asked.

"From what the boys have told me, no!" Lachie Drew replied, "and I'm not sure we'll see anyone either," he added, "it's bloody pissing down and my boys have got no cover at all. They are all soaked to the skin."

Stone didn't rise to the bait. He wasn't sure where Drew was but noted that he hadn't included himself as being wet. "Well, there are only two races left, so something needs to happen soon."

"I bloody well hope so, because the boys are finding it difficult just standing around, waiting. Having said that, we've got a bit of a problem."

"What's that?" Stone asked, intrigued.

"The fucking parking attendants!"

"What?"

"Yep, they keep asking the boys what they are doing hanging around the car park in the rain. I guess they think that my men are checking on some of the cars with an intent to steal them or at worst break-in?"

Stone could imagine the scene. He had hoped that Drew and his men would be discrete, but he now realized that it would have been difficult to watch the car from too far away, especially given the number of people parking in the area. If you weren't close you would struggle to see a single person moving or walking with intent towards Wingrew's car, particularly through the numerous rows of vehicles.

"So, what's the plan, now then?" he asked.

"We give it another hour. Then that's it. The last race will have been run and then the masses will start to leave. I assume you'll be leaving soon after that?"

"Yes, I will. But Wingrew will be leaving a little while later. He needs to make sure all our horses are ready to go back to the stables and he has to get himself ready for tomorrow."

"Okay, maybe whoever it is you are worried about, has decided that it's too risky for them? Would they know that *we* are around?"

"I would hope not, though they may suspect something," Stone stated. He was concerned about the lack of any attempt to approach the vehicle. Was there a game being played? The last thing Stone needed was for his secret to get out. He needed his tormentor to be caught and the Kruger Rands to be back in his safekeeping. Without them, it would be all over.....

"Give it until the last race, if nothing happens then okay call it a day," Stone said finally, ideally hoping to hear something positive from Drew in the next hour or so. The wait was beginning to jar. His nervousness was becoming more pronounced. He knew that his life depended on catching whoever was trying to steal the Kruger Rands from him and needing *Titan's Hand* to win the next race. One without the other would be a disaster.

Cannon had not seen Cummings or Peters again during the day. Since he had left them earlier that morning, it appeared that they had melted into the crowd. He wasn't sure how the Detectives and their men were monitoring the movements of all the Titan-H syndicate members, but he assumed that they were.

After the disappointment of the Topham Chase, Cannon and Telside had put it to one side and had concentrated on getting the Syndicate's horse ready for the next event, the main hurdle race of the day. With the rain continuing to fall, the track was beginning to yield even more. Large clumps of grass had been thrown up by the runners of the Topham and while the track staff had tried to repair what they could it was obvious that the *Titan* would be favoured by the worsening conditions.

Once the formalities had been concluded and the runners for the race had left the parade ring for the start, the Titan-H syndicate members, including Cannon and Stone, returned to the table in the Princess Royal restaurant to watch the race. Telside had said that he would watch from the grandstand so that he could collect the horse and bring it back into the necessary enclosure once the race was over. Cannon hoped that it would be in the number one box. Stone was hoping the same.

The blind man listened to the race on his TV. The result was not important. What really mattered was getting hold of the money that he believed rightly belonged to him. He had no alternative but to wait for the call.

"The crowd has thinned out quite a lot," Harris said, as he looked out through the restaurant window. Gaps, where previously there were none, were evident in the various stands.

"This rain hasn't helped," Swiftman replied, "I think a lot of people have gone home." He looked around at those seated at the table. Most, if not all, had been impacted by the change in the weather. He noticed that Melanie Freed was still wearing her coat. It was spotted with moisture at the shoulders and dark in places from the rain that had skimmed her umbrella as it continued to fall, the wind gusting at times, sending the rain parallel to the ground. Cindy Higgins was dressed as if for Summer, her knee-length floral dress insufficient to keep the rain off her bright yellow shoes. She was in deep conversation with Clairy, almost oblivious to the time. It was three minutes before the race was due to start.

Stone's heart was thumping madly. The race was at the halfway stage and *Titan's Hand* was in fourth place at least seven lengths off the leader. He sat next to Cannon who along with the others watched the race on one of the TV screens in the restaurant. The room was still close to 100 percent full and those within its' confines had the advantage of being warm and dry.

The rain had continued to fall. It was steady but still heavy and a low mist had begun to roll in making it difficult to follow the race. Without the TV it was almost impossible to follow the runners, particularly with the naked eye.

With three hurdles to go, *Titan's Hand* had moved up to the flanks of the leader. The sound from around their table began to get louder as the various syndicate members began to shout encouragement towards their horse. Cannon could see that his charge was travelling well having jumped each hurdle with economy and at speed. The jockey, *HR,* was sitting quietly on the horse's back, just waiting to make his move.

"Go!" Cannon said under his breath, as the *Titan* reached the second last hurdle still sitting in second place, a neck behind the leader. As if by telepathy. *HR* gave the horse a whack with his whip and a kick to the belly and the big roan surged to the front. The crowd on Cannon's table roared with delight as the horse put daylight between himself and the opposition. As each second passed, the horse drew further and further away. With one flight to clear, the horse was now five lengths ahead. After soaring over the last hurdle, the soaked jockey urged his mount on towards the finish line, the colours of the syndicate just about visible on screen, splattered with mud and dirt. Over the next fifteen seconds, the cheers grew louder and louder around the table and Cannon watched with satisfaction as *Titan's Hand* crossed the finish line almost twenty lengths ahead of the second-placed runner. He noticed the relief on Stones' face as the cheers died down. He stood up, smiled, and told the table that he would meet them all in the winner's enclosure in a few minutes.

Titan's Hand was blowing hard. The track going had been downgraded from soft to heavy just before the start of his race and it was obvious from the way the rest of the field had finished that it had been a tough race. *HR* was all smiles as he unsaddled the horse. Telside held the horse's head as the obligatory press photographs were taken. The syndicate members all stood together in the enclosed winners 'circle' safe from the rain, each smiling for the TV cameras as first Cannon, then *HR* were asked to comment on the result of the race. After the jockey had weighed in and the result confirmed the various syndicate members began to disperse, each in turn, saying goodbye to the other, shaking hands, kissing cheeks, and looking forward to the celebratory dinner at the Mercure St. Helens that had been arranged for them.

Cannon found himself alone with Harris. Telside having gone to ensure that *Titan's Hand* was washed down and that his groom settled the horse ready for the drive back to Stonesfield, along with *Statue of Ramos*. It would be a slow trip given the rain and the difficulty in getting away from the course due to the heavy traffic, but Cannon and Telside had discussed their plans earlier in the day, yet Cannon was still worried about Michelle's safety.

"A good day for you, Mike, indeed for *all* of us?" Harris said as they stood under the roof of the winner's stall. There was still one more race to go, *a bumper*, yet the course was rapidly emptying. The crowd was reducing in size quicker than usual. People were making their way home, the rain and the gloom making their stay unpleasant unless they were already intoxicated or had been placing winning bets, in which case staying until the end was preferred.

"Yes," Cannon replied. "I hope you backed him?"

"I did. Just a small one. A hundred pounds each way is my limit, and my share of the fifty-odd Thousand pounds prize money, ten percent, will do me," he said, knowing that it would go some way to get him out of the hole with regards to his underwriting commitment. He hoped that Swiftman would now be persuaded to buy some of the other shares available too. With *Titan's Hand* winning so easily, the Champions Hurdle in Cheltenham the following year would be very tempting. At nearly 200,000 pounds to the winner, it would be a worthy proposition, he thought.

Cannon nodded. "A sensible amount," he said. He was always pleased to see happy owners. He as a twenty percent owner of the horse was also a beneficiary of the victory. Michelle had been right. Buying into a horse that he was training, brought additional benefits in addition to the training fees. He was glad that he had listened to her.

Harris indicated that he was also about to leave. "So, I'll see you at about seven?"

"Yes, I'll be there. Though I'll need to leave around ten-thirty at the latest," Cannon answered, "I have another horse, *Thunderstruck*, racing tomorrow and I will need to be here nice and early. With it being the big day, Grand National day, a crowd of around one hundred Thousand is expected and the traffic will be much worse than today."

"If it continues raining, then I'm not sure how they are all going to fit under cover," Harris replied, looking at the sky, the angry clouds continuing to dispense their load.

"That's true," Cannon replied. "If it carries on overnight, I may even need to scratch the horse. If it's too wet the horse won't run. I don't want him to injure himself or have a jockey hurt either. Both could easily fall in very wet ground," he added. He still had to face the inquiry about Ray Brollo, plus attend the young rider's funeral, which would only take place once the coroner released the body to his family. Another fall, causing an injury or at worse death, was something he didn't want on his conscience again.

"Very well," Harris replied, "I'll be on my way then. I'll see you later."

With that, he placed a hand on his head, to act as a quasi-umbrella, and ran in the direction of the car park. Cannon watched him go, disappearing into the diminishing crowd as people headed in the direction of the course exits. Cannon smiled as shoes splashed through the various puddles. He saw some others, men and women, holding their shoes in their hands as they danced their way through the water. The on-track announcer said that there were still ten minutes until the off.

Cars were moving in all directions. The once straight lines were now haphazard. Horns blared and windscreens previously steamed up slowly cleared as air-conditioners did their job. The car park attendants struggled in the rain to keep order. Near misses due to impatient drivers and some that were clearly over the legal limit, being intoxicated, made it very difficult at times. The now nearly black sky still continued to drench the area. Drew's men were constantly moving, trying to keep an eye on Wingrew's car. It was almost impossible. They needed to dance between moving cars, people walking in front of them obscuring their view, and they had to contend with the persistent rain. They had spent hours watching people come and go. Their motivation was waning as the day turned into night. The rain and cold was seeping into their bones. Finally, the call came from Drew. It was time to abandon the exercise.

"I've called my men off," Drew said into the mouthpiece of his mobile, "nothing happened," he concluded.

"Okay," Stone replied. "Thanks anyway. I appreciate the help."

Drew concluded the call. He and his men deserved a drink and a meal. There was a *Harvester* close by…..

"I will see you back at our place," Stone said to Wingrew on his phone. "It seems like it was a hoax. My friends have left now," he advised.

"Okay, I just have a few things to do here," Wingrew replied, "I need to ensure the horses are securely boxed and settled before their trip home. I should be there in about an hour."

"That will be perfect. We can go together to the Mercure," he went on. "I guess our mysterious caller has *bottled it*. Let's hope that's the last we hear from them. All we need now is a good run tomorrow and we are home."

Wingrew knew what Stone was referring to. His two runner's the next day, were both high up in the betting. If the rain continued it would be even better, he thought.

"Fine. See you shortly," he said.

Stone was already changing out of his wet clothes when the phone rang.

It was Wingrew.

"Are you on your way?" Stone asked. For a few seconds, there was nothing but silence in response.

"No, I'm not," Wingrew replied. "In fact, I'm not going anywhere at this stage…the car…"

"What about it?" Stone replied.

The answer froze his blood.

"It's gone!"

CHAPTER 56

Stone was beginning to panic. The theft of Wingrew's car along with the gold coins was devastating. He was beside himself with anger and fear. The call from Wingrew was the last thing he needed.

"How the fuck is that possible?" he asked.

"I don't know," Wingrew replied, "I have absolutely no idea. I thought your *friends* were all over this?"

Stone was unable to respond. He was speechless, an ugly feeling inside him was beginning to ripple through his very being. His mouth was dry, his palms began to itch, and beads of sweat had begun to form at his temples. He needed to calm himself down, find a solution. His mind reeled, thinking, contemplating, calculating. Finally, he said, "Get back here as soon as you can, we need to talk, we can still get through this," he continued, "but we'll need to take the biggest gamble of our lives," he added ominously.

"And how do you suppose I get there?"

"I don't know, call an *uber* or something, but get back quickly. We've got to get out to the Mercure, or they'll be wondering where we are."

"Isn't the gold the most important?" Wingrew asked, "Finding it?"

"Yes, it is, but at this stage, I don't think we have a hope in hell of finding it. We don't even know who stole the car. It could have been *anyone*."

Wingrew grunted a response. He wasn't sure if there was a hidden implication in Stones' words. Did he hear Stone suggest that he, Wingrew, was the possible thief? After all, only the two of them knew about the gold. Did Stone not believe that the car was stolen? He only had Wingrew's word for it. He had no other evidence and Drew had said that the car was still there when he and his boys had left. All these thoughts crossed Wingrew's mind. He felt unsettled.

"What about the police?"

"Are you fucking mad?" Stone answered. "What are we going to tell them? That we lost over Three Hundred Thousand pounds worth of gold coins that we left in the back of a car to pay off someone who was blackmailing us?!"

"I just thought.."

"Don't be bloody stupid, Dom, we need to sort this out ourselves."

Wingrew stayed silent for a few seconds. He couldn't believe the mess he was in.

"I'll get there as soon as I can," he said.

Stone called the number.

"You fucked up!" he said, "I thought you were supposed to be keeping an eye on that car?"

"The boys didn't see a….."

"I don't care. Find it!"

He pressed the button terminating the connection.

CHAPTER 57

Cannon had met with Peters and Cummings an hour or so earlier. The two policemen had agreed to let Cannon address the syndicate members before they would act themselves. If Cannon was right, then it would be easier for everyone. At the request of Peters, Cannon had agreed to call Peters' phone surreptitiously so that the policemen could listen in on the conversation. They would be waiting in one of the hotel rooms. They would move to make an arrest once it became clear that Cannon's theory was proven correct. It was an unusual approach, but the challenge of trying to prove multiple murders without specific and direct evidence was a risk worth taking. Even if there was no confession, but there was an acknowledgement, then the police would have something more concrete to go on. At this stage everything was speculative. Cannon was hoping that he was right. If he was wrong then he would likely lose in several ways. He would lose the syndicate. He would lose the horse and more importantly, he would lose credibility. There was a lot on the line.

He called Michelle. She was aware of the horse's success having watched the race on the TV. She was sorry that she couldn't be with him, but he promised her that he would be home the next evening, Saturday night, though it would be late if he decided to run *Thunderstruck*. He would consider whether to do so once he knew what the weather was like the next morning.

He told her to be careful. He believed that he knew who had been prowling around the yard and had attacked Cynthia, but he wanted her to be vigilant, nonetheless. He had worked out what had happened, and his earlier phone call had confirmed how things could be done. He just needed to ensure that he was able to get the confession.

He told Michelle to text him if anything happened during the evening. With Peters and Cummings waiting to hear his theory play out, Cannon hoped that should anything happen down in Stonesfield, the two detectives would be in a position to make calls to the local police to get them out to the yard as quickly as possible.

"Yes, text me," Cannon had said to her. "It will probably be better than calling. With all the talking going on, I may not hear the phone ring, but with a text, the vibration will be easier to get my attention."

He hadn't wanted to tell her the real reason why she should text, that he would be using the phone secretly as an open channel to Peters.

Michelle had told him not to worry and had wished him a good night.

"A fantastic day," Harris said, patting Cannon on the shoulder. He was holding a small glass in his other hand, with which he pointed towards the rest of the syndicate members who were busying themselves at the private buffet bar. Food was being served by the hotel staff to their happy guests, each of whom was choosing what to eat from the various dishes available before returning to sit at the table bedecked in the syndicate's colours of grey and red. Red streamers stretched themselves amongst the maze of glasses, crockery, and cutlery laid out neatly across the table. Light grey serviettes with red flecks were folded into various animal shapes, a different design seated on a side plate at every place setting. "You must be extremely happy with how things went, Mike?" Harris continued. He hadn't stopped gushing about the win since the race had finished. Cannon noticed the slight slur in his voice.

Cannon nodded. "The horse couldn't have done any better," he said, for the umpteenth time.

Harris took a swig of his drink, emptying the glass. "I think I'll get another," and he walked over to where two hotel employees were acting as the room barmen for the night. Cannon watched him go. Once everyone had eaten, Harris was expected to make a short speech and then they would be free to enjoy the rest of the evening. It was at that point that Cannon planned to step in. He made his way to his nominated seat and joined a conversation with Swiftman and Mary Freed. He noticed Clairy and Higgins were deep in discussion, totally oblivious to the rest of the group. Aware that everyone was now eating, Cannon decided to join them. As he stood to make his way to the buffet, the door to the room opened and Stone and Wingrew entered. Stone smiled, hiding his concerns. Wingrew remained stoic. The two men had discussed a way out of their mess as they had driven to the hotel. Realistically it was highly unlikely that Wingrew's car had been stolen by someone acting randomly, and that being the case, Stone hoped that the nightmare as far as the blackmailer was concerned was over. That whoever it was, had achieved their objective, that they had what they had come for, and they would now disappear…forever. Both men knew that such thinking was a gamble, but if the blackmailer continued with any further threats Stone would throw everything he had to track them down and ensure that they would pay the ultimate price for crossing him. He would try to find out who they were, anyway. He wouldn't give up, but he needed to address his short-term problem first. Once that was resolved, he would refocus his efforts on finding his nemesis. In the interim, the following day, Grand National day, was his main focus. He had no alternative.

"Glad you could make it, Alex...Dominic," Harris said. "Please, grab a drink, have something to eat. It's a night of celebration."

"Thanks, Brendon," Stone answered, "we most certainly will." He turned to Wingrew, facing away from the group. His impression showed one of disdain for Harris. Cannon watched them closely, the body language of Stone was not lost on him. Wingrew could also not hide how he was feeling.

The two men eventually settled themselves down at the table, drinks charged and their dinner plates full. Cannon now seated with Harris and Swiftman continued to watch the room dynamics. The more he observed, the more his view about what was going on, solidified. Over the next half an hour, the room began to get louder. The laughter increased as the volume of liquid in the various glasses decreased. Cannon had moved to drink water after he had finished his first and only glass of a red cabernet. Tomorrow was the biggest day of the year for the general public with regards to jumps racing and he still had a runner on the card to look after.

It was just after 9 pm when Stones' phone rang. He excused himself from the table, then left the room, taking the call in the outside foyer. It was Lachie Drew.

"We found it," Drew said, his voice angry. The original loss of the car had wounded his pride. Having to *jump* because Stone had said so, had displeased him.

"Where?" Stone replied.

"About ten miles from the racecourse, at the Huyton Golf club."

"How did you...? Hey.....wait a second," Stone stopped himself. He suddenly realized what Drew had said, the implications. "Did you say the Huyton Golf club?"

"Yes."

"Near the safari park?"

"More or less, yes."

"Bloody hell!" Stone exclaimed, realizing the implication.

"What do you mean?" Drew asked, noting that Stone seemed to be somewhere else. "Don't you want to know about the car?"

"Yes, yes, sorry. My mind was reeling. Tell me about the car and how did you find it in just a few hours?"

Drew smiled inwardly, congratulating himself. His response, smug, self-promoting. "Friends," he answered. "I've got lots of friends...all over the place. I put out a request, and well, we found it. Parked in the golf club carpark, in the furthest corner, away from the strongest lights. Whoever had dumped the car hadn't closed the boot properly in their haste and the light was still on. It was a dead giveaway. It was easy for my guy to spot."

"Your guy?

"I have a *few* people who owe me a couple of favours," Drew answered.

"Security guards, barmen, drivers, green-keepers," he laughed, "and with a few texts to all or some of them, it's amazing how quickly you can get access to people and get results."

Stone didn't doubt it. He began to feel a little uncomfortable. He hoped he hadn't crossed the line when he had castigated Drew. He tried not to show it in his voice. "So, the boot was empty?" he said, already knowing the answer.

"Yes."

"And no sign of anything left behind by whoever stole the car?"

"No."

Stone thanked Drew for his help. He offered the car as an additional payment for Drews' services, but Drew declined it. He told Stone he would be sending his bill shortly. Stone dared not ask about the fee. He had enough to worry about.

Once he had terminated the call, he pondered on the information he had just received as he re-entered the room. The Huyton golf club was only 5 miles from the hotel. Everyone who was expected to attend the get-together was already there. He and Wingrew had arrived a little later than they should have, and everyone else was present. Given the car was taken near the end of the days racing at around 5 pm, to drive it from the course, dump it at the golf club, transfer the coins into another car, and get to the function before he and Wingrew did, was possible, but would be very tight in terms of the timing. If it was someone in the room who had stolen the car, then they were unlikely to have had time to change clothes from those that they were wearing at the track. His mind raced. He looked around the table checking to see what people were wearing. He spotted what he was looking for. Could it be…? Given what the unknown caller claimed they knew about him and Wingrew, and what it was said that they were involved in, was it possible that the blackmailer was staring him in the face? Was it coincidental that the car was dumped just a short drive away, close enough to take the coins and put them into another car and then drive on to the hotel? A multitude of thoughts raced through his head. The more he considered them, the more he began to believe that he was on the right track. He needed to let their tormentor know. He needed to get the coins back. His life depended upon it.

Harris tapped an empty glass with a dessert spoon. The conversation in the room slowly died down. Stone had earlier taken Wingrew to one side and filled him in on the conversation with Drew. In addition, he had shared his theory about those in the room. Wingrew was not convinced.

The Chairman tapped his glass a final time, then stood up from his seat.

"Ladies and Gentlemen," he started, sounding somewhat pompous, and a little drunk, "if I could have your attention, please?"

The room fell silent, his audience attentive. He looked at everyone's face in turn. He was a happy man.

"I just want to take a minute to thank you all for coming tonight, and for sharing in the success of *Titan's Hand,* given his magnificent win today."

He turned to Cannon and raising a glass from off the table, offered a toast to the trainer. The room collectively joined in the tribute to both Cannon and the horse.

"One final comment, if I may," Harris continued, "before I take my seat? ....When we started on this journey with Mr. Cannon, just a relatively short time ago, we had a number of fellow syndicate members who are sadly no longer with us." He looked around the table then focused on Wingrew. For a few brief moments, their eyes met, Wingrew sat uncomfortably in his seat. Harris continued with his speech. "It's been a difficult time for all of us and as guarantor to the syndicate I have found the past few months extremely difficult on a personal level," he looked at Swiftmann, "but I'm pleased to say that today's success has resolved that matter."

Stone stared at Harris. The words used by the Chairman seemed to have implications, hidden references. Stone would follow his instincts and confront the man once the formalities were over.

"So, in conclusion," Harris continued, "I want to dedicate the win today, and hopefully our future successes to those who are no longer with us. Thank you." With that, he raised his glass and asked the table to join him in a final toast. As the group did so, Cannon took the few vacant seconds to dial Peters' number from his phone that he had secreted on his lap. He then placed the phone face up onto the table. The screen on the phone went dark, but Cannon knew that the connection had been made. The line was open. Peters and Cummings were listening in. Unfortunately, even though they had other smartphones with the facility, they could not record what they were hearing as it would not stand up in court. The listening in was a means to an end. They were relying on Cannon to get the information they needed. If things went as hoped, an arrest was possible. If it didn't, then a killer could walk away from the room.

The last of the murmurs after Harris' toast were dying down. Cannon knew that he had to move immediately. If not, the group had the potential to begin to break up, disperse, call it a night. Cannon himself had an early start. He couldn't wait any longer. He tapped a glass to get everyone's attention. As silence descended, like Harris, he stood up from the table, then he began to walk around it, circling the group like a shark. All eyes were trained on him. He wasn't sure what the group was expecting him to say, but he knew that the message he was about to give, was not going to be received well by any of them.

"What I am about to say will shock some of you," he said, "but some of you will know my story *already*. Why? Because what I am going to share, is that the person who killed those that Brendon has just referred to.....is actually *in this room*."

As Cannon spoke the last few words, the room suddenly erupted with the sound of confused and angry voices. "What the..?" Harris shouted.

"Explain yourself!" Swiftmann called.

"Who? What?" Melanie Freed said, sounding confused.

Stone and Wingrew stayed silent. Stone realized that if Cannon was right, then maybe his nemesis would be *outed* for him? Perhaps the solution to what had been going on would be put on a plate for him?

Cannon put up both hands requesting the group to give him a chance to speak. Once he had their attention, he asked the bar staff and those manning the buffet table to leave the room. "It's a private matter, not a public one," he said, "so there is no need for anyone outside of the syndicate, other than Mr. Wingrew here, to be present." He took a glance towards his phone still showing a dark screen, still facing upwards on the table, hoping that Peters could hear what was being said. He continued to walk around the room, finally stopping at his chair which stood away from the table. Once the hotel staff had left the room, he said. "So, where to start? Well, I guess it's from the beginning. So let me start there." The room was deathly quiet, the silence almost intimidating. "The first question that needed answering was *why Titan's Hand* was sent to me to train? The answer was difficult to find, but once I had worked it out, everything else seemed to flow from there. It was the key to the door, a door that opened to murder."

"Hang on," Swiftmann interjected, "are you suggesting that because we decided to move the horse to you, that caused people to be murdered?"

"Yes," Cannon replied, "but only indirectly....let me explain."

"I should bloody well hope so," Clairy said. "It all seems a load of bollocks to me. People being killed over a horse?" he exclaimed. "It's unbelievable!"

Cannon nodded in agreement. He could see how someone like Clairy could find the idea strange. However, the truth was often more bizarre and complex than anyone could ever imagine.

Cannon continued. "Let's look at the horse first," he proposed. "You have seen how good he is. So why did he run so badly in the past? Why was he so inconsistent?"

There was a murmur in the group. Cannon looked towards Wingrew, who knew what was coming. He then looked at Stone, who remained statue-still, his face unmoved.

"The reason is quite simple, and I'm sure Mr. Wingrew and Mr. Stone already know the answer, don't you?" Cannon said, pointing towards the two men seated next to each other. All eyes turned to stare at them.

"I don't know what you mean," Wingrew said.

Cannon smiled. "Oh, but you do, Dominic."

Stone jumped in to defend himself and Wingrew, "Mr. Cannon, I'm not sure where you are going with this...this innuendo, but I must admit to being confused. How does moving *Titan's Hand* to your yard link to murder? And what do Dom and I have to do with it?" he said with a sense of bravado. "I mean even the police have cleared us of what happened to poor Fred Punch, and regarding the others, Sarah Walters and Peter Brown, we had nothing to do with that either."

Like a tennis match, the group turned back to Cannon, waiting to hear his riposte to that of Stone.

"Birmingham," Cannon said, leaving the word hanging in the air.

"Birmingham?" Clairy echoed, "what does that mean?"

"It's where it all came together," Cannon responded. "A simple sign, on the motorway when I was on my way to Nottingham. Without even thinking about it, the sign on the side of the road confirmed what I already knew, and with that, everything clicked into place."

Harris added to the chorus of confusion, asking Cannon to clarify what he meant.

"As I said, *Titan's Hand* was inconsistent before he came to me, but as you know he is a very good horse. So, the obvious question was, why? The answer itself is quite simple."

"And....?" Harris asked.

"He was being run the wrong way?"

"Wrong way?"

"Yes," Cannon continued, again looking towards Wingrew. "You see, when I began training him I noted how he was feeling his feet. How sensitive he was to the going and the pressure he was enduring when he landed from his jumps or when he went into a turn."

"Which meant?" Harris responded, believing he was talking for the rest of the syndicate members.

"Which meant that he has a preferred way of racing."

"I'm still not with you," Harris replied, his face contorted in confusion.

Cannon sighed slightly. He knew the explanation was necessary, but he had hoped that it would be much simpler than it was turning out to be.

"The horse likes to run counter-clockwise, on left-handed courses. All his wins were on such tracks. All his bad runs were on right-handed tracks. Today he was running left-handed, and he won easily. When I saw this during the first few training sessions, I made a mental note but wanted to test the theory. We did have a bad run at Ludlow, which is a right-handed course, and then his run at Haydock proved my point."

"Which proves murder?" Melanie Freed asked, her voice thin, but clear.

"No," Cannon responded, "but it proved to me that something was going on."

"And that being..?" Dick Swiftmann asked.

"That the horse and other horses were being used."

"To do what?"

Cannon looked at Wingrew, who turned his head away.

"Well, given it would have been impossible for Dominic not to know about *Titan's Hands'* quirks in racing, as he is a good trainer, I started to look at other results over time. It soon became obvious that some of his horses that should have won didn't and some who should not, did. So that got me thinking. Why? The more I thought about it, the easier it became….they were betting against their own horses."

Wingrew looked at Stone who shook his head slightly, suggesting to Wingrew not to rise to the bait.

"Including *Titan's Hand*?" Clairy asked.

"Yes, especially when he was running on the wrong track."

"The bastards!" Clairy continued.

"So, the question, of why, still needed answering," Cannon continued, ignoring Clairy's outburst, "and for that I needed the police to investigate something for me. What they uncovered, only confirmed the theory."

"Which is what?" Stone asked some sarcastically.

"That you were in trouble financially. That you were in debt. The cost of building your training facility, the barns, the visitors centre, the cost of running it, the staff costs, etcetera, far exceeded your income. In addition, your gambling habit had resulted in debts owed to bookmakers and they were calling in their loans. The police also found out that the banks had refused to lend you any more money as you had used up all the equity in the place and that you had borrowed almost Thirty Thousand pounds from a local drug dealer, an *ICE* importer, a racketeer. A friend of yours I believe. From your football days?"

Cannon stared at Stone, who didn't flinch despite their eyes meeting. He continued with his commentary. "I think you borrowed that money to gamble with. I think you came up with a plan to bet against your own horses when you knew they wouldn't win. Betting against a favourite and getting good odds on another runner must have seemed like a good way out of the mess, didn't it? And you have been doing it for months now, haven't you?"

Stone smirked. "It sounds like a good story, but you can't prove any of this, plus what does it have to do with the murders? Explain that!"

Cannon had anticipated the comment. He was also aware of how careful he needed to be with his language. Peters had to be fully convinced before the police would act.

"The answer to that is again quite simple," Cannon lied, "someone else knew what you were up to, and must have been putting pressure on you. Maybe blackmailing you? Both of you? Making you pay to keep them quiet. Keeping your secret safe," he said pointing at Stone, then at Wingrew in turn.

"And how did you conclude that?"

"I didn't," Cannon said, "but the police did. They've been investigating you for the past few weeks, watching. The final piece of the puzzle was a recent purchase of 300,000 pounds worth of Kruger Rands." Wingrew flinched, a tick at the corner of his left eye began to flicker. "The dealer let the police know about it as it was a very unusual transaction and done very quickly. The fraud squad did the rest, asking the obvious question, why? The answer being, *to pay someone off*, someone who knew what you were doing."

"All of which is very fanciful, Mr. Cannon, but again how does what you've just said relate to the murders of Walters and Brown?"

"The pay-off," Cannon replied. "Whoever was blackmailing you, wanted the money for a specific reason."

"Which is?"

"I'm not sure, but it seems to me that they wanted you to suffer. Perhaps they knew about your financial situation and wanted to make life more difficult for you, for something you had done? Payback perhaps?"

"There are several guesses in that comment, Mr. Cannon, all of which are just that, empty guesses," Stone replied.

"Very well Alex, if that's the game you want to play, we'll let the police decide when to show you their evidence. I suspect it will be very soon."

Wingrew was becoming concerned. He felt that Cannon knew more than he was saying. The comments to date were getting too close to the bone. He could see his future disappearing. Racing a horse with an intent to lose not only affected his status as a trainer but would result in a lost livelihood, possibly even lost liberty. The murders also concerned him, he was afraid that he and Stone would be charged with those as well.

"You are right, Mike," he said softly.

Stone looked at him, daggers flashing in his eyes, an attempt to stop Wingrew from talking.

"Go on," Cannon encouraged. He knew from his days in the police that once someone breaks, the dam often overflows.

"It's as you said. We *were* the subject of blackmail, and we *were* in financial trouble, so we tried a number of things to get out of the mess."

Stone could not contain himself. His standing as a successful racehorse owner, former England soccer player, and all that brought with it, was about to go down the drain if Wingrew cracked. "Shut up Dom," he said, "say nothing. It's all a guess. They have nothing, he's speculating!"

Cannon and the others were surprised by the extent of the outburst. The room became deathly silent, like a graveyard at midnight. All eyes were on Wingrew who stared downwards at the table. Eventually after what seemed like minutes but was merely a few seconds, Wingrew spoke again, his voice clear but his eyes still downcast. Stone looked horrified but had no way of stopping Wingrew's confession.

"The odd results, the poor runs, the gambles we took, including running *Titan's Hand* and other horses at unsuitable tracks were all an attempt to win back what had been lost. We also needed to build up a fund to pay off someone who was blackmailing us…"

Cannon hoped that Peters and Cummings were taking notes.

"Shut up Dom!" Stone again interjected, grabbing him by the shoulder, but Wingrew shrugged him off.

"No!" he answered, "no more lies, Alex. Enough! What we did was wrong, but I won't be accused of something we didn't have anything to do with… those murders!" He looked at all the people in the room in turn, before focusing on Harris. "I let you down, Brendon. I ran the horse at times knowing that he couldn't win but telling you otherwise."

Harris looked downcast. He was the representative of the syndicate, the de facto leader. It was he, that had introduced Higgins, Freed, Clairy, Brown, and the Punch's to the syndicate. Thank God that he had suggested a move of the horse to Cannon. If not, who knows how things would have turned out?

Wingrew continued to speak. "In some ways moving *Titan's Hand* to Mike here, was a great idea. You can see how well the horse has done since then. Mike is a good trainer, he worked out what was going wrong. I could have told him myself but that would have exposed what Alex and I were doing. It was wrong. I admit that, but we never intended to harm anyone. We just tried to solve a problem. It just got out of hand…"

"Leading to murder," Cannon jumped in.

"Yes, but that had nothing to do with us," Wingrew said, "nothing whatsoever," he pleaded.

"Not directly," Cannon admitted, "but indirectly it did."

Wingrew slumped back into his chair. Stone still full of bravado said, "So what does all this prove, Mr. Cannon, Mike? It seems to me that we still have no idea who killed Brown or Walters or indeed Fred Punch. All you have is Dom's outburst, which frankly proves nothing."

Cannon knew inwardly that Stone was right, but he also knew that the reason for the subterfuge, the need to pay off someone, using something so obscure as Kruger Rands, must have meant that someone close to Stone, knew what was going on. From his previous experience, the ghosts of murders he had witnessed and investigated as a junior policeman, all the way through to when he became a DI, always told him to look closely.

Look to relatives, friends, and lovers as they were often the perpetrators. During his conversation with Peters over the past few days, he realized that the attack on his house and on Cynthia had convinced him that someone in the syndicate was responsible. It had to be. The events seemed to be linked and he had felt that he was getting close to something. He had formed a view in his mind, and he had asked Peters and Cummings to investigate the backgrounds of each of the syndicate members to substantiate his thinking. What they had told him in response to his questions then, allowed him to respond to Stone's statement now.

Before he spoke, however, he looked around the room again. No one had moved since Wingrew had finished his confession. Everyone was still seated, seemingly rooted to the spot.

"Let me ask you a question, Alex," Cannon said. "Whose idea was it to open up the syndicate to more members, to reduce your share for example?"

Stone wasn't sure where Cannon was going with his question, but he answered it anyway, "It was mine."

"Did you explain why?"

"Yes, I told Brendon that I thought it was the right thing to do if a new trainer was to take on the horse."

"Because...?"

"Because we would no longer have the same control over what happened to the horse. Someone else would be making decisions about where and when he raced."

"So, you liquidated part of your shareholding?"

"Yes...so what?"

Cannon ignored the question, asking him, "Did you tell anyone that you needed the money?"

"Not really, no. I told Brendon as the syndicate manager, to see if he could find people to buy into the syndicate....and he did."

"Did you know any of the people before they bought in?"

"No."

"None of the names ring any bells?"

"No...what are you getting at?"

Cannon turned to Harris. "Brendon, when you were finding new members, excluding myself who was buying into the horse as well as training him, did you tell those here, Walters and Brown, who the existing members were? The likes of Alex, *Dick* Swiftmann, Sarah Walters, yourself?"

Harris thought for a second. "Yes, I probably did. I think it was a bit of a selling point. I'm sure Cindy, Melanie, and Tony can speak for themselves, but I'm sure Alex's name was a big plus."

"Did you know that Mrs. Freed and Cindy Higgins knew each other?"

"No, I didn't," Harris said, looking at both women in turn, "what does it matter?"

The room suddenly seemed a little colder. Melanie Freed who was sitting next to Swiftmann pushed a hand through her grey hair. She looked across at Cindy Higgins. Clairy who had been intrigued by what was being said but had looked bored was now suddenly alert.

"It matters Brendon, because three people from the syndicate have been murdered. It matters because of why they were killed, and by whom."

"And you are saying that …?"

"I am saying nothing Brendon," Cannon said. "The evidence is telling me however that it is because Melanie and Cindy knew each other, that the blackmail and the murders took place."

The inference in Cannon's comments caused an immediate cacophony of noise. Stone and Wingrew were suddenly extremely animated, shouting at Cannon to explain himself. Swiftmann was suddenly asking Freed about what had been said. Clairy likewise with Higgins. Harris had his head in his hands.

"Quiet please, everyone…quiet!" Cannon shouted above the noise. He needed to regain control, for his sake as well as those trying to listen in on his phone. It took fifteen seconds before Cannon could speak again. Once the room was still, Cannon continued.

"What was concerning me originally, was why Walters, then Brown were killed, especially so soon after Punch's death? It didn't make sense until I realized the only connection was this group of people, this syndicate." He waved his arm across the table. "It was only when the police conducted their investigation for me that things fell into place. That the pieces began to fit."

"I'm sorry, Mr. Cannon," Swiftmann moaned "but you are talking so cryptically that you have lost me and I'm pretty sure I'm not the only one. Could you please tell us what's going on?"

Cannon hoped his gamble would work. He had deliberately taken his time. He had deliberately done what Peters had asked of him. They needed a confession. The evidence was still flimsy, but Cannon was skilled enough to pretend that he knew more than he was letting on.

"When we first got together, Dick, you were the only person who didn't explain to everyone what your background was, or what you did for a living."

"I'm retired," Swiftmann replied.

"I know, but it was what you did before you retired that interested me. So, I found out, as I did with everyone else."

"And what did you find?"

"The answers," Cannon replied.

"Please tell us then, Mr. Cannon, and let's have less of the games," Clairy asked sarcastically. "We are all ears."

Cannon nodded. He had been here before. "When Sarah Walters was killed in Birmingham, an individual was seen escaping from the building then climbing into a car and leaving the area. That car was found a few days later, miles away from Birmingham, having been driven for hours before being dumped. That got me thinking. Why? Then when I found out about Mrs. Freed and Cindy here, the answer was as clear as day."

"In what way?" Swiftmann asked.

"Blackmail, jealousy, and ultimately revenge," Cannon said.

"For what?" Swiftmann again.

"For what *you* did….actually, for what you *didn't* do."

"Uh?"

Cannon decided it was time. He knew that the guilty parties would have listened to what he had said. He was now hoping that he had hooked them and that he could reel them in. "You used to be a soccer referee a few years ago, were you not, Mr. Swiftmann?"

"Yes. I was lucky enough to referee at the highest level, but I also worked in the lower leagues as well. The Premiership, League One and others."

"And the name Higgins means nothing to you?"

"No, should it?"

"Yes, it should. Because Paul Higgins was a player in a match you refereed. A match in which Alex Stone also played in." Cannon looked towards Cindy Higgins. He noticed her eyes beginning to tear up slightly as he spoke. "Do you recall that game? A FA Cup third-round match? Stones' Premier League side against a non-league side?"

"No. Should I have?"

Cannon transferred his gaze to Stone. He could tell that Stone's mind was racing, trying to remember what Cannon was getting at.

"It was a game where you made a decision. A decision that indirectly led to the deaths of Brown and the others."

"What?!" Swiftmann said, incredulously.

"Yes, a decision not to send off a player who had committed a bad foul, a decision that ultimately resulted in that very player being viciously elbowed in the face. He was ultimately blinded as a result of that elbow. That player was Paul Higgins. The man responsible was Alex Stone."

"But I refereed lots of games, how could…?"

"And I was cleared of any wrong-doing," Stone jumped in, "it was an accident."

"No, it wasn't!" Melanie Freed shouted. "You did it on purpose, and you ruined a life in doing so."

Stone stared at the old woman. He couldn't believe what he was hearing. Was she their tormentor? It hardly seemed possible.

Cannon's tactics were working. The background he had been able to discover with the help of the police, about each of the people in the room, was paying dividends. He needed to get the meat on the bones. He had the opening he needed. Melanie Freed had given it to him inadvertently. "When we first met, Melanie," he asked, "you said that you had no children and that you were a widow. Is that right?"

"Yes," she answered.

"But you had a brother, didn't you?"

"Yes," she replied, eyeing him suspiciously.

"And he had two children, didn't he?"

"Yes. But what does that matter?"

"Well, from what we have been able to establish, those kids, your niece, and nephew are Cindy and Paul Higgins, aren't they?"

Melanie Freed stayed quiet. Cannon stood and walked towards Higgins, but he continued talking to the old lady. "It's my guess that when Brendon told you about the syndicate and in some way suggested that Alex needed the money, which was why he was reducing his share, somehow, perhaps after overhearing something, you found out about what he and Wingrew were up to, and you decided to try and get back at him."

"They just threw him onto the rubbish heap!" Cindy Higgins suddenly exclaimed. Her outburst, her anger making everyone sit up and take notice. "Just like they did with me!" she added.

Melanie Freed was staring at Dick Swiftmann. "When Paul was blinded, there was hardly any compensation paid. He was effectively left on his own, to fend for himself......dispensed with like an oily rag. Dumped!" she said angrily. "Being a player in a semi-professional non-league team, their insurance didn't provide any sort of cover either. In the meantime," she pointed towards Stone, "*he* was getting all the accolades! Playing for England, earning a fortune, spending money like water on girls, booze, and gambling...and still having money to build up his fancy training operation. It's a disgrace!"

"So, you wanted to get back at him?" Cannon asked.

"I only wanted to get what Paul deserved. A chance...that's all," Freed said, "We weren't asking for much....just enough to ease the pain...but given his arrogance," she said, pointing at Stone, "yes I wanted to make him suffer for what he did to Paul."

"And that drove you to kill?" Cannon asked.

Melanie Freed looked at her hands. They were gnarled, lined, almost talon-like. She raised her face to the group, most of whom were still trying to come to terms with what they had heard so far. They waited for her to speak. When she did her voice was soft, calm, controlled.

"Can you imagine," she asked, "how it feels to be thrown away, treated like dirt, like shit on a shoe that needs to be scraped off? Can you?" she repeated. The empty response told her all she needed to know. "Of course, you don't," she added, "but I do! *We* do!"

Cannon knew that the old lady was ready to tell the full story. He realized that he and others may start to feel sorry for her, but he reminded himself that he was dealing with someone involved in three murders. He needed to keep perspective, and he needed more than he had heard so far. He pressed her to continue. He sensed that when she spoke, her statement would be somewhat cathartic. As if she needed to say her piece that justified her actions. She pointed at Cindy Higgins who was still seated next to Clairy, but now a few feet apart.

"When Cindy had her accident, a toppled pan of scalding water knocked over by a visitor at her home, she lost her modelling career. Like Paul, she was wanted one day, and dispensed with the next. A clothing and swimsuit model with burns and ugly scars to her arms and legs are a no-no," she said. "She was told that her services *were no longer needed*, and overnight she lost her job, her confidence, and her self-esteem. Thrown out with the trash….just like that," she added, clicking her fingers and spitting out the words. "The bastards! To treat anyone like that. To dismiss them both without a *thank you* or a *can we help*? But no, it was just goodbye, au revoir and piss off! It was just disgusting!"

Cannon was beginning to understand the anger Melanie Freed was feeling, but what he needed was a confession to the murders. So far he still had nothing concrete. He had allowed her to carry on talking, but she was rambling at times, and the ghosts from the past were beginning to gather in his mind. We know why they stalked and blackmailed Stone, the ghosts said to him, but *why kill?*

They asked him again….*why kill?*

"A number of people from this syndicate were murdered, in cold blood," Cannon said, looking straight at Melanie Freed. Her eyes, now rheumy, held his gaze. "People who had nothing to do with Paul or Cindy, so why did they have to die? For what reason?" he asked, incredulity in his voice.

"For being smug, for being rude, arrogant, dismissive….just like all the others!" Cindy Higgins said. "Need I go on?!"

The comment from Higgins confirmed what Cannon had expected.

"You mean jealousy?" he asked, his voice vibrating. "What gave you the right…?"

"I had every right!" Higgins shouted, resulting in Clairy moving his chair even further away from her. "I had every right," she repeated. "They were just like everyone else. They dismissed people. They were just like those who threw me away, threw Paul away. You saw how Walters acted when we first met! You saw how Brown ridiculed me as a rep! They are *all* the same. Selfish, money-grabbing bastards!"

She stopped. Her breathing was slightly laboured. She looked around at confused faces that stared back at her. They understood her words but were shocked at the sentiment. Cannon thought for a second, his previous life came knocking on the door of his mind.....

Death had not forgotten what had happened to Paul Higgins. *He* had just come to claim his prize.....these other victims. A prize built on human emotion and the desire to win at all cost! Greed! Trampling on anyone to reach the top irrespective of the bullying or the hurt that occurred along the way. Behaviours that caused the mental health failures that Cannon could see in front of him.

Death didn't need to worry about being forgotten, the living made it easy for *Him*.

Peters and Cummings waited. They continued to listen. They had everything they needed for now, but Cannon had not finished, and they allowed him the opportunity to get the information they needed regarding the death of Fred Punch. It was the last piece of the puzzle. They would make the arrests shortly.

The room was silent. After the confession, the gap in time before anyone reacted was filled with glasses being drunk from. It seemed that suddenly everyone had dry mouths. The scotch, gin, beer was consumed in a flurry of activity. Cannon watched. Cindy Higgins had left her seat and had gone to sit next to Freed. They had embraced each other, crying, sobbing. The men in the room, except for Stone, remained quiet, giving the two women some space. Stone was not so kind.

"So where is my fucking money?!" he shouted. "Where are my coins?!"

Wingrew tried to calm him down, suggesting that Stone give the two women some space. "No," he replied. "We need those coins, Dom. We need to get them back. Where are they?" he shouted at the women again.

Cindy Higgins turned to face Stone. "You'll never get them back," she said. "They are in a safe place. A place where you will never find them."

"You bitch!" Stone shouted, standing up and trying to reach across the table. His hands aimed at Higgins's throat.

Glasses, crockery, and cutlery went in all directions, some crashing onto the carpeted floor, others spinning on the table sending dribbles of liquid onto laps and across the tablecloth. Cannon and Clairy pulled Stone back into his chair.

Harris and Swiftmann stood up before moving their chairs further away from the table. While Stone tried to get his breath back, Cannon reminded him of his own situation. While he was on the end of an extortion plan, he was also guilty, along with Wingrew, of serious fraud. The BHA would not look kindly on their actions, nor would the police. Cannon turned to Cindy. "Why Fred Punch?" he asked.

"I didn't kill him," she replied, "I had nothing to do with that."

"I didn't say *you* killed him. But *you* did, didn't you?" he stated, pointing at Tony Clairy.

The former footballers' face dropped. "What?" he answered, "are you mad?"

"No, I'm not," Cannon replied, "and I know what happened."

"Really?" Clairy said. "Tell me…" a smirk across his face.

Cannon took a deep breath. He had been successful in getting confessions to two murders. He was hoping for a third time lucky.

"Photography," he said.

"What?"

"Photography," Cannon repeated. Clairy looked confused. "You are a Professional Photographer, are you not?"

"Yes,"

"So, you know how to manipulate an image?"

"Using software, of which there are many types, yes of course I do. *Lightroom* is an example and is one of the most popular," he said, "but what does that have to do with me? I'm a nature photographer. That's my job. That's what I do." He looked at Cindy Higgins, his face showing the embarrassment of his lie. He had taken many pictures of her during their trysts. She looked at him with contempt. Here was another man who took advantage of her. Her hatred for him was evident.

"You killed Fred Punch, didn't you?" Cannon said.

"What? What are you talking about?" Clairy replied.

Cannon sighed. It was always this way. Denial, despite the evidence….though in this case it was still circumstantial. "You knew the Punch's didn't you? Before the syndicate opened up to others, you, me, Cindy, the rest?"

"No,"

"Well, I know you did," Cannon replied. "You worked with them as a 'Still's Photographer' on some of their documentaries, didn't you? The evidence is on their film credits. I asked the police to check up on you once I realized the link. The Punch's and you said that you were involved in film and photography. It didn't ring any bells for me until my home was attacked, and my CCTV images messed with, then it all clicked."

"And you think that was me?" Clairy said.

"Yes."

"Well, you are wrong about that, and you are wrong about me killing anyone."

Cannon stayed quiet for a moment. Thinking. He had hoped that it would be easier than this. Suddenly his phone buzzed. Michelle! The phone was still sitting on the table, the line still open to the listening policemen. He had forgotten that Michelle couldn't call even if she had wanted to. She would have received an engaged signal. He picked it up and without losing the line, looked at the message.

'There is someone here. Shadow outside. Security lights came on now gone off. Dare not try to get to the CCTV screen in the tack room. Need to stay inside. Am scared. What to do?'

Clairy waited, fuming, while Cannon typed back an urgent response, *'Call local police. Call Rich. Stay calm'*

He was confused himself now. Worried that he had made a mistake, that he had left Michelle in danger. Then it hit him! How could he have been so stupid? He had been so obsessed with one solution, that he had forgotten the most obvious. It wasn't about Clairy, but it *was* about jealousy. Film, models, revenge, they were all linked.

While Cannon had been responding to Michelle, the room had begun to fill with voices, murmurs. Separate conversations sprang up. Clairy shaking his head and remonstrating with Harris. Swiftmann was angry at Higgins and Freed. Stone was still trying to figure out how to get his money back. Wingrew knew that his career was over. Fortunately, however, he realized that it was Stone alone who would have to answer to his creditors.

Cannon took the opportunity of asking Peters and Cummings to come through to the room. The two policemen were quick to do so. They ensured that there were other resources outside just in case anyone tried to leave. No one did. They made the arrests.

Cannon turned to Clairy. "I was wrong, I thought you were guilty but now I know you're not. I'm sorry," he said. "Though the murder of Punch is still definitely linked to you and Cindy Higgins," he continued. "You may not have killed him, but you *did* set it in motion."

Clairy just stared at Cannon, relieved that he had avoided being arrested, but still devasted to hear that Cindy Higgins, someone he had been sleeping with regularly, was a killer. How close had he been, to being the next victim, he thought? He watched as she and Melanie Freed were escorted out of the room by Cummings. Peters took charge of Wingrew and Stone.

From a full room, only Harris, Swiftmann, Clairy, and Cannon now remained. They sat in silence, the success of the day lost in the midst of what had just been said. Cannon looked at his phone again. There were no more messages from Michelle. Had the police arrived in time?

CHAPTER 58

The door opened slowly. The silhouette, dark, foreboding, stood in the entrance, a large knife held in the right-hand glinting in the cold moonlight. Michelle hid behind the dining room chair. She could see through the gap at the top between the fabric and the frame. Her eyes were now accustomed to the dark, ever since the lights went out. The figure walked slowly into the house, shutting the door behind them. The door had been unlocked because Michelle in her haste to contact Cannon had forgotten to lock it. The cars in the driveway still needed to be unloaded. They hadn't got around to it yet.

"I know you are here," the intruder said, "show, yourself!"

Michelle did not move. She held her breath as the figure began to move slowly around the room. It would only be a matter of seconds before she discovered where she was hiding. As the figure walked around the edge of the dining room table, Michelle shot up from her hiding place, and ran towards Cannon's office, hoping to be able to lock the door. The intruder screamed abuse, chasing Michelle, only a few yards behind her, the knife raised ready to plunge into Michelles' back as she tried to flee.

"Come here, you bitch!" the intruder screamed. Michelle pushed over the chair at the end of the table trying to create an obstacle. It gave her a few seconds grace as she ran down the hall, her pursuer now ten yards behind. Michelle ran past a few open doors heading towards the office, as she did so, she noticed another figure standing just inside one of the doors. She continued running when suddenly a scream rent the air. The intruder fell to the floor. Cassie held the hammer that she and Michelle had taken from the tack room earlier in the night. They had heeded Cannon's warning. Michelle reached for the knife that had skidded along the hallway floor, her hands searching in the gloom. The slumped body lay in the passage and seemed to have cracked its head on the wall after Cassie had struck them from behind, right between the shoulder blades. Thank God Cassie had arrived when she had. They had been talking about the *wedding* plans when they had been alerted to an intruder. They hadn't even had time to remove Cassie's suitcase from the car. Michelle knew that Cannon had been cautious and asking Cassie to spend the night at the yard while he was in Liverpool was a sensible idea. One which now proved to be life-saving.

The figure lay prostrate. Cassie went outside to turn the power back on and then in turn, switch on all the lights in the hallway and the rooms that ran off it. She realized that if the figure roused from their unconscious state the bright lights would confuse them for a few seconds at least. As she moved from each room, she told Michelle to lie across the legs of the figure to keep them still if they awakened. Finally, Cassie came back into the hallway holding some string twine that she had found in a kitchen drawer. They pulled the arms back of the now reawakening figure and began tying them together. As they did so, they could hear a couple of cars pulling up outside the house, headlights and blue lights flashing. They heard Rich come through the front door, calling out to Michelle. Shortly behind him, two policemen followed. Just as the men entered the house they saw Cassie and Michelle frog-march the intruder from the hallway, Cassie holding a large knife in a small hand towel to protect any fingerprints left on the handle. The intruder raised its head from sagging shoulders as it was dragged along on groggy legs, looking dejected, sheepish, into the faces of the policemen. Shocked at the appearance of the intruder, blood now smeared down one side of the head through a deep bloodied cut that matted the hair, a result of hitting the head on the passageway wall, the police seemed to find it incredulous that the intruder was a woman.

CHAPTER 59

The next day was a blur. After the events of the previous evening, and the attack on Michelle, Cannon was quite shaken up. He had worked out previously that the intruder was Mary Punch, but he had not been able to prove it. The issue with the CCTV had been the biggest problem that he had needed to understand, to solve. He had realized and had been able to verify through his earlier inquiries, that someone could break into the system and project an image on the main recording device that wasn't true, live, or realtime. For someone who knew about film, and how to operate video as Mary Punch had done for years, it was actually quite easy. She had been able to create loops which unless you spent time watching repeatedly, would seem to suggest that the CCTV cameras and recording system were seeing live pictures but were instead images from previous recordings or were 'stills'.

Her knowledge of such techniques had allowed her to enter Cannon's yard and remain unobserved as she threw bricks into his bedroom, attacked Cynthia, and eventually entered the house. Later it was established that she had been able to manipulate the film at Stones' yard as well, resulting in the murder of her own husband, and pretending that she had nothing to do with it.

Cannon ran *Thunderstruck* mostly for the benefit of the owners. It was in the race just before the National itself. By the time the race started, the crowd had swelled to near capacity and the horse was still learning to race again after its recent throat operation. Not in the betting, the horse was not expected to be particularly competitive in the field of sixteen runners. Surprisingly, however, the horse ran extremely well. There was no sign of any 'choking down' and he finished a gallant fifth, only twelve lengths behind the winner. It was a good sign for the future and the owners were extremely pleased with the outcome. With prizemoney being paid down to eighth place, the horse more than paid its way.

DI Cummings had already been down to Woodstock on the day after *Titan's Hand*'s race to take Mary Punch into custody. The murder of her husband in Cummings' jurisdiction meant that the case, as agreed with Peters, was one that he should prosecute. He had taken her back to Cheshire and she had already confessed to the murder.

"How did you know about Mary Punch?" Peters asked as he sat with Cannon a few days later reviewing the events of Aintree and at Cannon's stables.

"I didn't initially," Cannon said. "I thought that Clairy was the killer. I got it completely wrong, didn't I?" he admitted.

Peters nodded but understood where Cannon was coming from. Cannon had shared with him some of his thoughts about the night that Fred Punch was murdered. "There was so much going on, that it was almost impossible to establish what had happened or indeed why," Cannon had said. "The accidental grabbing of the pitchfork handle by Stone hadn't made it any easier either. I guessed much later that Mary Punch must have worn gloves at some point, which she somehow concealed, probably in her jeans pockets, while she pretended to be in a state of shock. She certainly had me fooled for a while."

Peters contemplated the next question before asking it. So far, despite the arrest, Mary Punch had not been willing to provide an answer. He believed Cannon knew. "What I don't understand," he said, "is why? Why did she kill him?"

Cannon had thought about the murder for quite a while. He had needed to think through all the angles, as he had with Melanie Freed and Cindy Higgins. The pieces there had only begun to fit once he had worked out what Wingrew and Stone were up to, the running of their horses with an intent to lose. He had needed to understand the why to that question as well. As his thoughts had become clearer, the issue of blackmail seemed the only obvious answer. But as far as the murder of Fred Punch, it was not easy to determine. He had needed to think in a similar vein, to find the connection.

"To answer that," he replied, "I need to let you know that it was because I assumed some things that were wrong initially, about Clairy in particular. It was only after I was able to recalibrate my thinking that I finally worked out the why, and with Mary now confessing to Fred's murder, it all makes sense."

"I'm not with you, she still hasn't given us a reason why she killed Fred."

"Well as you heard me the other night at the hotel, when we finally got the confession from Cindy," he said, "there needed to be a link, and in the Punch case, it was a film, one of the documentaries that the Punch's had made."

"Go on," Peters requested.

Cannon obliged. "I did some digging, some research on them both, after Fred's death, and I found out that one of the films they made, related to the fashion industry. During the making of the film, it seems Fred Punch had formed a *friendship*, shall we say, with Cindy Higgins, who was one of the models portrayed in it. It was before Cindy's accident and Mary found out about it a few months later. That was a few years ago, but when the *Titans-Hand* syndicate was formed, and we all met at Stones' place, memories of the affair must have come flooding back and I guessed that Mary realized that Fred was still somehow attracted to Cindy. There were signs during our initial meeting. I noticed them but thought little of it...as I said earlier...*initially*. The green-eyed monster must have raised its ugly head and after an argument which none of us witnessed, because they went off on their own that night, she killed him in a fit of rage."

"Was Cindy still interested in Punch?" Peters asked.

"I'm not sure," Cannon replied, "though it's doubtful. After her accident, it seems like she was extremely distressed about what had happened to her, how she was treated. It was almost a mirror image of what had happened to her brother. She had been cast aside like a leper, yet her determination over the years, very noble though it was, remained to try and find a way of helping him out of his predicament, to provide him with a better future, one she felt he deserved. Seeing Fred Punch again, and the hate she saw in Mary's eyes, along with the jibes from Brown and the arrogance and dismissive nature of Walters just sent her over the edge."

"And going back to Mary Punch and her attacking Michelle?" Peters asked.

"I can only assume that she thought that I was getting close to working her out, and that's why she tried to intimidate us. It was the CCTV problem at the stables and the obvious link to photography and film that finally gave her away....once I'd made the connection," Cannon replied. "In addition, the timing of the incidents at my stables as you know didn't quite fit with the movements of Clairy. Fortunately, your inquiries were able to verify that he was with Cindy Higgins during some of that time, but it certainly wasn't definitive."

The Detective nodded, a grim smile slowly creased his face. "Two people dying in such terrible circumstances though," he said, "and the body of Sarah Walters, or what was left of her, was a sight I don't want to see ever again," he added. "I know I've seen many dead bodies, but for someone to be murdered in that fashion, just because of their views about others, was unjustifiable."

Cannon didn't reply. In his own time in the force, he had seen the entire gamut of human emotion and how that played out in people's actions. He had seen the worst in both men and women. He was continuously trying to escape from it. He wasn't sure if he ever would.

CHAPTER 60

The funeral of Ray Brollo was a sad affair. His body was released by the coroner after the investigation into his death was completed. The conclusion was that incident was a result of nothing more than a tragic accident. Cannon, Rich, and the rest of the riders involved at the time were cleared of any wrongdoing. The number of mourners attending the service surprised Cannon. There were well over a hundred. Many were from family and friends, others were workout riders, and also some well-known jockeys. The church, St. James the Great Parish Church, a half-mile from Stonesfield, near Witney, was full, overflowing.

Cannon watched as the coffin was taken into the cemetery lot to be buried a short walk away from the church itself. Mourners took their time dropping handfuls of earth onto the coffin lid, in a final mark of respect, before retiring to attend a small wake in the St.James Church Centre located at the edge of the church grounds.

Cannon and Rich left the family in private to say their final farewells.

The loss of Ray Brollo moved Cannon. He discussed his feelings with Michelle and Cassie. Between them, Cannon and Michelle mutually agreed that they would postpone their wedding until after the trials of Mary Punch and the others.

Michelle and Cannon were going to be first-hand witnesses in the Punch case. Cannon was also expected to be key in the blackmail case of Stone and Wingrew and to provide supporting evidence linking the murders of Walters and Brown. Cummings and Peters still had to prosecute the case and justify to the DPS that they had enough evidence to obtain a conviction, but the confessions the police had heard through Cannon's phone were expected to be enough to start the process. This would eventually lead to formal written confessions that the police needed as part of their case.

The late spring wedding would now be postponed until early Autumn.

Cannon had promised Ray Brollo that he would take on a conditional rider, an apprentice, before the young man himself had been killed. He had hoped that Ray would be that very person, someone that Cannon really liked. A youngster keen on the game of jumps racing, full of positivity for the sport. Cannon started the *Ray Brollo Apprenticeship Trust* which he intended to use to fund his first conditional jockey to be attached to his stable. It wasn't long before he found the right person for the job.

The gold Kruger Rands that Cindy Higgins and her aunt, Melanie Freed stole from the back of Wingrew's car were never found. Both women never disclosed what they had done with them. Paul Higgins was never charged with any crime. He was ultimately deemed to be innocent. Neither an accessory nor a beneficiary of any criminal activity.

He had hoped to move from his flat much earlier than he was able. A few months after the arrest of his sister and aunt, he received a letter in braille from a local lawyer and shortly thereafter, a visit from a financial consultant who made him aware of a deposit in his name, of over 300,000 pounds. It seemed the donor or donors wanted to be kept anonymous, but he knew where the money had come from. He cried at the news and realized the sacrifice others had made on his behalf. He had lived with blindness for years, locked away in the dark. Now others who loved him were stuck in their own darkness.

He wasn't sure which was worse, loss of sight or loss of liberty?

ABOUT THE AUTHOR

Other books in the Mike Cannon series:

- *Death on the Course*
- *After the Fire*
- *Death always Follows*
- *Death by Stealth*

A former Accountant with a lifelong love of horseracing. He has lived on three continents and has been passionate about the sport wherever he resided. Having grown up in England he was educated in South Africa where he played soccer professionally. Moving to Australia, he expanded his love for racing by becoming a syndicate member in several racehorses.

In addition, he began a hobby that quickly became extremely successful, that of making award-winning red wine with a close friend.

In mid-2014 he moved with his employer to England for just over four years, during which time he became a member of the British Racing Club (BRC).

He has now moved back to Australia, where he continues to write, and also presents a regular music show on local community radio.

He shares his life with his beautiful wife Rebecca.

He has two sons, one who lives in the UK and one who lives in Australia. This is his fifth novel.

Printed in Great Britain
by Amazon

79878096R10159